Her Butterfly Diary

B. L McGrew

Holly —
Thank You so much
for your support!
I hope you enjoy Her
Butterfly Diary

For the army of people who have supported me *every* step of the way, I thank you and I love you. I am filled with gratitude when I think about *all* you have done to help me get to this point. My dreams have come true and I did not do it alone. Family, best friends, friends, and my online reading community, you all have had a *major* hand in this and I am forever indebted to you.

You all know exactly who you are.

Preface

Dear Diary,

Chapter One: The Million Dollar Question

February 2014

I'm not really sure how this is supposed to work. Am I really supposed to sit here and pretend all of my problems are going to go away because I wrote them down?

Bullshit.

I mean, I'm not a negative person. But all of this seems like some psychobabble created by therapists to make their jobs easier. Forcing me to write my feelings, only to have you dissect them into something they're not?

Fine, call me a pessimist, but this? This is definitely bullshit.

Impatiently, I sat and watched my therapist –Dr. Gleasyn, read my first diary entry. I was forced against my will to sit down and write *whatever was on my mind*. She said she wouldn't give me a prompt or writing exercises like she did her other patients –*yay me*. My sarcasm was just as blatant when she said the words to me last week. She said she wanted me to have the free will and creativity to write what I saw fit. That I didn't even have to look at it like it was a diary if I didn't want to. It didn't matter to me what she wanted to call it, it was *bullshit* and a waste of time.

Dr. Gleasyn's eyebrows furrowed as she stared at my words contemplatively. I can tell she was reading it more than once because I didn't write much, and she was taking an annoyingly long time to speak. Finally, she looked up and sighed softly. She closed the diary and placed it on the small glass coffee table sitting between us. She cleared her throat then looked directly in my eyes, her green eyes trying desperately to read my body language. I was trying to control the urge to roll my eyes; it was a battle I knew I would soon lose.

"Well," she said as she took her glasses off and placed them on the collar of her purple blouse. "Do you think that's why I wanted you to start this diary?" Her voice was very calming, but I wasn't going to be fooled. She was a nosey pariah who always wanted *too* much from me. She always wanted to know too much about my thoughts, too much about my dislikes, too much about anything that even remotely resembled being personal.

"Yes," I said as I stared right back at her while she studied me, like she *always* did. She was trying to pick apart why I wore a certain color, or why I painted my nails last week, but not this week, why I wore my hair up or down. She always wanted to know *why*. It was very irritating.

She picked the diary back up and opened to the first page, *the only page*. She skimmed over it silently *again*. I sat there annoyed beyond comprehension. Gouging my eyes out ranked high on the list of things I'd rather be doing than sitting here.

"You say here that you're *not a negative person,* why did you write that?"

Sigh.

"I don't know," I answered flatly. I finally look away towards the large patio- like window that oversees the parking lot. I started counting the cars. That was more enjoyable than having to pay attention to this nonsense. The off- white nearly tan walls and extremely tall ceiling in this office made me feel like I was in an asylum. Every time I was here I felt like I was one wrong choice of words away from a straightjacket. That's why 90% of the time my answer was *I don't know.* It was much easier that way.

She didn't say anything for a moment as I counted car number twelve. I could think of one million places I'd rather be than to sit here and watch her try and put a magnifying glass on what she believed were my innermost thoughts. There was no deeper meaning in my words; a *breakthrough* wasn't on the horizon.

"*Call me a pessimist,*" she stated out of the blue. "Do you know why you wrote that?" She leaned towards me slightly with an insightful look on her face as if she truly thought I would answer that question or *any* question. You would think as a therapist she would pick up on this pattern. I had nothing to say. There was nothing to overanalyze.

"I don't know," I say quickly, my tone still flat and uninterested, my eyes still staring at the cars piled into the small parking lot.

I could feel her looking at me, her gaze felt poignant in a way, but I still kept my eyes locked out of the window. "Are there people in your life who think you are negative? Someone that might call you a pessimist?" she quizzed, her voice soft and almost hopeful. I snorted angrily and finally looked back towards her –my eyes beaming with contempt.

"Besides the people who think I'm the devil for giving that baby up for adoption?" I snapped.

She stared for an exaggerated moment unfazed by my outburst, and then sat back in her chair writing in her notepad. She exhaled softly before looking back up towards me. I glared in return.

"…*that baby?*" she emphasized carefully. "Why is it so difficult for you to say *my baby?*"

"Because it's not *my baby!*" I nearly yell at her, my voice angry and almost acidic. I hopped off of the couch, grabbed my bag, and stormed out of her office.

That was the sixth session and the sixth time I stormed out, each time the subject was *that baby.*

I ran out of the front doors of the building right into the parking lot where my mother was waiting. She had a doctor's appointment in the area and decided it would be easier to stay and wait for me than to drive all the way home and come back. I insisted on walking, but my mother wasn't the negotiating type. Her mind and plan were already made and therefore set in stone. I knocked on her car window impatiently, startling her from the book she'd been reading. She sighed and unlocked the door, throwing her book in the backseat.

"Why do we spend all of this money on getting you help if you're never going to stay for an entire session?" She said angrily, her voice tired and exasperated. She looked exhausted. Light purple shadows tracing the curvature under her eyes, her dark brown hair in a messy bun with tendrils of hair sprouting in different directions from the root.

"That's the million dollar question, isn't it?" I stated. I put my headphones in. "I never asked for help, remember?" I add, looking out of the car window.

She didn't say anything as she pulled out of the parking space.

It was true, I'd never asked for *help,* but the world around me insisted that I get it. It was like everyone was waiting for me to have a meltdown. Everyone was waiting for me to feel regret or to *open up.* Neither of those things was going to happen. I was fine.

"Can you drop me off at Matt's?" I asked as she turned down our street.

She sighed before nodding.

No other words were spoken between us, mostly because I was drowning her out with the music blasting in my headphones. In less than ten minutes we were parked in front of Matt's house. I grabbed my bag and hopped out of the car.

8

"I'll be home by seven." I say, closing the door before hearing her response.

I walked in the side door, headed right towards Matt's basement. He was sitting on his old and tattered brown couch playing a video game.

"It's 4:25pm." He said flatly, not looking up from the game. I could already feel the tension and frustration in the room and I hadn't even sat down yet.

"I'm so glad *telling time* stuck with you since elementary school," I replied. I dropped my bag on the floor and sat down next to him. He sighed, and then stopped the game before turning to make eye contact with me. His dark eyes glaring at me, I felt like a child about to be reprimanded.

"Why are you here so early?" I could see the aggravation on his face as he asked the question.

"Sorry, if you didn't want me to come over all you had to do was say so."

"Zoe, you know what I am talking about," he said with annoyance in his tone. "Your appointment started at 4pm, you couldn't even last ten minutes this time?"

"That lady is a quack!" I rebut, I wasn't the bad guy in this scenario. Dr. Gleasyn had no clue what she was doing. "All she does is ask me the same damn thing over and over just with different wording. I'm not at fault here."

"What's the point of even going if ..."

"*Exactly,*" I interrupted. "What's the point?" It was quiet for a moment as we glowered at each other, neither one of us wanting to ease our stance –per usual.

"Forget it." He finally said. He turned the game back on ending our *conversation*.

It was very common for my best friend and I to argue about pretty much everything under the sun. A hot topic lately has been my inability to stay at an hour long session for longer than fifteen minutes. This was the sixth time a conversation like this has been had.

"What is this? Death Con Two?" I asked trying to lighten up the air a bit. If I wanted to get yelled at about not finishing a session I would've just went home with my mom and let her go to town berating me for my lack of *whatever it is* I was apparently lacking.

"Three," he replied. A few moments passed before he spoke again. "Next level. You in?"

And just like that this argument was over, for now. I picked up the controller and played Death Con III with Matt for about two hours before his mom came down stairs.

"Oh," she said unamused, her barley there smile was clearly all for show since Matt was right there. "...hi Zoe I didn't know you were down here." She wasn't the biggest fan of mine ever since the whole *having a baby at seventeen* thing.

A part of me still wonders if she truly thinks Matt is the father of the baby –how morbidly disgusting that would be. The fact that the question ever came out of her mouth still makes me sick to my stomach.

"Hi, Mrs. Hunter, I was just leaving." I say evenly.

"No you weren't?" Matt said. "Stay for dinner?"

A silence fell over the room. It was depressingly hilarious how oblivious Matt was. He believes his mom still likes me. That she and I were as close as we'd always been. He had no clue that she secretly thinks I seduced him, got pregnant, and then gave her first and only grandchild up for adoption.

Sigh.

"No. It's okay," I said as I stood up grabbing my bag off of the floor. "I told my mom I'd be home by seven."

"Oh, well let me drive you," he offered, jumping up from the couch. I could see the frustration on his mother's face as she uncomfortably put her hair behind her ear avidly avoiding eye contact with me.

"Cool," I said as he headed towards the door. "Have a nice night, Mrs. Hunter." I said walking past her. She just nodded and smiled unconvincingly.

We are sitting in the car as some band I've never heard before plays in the background. Matt sighs and I know he's preparing to say something that he knows I'm not going to want to hear. "I was thinking…" he began.

"Oh boy," I said annoyed.

"Maybe the issue is talking to a stranger? I mean you can talk to me, you know I wouldn't tell anyone your business," he offered sincerely.

I took a deep breath. Though I was frustrated about having to have the same conversation over and over again, I knew that Matt was just trying to be a good friend.

"There isn't anything to talk about, Matt," I try to say calmly, but I could feel my nerves starting to falter. I looked out of the window and started counting the trees hoping this would prevent me from yelling if this interrogation went too far.

"Yes there is," he countered, "how about the fact that I am your best friend and I have no idea who the father is? I didn't even know you liked anyone let alone enough to get preg…"

"Matt," I interrupted, staring in his eyes pleadingly. "Stop, okay? Just stop." I looked back out of the window trying to coax these tears from falling down my cheeks. There weren't too many things I hated more than crying. I'd done enough of that over the last year to flood two lifetimes with tears.

He sighed. "I'm sorry," he said solemnly. "I just wish you would let me in… or *anybody* in."

It was quiet for a moment and the air between us was thick. I did hate not letting him *in,* but this was my life and it was something that I'd decided to handle on my own. I wish people would understand that everything was fine, that it was time we all moved on.

"Something isn't right with you and I know you know that," he continued. "Everything is different. *You* are different and I miss you."

I sniffle. I was *not* about to do this tonight. This horse had been dead for quite some time now, but everyone around me wouldn't stop beating it with sticks. I inhale ignoring the tightness in my chest. There would be no full blown breakdowns in this car.

"I'm going to be late," I say softly. Matt didn't say anything for what felt like an eternity. I hated that I had nothing to say to him, I hated that he was constantly there without reason and I couldn't even give him crumbs. I can feel his eyes on my profile, I knew he had more to say, but he just shook his head and turned the key into the ignition.

Later that night in my room I sat down at my desk and sitting there was that damn diary that I'd left in that quacks office. My mother must've went back to get it. I was willing to bet money that she read what I'd written. I didn't care. I could only imagine what she said to Dr. Gleasyn.

I stared at the butterflies on the cover of the diary. I stared at them for almost an hour. I don't know what I was expecting, but I just sat there counting them over and over. Matt's words kept playing in a loop in my head. Maybe talking to a stranger *was* the problem. But, there was no way in hell I could talk to someone I actually knew, that was a nonstarter.

I angrily wiped a tear from my cheek and opened the diary. I read the words that I'd written and almost laughed. I wouldn't want to deal with me at all if I were Dr. Gleasyn. I picked up a pen and pressed the black ink to the paper. I wiped another tear away with my free hand.

February 2014

Dear Diary...

I hate crying.

I closed the diary and exhaled. I was fully aware of the questions that would be thrown at me from that quack, but I was told to write what I felt and at this particular moment that is what I felt. I never wanted to cry again, it was weak and served no purpose.

Chapter Two: Hating, *everything.*

I hate school. Not your typical teenage angst type of hate, but I truly, deeply, and unequivocally hate it. And the way people spoke about me and *to* me you could definitely tell they truly, deeply, and unequivocally hated me too. It didn't help matters much when I refused to transfer schools when I got pregnant. Insisting on playing volleyball in gym with a stomach that was bigger than the ball, wanting to be included in everything and acting as if nothing had changed –it wasn't one of my brighter moments.

I was in lunch now, my favorite time of the day because I didn't have to socialize with the Barbie's of the school and I got to eat –my favorite pastime. Sometimes, I did miss eating lunch with Matt. He transferred to a private high school last year to up his chance of getting a football scholarship. Smart move, this place was a shit hole in my eyes.

"Slut," someone coughed as they walked behind me, bumping my chair. I didn't even have to look up from my pizza to know it was Erica Taylor. She was the typical popular cheer captain type. It sickened me how unbelievably cliché this entire scenario was. I felt like I was in a cheesy teen movie from the 80's.

"Good job Erica, maybe next time you can string an entire sentence together?!" I said loud enough so I knew she and her clan of minions would hear.

"What did you say to me?" she turned around walking back over to my table. Her hand was on her hip as she glared at me. Her nearly bleach blonde hair in a high and neat ponytail, her face painted in almost Ronald McDonald levels of makeup. I was cringing from the cliché overload.

"Aww man," I said with mock sympathy in my voice. "Too many big words?" I glared right back at her, not intimidated by her or her group of brainless puppets in the least. "Would you like me to break it down for you? Say it slower? Take out the unfamiliar words?"

The anger that flashed across her face was refreshing in many ways for me. I could literally see the wheels turning as she tried to think of a comeback. Wouldn't it be great if she were able to figure out something clever to say that had nothing to do with the fact that I was pregnant fourteen weeks ago?

"That's a lot of food. Remember, you're only eating for *one* now."

Man, didn't see that one coming, I thought sarcastically. Before I could respond Mrs. McCabe walked over. "Erica, move it along. Your food is getting cold." She ordered.

Erica rolled her eyes and walked away, her peasants following suit.

"How are you Miss. Oakley?" Mrs. McCabe asked. She was my counselor. She was the one that suggested to my mother that I see a therapist. She was a nice lady for the most part, but I wasn't a big fan of hers at the moment. Her meddling is why my Thursday afternoons were no longer free.

"I'm excellent, how are you?" I could hear the heavy sarcasm leave my lips as I said the words. Sometimes I couldn't control it. She stared at me for an exaggerated moment before she responded. She clearly detected my mocking tone.

"I'm excellent as well," she paused for a moment and all I could think was *please don't sit down, please!* "I haven't seen you in my office in nearly seven weeks." She states, her somewhat large stature moving in towards me.

It wasn't a question, so I didn't respond.

"Why is that?" She added after I went back to eating.

"Busy, busy, busy," I halfheartedly smiled. "A lot of work to catch up on since I missed six weeks due to the fact I had to push a kid out of my vagina."

She just stood there staring at me. I went back to enjoying my room temperature pizza. I should've gotten the pepperoni.

It amazed me how everyone wanted me to talk about that kid, but when I actually brought it up they suddenly fall quiet. They look at me like I'm insane, how hypocritical.

"I would like to speak with you in my office before the end of the week, okay?" she was frustrated with me and I truly didn't know why. I'd answered her honestly, what else was I supposed to say?

I nodded and she walked away her annoyance spilling over in the way she turned around.

I hate school.

***

"Sweetheart!" I heard my mother call out before I was even fully in the house. I sighed before turning the corner. I was not prepared for that level of enthusiasm after a long and annoying school day.

"Yes?" I said, entering the kitchen. Sitting there at our large, dark wood kitchen table was my mother's husband. I stopped suddenly in my tracks, my heart sank. Quickly anger and frustration boiled in my chest. I had to quickly regroup myself.

"Look who is back from California early!" She beamed. I couldn't scrounge up the same type of excitement she had if I were paid to.

I placed my backpack on the floor next to the fridge.

"How ya doing?" he asked as he took a sip of his beer. I was trying so hard not to roll my eyes or scream in his face. He wasn't supposed to be back yet.

"Peachy," I answered flatly not making eye contact with him. I grabbed a drink out of the fridge, picked my bag back up, and then walked towards the stairs. I needed to be out of this kitchen.

"Where are you going?" My mother asked disappointedly. "I thought we could eat together? We haven't sat down together as a family in months."

I almost choked over the word *family*. Oscar was *not* my family. He was an enormously large, controlling, and terrifying man my mother met three years ago on a cruise and married four months later – nothing more –nothing less.

"I have a lot of homework to do," I lied, trying to edge my way out of there.

"It's fine. I bet she has a lot of catching up to do still." Oscar nodded, looking me directly in the eyes.

I could feel the bile trying to rise in my throat. I bit my lip, diverted eye contact, and headed towards the steps. "Yep," I said.

When I got to my room I sat down at my desk, I closed my eyes, and slowly took a deep breath in, holding it for a few seconds before letting it out slowly.

I hated Oscar too.

It was a deeply engraved and seared into my soul kind of hate. I hated him more than school, more than my therapist, more than my best friend's intrusive and personal questions. There honestly weren't too many things I liked in my life. The thought of all the things that bothered me or made me angry was a list so long that it would be easier to just list the things I could actually tolerate.

There, sat my diary. *Again*, I was transfixed on the same butterflies – of course they hadn't changed. They were the same as they'd been the day before. Just like *I* was the same as I'd been the day before and the day before that. I opened it to the third blank page and grabbed my pen. I pressed the pen to the paper, but I couldn't move my hand. I knew what I *wanted* to write, I knew what I *needed* to write, but something wasn't clicking, everything felt disconnected. I was beginning to think I wasn't wired correctly.

My brain was running a marathon while my heart was being lazy, sad, and unmotivated. It was like my arm went numb just like the rest of me.

My phone's blaring ring yanked me out of my trance. It was Matt. *Who else would it be?* I thought to myself.

"Hey," I say.

"What's wrong?" He asked immediately. God, he was so good at picking and choosing when to be perceptive.

"Nothing," I lie trying to placate my tone as to avoid more interrogating from him. "Math will be the death of me. What's up?"

"Me and Alicia are going to the bonfire, go with us?" He had excitement in his voice. Almost as if he didn't know me at all.

"Pass."

"You can't stay cooped up in your house every day," he quickly rebutted. "Plus, Alicia said she misses you." His voice was pleading –borderline begging.

Alicia was his girlfriend. They'd been together a little over a year. She was probably one of the nicest and most genuine people I'd ever met. Other than Matt, she was the only person who didn't judge me when I got pregnant. The last time she'd seen me I was in the hospital giving birth. I remember getting so emotional when she showed up with a teddy bear for the baby and flowers for me. If Matt screwed this up with her I was going to personally kick his ass.

"Ugh, fine," I conceded. "But I'm only going for Alicia," I added with effect.

"See you in an hour!" He hung up quickly, like he knew I'd change my mind if he stayed on the phone any longer. He was right though; I needed to be out of this house, especially now since Oscar was back. I looked at the blank page of my diary and finally wrote something.

February 2014

Dear Diary ....

Going out, I'll even try to have fun.

***

"How long was he supposed to be in Cali?" Matt asked as he took a swig of his beer.

"Three more weeks," I rolled my eyes, not really wanting to have this conversation.

"Why do you hate him so much?" Alicia asked. Her soft voice and peaceful demeanor was always so welcoming and comforting to be around. She was sitting on the ground between Matt's legs; her back facing him as he played with her now straightened dark hair absentmindedly with his free hand.

"He's an asshole," Matt answered for me. I nodded in agreement, because that much was true.

"Very specific," she said sarcastically, leaning forward to put her slender hands closer to the fire.

"It's true," I said quickly, but wanting to change the topic. "I'm gonna go for a walk." I got up from the log I'd been sitting on and started walking. I was feeling a little suffocated with the small group of teens I barely knew huddled around the bonfire. I needed some breathing space.

"I'll go with you," I heard Matt say, getting up before I could object. "You cool?" He asked Alicia. She nodded. "Yea, I'm gonna go up that trail with the girls, meet you guys back here in an hour or so."

I'd already made it a few yards away; as I heard Matt jogging to catch up.

"I kind of wanted to be by myself." I muttered under my breath, burying my hands inside the pockets of my thick jacket.

"So what?" he shrugged. We were walking quietly along the nearly frozen lake, it was beautiful and eerily serene – I inhaled slowly. We were almost far enough from the bonfire that we couldn't hear their voices anymore. The open space felt so good, I could walk for miles in this cold weather. From where I was walking it looked like the beach was never going to end.

About ten minutes went by before Matt broke the comfortable silence. "Tomorrow you have a session…" he trailed off.

I sighed. "That is correct." Matt was in the process of ruining my peaceful moment. I clenched my jaw and looked toward the frozen lake, trying to avoid all eye contact with him. Just like the cold sand beneath my booted feet, the lake looked like it would never end as well. The sun was barely noticeable as it played tag with the horizon. The beautiful soft pinks, oranges, and purples were prominent enough to break through the gray clouds that had dominated the sky for most of the day.

"Can you promise me you will stay for the entire hour?" He pleaded. And there it was my peaceful moment trampled on. "Before you bite my head off just…you won't let me or your mom or anyone help you…"

The anger and frustration overflowed my chest and I couldn't hold it in anymore. "I don't need help!" I yelled, surprising myself. "I never once said I needed help! I am fine –I got pregnant, I gave the baby up for adoption and that's it. This happens to millions of women! Go ask *them* if they need help. Having that baby doesn't define me. Can I have one minute, one fucking second to just be Zoe? Not the slut that got pregnant?"

I was pissed that in the middle of my anger tears produced. I'd promised myself that crying over something I couldn't change was useless, but here I was again, with my tears betraying me. I wiped them quickly looking back towards the horizon; maybe its beauty could calm my nerves.

The sun was gone and the colors were long faded. There was just a blackened night with gray hues softening its potency. The beauty I'd admired just moments ago was no longer there. I sighed and more tears fell.

"Zoe, I didn't mean to make you feel…" He was trying to find his words. I'd never blown up at him like that on *this* subject before, but I was tired. I was so tired of always having to defend my choices and my actions. "You're not a slut. No one is calling you a slut."

I laughed, thinking about the fact that I was literally called one a few hours ago during lunch. I probably looked like a sociopath, tears streaming down my cheeks at the same time.

"It's not funny. I never meant for you to think any of that. I don't know what to say. I just want you to be happy."

I let his words set in before I could respond. "Happiness isn't meant for everyone."

Those were the saddest words I could've ever spoken, but in that same sense I'd never said truer words. There were winners and losers at life and it was clear what side of the spectrum I belonged to.

A hollowed feeling washed over me, as I fought vigorously against the fresh tears that wanted to escape.

"That's not true, Zoe…"

"I'm gonna walk home," I interrupt. I felt like I was scarily close to a breakdown and Matt was one of the last people I needed in this world to see that. He would feel responsible or try to figure out why I was losing it which would ultimately just make me cry even more. "I really do have a lot of homework." I lied.

"No," he interjected, "let me drive, it's dark. I'll go get Alicia." He went to walk away, but I grabbed his arm.

"I want to walk and plus she's almost halfway through the hike. I just need to be alone." He's just staring at me, contemplating whether he would persist or not. Finally he nodded.

"Fine, I'll see you tomorrow after your appointment?" He asked expectantly. "Text me as soon as you walk through the door so I know you made it."

"Yea, okay," I responded as he started to walk away. "Matt!" I called out. He stopped and turned around. "Thank you for being such a good friend." It wasn't his fault that I wasn't a good communicator. No matter how closed off I am he's always there. He needed to know that though I didn't always show it – I did truly appreciate him and his patience.

I could sense the smile in his eyes. "I'm the only one that can tolerate your shit, Zoe." He said with a smirk.

"This is true," I smiled and walked away. It was a nice and quiet twenty minute walk. When I made it home I stood in front of my house for a good ten minutes before my mother opened the front door.

"Zoe, what the hell are you doing?" She was startled. If I were being honest I would say *"I don't want to go in the house because your husband is there, I don't want to go in the house because you always bombard me with one thousand questions, I don't want to go in the house because that diary will be glaring at me as soon as I step foot into my bedroom."*

"Enjoying the scenery," I said unenthusiastically, my sarcasm marinating every syllable.

"Oh, well get in its getting late and its cold. Where were you? I thought you were doing homework? Did you get dropped off?"

Only nine hundred and ninety seven more questions to go.

I went straight upstairs when I got into the house, locked my bedroom door and threw my diary in the trash.

I lay down on my bed fully clothed, staring at the ceiling. I felt paralyzed. It was hard to explain. I felt like I was stuck in a moment so cemented in time, that there was no way I would ever escape it, no matter how hard I tried. It was stronger than quicksand. I felt muted and unhinged. I was always drifting away, unable to put up a fight. Some days I wasn't even sure if I wanted to.

I was in a perpetual state of drowning, and reaching the surface wasn't a possibility.

I got up slowly and fetched the diary out of the trash like I knew I would.

February 2014

Dear Diary ...

It's too cold for a bonfire.

I slammed my pen down. I was frustrated that I couldn't put my thoughts down on paper, frustrated that I couldn't construct a full written sentence without wincing or crying. Dr. Gleasyn was going to have a field day. I should at least get extra credit for trying.

Chapter Three: Shifts and Change

There was an away game for one of the sports here at my school. I don't know, Basketball or Football probably, that was beside the point. Erica and her brainless followers were there and not here so that meant that my normal *level ten shitty day* would drop down to *a level six shitty day*. This was saying a lot.

I could actually enjoy my lunch for once. This was starting to make me love sports again. Look at the joy it was bringing me?

"Can I sit here?" An unfamiliar voice said, essentially ripping me from my semi happy bubble. There stood a tall, somewhat muscular boy with dark brown hair and matching dark brown eyes. I'd never seen him in this school before. He stood there looking expectantly at me.

"Umm," was all I could manage to say. I wanted to say *no*, that's my kneejerk reaction when it comes to speaking to people in this school. I wanted to say *go away*, but I also didn't want to be rude to someone who hadn't actually *earned* the receiving end of my rudeness.

"I'm new here." His deep voice spoke as if I should feel some type of sympathy for him. He should be lucky that he is just now being subjected to this hell hole. I'd had to suffer for three years here with one left. "Never mind, sorry I bothered you." He said as he began to walk away. I forgot that my inner dialogue translated to radio silence to the outside world.

"Wait, I'm sorry," I said, "yea, its fine. I'm almost done."

He nodded, and then placed his tray down before sitting. "Thanks."

"Yep,"

It was quiet. The awkward *maybe I should fill the air with noise* kind of quiet. I picked at this salad as if I were actually going to eat it. I looked at it with so much distaste it could've easily been a plate full of maggots and it would've garnered the same facial expression from me. I don't know why I thought I would enjoy this. The last green thing I ate was a skittle.

"Not a salad fan?" The new kid asked. It pulled me out of my headspace. Small talk? Not really my thing.

"Yea, no… not at all," I pushed the plate away and opened a bag of chips. "The person in front of me took the last cheeseburger." I said with an eye roll. Potato chips and chocolate would salvage my meal.

"Uhh…I think that was me," he pointed to his burger and come to think of it a tall dude with a dark colored shirt and brown hair *was* in front of me.

24

"Wow, you're the reason I was subjected to salad?" I said with mock anger. "Had you transferred a day later, I would be enjoying that burger right now." I added for affect.

He didn't say anything as he grabbed a butter knife and split the burger into two. He grabbed half to put on a napkin and then slid his entire plate – fries included – to me.

"I was just joking. You can eat your food." I pushed the plate back towards him.

"No, I insist," he pushed the plate further towards me again. "Think of it as my rent for occupying space at your table."

"Rent?" I repeat, he nods and smiles. I look down at the burger and I can feel my stomach rumbling. What the hell, if he's offering. I picked up the burger, "In that case." I took a huge bite and of course ketchup and mustard dripped down my chin. I could hear him laughing as he handed me a napkin. I should be immune to embarrassment at this point in my life, one would think.

"One thing to know about me…" I began to say sarcastically, the embarrassment circling me – my mouth was still full of burger, "Is that I'm a lady with class and high standards of sophistication. Clearly," I put the burger down and grabbed the napkin –wiping the mess off of my face.

"I can absolutely see that." He smiled and handed me another napkin.

We were quiet for a moment and this time it didn't quite feel like we needed to fill the space with noise. I enjoyed that half of burger, when I was done I scooted the plate to the middle of the table so we could share the fries. I didn't socialize with anyone in this school, really. It was weird sitting here with this stranger; but in the very short time I've been in his presence he didn't seem like a mindless teenager like 90% of the population in this school.

Also, he didn't know who I was so he was unable to judge me based off of rumors. It was refreshing that I was sort of able to be more *myself* in this moment than I'm usually capable of being when I am here.

"Thanks," he said with a gentle smile as he grabbed a few fries.

"Where are you from?" I asked out of the blue. I needed to know who would actually decide to come to this high school. He had to be an out of state-r; I was willing to bet money on it.

"Nebraska," he said simply. I wasn't going to lie; I probably couldn't find Nebraska on a map without labels if you paid me.

"What brings you to Ohio? We don't have anything but sports and cows," I stated. "From personal observation, of course," I added.

He laughed, "Pretty much the same in Nebraska." He shrugged before continuing. "My dad got a job out here. I had a choice, stay back with my mom or move out here with my dad. I chose the lesser of the two sociopaths." He didn't laugh or smile, but I could hear the sarcasm saturating his words, he was speaking my language.

"God, can I relate," I said with an eye roll. "I always contemplate calling somewhere to see if I can get my mother admitted anonymously."

He laughed and ate another French fry. "Is your dad equally as insane?"

"I don't know. When you find him ask him for me."

"Oh, I'm sorry," he said quickly, his tone changing. "I didn't mean to…"

"What? Oh! No, I'm fine. I didn't mean for that to sound so woe is me." I interrupted. It was as if sarcasm was my first and second language and because of that I could quickly make situations awkward unintentionally, it was a gift and a curse.

26

It was quiet again. I could feel the heavy blanket of uncomfortable silence cover us fully. I looked around the lunch room and saw Mrs. McCabe eyeing me from across the room. I perched my eyebrows in confusion, then looked back at the new kid. He was already staring at me contemplatively.

"So," he said casually, "you've lived here your whole life?"

"Unfortunately," I rolled my eyes.

"It can't be *that* bad?" He questioned sympathetically. If I wasn't mistaken I could actually hear a note of real remorse in his voice.

"You'd be surprised." I mumbled under my breath. It wasn't so much that it sucked here, it was the fact that *circumstances* in my life made the people around me suck. But the new kid didn't need to know that.

I pick up a couple French fries and stare at the plate because the new kid is still looking directly at me. I can feel it. I know that one of the keys to holding a conversation is eye contact, but it made me uncomfortable. What made it even more uncomfortable was eye contact when no words were being spoken. I clear my throat before speaking.

"Do you miss it?" I asked, finally looking up from the plate. He looked at me for a moment longer before answering.

"I miss my mother and a few friends, but I needed the change and I like it here." He said with a soft smile.

He seemed like the *happy* type, the kind of people who wake up super early in the morning with a smile on their face, ready to conquer the world. He seemed like the kind of person that people like me would want to punch in the face. Not because he was annoying, but because his life appeared to be shiny and sunny. I wasn't the shiny and sunny kind. I was the kind of person who had a dark black storm cloud surrounding her that repelled the happy people.

"How long have you been here?" I asked.

"Just a few days, but I have a sneaky suspicion that I made the right choice coming here." He held eye contact with me for a moment before I looked away, looking at the rain slamming against the cafeteria window. It had been such an abnormal winter, we hadn't really gotten any snow – just frigid temperatures some days and rain the other days. As much as I complained my whole life about hating snow, I was actually missing it.

It was quiet again for a moment. I was entranced watching how hard the rain was pouring. "What class do you have next?" He asked, snapping me out of my trance. Before I could answer Mrs. McCabe walked up.

"I need to speak with you in my office." Her voice was clipped and impatient.

I wanted to object, but the bell rang.

"Mr. Jordan, you will be late for class." She said to him, standing at the table. He looked at me with an arched eyebrow as if to say *what was her problem?* I shrugged before he grabbed the tray and walked away.

"I'll see you in five minutes Miss Oakley." She ordered then she walked away.

Her tone and demeanor irritated me, but I gathered my belongings and did as I was told.

I sat impatiently outside of Mrs. McCabe's office waiting to be summoned. I couldn't understand everyone's obsession with talking. Why does every thought or every feeling you've *ever* had need to be discussed? Some things should be left unspoken, just for you and your demons to grapple through.

Between the quack I would be seeing after school, my mother, Matt, and Mrs. McCabe I felt like it would be much preferred if my life was played out for them on a reality television show. It would save us all so much time.

What I needed everyone to know was that silence didn't always mean pain and speaking didn't always mean healing.

"Come on in," I heard Mrs. McCabe say behind me. I inhaled and counted to five before getting up from my seat.

Her office is bright, the many colors are loud. I think this was her attempt at appealing to young people, but for me – my retinas alerted me to leave every time I was in here. I sat down on a fluffy red chair; I would imagine this bright and tacky chair being in a corny soap opera.

"So I wanted to speak with you about your future."

I waited for her to elaborate. I could've taken a wild guess that she would want to speak with me about my future. That *was* her job essentially.

"Do you plan on going to college?" She asked as she tried to sustain eye contact with me.

"Yes, I do plan on going to college." I nodded mechanically. I didn't know where this was going but my attention span was not cooperating. I started counting the pictures of past and present students she had displayed on her wall. I'd gotten to twenty-four before she asked a follow up question. I guess she wanted me to elaborate.

"I just want you to stay focused, okay?" She added with a much stronger and less motherly tone. I wasn't sure if she meant in this very moment as I counted picture thirty -one or in general. So I nodded.

"I don't want you to let bullies, or being overwhelmed, or *boys* distract you from your goals." She looked at me as if she pitied me. Her glasses sitting on the tip of her nose as her large hazel eyes pierced through me.

I just stared at her blankly. She did *not* want to go there.

"Care to elaborate?" I'm trying to keep the acid from spilling from my lips, but I could sense the sharp turn this conversation was about to take.

"Your freshmen and sophomore years you were a top student and …" she paused, taking in a quick breath before she continued. "We can't avoid the elephant in the room," I was done counting the pictures. She had my *full* attention. "Last year you got involved in situations that led to a pregnancy. As I see you sitting there with Mr. Jordan I fear the path you could be headed down again" I let her words linger there for a moment as I processed them.

I wondered if smoke was coming out of my ears. You see it on cartoons all of the time, but in this moment the rage and anger and *shock* that are cascading up and down my entire body made me feel like I would combust. *I got involved in situations that led to a pregnancy.* So what now, I'm so tainted that if I even glance at a human who happens to have a penis I'll get pregnant? Or no better yet, I'm such a whore I'll just throw myself at him. I just won't be able to contain myself and these hormones?

I couldn't find the words, I was livid. My blood was boiling and my head was pounding. I wouldn't dignify her comment with a response, because what would the point be? I grabbed my bag and stormed out of her office. I could hear her in the background calling out for me, *"Zoe! That's not what I meant. Let me explain to you! I just want you to protect your future!"*

I ran out of the front doors of the school and slumped onto the drenched steps, the rain hadn't stopped. I wanted to cry, I wanted to cry until every tear was gone from my body, but I refused to do that here, *especially* here. I could feel that my face was red, my breathing was uneven. Mrs. McCabe had crossed a line today. I wanted to tell my mother but who was I kidding? I'm sure she'd agree and send me right back to her office to be berated more.

Pulling me out of my thought was the loud roar of three school busses pulling up in front of the school. The first bus emptied and of course just to add the cherry on top of this wonderful day I was already having – it was Erica. Maybe giving up that baby did affect me? It affected my karma because I kept getting screwed by it left and right.

"Leaving early to pick up your bastard child from daycare?" She said as she walked by, her friends giggling behind her. I didn't say anything. I needed to realize that what I said to Matt would never be true. That baby *did* define me. I would never be *Zoe* again. I would always be the girl that got pregnant. I couldn't escape it no matter how hard I tried, no matter how normal I tried to live my life. It was who I was to them.

I couldn't stay here another second. I decided I didn't care if I got in trouble or if they called my mother, I was done with this school day. I had to get away.

***

"Zoe?" I heard Alicia say confusingly. I looked up and now I'm embarrassed that I'm even here. "What's wrong? You've been crying should I call Matt?" She asked panicked.

"No!" I said abruptly. I'd been sitting on her steps for thirty five minutes, thanking God that the rain had finally stopped. Those thirty five minutes where I should've been sitting in my therapist's office. I didn't know who I was more afraid of hearing from, Matt or my mother at this point.

"Okay, its freezing, come in." I stood up and she immediately put her arm around my shoulders as we walked through her front door.

"Mom?" she called out, "I'm going upstairs with Zoe." She yelled as we shuffled up the steps. Her house was so cozy, a very warm and homey feel. Pictures of her and her older brother were on every inch of the walls leading upstairs.

"Okay, hi Zoe!" Her mother answered from a different room. I met her mother a couple of times, she seemed very sweet. She and Alicia had the same demeanor – always warm, comforting, and soft spoken.

"Hi Miss Spencer," I said just loud enough for her to barley hear me. We were in Alicia's room. I'd only been to her house a handful of times, each time I was with Matt. We sat on her bed and the quiet lingered. I guess I should be the one to start speaking. I am the one who showed up unannounced.

"I don't even know why I'm here." That was the honest to God's truth. Leaving school early today I just couldn't imagine sitting in my therapist's office. I couldn't go home *obviously* and if I went to Matt's he would be angry with me and then want to talk about it. I felt like Alicia was the most neutral person I knew. I felt like I could escape the hounds while in her presence, even if only for a few minutes.

"Well, you're hiding from your mom and my boyfriend for starters?" She chimed in.

"Perceptive," I nodded. "I'm sorry to bombard you like this."

"No, are you kidding me? I always want one on one time to hang out with you. I think Matt never relays my messages because he's afraid we will start shutting him out." She smiled.

"Highly likely," I tried to force a small chuckle out. It got quiet again before she spoke.

"You can hang out here as long as you'd like, but I can't lie to Matt when he calls me."

That seemed like a fair deal. I hope she didn't expect me to explain why I skipped my afternoon classes, or expect me to talk about how I'd been slut shamed by a high school counselor and a high school bimbo. Maybe with a little mental coaxing I could treat this situation like getting in a pool for the first time after a long and cold Ohio winter. You put your toe in, it's frigid, but you slowly submerge your entire body in the pool. After a while it isn't so bad. It's as if you and the water are the same temperature.

Maybe I could say a little? Maybe it wouldn't be so bad to see what *talking* felt like outside of my sarcastic remarks.

I went to open my mouth, but it was like the words got frightened at the open space and ran backwards. I inhaled and bit my lip.

"Do you want to stay for dinner?" she asked. I knew there was no way between my mother and Matt that I would be able to be here long enough to enjoy a home cooked meal. In ten minutes my mother was going to be calling my phone in a complete panic when she is told that I never showed up for my appointment. Then, she will call Matt who will freak out and call me thirty times. He will call Alicia and be shocked that I was here the whole time. I have about twenty more minutes or so of unsolicited *freedom*.

"No, it's okay. Thank you."

"Do you want to talk?" She asked. Her voice was so unsure. I wondered what horror stories Matt scared her with in regards to my communication skills or lack thereof.

"Not really," I said. "I don't want to be rude, it's just…"

"I understand," she interrupted, "as long as you know that I am someone who can be here for you when you're ready."

I was able to control my eye roll. She was being a good friend, she didn't know that people assuming I was on the verge of being *ready* to talk is what pissed me off the most. Everyone was on pins and needles waiting for me to be *ready.* They were wasting their time.

33

"Hey, did Matt ever send you that link to that group I saw over winter break?" She asked as she got up heading to her computer. I loved how she moved on to the next subject. She didn't linger or dwell like everyone else I knew.

"No, he didn't," I said almost relieved. I was relieved that I could be here and not be scolded for not wanting to share my every thought. I was basking in the fact that I didn't have to talk about the many skeletons in my overflowing closet.

She started playing the band and it was nice. I would definitely put them on my list of albums to download and concerts to go to. We were on the fourth song when my phone rang. It was my mother. I stared at my cell as my mother's name blinked across the screen. Alicia turned down the music to a whisper. I was going to have to face my mother sooner or later.

I inhaled.

"Hello?"

"Zoe! Where are you? Are you ok?" Her voice screeched, I actually felt bad for causing the panic I could detect in her voice.

"I'm fine. I'm on my way home now." I lied, looking in Alicia's direction.

"Wait, did you *intentionally* miss your appointment?" The panic in her voice quickly turned to anger. "I'm so disappointed in you. I can't even talk you right now."

Then she hung up. I didn't know what was worse, her yelling or her being so mad she couldn't even speak to me? I sat there for a moment staring at my phone that was now in my lap. I inhaled and exhaled slowly.

"I can drop you off?" Alicia said softly as she got up heading for the door. "I'll just have to get my mom's keys."

34

"It's okay, I'll walk," I answered as I stood up, grabbing my bag. "Thanks for letting me awkwardly encroach on your personal time and space." I said with a forced light chuckle.

"No, you're fine. I enjoyed it. Like I said, I'm always telling Matt me and you should hang out more. You're always welcomed. I hope you know that?"

I was not good at the whole *meaningful dialogue and interchanging of sentiments* thing, if that wasn't noticeable enough already. I just smiled, nodded and walked out of the room.

It had been a mild winter in mid-western Ohio thus far, but the cold air was stinging my skin as I walked against the light breeze. You could almost smell the snow that was to come. I was taking my time walking home, the urge to speed up and get out of this cold was battling with the urge to run away and never come back all to avoid that house. It was about 50/50 at this point.

My phone rang and it was Matt. Sometimes he didn't feel like my best friend. Sometimes he felt like a disapproving father or an overprotective older brother. I couldn't handle dealing with him and then having to hear my mother scream at me tonight. I pressed ignore and kept walking, I'm sure Alicia would fill him in.

I wish people would just move on past their frustrations and anger. What is done –is done. Missing that session is over with, yelling at me, and being angry about it can't send us back in time. I would never understand why people harp over things that are no longer in their control, why people feel the need to discuss things to death. The world keeps spinning, time keeps ticking, why do we obsess over holding onto that rope? That's something I would never understand.

I hadn't realized I was in front of my house and slowly walking up the porch steps. I was on autopilot. I think I'd been on autopilot for the last year if I'm being completely honest with myself.

"Can you even comprehend how terrified I was?" I heard my mother yell but five feet from my face. I wasn't even fully in the house. I guess she has found the words that she claimed she hadn't had earlier on the phone.

"And I called the school, Zoe. They told me you weren't in your last two classes? Where the hell were you?" Her voice screeched. I wasn't able to snap out of my autopilot, I was just so depleted from the day, this day that seemed like it would never end. "Answer me!"

"I…" I began to say, but the look in her eyes caused me to stop. I didn't want to argue and I didn't want her to lose it completely.

"So help me God if you were at a boy's house, I will *not* go through this again with you. You know what you put this family through! I won't tolerate it *or* you…"

Her *words,* those daggers, its shrapnel, the scratches that scarred my spirit, it was official there wasn't a person who didn't see me as a whore not even my own mother. I was forever marked. Zoe died the day those two blue lines popped up on that pregnancy test.

I stared at my mother directly in her eyes, I wanted her to see *me* I wanted her to remember her daughter. In her eyes I can tell she didn't know me, I didn't know her. I didn't know anyone anymore. I was unfamiliar with the faces of people who claim to be family and friends, the people who claim they want to *help* me. I was unfamiliar to myself. I, who would have never let words hurt me, I, who would have never been rendered speechless, I'd lost me. Just like everyone else had.

My tears betrayed me. "I had a really rough day, so I went to Alicia's. You can call her mother." My voice cracks. "You don't have to worry I don't plan on sleeping with all of Ohio and getting pregnant again. I would never want to burden you or *this family* more than I already have." I walked past her heading up the stairs.

"Zoe, wait!" I heard her call behind me.

I was in my room, door locked, and the lights off. That same hollowing feeling I always get encompassed me completely.

This last year I'd blocked out things, *dark things*, things that I promised would never see the light of day, but I was tired. I was so tired of being the punching bag, of being the one to be blamed and ridiculed. I sat down at my desk opening my diary. I was going to write my truth. I was going to write about when I got pregnant. I was going to empty every single thing on that paper and watch the world around me explode. I was going to watch my therapists face as she read the words, I was going to absorb her reaction when she sees all that I'd been through, all that I'd been carrying with me.

I picked up the pen and let the words rage out of me. Every detail I penned to my butterfly diary. The pages were wet from my tears, my eyes swollen, and my anger palpable. This hurt. It physically hurt seeing these words on this paper. Thoughts that I'd buried deep and far away were now out alive and breathing, staring me boldly in my face. I felt like I was going to be sick.

I closed my eyes pushing a few more tears down my cheeks as I exhaled angrily. I finally closed the diary and stood up. Everything I couldn't say was right there. Everything was out in the *–figurative –* open for the entire world to see. I stared at the butterflies on the cover of my diary for a long time, counting them over and over again before I was finally able to force my legs to walk out of my bedroom.

I got in the shower and let my mind wander about random and frivolous things, like an upcoming math test I had that I hadn't properly prepared for. I thought about skipping lunch tomorrow so I could avoid seeing Mrs. McCabe. I thought about the oddly nice new kid who shared his burger with me today. Realizing that within this crappy day the sunny and shiny boy had been the only *okay* thing about my day. I thought about the inevitable conversation I was going to have with Matt tomorrow once he finds out I was at Alicia's instead of therapy. I thought about why I'd missed the session, how upset my mother got – what she assumed… –I let my train of thought derail.

I turned off the water, grabbed my towel, and went right back into my room locking the door. When I sat down on my bed I looked up and sitting there was my diary. It looked bigger. It looked like it was taking up more space on my desk than it had before.

I inhaled, getting up to put my old ratty t-shirt on. I turned back around and the diary was still there, *obviously* where would it go? I got back into my bed pulling the covers over my head and like a freight train skidding to an abrupt stop the diary was screaming, the diary was on fire, the diary was banging itself on my desk.

I yanked the covers off of my head and turned around to see the diary just sitting there. It wasn't screaming, it wasn't on fire, and it wasn't banging itself on the hard wood trying to get my attention.

But, I felt like it was glaring at me, it was pretentious, and indignant. It knew it had all of my secrets. It knew it was capable of imploding my life and the lives of the people around me.

I was manic and anxiety ridden watching it hold my words, words that I could never get back. Like a crazed person I jumped out of my bed and nearly ran to my desk grabbing the diary. I yanked it open and violently ripped those three pages out that I'd just written. I tore the pages into pieces so tiny that they could have easily been confused as confetti. I threw the pieces of confetti into the trash and then poured my bottle of water over it just to ensure the pieces could never be put back together.

I sat down in my chair nearly out of breath. My shoulders slumped as I stared at my trashcan. Unable to cry for some odd reason; my hands started to tremble. I counted the butterflies on the cover of the diary again and again, slowly and methodically until I was able to calm my unsteady body.

In that moment I realized that like the wet and ripped pages of confetti, I *too* would never be put back together.

Chapter Four: No Coincidence

I was so sleepy. Losing your mind could do that to a person. Last night I'd gone thoroughly insane. Last night I let an inanimate object terrorize me. I wondered if what happened was considered a mental breakdown. I slept probably an accumulative of two hours. I was a real life Zombie. I didn't even look in the mirror at myself; I didn't want to deal with my face right now.

I decided today to take my lunch outside, maybe the fresh air would wake me up and breathe some spirit into my lifeless body. Also, Mrs. McCabe wouldn't be able to approach me. It had the potential to be a win/win situation.

It was much too cold to eat outside, but the abnormally quiet atmosphere was strangely calming. I closed my eyes for a moment and took a deep breath in. The frigid air pinched my lungs, but it did give me a jolt of energy that I so desperately needed. I opened my eyes to see the new boy walking out of the cafeteria. He was already looking in my direction when we made eye contact. In that same moment a bright smile shot across his face and reflexively I smiled in return.

I hadn't noticed yesterday or maybe I just wasn't paying close enough attention, but he had a very nice smile, the kind of smile they use in ads for dental offices. I looked away when I realized I was just staring at him like an ultimate creeper. He walked over to me with an orange and a can of pop in his hand.

"You probably think I'm a stalker at this point?" He said with an impish smirk on his face.

"A little," I nodded. I scooted over so he could sit down.

"Thanks," he put his can down and began to peel his orange.

"Was the lion's den too much for you?" I asked as I took a bite of my candy bar. The first thing I'd eaten today and the same as the last thing I'd eaten yesterday.

"If I'm being honest, I didn't want to eat in there by myself. It already sucks being the new kid I didn't need to be the new kid who sits in the middle of the cafeteria by himself peeling an orange," he laughed. "I have a reputation to uphold."

"Hmmm, a reputation," I say with a light chuckle. "What? Were you some kind of big deal in the dog eat dog world of *Nebraska*?" I tease with an arched eyebrow.

He laughed and the sound was light and easy. He was *definitely* too sunny and too shiny. I felt like my dark black storm cloud would leave smudges on him just for the simple fact he was sitting this close to me.

"Yea," he said through his laughter. "I left some unfinished business back home, I can't let word get out that Ohio turned me soft."

I nodded with my laughter, noting that I was on school property with an actual *smile* on my face. I couldn't remember the last time I'd shown my teeth here, I'd never really had a reason to.

"Definitely wouldn't want to hurt your street cred." I winked. He held our eye contact as our laughter subsided. I looked away again, taking a sip of my pop. I was realizing that he did that a lot in the very short time I've known him. He would try to sustain eye contact as if he were trying to communicate some secret language without using words. It made me uncomfortable.

"I was actually looking for you," he said out of the blue. "I mean, I didn't know you were out here. I was looking for you in the cafeteria. I was going to offer you some fries to occupy your table." He paused then added. "I'm glad I found you."

I could feel his eyes still on me as I pretended to focus on my can, my chest felt warm in a weird way. "My rent is now candy bars not French fries." I state lowly trying to quickly change the vibe.

"Noted," I see him nod in my peripheral. "I'll have a candy bar ready for you Monday." he added casually.

"Monday…" I repeated, finally looking up at him.

"Yea," he answered, "if that's okay with you?"

It's quiet for a moment as I tried to suppress a smile. "I like Kit-Kat's," I said nonchalantly as I pulled one out of my bag to open. He laughed and shook his head.

"Kit Kats are my favorite," he started peeling his orange again, "looks like we have that in common." He held a slice of his orange in front of me. "Here."

"No thanks," I replied cringing away from his hand. I put an entire Kit Kat piece in my mouth and started chewing rapidly as I eyed him incredulously. He laughed again. The sound was even lighter and brighter than before. It was almost infectious.

"I've only known you for less than twenty four hours and I can already tell you *need* to eat this piece of orange," he continued to laugh leaning his entire body over holding the orange closer to my face. "Your diet consists of potatoes and chocolate. I'm truly worried about your insulin."

"I'm allergic!" I lied, shooing the orange out of my face, as he continued to jab it towards me. I was truly acting as if it were poisonous, one hand shooing it away, my leg up as if I were protecting my entire body from the orange ever touching me.

We were both laughing hysterically as I realized his mischievous plan. "Wait," I said almost breathlessly. "You're just offering me something because the polite thing for *me* to do would be to offer you a piece of my Kit Kat bar?"

41

He looked at me with one eyebrow raised, that was all the confirmation I needed.

"Well, I don't have manners." I said quickly turning my body directly faced him to shove another Kit Kat piece into my mouth.

"Wow," he shook his head in mock disappointment, amusement lighting up his deep chocolate eyes. "I thought we were friends?"

"Are we?" I said automatically. The air between us is still and loaded with unspoken words, I cleared my throat prepared to change the subject, but he beat me to the punch.

"I just realized I don't know your name?"

"Oh, it's Zoe."

"Aiden," he answered. It's quiet again. I looked over at him as he forced himself to finish his orange, thankful that he was done using it as a weapon on me.

"Here," I said holding out a piece of Kit Kat towards him, he smiled brightly. Now that I was up close I could definitely confirm that he belonged on a dental office brochure or billboard.

"We *are* friends!" He exclaimed as he put the whole thing in his mouth. I smiled and rolled my eyes. "Thank you." He said –his mouth still full.

"Welp," I shrugged, "that's what *friends* are for, right?" He paused and again he tried to sustain eye contact with me. This time I didn't look away. I still felt like he was trying to communicate with me soundlessly or maybe he was trying to look right through me? That same warm feeling filled my chest and it almost made me squirm.

"Yes," the enthusiasm in his voice nearly faded, but that sunny and shiny glint in his eyes was still there. "That's what friends are for." He repeated in a much more serious tone.

I bit my lip then reluctantly turned away from him. So we were friends –that much was clear. It would be nice to know someone here who didn't know my history or reputation at this school. I knew sooner or later he would find out things that really aren't anyone's business. I would hope that he would give me the benefit of the doubt.

"Well, I'm going to be late to class," he said grabbing his unopened can of pop. "I'll see you Monday. Kit Kat in hand," he added, giving me thumbs up. I teasingly gave him thumbs up back and he walked away.

Today wasn't bad so far, I managed to stay awake in my first three classes, I managed to avoid Mrs. McCabe, and I managed to kind of make a friend who didn't know I was known as the school whore. It was almost cause for celebrating. The bell rang and I knew I would be late to class, *again*. I really needed to work on that.

I got to class, everyone was seated already. I walked in head down headed towards my normal seat. I sat down immediately getting my notebook and pen ready.

"Wow, you're stalking *me* now?"

I turned and sitting in the chair that was always empty was Aiden, a surprised smile resting on his face. "What are you doing here?" I asked him abruptly – caught completely off guard.

"What are *you* doing here? You weren't here yesterday?" He asked with the same level of surprise in his voice.

"Oh…" I said, "I left early yesterday"

"Oh…" he nodded –us both not knowing exactly what to say next.

"Well, I have claim on this table too," I finally say. "Looks like you owe me *two* Kit Kat bars." I smiled humorously at him.

"Hmm," he said with a smirk, "what if I mix it up a little, how about a Kit Kat and a Snickers bar or something?"

"Sorry," I shrug. "It's a very strict *Kit Kat's only* clause." He snickered. "I wish I could change the agreement, but it's out of my hands." I add.

"Is it now? Who do you suggest I speak to about this?" He asked in mock seriousness, "I think this clause is highly discriminatory to other delicious candies?"

"Well, I..." I began to say, but was interrupted by my math teachers booming voice.

"Miss. Oakley and Mr. Jordan would you like to share whatever it is you're talking about with the entire class? If not please refrain from disrupting the beginning of my lesson." Mr. Knight said from the front of the classroom. We both turned from each other and immediately started writing down notes.

Class was long and agonizing. I could guarantee that I would never use any of this information as an adult. High school curriculum was a joke. I glanced over to see Aiden writing quickly his eyes intent on the smartboard. He was studious; I bet he was super smart, I bet he completely understood this mess. We didn't say a word to one another for the entire one hour and fifteen minute class. The bell finally rang and we looked at each other at the same time.

"You understood all of that didn't you?" I accused him jokingly.

"I'm kind of good at math," he shrugged. I could tell he was proud of that fact. I would be too if I had the ability to understand it.

"*How* good?" I raise one eyebrow.

"I took honors math in Nebraska and the only reason why I'm not in an honors class here is because it's required to take this class first, and then get admitted. Something weird with my transcript, I don't know..."

I just looked at him with my eyebrows furrowed.

"What?" he said incredulously.

"New deal," I said forcefully. "Rent is now you being my math tutor?" I was joking to be honest. There wasn't enough tutoring in this world that could make me understand any of this.

He smiled then extended his hand, I shook it and he nodded. "Deal," he amended. Maybe it was just me or maybe it was him, but we held hands longer than we probably should have.

"Well," I said pulling my hand away and clearing my throat. "I don't want to be late, I'm pretty much known for that."

"Me either," he agreed, putting his hand in the pocket of his hoodie. "See you later."

"See ya…" I walked past him in the small space around the chair to hurriedly leave the classroom. I exhaled as soon as I got into the hallway. Again, a warm feeling swam through my chest, it was unfamiliar and uncomfortable and at this point *annoying*.

I got to my last class of the day early. That was a first. I sat in the back like I always did. As far away from the board as I could possibly be. My train of thought was interrupted by my phone buzzing in my pocket.

Just trying to figure out why I haven't heard from you in two days?

The text was from Matt, I'd completely forgotten that I'd ignored him last night.

I sighed before responding. *I'm sorry. I'll call you tonight.*

I watched as the little bubbles blinked on my screen.

Come over after school

45

I have a lot of homework I texted back

So you are avoiding me, what happened?

I stared at the text for what felt like an eternity before responding.

Fine, see you tonight.

He texted two thumbs up.

I have been told that I have a tendency of pushing people away. I didn't think it was intentional. Matt would never allow me to push him away even if I tried though. He was permanent and that made me feel safe in away. I hated for him to be angry or frustrated with me, but that was pretty much the packaging that came with being my friend.

Class was about to start, the loud scratching of chairs and conversations filled the air as students rushed to their seats. One more hour and I would be free for the weekend. I lived for the weekends, no obligations, no people, no having to communicate with the outside world if I didn't want to. I would marry weekends if I could.

I looked up and my eyes nearly bugged out of my head, I had to quickly regroup before speaking. "Aiden?" I say, I didn't mean for it to come out as a question, but it did. He hadn't noticed me as he walked in the classroom already heading in my direction. When he saw me a huge smile stretched across his face.

"Wow," he said placing his bag on my desk. "*Three* Kit Kats a day five days a week? I'm going to have to get two jobs to afford this rent …"

I smirked, and a sound that was supposed to be a chuckle escaped my lips. "Weird, yea…" is what I said. Not exactly responding to his statement, but responding to my inner dialogue, this was weird.

46

"Assuming this seat isn't taken?" He said.

"It's free," I said lowly scooting my chair over slightly.

It was quiet for a moment and I was not going to let my overanalyzing of Aiden ruin the fact that he was kind of a friend now. I could feel this awkward vibe about to take over and I didn't want that. "Let me guess," I say breaking the slightly uncomfortable silence, "you were in honors classes for History as well?"

He just stared at me and I couldn't help but laugh. "You think you have me pegged?" He said jokingly.

"Somewhat. Yes," I answer honestly.

"Let's hear it?" He questioned. I looked at him for a moment before responding.

"Okay, I think of you as shiny and sunny."

"Shiny and sunny?" He repeated confusingly.

"Yea," I answer. "You are that good kind of person. The *real* kind of good not the for show kind, you're the kind of person who walks little old ladies across the street. You're the type that probably volunteers in soup kitchens on Thanksgiving and still rushes home to help your mom cook." I nodded realizing that there was no way I was wrong about him, you could just tell. "You probably keep extra umbrellas in your car just to pass them out to people at bus stops when it rains." He's staring at me intensely not giving me any indication if I were spot on or way off. "Assuming you have a car." I added.

"Hmm," was all he said after a few seconds of silence. His eyes were still staring directly into mine. "In twenty four hours you know that much about me?"

I swallowed then nodded. It was weird, my gut told me that everything I was saying may not be exact, but I was sure as hell in

47

the ballpark. I bet he's fooled a lot of people with this edgy exterior, borderline *bad boy* look he has going on. Though I did not truly know him, he wasn't fooling me.

"Well?" I say.

"What?"

"Am I right? Do I have you pegged?" I questioned. His eyes never broke from mine and for the first time I was okay with the warmth I felt in my chest as I stared right back at him.

"I can't divulge *all* my secrets. I just met you, Zoe." He said teasingly, he smiled brightly – his teeth were seriously ridiculous. I smiled and finally blinked away looking down at my notebook.

"I'm trying to peg you," he said out of the blue, causing me to look back up. "I have fragments for sure, but not the entire picture."

He couldn't peg me because dark black storm clouds were erratic and unpredictable. He couldn't peg me because *I* couldn't peg me. I didn't say anything because I wasn't exactly sure I wanted to hear how I was viewed from the one person in the world who didn't think I was a whore.

I turned away from him, not responding to his statement. I picked up my pen and wrote the date down. I could feel him staring at me, I knew he was studying me and I felt oddly exposed as if he could actually figure out things I never wanted anyone to know if he tried hard enough.

"Zoe…" he said, but was interrupted when the teacher started speaking. I exhaled and kept my eyes looking straight ahead.

This history class was dragging and it didn't help that I was avidly trying to create a bubble around me so Aiden couldn't see me. I felt so childish, it had been over thirty minutes and I didn't look over in his direction or say another word to him all because I was afraid of his opinion. I truly questioned my sanity sometimes.

Finally, I casually and discreetly looked over at Aiden. He was focused on his notebook, but this time I realized he wasn't writing notes he was sketching. He was drawing a girl with flowing dark hair; her face was shaded in like a shadow as if she didn't have an identity. The hair covered half of her nonexistent face lying well past her shoulders. She was sitting on a bench with her eyes closed, looking up at the sky. She looked peaceful, but even without seeing her face she looked morose and contemplative.

It was beautiful.

Another talent that Aiden possessed, I wondered if there were things he was *not* good at.

"Miss Oakley," I snapped out of my reverie when I heard Mrs. Brennan call my name. "Could you read the paragraph aloud, please?" She requested.

I looked down at my book and didn't have a clue where we were, I felt Aiden bump my knee with his knee. "Page 315, second paragraph," he whispered quickly.

I smiled to myself and began reading, Mrs. Brennan being none the wiser. I wasn't absorbing anything I was saying, my autopilot had some benefits. I was trying to figure out how Aiden knew where we were in the book while drawing that beautiful picture of the faceless girl.

Class ended five minutes early by the grace of God. I originally planned on leaving the classroom without saying a word to Aiden. I'm sure he thinks I am weird now anyways, but he'd helped me today. I wanted to at least thank him.

"Hey, thanks," I said to him as he started putting his things in his book bag.

"No problem." He said with a soft smile, standing up from his seat.

"I have a question," I said as he closed his notebook. I was intrigued by his sketch. I wanted to know more about this faceless woman who was somehow so stunningly beautiful. It really wasn't my thing to pry or ask a lot of questions, but I really wanted to know.

"Yea?"

"I saw your sketch, It's…she's beautiful." I realize immediately that wasn't actually a question. I wasn't exactly good at giving compliments either, but I had to give credit where credit was due. I instantly wished I hadn't said anything because the look on his face was telling me he didn't want me to see that picture and didn't want to talk about it.

"Sorry, it was just… right there and you're very talented." I added as I grabbed my bag and stood up to walk away.

"Wait," he said. "Sorry, I sketch a little for fun. It's… private."

"Oh, well you're amazing," my words made me want to vomit. I didn't use words like *amazing,* but that's what it was. I wanted to tell him that someone with that type of talent shouldn't keep it a secret, but it most obviously wasn't my place to say that.

He didn't respond he just stood there looking at me. He reminded me of myself in that sense unable to take a compliment. I couldn't blame him honestly, but now I know I have definitely ruined any chances of a continued *friendship*. Between me acting weird at the beginning of class and now intruding on his personal and private art, I'm sure he won't be sitting with me or bringing any Kit Kats Monday.

I exhale. "Okay, bye." I say awkwardly as I turn to walk away. I want out of this classroom as quickly as possible, but I am stopped in my tracks when I hear him say my name.

"Zoe, hang out with me tomorrow?" He said the words quickly, but he was sure of himself. He said the words as if he was debating this entire time whether to ask me or not.
I turned around looking at him directly in the eyes. "I mean, I would like to take you on a date." He added his words slower and clearer. I blushed. I don't think I'd ever done that before, it felt weird and I didn't like it.

"A date?" Like an idiot I repeat the words back to him as if they would become any less true. I'm thrown off because just seconds ago I was pretty sure he was never going to talk to me again.

"Yes, I would like to take you on a date." It was as if his nerves had dissipated. He was confident and apparently prepared for any answer I was going to give him. I hadn't been on a formal date. No one had ever asked me to go on a legitimate date before.

As I stand here looking at Aiden who I hadn't noticed before, but his large brown eyes and his warm beach sand skin made him attractive –*very attractive*. I'm realizing that I *want* to go on a date with, which is surprising me completely. I want to talk to him outside of this school. I want to know what other talents he had besides academics and sketching.

"Sure," I said simply. I felt my nerves start to scatter sporadically throughout my body. I inhale, and then smile. Again, I'm blushing. I felt like a dainty school girl from the fifties, all I needed to do now was bat my eyelashes or something.

"Okay, cool," he says, his smile matching mine. "I'll pick you up at your house around seven? I'll need your address."

My mind flitted back to the argument my mother and I had last night, there was no way he could come to my house. There was no way she could know I was going on a date. She already thinks I'm a whore who will get pregnant again. I didn't need to give her anymore ammunition.

"Uhh," I choke out, "my mom is a little overprotective. Maybe we can meet somewhere?" That was as close to the truth I would allow myself to get.

"Okay, no problem. Here's my number. We'll text."

I pulled out my cellphone and he put his number in it. We just stood there for a moment in the silence and it didn't feel awkward at all, I was the first to break the trance.

"I'll see you tomorrow," I said softly as I walked away, he nodded with a smirk.

Again, I exhaled as soon as I got into the hallway, trying to gather my thoughts. I pulled my cellphone back out and texted Matt to let him know I was on my way. He replied immediately asking me to pick up some French fries along the way.

Matt was my best friend and he had been since we were five years old. I told him *almost* everything, but as I walked to his house I debated whether I should tell him about my date with Aiden. I was used to my mother disappointing me, but if I told Matt and he assumed the worst it would ruin me, it would ruin how I viewed our friendship. I decided it was my personal business and not for anyone else to dissect like they did everything else in my life.

I got to Matt's and walked right down to the basement.

"Hey," I said as I plopped on the couch, handing him his fries.

"Thanks," he stuffed a handful in his mouth. "So…"

"I'm not avoiding you." I say simply leaning over to grab the remote.

"You skipped your session to hang out with Alicia?" He questioned. Which was annoying because obviously that's exactly what happened so why ask the question?

"Yes."

"I don't want to argue, Zoe." He said frustratingly.

"So let's not," I rebutted. It was quiet for a moment as I surfed through the channels. Nothing was on of course.

"It's like you're moving backwards." He finally said, shifting his entire body in my direction. So he *did* want to argue.

"Look, you wanted me to come over. I'm here, but if we are going to have a bash Zoe- athon I'm going to leave."

"I just want you to act like I'm still someone you can turn to? It's like you clump me with your mom and your therapist and it isn't fair. I love you Zoe and I just want the best for you. I don't want you to treat me like someone you have to hide and run from."

I felt horrible listening to his honest words. I never wanted him to feel like he was just another person. Maybe I was being a little hard on him; he was only trying to help. He was trying to be there for me and I wouldn't let him. He was right, it wasn't fair.

"I'm sorry," I finally muttered. "I'm just so tired of everyone wanting me to live in the past. I don't want to talk about the last year, it's over with and we can't change it. Aren't you tired of having the *same* argument? Can we just please move on? Please?"

He looked at me for a moment before grabbing my hand and squeezing it tightly.
"Okay…" he finally answered. "I'll leave it alone."

It was quiet for a moment when his mom came down the stairs. "Hello," she said flatly. She truly hated me. Matt let go of my hand and grabbed the remote, his mother's eyes were locked on that entire transition. "Is *Alicia* coming over tonight?" The way her eyes pointed daggers at me was almost enough to make me burst into laughter or tears. I wasn't sure which one at first.

"Is she?!" I exclaimed over enthused. "When I was over her house *yesterday* she didn't say she would be here... I would love to see her again!" I glanced at his mother and the annoyance that spilled from her was oddly satisfying. Matt –my oblivious Matt –looked at me strangely then answered his mother. "No, she is going out of town to see her Grandma this weekend. Zo is staying though." He added as he continued to surf through the channels.

"Oh, okay..." she said before pausing then walking back up the stairs.

"Dude," I said flatly. "How do you *not* see it?"

"See what?"

"Your mom hates me, she openly despises me."

He sighed then rolled his eyes. "That's all in your head, my mom loves you. She always has."

Matt was too smart and too in tuned to the world around him to be this clueless.

"Things change..." I trailed off.

"Like?" As soon as he said the words he realized what I was referring to.

"*That* didn't change anything." He finally answered glowering at me.

It was amazing how he could not see it. The, *that* he was referring to was a surprise pregnancy. I so badly wanted to tell him about his mother pulling me off to the side and asking if the baby was his. I remember the shock that traveled through me, the anger that blazed through my body, the sadness that knowing my best friend's mother, someone I viewed as a second mother for over a decade would never look at me the same. How in her eyes I saw that she didn't believe me when I said he wasn't the father that Matt and I were so platonic

54

we might as well have been blood related. She didn't say the words, but I knew she didn't believe a thing I'd said to her.

I sat there watching my oblivious Matt defend his mother. I wanted to tell him that story, but I needed to stick to my own motto. Don't harp over things that happened in the past, things you can't control. I wouldn't bring up a conversation that happened nearly eight months ago, a conversation that could cause an argument between Matt and his mother.

"Okay, Matt," I conceded. "I don't want to talk about it anymore." I shake my head facing the television. "Movie?" I suggested. There were over two hundred channels and nothing to watch on a Friday night.

"Scary?" He said getting up walking towards his shelf of DVDs.

"Only, if you're driving me home." I answered.

"Deal."

Chapter Five: Almost Perfect

It's 6:25pm and I have to leave to meet Aiden. I'm sick to my stomach, I want to scream, and also I want to cocoon myself into my bedroom and barricade the door shut. I was so unbelievably nervous, I was acting as if I didn't already have an easy rapport with him, that I hadn't already felt comfortable around him.

I was blowing this way out of proportion. I knew that, but I couldn't help it.

"Zoe?" I heard my mother say as she knocked on my door. We hadn't said a word to one another since our Thursday night argument. She opened the door slowly to find me sitting at my desk wearing clothes I'd never worn before.

"You look nice," she said softly as she sat on my bed, "going out tonight?"

"Don't worry; I'm not planning on getting pregnant." The words are acid on my tongue, the volcano in my chest erupting. "Clearly, I'm too fertile for my own good."

"Zoe, listen…" she snapped angrily. "What I said was out of line and I know that. I was angry and I felt like you were being sneaky and…I'm being the bigger person. I didn't mean to make you feel…"

"Like less of a person?" I interrupted, "like a whore?" I added bitterly. She looked down and then back up –tears brimming out of her eyes.

"I don't think you are a whore and those will never be my words," she sniffled. "I never meant to make my baby girl feel like less of a person."

It was quiet in the room for a moment as I refused to let my tears escape my eyes.

"We have to be honest with one another, Zoe," she finally said, "there is so much I don't know or understand about you. I just want you to let me in." She sighed. "I figured since you couldn't let *me* in that maybe those sessions with Dr. Gleasyn would help you."

I was absorbing my mother's words but I was disconnected. I felt animosity towards her, I felt anger and frustration and I knew exactly why but it didn't matter *why* at this point.

"I just want you to be happy." She added as she wiped away another tear.

I looked directly at her, feeling vacant as I said the words. "That's not meant for everyone." The words hurt as I said them, practically the same words I'd uttered to Matt when he'd said the same thing to me.

"Zoe…" she began to say, pain rippling across her face.

"I'm going to be late," I interrupt. "I'll be home before 11pm." I stood up and headed towards the door.

"Zo!" she said stopping me in my tracks, "I love you."

I paused at the door for a moment, my back still facing her as I exhaled, "You too, mom." I walked out of the door and out of that house.

It was about a fifteen minute walk to the park where I was meeting Aiden. I thought it was odd that he wanted to meet here. I was expecting a movie, maybe dinner. He obviously had other things in mind. About two minutes go by before I see Aiden walking up with a huge wicker basket.

"Hey," he said, "you ready?"

"Picnic?" I asked with slight surprise in my voice. It was about forty two degrees out, not exactly picnic weather.

"Not exactly…" He said as he grabbed my hand. I felt a pinch of electricity but I ignored it and followed where he was leading. He walked us over to a giant oak tree, its leaves were gone for the winter but it was still beautiful. He placed the basket on the ground, opening it up and pulling out two fleece blankets. He spread one on the ground and then placed the other one over my shoulders.

"Thanks," I said as he continued to pull things out of the basket. Surprisingly, it really wasn't a picnic. He pulled out three game boards, playing cards, a large sketch book, colored pencils, and water colors.

"Have a seat," he said as he sat down and pointed to the ground next to him. "I almost forgot," he added as he dug through the basket, "here." He handed me a giant bag of mini Kit Kat bars. I burst into laughter.

"I think this is the best gift I've ever gotten!" I said between giggles.

He laughed along with me, "I figured that should buy me a couple weeks?" He smiled.

"Yea, you're paid for through spring." I say as I place the giant bag on the blanket next to me. "What is all of this?"

"Well, seeing as though I don't start my new job until next Thursday I couldn't exactly take you on a nice classy date like I wanted to..."

"Aiden, I don't care about stuff like that." I interrupted.

"I figured as much but *I* wanted to do that for you. So, this will be sort of a place holder until our *real* first date after my first check." He was studying my face to gauge my reaction.

"This isn't a real first date?"

"No," he answered simply. "I plan on wowing you on our first date. *Tonight,* I plan on kicking your butt in Taboo, Picnic Panic, Jenga and Black Jack." He smirked.

"This is probably the sweetest thing anyone has ever done for me," I say lowly, smiling right back at him. "But, I'm going to kick your ass and it will be embarrassing," I glared at him. The humor in his eyes almost makes me break my serious hold.

"Oh, so you're competitive?"

"With worthy opponents? Yes. With you? Not so much." I shrug nonchalantly.

His smile beamed brightly as he grabbed the Jenga box and dumped all of the blocks onto the blanket. "You don't know who you're dealing with. Prepare to eat your words."

I'm trying very hard not to laugh at how intensely he is saying these words but he was being such a dork in the most appealing way, "This isn't a flat surface?" I questioned.

"We will use the bottom of the picnic basket."

"You have this all planned out, don't you?" I question. I grabbed the basket and flip it upside down. He looked up at me with an arched eyebrow and started stacking the blocks on top of the basket meticulously. He was trying to be intimidating. I bit my lip to hold in my laughter.

We played Jenga for at least thirty minutes he won three games and I won four. There was a lot of yelling, throwing of blocks, and some explicit language, but nothing overshadowed how much fun I was having.

"Luck," he stated flatly, placing the blocks back into the box.

"Aiden, I never would have imagined you being the sore loser type. It's not becoming of you."

He smiled and threw a Kit Kat at me. "And abusive? My God!" I said in mock horror as I picked up the Kit Kat and opened it.

"That's like, what? Your fifth one?" he asked comically.

"Sixth actually," I say, shoving the entire mini in my mouth.

"I want to know how many cavities you have?" he's laughing shaking his head, "I *need* to know." He closed the Jenga box and threw it back into the basket.

I shrug with a smile.

He was shuffling through all of the things he pulled out the basket when the sketch book caught my eye.

"Hey," I said. I repositioned myself so that I was now sitting with my legs crossed up under me. "What is the sketch pad for?" My mind flitting back to the beautiful sketch he'd drawn yesterday. I was hoping he would draw another. He paused for a moment as if he were contemplating something then he finally grabbed it and handed it to me. I opened it and there on the page was the beautiful faceless girl, the same girl he was sketching in history class but this time she wasn't sitting on a bench she was sitting in a tree. Again, her hair covering her features but she was stunning. It was ridiculous how talented he was.

"This is beautiful," I said simply because I couldn't say anything else.

"It's you."

You could hear the uncertainty in his voice. You could hear how nervous he was to share this with me; something that he'd said was private.

I stared at him in complete shock, this beautiful drawing and the one from class yesterday was me? I wanted to know more about this girl. I wanted to learn everything there was to learn about the faceless girl and it was me the entire time? I didn't realize how long I sat there silently with my mouth gaped open staring at Aiden.

"That's creepy isn't it? It wasn't supposed to be creepy. It's just that…"

"No," I interrupted him, "it's beautiful, it's… it's too beautiful to be me I don't understand." I was truly captivated and confused, *should* I be creeped out? If that was the normal reaction I was supposed to be having, then I was far from normal. "I don't understand how this could be me?"

"Too beautiful to be you?" he repeated, "I don't think you see yourself very clearly."

The blush covered my entire body. I looked back down at the sketch. And I felt something rumble in my chest a feeling I'd never experienced before. It wasn't the same as the warm feeling that would fill my chest when I was around Aiden. *This* rumbling almost devoured my chest completely. I looked back up at him and he was still studying me. He was trying to figure out what I was thinking.

"Her face," finally able to string together my thoughts, "why is she…I mean, why am I faceless? Does that mean something?" I asked honestly. Maybe it didn't mean anything, or maybe it meant everything? Maybe that's just how he drew all of his pictures. Either way I still needed to know.

He looked at me for a moment. I could tell he was trying to figure out how to word it properly. I waited patiently, looking back down at the drawing, wishing I could figure out what was wrong with her – with *me*.

"Can I be honest with you?" He asked. I nodded, still not looking up from the drawing.

"When I said I couldn't peg you yesterday, this is what I meant."

I looked up at him confusingly waiting for him to continue. He looked as if he were nervous to continue, like he thought I would be upset with what he had to say.

"It just feels like you are in this bubble, that you allow *just* enough in or out but never all of it," he sighed. "I'm not making sense. I'm sorry."

"No," my voice cracking, "keep explaining." I felt like an open live wire. Aiden was tap dancing around some version of my truth and it was terrifying but I wanted –no I *needed* to know exactly what he was thinking about me.

"I thought I could figure it out if I drew it. I wanted to draw your essence. The things I am actually able to see and feel when I'm around you." He looked like he was uncomfortable trying to explain. "I think you're beautiful Zoe, but there is something behind your eyes that's …" he trailed off searching for the right wording. "There's a disconnect I think. I don't know. Maybe you're not happy? And you're tired of pretending to be? Your eyes give you away almost. I wanted to sketch a picture of how beautiful you are without that pain or whatever it is dominating the sketch."

I was at a complete and total loss for words. I was just staring at him wanting to tell him how spot on he was, how he had me completely pegged but I couldn't do that. I couldn't reveal parts of myself to this person I'd known since Thursday. I couldn't tell him things that the closest people in my life couldn't even get out of me. He knew so much and he thought he didn't know a thing.

Is this what my mother saw? Is this what my therapist, and Mrs. McCabe saw? Is this what Matt saw? I wasn't fooling anybody if some boy from Nebraska could peg me after only two days of knowing my existence.

A tear fell from my cheek and I was immediately embarrassed. I wipe it quickly and turned my head slightly.

"I'm so sorry Zoe," regret in his voice. "I wasn't trying to hurt your feelings or make you feel like …"

"You didn't do anything wrong," I said wiping another escaped tear from my cheek. Aiden was something special that was for sure. I wish I had the ability to tell him why there was pain behind my eyes. I wish I could explain to him how many horrible experiences I had to deal with consecutively over the last year.

"Can you draw another?" I asked him while handing him the sketch pad back. I didn't know I was going to ask him to do that.

He nodded as he turned to a clean page. "…with my eyes?" I added. I wanted to see this pain that he says he sees. The pain that I don't see when I look in the mirror, a pain that I didn't think was visible to the world even though people in their own way had been trying to tell me all along. I knew exactly what the pain was but I'd only felt it, I never saw it in human form. I never saw it disguised as me.

He started sketching and I just sat there replaying his words over and over again in my mind. Who was this kid? Why did I feel like I'd known him my whole life? Everything about this was odd and different, especially for a first date. A part of me wanted to get up and leave but another louder and more present part of me wanted more. I wanted to stay. I didn't want to move an inch from this spot.

The cold air was soothing against my flushed skin. I felt so exposed. What shocked me most is that it wasn't a horrible feeling –not as horrible as I would've thought it to be. To be seen so clearly by someone you barley knew should be terrifying and it was in a sense but my chest felt open in a way I hadn't experienced before. The dormant places in my being were being lit by dim rays of light. I was so uncomfortable but I was cemented here.

He found it somehow –those dormant places. He didn't know what *it* was but he knew it was there.

After a few minutes Aiden placed the sketch pad back on my lap. I stared at it for what felt like an eternity before I could even think of a single word to say. This girl was so sad and vulnerable. She looked like she'd been crying for weeks, maybe months. She looked like there was a scream buried in her chest that she needed to let out but hadn't, it was trapped. She had a beautiful smile, it was radiant even –but it wasn't real. It was not genuine. Her eyes made me want to cry, her eyes had seen things that they would never share with the outside world. She looked like she was being held together with tape and glue. She was falling apart.

She was most definitely me.

I felt the tears welt up in my eyes, but I wasn't going to do this, not here. It felt like whatever the connection was between Aiden and I had gotten too strong, too serious, too quickly. I took in a deep breath and closed the sketch pad.

"You're very talented," I said calmly. "That was really good," my voice was placid and unenthusiastic. I didn't want to feel exposed anymore. I didn't want my chest wide open. I wanted to switch off those dim rays of light and let my dormant places fall back into their dark corners quietly and unbothered where they were comfortable and safe.

He didn't respond. He just studied my face for a moment. I still felt exposed and it was almost making me angry. I turned my head away looking out towards the open park. There weren't a lot of people out so it was peaceful and serene. I started counting the trees. I needed to calm my racing heart somehow.

"I feel like this was a mistake?" Aiden finally said. His words were crushing, damn near debilitating but he was right. This whole thing *was* a mistake. I wasn't ready to date. I wasn't ready to like anyone. I wasn't ready to *be* anything to anyone and I probably never would be.

This was our first date and it got way too heavy. He was seeing that I came with much too much of a load to carry and I could not blame him for wanting to get out before this went any further.

"Okay," I said while taking the fleece off of my shoulders preparing to stand up.

"Wait," he grabbed my wrist. I stopped midway eyeing him confusingly. "Where are you going?"

"I'm going home?" I looked at him as if he were absurd. He was looking at me the exact same way.

"No Zoe, sit down. Please," he said while shaking his head. "I meant it was a mistake for me to say all of that. I don't know what I was thinking. I'm sorry."

"Don't apologize. I asked." I say lowly. He still had my wrist in his hand as I slowly sat back down. He gently moved his hand from my wrist to my hand and I avidly ignore how hard my heart is pounding in my chest.

"But still, on our first date? It wasn't the right time." He looks down at our connected hands and then back up at me. "I just, I wanted to be honest with you."

"It's not our real first date." I was trying to lighten up the severely intense mood. I didn't acknowledge what he said about being honest because right now and every other time in my life I was not the poster child for honesty and transparency. He smiled then interlocked our fingers. The rumble in my chest that I felt earlier was now cascading throughout my entire body. I could feel heat rise to my cheeks and boil in my stomach. I needed a word for what I was feeling; I desperately needed it to be defined.

"Zoe, you're going to think I am crazy and I probably am but I have to say it," his words are rushed and he looks nervous. I didn't know what he was going to say but the electricity flowing between our interlocked fingers was causing my heart to continue to beat uncontrollably, my stomach to flutter, and my thoughts to jumble.

"I really, really like you and maybe I'm missing the mark here, but you feel that, right?" He lifts our connected hands in the space between us. So it wasn't just me, I wasn't a crazed lunatic imagining things. These intense and confusing feelings were traveling intermittently down a two way street.

I nodded, not capable of finding the right words because I was overwhelmed and confused. I was hyperaware of each breath I took, of each breath he took. I was completely and utterly aware of how passionately he was looking into my eyes. I could feel his heartbeat through his fingertips. His deep chocolate eyes were casting an unsolicited spell over me as I stared right back at him. I exhaled and the words came out with no guard.

"I like you too," I said softly. The anxiety I thought I would experience uttering those words never came. It felt right to say it because it was the truth. I did like him. I liked him a lot –probably more than I should for only knowing him this short time, but I didn't care. I didn't even recognize myself right now. I was a different person with him. I didn't have to be the school whore, or the liar, or the damaged girl who is sarcastic and rude. I could just be me, whoever that *me* was flourished when she was with Aiden.

He smiled and squeezed my hand twice. "Well, I'm glad we are on the same page."

"Yea," I nod, "that had the potential of being super awkward for you." We both laughed lightly.

"…and I'm sorry if I made you feel uncomfortable with the drawings," he added, looking sympathetic. "It's just ever since I sat with you Thursday you're all I could think about." He placed his other hand on top of our intertwined fingers. "I was going to play it cool but then us being in the same classes and you seeing the sketch. I just don't see the point in waiting if you know what you want."

I nodded because it was all I could do. *I* was what he wanted? I was rendered speechless, I felt like he and I were having a conversation outside of this realm. This is the kind of thing that only happened in movies or on television. This kind of thing didn't happen in real life.

I felt like I should be wearing a warning sign that said damaged goods, that there were pieces of me that he would never know. I wanted to tell him that I'd given up a baby for adoption. I wanted to tell him before he found out from someone else, but I didn't want to ruin this moment. I wanted to hold onto whatever this was for just a little while longer before the inevitable happened.

"This," he began, giving my hand a gentle squeeze and lifting it up between us, "I want to see what *this* is. I want to see where *this* goes?"

"Me too," I say breathlessly. Feeling like I'd just run a marathon. My heart was still unable to control itself.

With little words, so much was said. There had to have been another life where we'd known each other but weren't given enough time together. The universe was giving us more time, a second chance or something. I felt like we were connecting *again* and not for the first time, that we'd been down this path before. I felt insane even thinking like this. Three days ago I didn't even know he existed and somehow right now in this overpowering moment I couldn't picture him not existing. It made my stomach flutter again but in a new and nearly unsettling way.

"One more thing," he said seriously, his face set in an intense scowl. I was confused. "Just because I like you doesn't mean I'm going to go easy on you in Taboo."

I laughed because he caught me off guard. I exhaled, feeling my nerves slowly falter. I grabbed the box and tossed it to him. "Let's go, you clearly didn't learn your lesson the first time around."

"I was just warming up. Jenga is for amateurs, Taboo is the real deal."

I rolled my eyes.

Hours went by as we played different games and talked about almost everything under the sun. I felt like I was catching up with a long lost friend. I felt a pull towards him that was terrifying. I didn't know what to do with that feeling; I could feel us moving much too fast but I didn't help slow it down. I wanted to know as much as possible about him. I wanted him to know as much about me as I was capable of offering.

"It's getting late," I say regretfully. I didn't want to leave but I'd given my mother enough heart attacks this week. "I have to be home by 11pm."

"I'll drive you home," he paused, remembering what I'd said yesterday, "If that's okay? I can drop you off up the street?"

I smiled. "Thank you, but I like walking."

"Well, then I'm walking with you," he started putting everything in the basket. "I'll stop at the end of the street?"

I smiled again and didn't object. I felt calm around him. He was able to see me with fresh eyes, no preconceived opinions. He was learning who I was without the stigma attached. He was the only person in my life who didn't know all of the ugly parts that everyone else thought they knew.

We walked hand and hand and not for a second did I feel self-conscious or nervous. It just felt right. It felt right to be holding hands with Aiden on this day, at this moment. It felt important.

"I'm right up here," I said as I stopped walking. I'm standing directly in front of him now staring at our connected hands.

"So…" he said walking towards me slightly closer. "I'll, uh…I'll text you when I get home?"

I smiled and nodded. "…and don't be too hard on yourself when you get home, it is super hard to not say the words on the card, even though that's the whole point of the game."

"That didn't count because everyone knows you can't play Taboo with two people."

"Ummm," I looked at him incredulously, "*you* brought the game?"

"An oversight," he shrugged.

I smiled and shook my head because he was ridiculous.

"I really have to go now. My mom can be a tyrant," I say lowly. "I'll be waiting for your text." I immediately regret saying that, it made me sound so needy.

"The second I walk through the door your phone will buzz." His perfect teeth seeming whiter against this blackened night.

"Okay."

Again, there are unspoken words in the space between us. The energy is tangible it was as if one could physically reach out and touch whatever it was going on between us. I can feel him leaning in towards me and I brace myself, not sure what to expect. Softly, gently, delicately his lips are pressed onto my cheek, I exhaled softly. This was a pace I could handle. Warmth radiated in my chest and at the very spot his lips were just located.

"Have a goodnight, Zoe Oakley," he said with a soft smile, and then he walked away.

I stood there for a moment watching him walk until I could no longer see his tall frame in the shadows. My face was hot and my heart was *still* beating erratically against my ribs. I took a deep breath in then exhaled slowly before walking home.

I walked through the front door and the television was blaring in the living room. I peeked around the corner to see Oscar asleep on the couch with an open beer in his hand. I tip toed past the living room to the steps trying my hardest not to wake him as I tried to make it to my room.

"Zoe!" I heard his voice grumble loudly, forcefully, causing me to jump. My stomach lurched as anger and annoyance flooded my entire body. I turned around and stood at the entrance of the living room not saying a word.

"Get me a beer." He ordered.

I bit my lip and turned to the kitchen. I grabbed a beer out of the fridge, opened it and headed back towards the living room. I was startled and almost dropped the beer on the floor when I looked up to see Oscar standing in the kitchens entry way. I swallowed and handed him the beer.

He snatched it and took a swig, still standing in my way.

"Where were you, dressed like that?" he questioned. His beady eyes were looking me up and down. I wanted to throw up; it felt like bugs were crawling all over my skin.

"Is my mother upstairs?" I said. I'm angry at how unsteady my voice is. He took a step closer and another drink of his beer before answering.

"No, she went out…"

In that moment my stomach lurched again, my palms were sweaty, and my heart dropped. I was completely frozen in time; it was as if my feet were cemented to the kitchen floor.

"I have homework to do." I said shakily as I was finally able to gain motor control. I tried to walk around him but he stepped to the side blocking my way out with his large frame.

"Oscar, please…" I'm now irate inside at how defeated and weak and *small* my voice is. How afraid I must sound or appear to be. How afraid I *actually* was. Why didn't my mother tell me she was going out? The rage filled me wholly.

"What? You haven't said more than three words to me since I've been back from Cali. Can't a stepfather reconnect with his stepdaughter?" He took another step towards me and instinctively I clenched my fists. My nails digging into my palms so deeply I thought I was going to puncture the skin. I was cornered, the kitchen table making it impossible for me to move further back. He slowly moved a piece of my hair out of my face and placed it behind my ear.

"Such a pretty face, such a shitty attitude," his voice was gravelly and deep my body shuddered in disgust. I swallowed and closed my eyes taking a deep, but shaky breath.

"Haven't you missed me?" His voice lower as he stepped even closer, his body almost pressed against mine.

I was preparing to run or scream or whatever I had to do to get out of this house. In that same moment I hear the front door open and I exhale exasperatedly almost falling forward once Oscar backed away from me.

"Oscar? Zo?" my mother called out as she walked into the house. Oscar walked out of the kitchen quickly to meet my mother around the corner in the foyer.

"Yea," he answered, "we were in the kitchen catching up. You're home early?"

"Ugh, this is why I never make plans to go out." I hear my mother say as frustration saturates her voice. "Tammy and I were waiting for over an hour for Lisa to come and she cancelled! Mind you she had the tickets and I was not going to drive forty five minutes to get them from her. It was such a mess."

I was dizzy and angry and wanted to burn this house down. I would not let these tears fall. I did not want my mother asking me what was wrong. I needed to get upstairs and stay there until school Monday.

"Hey," I said in a hurry hoping she didn't hear the crack in my words. I darted out of the kitchen, my back facing her, rushing up the stairs. "I have a lot of homework." I yelled behind me before making it to my room.

I slammed the door shut and locked it. I stood there breathing heavily looking at my room. The light purple walls covered with ripped and tattered posters of bands I don't listen to anymore. Dirty clothes piled on the floor in front of my tall cherry wood dresser. My dark blue carpet that didn't go with anything else in this room was worn and dull.

Flashes of real life nightmares paralyze me as I look at my bed. New bedding, new mattress but it was the same – *everything* was the same. Nothing was ever going to change.

I was trapped.

I ran over to my garbage can dumping its contents onto the floor. I frantically tried to put those ripped confetti pieces of paper back together. They needed to be mended they needed to be *alive* again. The wet torn paper was illegible. There were no words, just smudges and smeared black ink. The words I'd written were in the void, they were gone and spiraling further and further away from my reality.

I suddenly collapsed to the floor, my body feeling listless as I began to sob. I was suffocating, the walls were closing in. It felt like my heart was going to rip itself from my chest. The ceiling was starting to cave, the rubble burying me completely. Where was the air? How do I breathe? I couldn't remember.
I curled my body into the fetal position as if I were holding my body together. It felt like if I were to move I would break apart. I couldn't hold all of the pieces together by myself – I needed to be saved. I didn't want to drown anymore.

There was no one here who could help. There was no one in this entire world who could remove the cement blocks from my feet quickly enough to prevent my body from plummeting to the ocean floor. I had to save myself; I had to be my *own* life jacket.

I started thinking of things that made me happy; my childhood, Matt, my music, *Aiden*. I thought about his warm hand cradling mine, his smile that always seemed to make me smile, his lips lightly pecking my cheek. I began to breathe more deliberately, my heart was beginning to regulate its rhythm, my tears were still swimming out of my eyes but I managed to at least calm myself. I took a deep breath in and closed my eyes, lying on the floor for a few more moments until I was completely functional.

I finally stood up slowly and sat at my desk. I looked down at my failed attempt at putting together the pages I'd torn out of my diary. I turned back around to my desk and stared at the butterflies on its cover. I inhaled and exhaled before opening it. I grabbed my pen and began to write.

February 2014

Dear Diary...

Today was almost perfect.

I put the pen down timidly, closed the diary softly, stood up slowly, and went to bed shattered like I did every night.

***

I barricaded myself in my room for the rest of the weekend, only leaving out to use the bathroom. I debated whether I should pretend to be sick so I didn't have to go to school today but this house was the problem. I needed out of it.

I was actively ignoring and avoiding Aiden. He'd texted me Saturday night a couple of times then again last night asking if I were okay, asking if something was wrong since he hadn't heard from me. Of course something was wrong *everything* was wrong, but I couldn't tell him that he wouldn't understand and I wouldn't expect him to. I liked Aiden; I liked him so much that I wanted to protect him from me. I wanted to keep my dark black storm cloud as far away from him as possible, no matter how much it hurt.

I stared at the large cafeteria doors and inhaled, I turned and stared out of the window looking at where I sat outside Friday and exhaled. I contemplated just skipping, maybe hiding out on Alicia's porch again but that wasn't a good idea the last time I did it. I turned and walked outside deciding to head to the bench. When I rounded the corner, there stood Aiden with his back against a tree. He was already looking in my direction, it was clear that he was waiting for me.

I stopped walking, frozen in my steps. Only milliseconds went by before I turned around and darted off walking quickly around the school building.

"Zoe!" I hear Aiden calling behind me but my feet kept moving, my brain not having a plan or a destination. My heart was angry and fed up with my antics. As I nearly ran away from him, I knew I was being absurd. I knew I couldn't avoid him forever, that eventually he and I would have to talk. I just wasn't ready now; I had too many things on my mind to have to worry about what it was I was feeling for Aiden or what it could possibly be. He couldn't be a priority in my life and a person like him deserved to always be the priority.

"Zoe, wait!" I hear again but this time he sounds much closer, before I could even process it, I felt him grab my arm turning me around to face him. "What the hell?" he said angrily and out of breath.

I looked down at my feet, trying to force my tears to stay in. I didn't have time for this. I didn't want to talk to him or anybody right now.

"Why are you ignoring me?" the anger and confusion that saturated his voice made my stomach lurch. I was realizing that being around him would taint him and trying to stay away from him would hurt him. Aiden just *knowing* me was already affecting him in ways that he didn't deserve. I wish he would've just stayed in Nebraska, met some normal likable girl there, he traveled all this way to have to deal with this shit. It wasn't fair.

"Please, just drop it." I manage to say.

"Just drop it?" He repeated confusingly. "Did I do something? I'm so confused I thought that we…"

"*You* didn't do anything," I say interrupting him finally looking up. That was a bad idea because his chocolate eyes were so sad and confused and it was all because of me. "You're perfect." I add as a tear fell from my cheek.

"Zoe, you have to tell me what's going on?" His anger was metamorphosing into anxiety.

"I just…" I knew that the words I was about to say were going to hurt, but if I wanted to protect Aiden from my toxicity I had to say them. "I think we got caught up in the atmosphere Saturday. You're a nice guy. I just don't think this is something we should pursue."

I bit my lip. Another tear managed to escape my eye.

He just stared at me, just like he had a few days ago. It felt like he was seeing right through me, like he was trying to communicate with me inaudibly. His facial expression didn't change, his breathing didn't hitch, he just studied me and I stood there allowing him to.

"I shouldn't have led you on," I add, trying to sound more confident, "…and I was immature to try and avoid you. I just think it's easier to call it now before it gets too serious. I'm sorry for wasting your time." And that was the whole truth. I *was* sorry for wasting his time, for leading him to believe that this could ever be anything.

We held eye contact for a second more before he clenched his jaw and turned around to walk away. He never uttered a word, but the look on his face said it all.

I exhaled loudly as if I'd been holding my breath that entire time. The flood of tears I'd been holding in finally overflowed down my cheeks. It felt like an anvil that was covered in gasoline and set on fire was placed on my chest. Everything I said to Aiden was true in a sense; he didn't know what he was getting himself into. It was bad enough that people who have known me for years have to deal with me. I didn't want Aiden to be burdened in anyway, it would be inescapable. I had to let him go before this went too far.

I stood there for a moment longer watching him walk away. Once he was out of sight I sat down on the cold wet grass and cried into my hands. It didn't feel like I was crying just for Aiden, I was crying for everything all rolled up into one. My entire life was shit. I was suffocating in all areas and the *one* good thing I'd experienced in this past year I'd manage to ruin in a matter of days.

I was furious at the fact that I was crying here of all places. I wished I could leave, I didn't want to be here but I knew I had to stay. I knew I had to endure classes with Aiden every day for the rest of the year. I had to be around him knowing he hated me, knowing that I *made* him hate me. I sat in the grass for twenty minutes until I heard the bell ring. I got up slowly wiping the remainder of my tears from my cheeks. I walked to class slowly; with each step dread filled me.

I walked into the classroom and every seat was taken except for the seat next to Aiden, *my seat.*

I looked down while I walked down the aisle way. I had no way of knowing if he saw me before I pulled the seat out and sat. I did not look over at him, I did not know if he looked over at me. The silence was screaming, it was deafening and obnoxious. I could feel the unspoken words physically in the open air bouncing around between the both of us.

Class started and I couldn't pay attention, my focus was on every single thing Aiden did. Though I had not looked at him directly, I was hyperaware of his presence. When he cleared his throat, repositioned himself in his seat, picked up his pen –everything had my attention. I so desperately wanted to see his face this up close to see how angry he was, see if maybe one day in the future he could forgive me for leading him on.

The bell rang and before I could even decide whether I should look over at him or not he was already up and rushing out of the classroom.

I exhaled slowly, determined not to cry anymore today. I didn't know why I was being this way. I did this, what was I to expect? Was he supposed to be okay with the fact that in less than forty eight hours I'd flipped completely? He had every right to be mad and hate me. But even knowing that still made me feel sick to my stomach.

I got to my last class of the day a little early and the first thing I did was scan the room to see if Aiden was here. He wasn't. I sat down in my normal seat and watched the door. I wasn't even sure if I blinked. The final bell rang as all of the students got settled. Class had begun and Aiden was still not here. I sighed and felt a hot knot in my throat form. Was he missing class because of me? I had to tell myself that I was hurting him just a little bit now to avoid hurting him a lot later. It made sense to me.

The class dragged, my eyes still darting to the door every few minutes. Even when there was only ten minutes left in the class I half expected to see him come in. The bell rang and it snapped me back to reality. Every student was rushing out of the door, I just sat there. I sat there until the entire classroom was empty, even my history teacher left before me.

"Miss Oakley," she said as she gathered the last of her belongings, "If you're staying to do homework, please close the door after you when you leave."

I nodded, and then she was gone. I sat there for a moment longer before grabbing my bag and finally readying to leave. I was walking out of the door with my head down, debating whether I was in the mood to go to Matt's. I didn't want to go home, but Matt would know something was wrong with me and I did not want to talk about Aiden. *Hell*, Matt didn't even know Aiden existed.

"It's bullshit."

I hear from in front of me, startling me out of my thought. I looked up immediately and there stood Aiden. I couldn't quite figure out exactly what his demeanor was but I knew anger was one of the leading emotions in his words.

"What?" I say unsteady, my guard was completely down so I didn't have time to think.

"What you said outside, all of it. It's bullshit."

"Aiden…"

"You got scared so you're pushing me away. Why?" He interrupted. The fire yielding anvil was back, lying on the center of my chest.

There were a few students still lingering by in the hallway. I looked at them then back at Aiden. I turned around to walk back in the class room. He followed, closing the door behind him.

"I didn't want to hurt you, Aiden."

"But you did." His words were honest and though they were simple they gutted me. I had to remind myself of what I'd said earlier.

"I'd rather stop this now before it gets too heavy and I end up hurting you more later on." I swallow, my throat is dry but my eyes are wet, tears trying to make their way back to the surface.

"Why are you so sure you'd hurt me? What is it, Zoe?" he doesn't have anger anymore, just pure concern in his eyes and voice. "Why are you so okay with being unhappy?"

His words bothered me to my core, they downright enraged me. No matter how *connected* Aiden and I might be in some weird way he absolutely did not know me and he had no right to assume he did.

"I never said I was unhappy!" I snap, slamming my bag onto the floor angrily. My reaction surprising me but my anger overshadowed that feeling. "You are a stranger, stop acting like you know who I am! You draw a fucking picture and you think you're in my head or something? You do *not* know me!" I was sure if the people in the halls were still there they most definitely heard me. I couldn't believe how loud I was, how infuriated I felt. I knew that my emotions were irrational but I didn't care, I couldn't care if I tried.

78

Aiden exhaled, he didn't look like he was mad at me for screaming and cursing at him. He looked contemplative and sympathetic. This only upset me more. Why couldn't he just see that I had problems, that I was crazy and obviously hot tempered? Why wouldn't he just let whatever we had fizzle, he would be so much better off without me and the massive amount of baggage I brought along for the ride. He took a small step forward before he spoke.

"No, I don't know you but I *want* to know you, Zoe." His voice is calm as his eyes are looking directly into mine. I'm still fuming but I can't figure out how to look away from him. "What I do know is that you like me, I know that you have stuff going on in your life that you don't want to share with me and that's understandable and I wouldn't expect you to. We just met, I get it. But after everything we talked about Saturday you're willing to just wash your hands of me like I don't exist at all?" he questioned sincerely, "I don't believe that's what you want. I may not *know you* in that sense but like I told you before your eyes give you away every time."

I was just staring at him, he was so calm and I was so angry. I was frustrated that he was making this more difficult than it had to be. I was frustrated that every damn thing that came out of his mouth was accurate and he knew it.

"I don't understand why you would want to even deal with me at all." I say lowly, slowly I'm starting to find my resolve, "*Especially* now."

He shook his head, and then shrugged, "I'm attracted to everything about you Zoe, I don't know why – I just am and if you do not want to pursue this solely because you're scared I'll have a hard time accepting that. But if you have reasons apart from that, then I'll walk away and that will be it." He took a step closer, "So? Is there anything standing between us right now that isn't just fear?" his voice was low but confident. I swallow and bite my lip.

"My life is complicated." I finally say, hoping that somehow that would be enough. But Aiden was persistent –clearly, I knew it wasn't enough. "*I* am complicated," I add as I quickly wipe a tear from my cheek because there were so many layers to that statement that he would never know.

"I'm gathering that." He said offhand, "…but I'm good with complicated. *Believe* me." He answered with a strange and saddening look in his eyes. His words made my chest constrict because it was the first time I was seeing an Aiden that wasn't sunny and shiny. Whatever memory or thought he was having was probably why my behavior wasn't derailing him, why my inconsistency wasn't alerting him to leave and never speak to me again. My curiosity was peaked to the highest level, but I had to focus on the situation we were in right now. I inhale and exhale quickly.

"I can't be who you want me to be. Or who you would need me to be." I say lowly as I give up on forcing the rest of my tears to stay in place. I wiped them away as they fell one by one, my eyes still locked with his. I couldn't believe I was standing in front of him crying like this, but every emotion I was feeling in regards to everything in my life was overwhelming.

"I don't want you to be anything but you, Zoe," he slowly lifted his hand. I could see he was trying to weigh what my reaction might be. I just stood very still. He rested his palm on my cheek. "I don't have any expectations. I just want to see where this goes. Okay?"

The warmth, the rumbling, and now the little fluttering wings of butterflies in my stomach had taken over my entire body. All I could do was nod. Everything I'd told myself over the weekend and this morning was now invalid. I didn't want to be away from him, what a strange and terrifying feeling to have. No matter how hard I tried to push against it I loved how I felt when I was with him, even moments ago when I wanted to bite his head off.

I realized that Aiden wasn't going to let me push him away and in a very bizarre way it made me want to be near him even more. I thought I was protecting him but he wasn't allowing it and as I stood there melting into his sincere eyes I didn't want to fight against it anymore.

My cheek felt hot under his touch, reflexively I leaned my cheek into his hand and before I could catch back up to real time his other hand was on the other cheek. Then gently, I felt his lips press against mine. It was like an earthquake shattering my foundation at once. His shiny sun had collided with my dark storm cloud making an explosion of light and sound that caused the ripples of the tide to wipe away any doubts or concerns I'd had about this.

He pulled away from me after a few moments, his hands still cradling my face. "I'm sorry. I couldn't help it." He said lowly.

I swallowed and looked at him confusingly. My mind was running a million miles a minute. I was trying to find my place back in this world, in this school, in this room, in this moment. "Huh?"

He smiled. "Are we okay?' He said softly, hope in his voice. "Or are you going to say this isn't want you want and make me beg for another date?" he shook his head, "I don't like begging." He added with slight humor in his voice.

I paused. Realizing that even though I truly thought it would be for the best there was no way I could stay away from Aiden. As long as he could tolerate me, I wanted to stay around. It would be ridiculous to pretend we didn't have feelings for each other, even though I wasn't familiar or sure of what these feelings were. I inhaled and blinked slowly.

"We are okay." I finally say. I could see the relief conquer his features as he dropped his hands from my face and grabbed my hand.

"Can I ask you something?" He squeezed my hand; I nodded. "Promise me that we will just talk out any issues that may come up. Avoiding me, running away, telling me whatever pops in your head? Please don't do that, we can just talk. Okay?"

I nodded, it didn't seem like he was asking too much. "Okay." I add. "I'm sorry."

"Water under the bridge," he said, "all of this was because I beat you in black jack?" his serious tone not changing. I still had tear streaks down my cheeks as I smiled.

"I don't like losing." I shrug, reaching down to grab my book bag. He grabbed my hand when I stood back up as we walked towards the door. He just laughed and opened the door for me.

"What are you doing for the rest of the afternoon?" he asked.

I'd planned on possibly going over to Matt's, but I hadn't spoken to him today yet.

"I don't know, why?"

"Wondering if you wanted to grab some ice cream with me?"

"It's forty six degrees out?"

"It's ice cream, Zoe. There are no rules." He answered immediately.

I smiled, and then nodded. "Okay, ice cream sounds good." As we walked hand and hand down the empty hallway. I could feel a soft smile resting on my face.

This was not how I expected my Monday to end but I was definitely okay with it.

Chapter Six: Axis

It's been about a month since Aiden and I started dating. Two weeks ago I finally decided I needed to introduce him to Matt and Alicia. As predicted Matt was rude to him initially, but I'd warned

Aiden that Matt wouldn't like him even if he were the Pope. Luckily, a couple days ago we all had a movie night that somehow turned into a boys vs. girls game night in Matt's basement. I caught the two discussing a new video game that comes out next month and it made me smile, seeing my two favorite people not being assholes to each other.

"Aww," I remembered Alicia leaning over to whisper to me, "male bonding is such a delicate flower."

I laughed and nodded in agreement.

I've been to five therapy sessions in the last four weeks. I had to make up for the one that I skipped. I wouldn't say there was an improvement in my participation, *but* my diary entries were getting a little longer and I did stay for the duration of the sessions which is a pretty big deal for me.

I've been spending all of my free time at Aiden's. Sometimes we don't even plan anything. I just come over and lay on his floor while he sketches or does his homework. I felt like I was in a different world when I was near him. It was intoxicating. *He* was who I escaped to when being *Zoe* was just too much. The Zoe I am when I am with him is who I wished everyone else could see and know.

"You should go to the pep rally with me next week." Aiden stated as he got down on the floor next to me.

"Ew, why would I subject myself to that?"

"Because that's what normal teenagers in high school do." He countered, tapping his index finger against the tip of my nose.

"I'm not normal, or have we not had this conversation yet?" I replied shooing his hand away from my face.

He sighed and flashed his beautiful smile and big brown eyes at me. "Please?" He never played fair.

I rolled my eyes and sighed exasperatedly. I guess he took that as a *yes.* He leaned over and kissed my lips. "An hour," I said sternly my eyebrows furrowing from annoyance.

"Tops," he held out his pinky finger as the official pinky promise oath. I latched my pinky to his and then he pulled all of me to him.

"Can you stay for dinner tonight?" He asked between kisses, "my dad only knows how to cook spaghetti but it *is* edible?"

"I love spaghetti." I answered as we continued to kiss. We kiss a lot; it's probably my favorite pastime, easily taking the place of food now. And for me that's saying *a lot*! He positioned himself over me and began to kiss my neck, then my lips again. I always turned into putty when he touched me.

His hands were everywhere, gently roaming areas they'd never roamed before. It was getting a little intense when suddenly his hand was hovering around the zipper of my jeans.

"Aiden," I said as my words were muffled by our connected lips. In that same moment he went to unzip my jeans and I snapped. It was like an alarm went off. It was blaring and glaring and screeching, "No!" I yelled, pushing him violently off of me and jumping up from the floor. Aiden jumped up with me –the look of shock and fear plastered on his face.

"Zoe," he says panicked, "I'm so sorry I thought…"

"I have to go…" I say quickly as tears stream down my face. I grabbed my bag a darted out of the door racing down the stairs.

"Wait, Zoe Please!" I heard Aiden running behind me. But I didn't want to talk to him; I didn't want to look at him. I was embarrassed. He didn't do anything wrong, he was being a normal boyfriend doing things that a normal teenager would do and I freaked out because these damn skeletons of mine wouldn't stay in their closet. I knew Aiden, I knew if I would've just said I wasn't ready he would've said okay and that would've been the end of it. I knew I

84

would ruin this. The second he told me he liked me I knew I would find a way to sabotage this.

"Zoe!" he said again as he finally caught up to me. He grabbed my arm and turned me toward him, "oh my God, I am so fucking sorry. Please you have to believe me. I feel like a pig. Please don't think that all I want is to …"

"You didn't do anything wrong," I said wiping my tears from my cheeks, "I just… I freaked out and I'm embarrassed and I'm sorry."

"I shouldn't have assumed." He grabbed my hands, "I'm sorry, please come back?" he took his thumb and wiped one of my tears away. I exhaled and wrapped my arms around his neck.

"I'm not ready to…" I trail off, "I'm not sure when I'll…"

"It doesn't matter." He interrupted, "We don't have to talk about this right now." He says as he pulls me closer to him and I exhale, but my chest is still tight. My thoughts are everywhere, almost impossible to sort through.

I needed to tell him about the baby. He needed to know what he was getting himself into. I know we were young and maybe I was unexperienced in this area but he and I had something very special – at least it felt that way to me. I couldn't keep hiding this part of me from him. It was only a matter of time before he started hanging around people other than me, people who would tell him.

I didn't want to hurt him like that.

"Remember," he began to say. "We can talk about anything and everything when you're ready. Just please don't run away."

I nodded as we stood there hugging for a few moments.

"Hey," I said as I pulled myself from him, "I'm gonna go but I'll be back in time for dinner."

"You want me to go with you?"

"No," I said as I gave him a kiss on the cheek, "I'll be back in an hour or so."

I walked and I walked and I walked, twenty five minutes to Matt's house. I went straight downstairs. He was sitting on the couch on the phone. I sat down next to him and when he saw my face his eyes bugged out of his head.

"Alicia, I'll have to call you right back." He hung up and then turned his entire body towards me. "Why are you crying what happened?" the anger that oozed out of his body was scary. He was definitely my protector, even though I didn't always need or want it.

"I haven't told Aiden about the baby or the adoption and I'm afraid he's gonna end this and hate me for lying to him." There was a time when I wouldn't let a tear drop from my eyes if my arm was on fire but it seemed to be all I've been doing lately –especially this last year. "We keep getting closer and closer and this secret is just looming over my head. It's lose/lose, when he finds out whether I tell him or not he isn't going to want to be with me and he will probably have questions. He will probably ask questions that aren't anyone's business but mine."

Matt didn't seem to have any words, he just pulled me to his chest and wrapped his arms around my shoulders. He let me cry there for a few minutes before he said anything.

"Aiden is a good guy," Matt finally said, "he's not good enough for you but he is a good guy."

I smirked and sniffled at the same time.

"I think you should give him the benefit of the doubt. You guys are like an old married couple. I think he can handle this and if he can't then he isn't meant to be in your life."

"Thank you," I said exasperatedly. This is why he was my best friend, I needed a breather, I needed to hear some positive words because sometimes I spiral out and it's hard to find my way back on my own.

He gave me a kiss on the forehead before I got up to leave. "I have to head back, his dad is making spaghetti."

Matt looked at me incredulously, "You hate spaghetti?"

"Yes, with a burning passion." I smiled and shrugged before walking out of the basement.

***

I must've truly fallen head over hills for Aiden because here I sat at a high school pep rally. This was what my personal hell consisted of. If the government wanted to torture classified information out of me *this* would do the trick.

"Admit it," he said in my ear, I could barely hear him over the screaming. "You're having fun."

I looked at him square in his eyes with absolutely no expression on my face. He burst into laughter then pecked me on the lips. When I looked up Erica was glaring at me and I felt a knot form in my stomach. She was evil but there was no way she would be the kind of evil that I see in her eyes right now. Right?

"Maybe we should go." I whispered in his ear. I see Erica walking over and I want to grab my boyfriend and yank him out of the gymnasium. She was cheer captain shouldn't she be cheering the entire time?

"You're really not having any fun?" He asked surprised. "It's only been thirty five minutes, you promised me an hour."

I exhaled as Erica stood right in front of us. "Excuse me," she said, "we are sitting up there until it's time for our routine."

I was panicking for nothing; I scooted over so that her and her friends could sit on the bleachers behind us, a little too close for comfort but it was okay for now. I had twenty five minutes before I could leave.

Aiden was in his own world watching the steppers do a dance routine, I was completely zeroed in on Erica, and my radar was waiting for an alarm to go off. My panic started to dissipate after about ten minutes.

"Hey," Aiden asked, "do you want water or anything?"

"No, I'm good."

"Ok, I'll be back." He kissed me again then walked down the bleachers and out of the gym.

"So..." I heard Erica say and I knew it was directed towards me. "... The new boy is your boyfriend? How cute. Does your bastard baby call him papa?"

"Hilarious, Erica... You win, okay?" I hated saying the words but I needed to make sure she had those comments out of her system before Aiden got back. I was going to tell him, but it needed to be on my own time.

"Wait, he doesn't know does he?" She questioned with pure astonishment in her voice. I didn't say anything because what was there to say.

"Okay, don't worry. Your secret is safe with me and the *entire school.*"

I turned around to face her; I had so much I wanted to say but knew that at this moment she held the upper hand so I couldn't. Pride was by far the toughest pill to swallow.

"I would appreciate that." I said, trying not to speak through my teeth. She winked, and I felt uneasy.

"Here." Aiden said as he sat back down. It was a Kit Kat. I smiled. *God, don't let me ruin this.*

"Thank you." I said as I broke off half to give him. It's quiet for a while and I am hyperaware of Erica, when was it her time to cheer? I was ready to remove the stack of bricks that were piled on my chest.

"Hey Chrissa," I heard Erica say, her voice louder than it truly needed to be. "Did you know that in the state of Ohio you need *two* signatures to give a child up for adoption, the biological mother *and* the biological father?"

It was like ice devoured my entire body as soon as I heard her words, I couldn't believe she was doing this; did she truly hate me this much? I felt like I was going to have a panic attack.

"I'm not feeling well," I said quickly to Aiden, "I think we should go."

"Seriously? What's wrong?" He said concerned.

"So…" I heard Erica continue. "The only way you can give your child up for adoption with one signature is if the other person died or if you declare to the state that you don't know who the father could be…my dad works for the state and I get to see *everything.*"

I can feel my body begin to sweat, "Yea, I'm just sick can we go please?" I said standing up; he stands up beside me grabbing my hand.

'Zoe!" Erica said loudly everyone in our section now looking at me. "Isn't that what you did when you gave your baby up for adoption?

There's no signature on the record besides yours and no documentation saying the father is deceased, so you had to declare to the state that you had no clue who the father of your baby was, right?" She looked at Aiden, then back at me. "Oops," she said with a shrug.

I was standing there in complete and total shock. All eyes were on me but the only person that mattered was Aiden. I couldn't even look at him; I snatched my hand from his and ran out of the gymnasium. I could hear him call out after me but he didn't follow and that was all the confirmation I needed. My biggest fear had come to life, I waited too long to tell him the truth and now our relationship was over because of it. It was a gut wrenching and sobering feeling to know he would now view me differently –that what we had would just become a painful and fleeting memory.

Somehow in a blur of anger and tears I ended up at Matt's house. I ran into the basement breathless with a sob in my throat only then realizing he was still at school.

"I'm sorry. I...I'm going." I said hurriedly.

"Zoe," Mrs. Hunter said, she was standing in front of the washer and dryer. "What's wrong?" the concern in her voice surprised me. It was the first time since finding out I was pregnant that she didn't say my name with contempt in her voice. I wondered how bad I looked. If it was half as bad as I felt then I understood her concern.

"It's nothing..."I shake my head back and forth, "I'm leaving."

"You're crying and you're standing in my basement in the middle of a school day." She said as she sat on the couch. "Sit."

There was a time that this wouldn't have felt uncomfortable. I would come over here all the time when Matt wasn't here. I would sit in the kitchen and talk to Mrs. Hunter about school or softball. She would cook for me while I waited for Matt to come home from his grandfather's house but our relationship hasn't been the same, my pregnancy would always be the elephant in the room. I sat down on the opposite end of the couch.

"Are you going to tell me what's wrong or should I call your mother and let her know you're here?"

I closed my eyes and wiped the tears from my cheeks, I took a deep breath in before opening them.

"I have a boyfriend, Aiden…" as I said the words I was wondering if I should have said *had* a boyfriend, the thought made more tears fall. "He's new here and… he didn't know about the baby."

"And he found out?" She guessed correctly. I nodded and continued to wipe my tears. They seemed as if they would never stop. "He didn't find out from you…" she guessed correctly again. I nodded.

"I was going to tell him, I just …"

"You were scared." She was three for three. "He really should've heard this from your mouth Zoe."

"Why? So he can treat me like everyone else does?" I didn't mean to snap at her but I was so frustrated. "He was the *only* person who saw me for me." It was quiet for a moment before I continued. "Not even Matt treats me the same even though he thinks he is….*you* were like a second mother to me, and before this moment you haven't even looked me in the eye since finding out I was pregnant."

She didn't say anything but I saw her quickly wipe a tear from her cheek.
I couldn't believe I was opening up to her but I wanted her to truly believe me. "Your son and I have never even *thought* about kissing. Let alone…"I trail off, shaking my head and wiping more tears away. "It's never been an option, it's never been on the table and it *never* will be. You have to believe me when I tell you I did not give your grandchild up for adoption. The baby was not his and there was absolutely no chance it could've been." I should be empty by now, at some point all the tears were supposed to stop, right?

91

Mrs. Hunter moved over closer to me and wrapped her arms around me. "I'm so sorry Zoe," I could hear the sadness in her voice, "I'm sorry I wasn't there for you." She sniffled.

I wished this was the kind of moment I could have with my own mother but that would never happen. I was too far gone from her, she was too far gone from me. She was Oscars. I was just there until college took me away.

I sat there in her arms for a few minutes, letting my tears fall unguardedly. "I'm breaking mom code but you can stay here until Matt gets home, I'll bring you some lunch." She said softly as she kissed the top of my head.

"Thank you." I said still enjoying her embrace before she got up.

She went upstairs and I could feel my phone buzzing in my pocket I didn't want to look at it. I had nothing to explain. Aiden knew the truth, and he knew that I lied to him. I didn't need to see him or hear the anger in his voice. I sat there ignoring the phone; it kept ringing and buzzing so I turned it off. I sighed because I felt disconnected from the world. It was a frightening yet freeing feeling to know that no one could contact you. I closed my eyes, but was startled by three loud thuds from the outside basement door.

I got up and peeked out of the window to see Aiden's car. *Damn it.* He knew me so well. A knot quickly formed in my stomach.

"Is everything okay down there?" Mrs. Hunter yelled down.

"Yea, I'm going outside for a bit." I called back up. I'm standing in front of the basement door with no foreseeable way to handle this situation. I'd never been broken up with before, I'd never been in a relationship before…I'd never felt this way about anyone ever before. I could feel more tears beginning to welt in my eyes. I took a deep breath in and held it longer than I probably should have. I knew once I exhaled I'd have to open the door and face him. I put myself in this situation. Aiden deserved better than a liar, and a whore for all he knew.

I opened the door and there he stood. I couldn't figure out what emotion he was exuding but I could tell relief covered him once he saw my face. I stepped out, closing the door behind me.

"Zoe," is all he said exasperatedly. I had to swallow. The knot was now lodged in my throat. "We need to talk about this...I'm so confused and you're ignoring me. I just..."

"There's nothing to be confused about," I interrupt, "I'm a whore who got knocked up and gave the kid up for adoption almost five months ago. Erica crossed all of the T's and dotted all of the I's. It's pretty self-explanatory." I said looking everywhere but at him.

"Don't do that...don't do that to *me.*" He said angrily.

"Do what...?"

"Your sarcastic *I don't give a shit* shtick. This is *us* talk to me like I'm someone you care about." He snapped.

"What is there to talk about, Aiden?" I snapped back finally making eye contact with him. I could feel my soul melting; I could feel this relationship slipping through my fingers, an ache wrapped around my core. "We argue about me lying to you, about me being a slut and then we break up. I'm saving us the argument."

"Slut? Break up? Zoe, sometimes you just..." The anger is spilling out of his pores as he tries to find the right words to express himself. His eyes are smoldering with frustration and confusion.

"I'm not here to break up with you. I want to talk about this. I want to know what's going on. Am I surprised? Yes, I am but I don't expect you to tell me every single thing that's happened in your life in a month's time. We all have our issues and crosses to bear. *Everyone* has things they aren't ready to share but what I'm most pissed off about is the fact that you're acting like you don't give a damn about me." He grabs both of my arms and tries to look into my eyes. I don't allow it.

"Every single turn, every hiccup –you run. You can't keep running away when it gets sketchy!" He says passionately. "How many times do I have to chase you and tell you how I feel about you before you finally start to believe me? Why don't you understand that I am here? That I *want* to be here with you?"

I'm looking down at my faded converses trying to control my breathing. I felt like I was edging close to hyperventilation. He was right, I did run and I wanted to run right now. I didn't want to have this conversation anymore. I had too many emotions I was trying to identify and reign in at once. It was overwhelming, it would be easier to just not deal with any of this at all.

"I'm not going to let you push me away like you do to everyone else in your life. I already told you that." His voice was softer but still intense and full of passion. "Zoe, look at me?" He nearly begged. "Talk to me."

"I'm giving you an out." My voice is barely a whisper as I wiped the tears and finally found the strength and resolve to yank myself from his hold.

"I don't want a fucking out!" He yelled. It startled me, forcing more tears to fall.

The passion burning in his eyes made me feel like my body was set ablaze. The urge to run away was even more encompassing, he truly was right running, shutting down, and disappearing was all I knew. I was damaged goods; this beautiful, intelligent, and fervent boy deserved somebody so much better than me. He deserved so much more than I could ever possibly give him. I tried to let him go before, I tried to tell him this wouldn't work –that I was *complicated* but he wouldn't *let me* let him go. He let his feet submerge and dry into the cement.

"I think you should leave." My words were wavering because I didn't want him to leave. What I wanted was the best for him and that couldn't be me. It would never be me.

"What?" He said disillusioned. "Zoe, don't do this...we just need to talk. You promised me we would talk." His voice is calmer, but I could see fear in his eyes. He was feeling this relationship slip through his fingers as well. I had to look away as I took a step back. "I'm not leaving until you talk to me, until I find a way to fix this." He stated firmly.

"*Fix*? There is nothing to *fix*! You didn't break anything, this is *not* on you!" I didn't know why I was yelling at him but that word hit a trigger for some reason. Everyone around me wanted to *fix* me, wanted to *help* me. Why couldn't things just be the way they were? I was fine. I needed the world to just leave me alone. "I didn't let you in my life to *fix* me! I didn't need that!"

"What the hell are you talking about Zoe? I didn't say that I was going to fix you, don't put words in my mouth!" He shouted back. "And you *let* me in your life? Why then Zoe? What was the point if you were just going to walk away? What did you need then?"

"I thought I needed someone to love me!" I blurt out and I can't believe those words have left my lips. Now more than ever I want to run. I want to escape this moment and pretend it never happened. I was a lunatic and if he didn't want to break up with me before I knew he would now.

"Well I do," he says urgently. His voice was still loud, "I love you!"

The air is still, cars are driving by, some birds have yet to migrate, war and poverty are plaguing the world, people are dying, babies are being born, the stars are aligned, and while the world still spins on its axis I'm standing here frozen in time in front of a boy who says he loves me.

He exhaled and grabbed my hand. "This was not how I imagined saying that for the first time."

I shook my head. "You deserve someone who can give you everything…" I whispered, wiping yet another tear from my cheek. None of this made sense, there was no way someone like him could love someone like me.

"You deserve that *too.*" He said softly. "I know we are young and stupid but I know what I want and I know that I don't want to be away from you."

I stood there a moment longer, remembering when I had a mental breakdown on my bedroom floor a month ago. I remember feeling like I was drowning. I told myself I needed to be my own life jacket, that no one could remove the cement blocks from around my feet. That no one could save me but myself. I forced myself to think calm and happy thoughts and the one person who was able to bring me closer to the surface was Aiden.

I thought about him and his smile and his touch, we'd only been on one date and he had that type of effect on me. I realized in that moment that I wasn't my own life jacket that I hadn't saved myself that night. *Aiden* had helped me. He was there for me and he didn't even know it. In the park I wondered what his purpose in my life would be. I wondered why every moment felt important, and now I knew. It didn't matter that we were young; it didn't matter how it looked, all that mattered was how he felt and how I felt.

"I love you." I said abruptly. I said the words as a statement, as a declaration. I said the words with assurance and confidence. Not as a response but as an affirmation. I loved him and he was right it *was* stupid and it was fast but it was true. I loved him and he loved me. Whatever was going on around us had to take a backseat right now because in this moment it's only the two of us and in this moment I realize I am capable of being some degree of happy despite everything else.

He hugged me and we just stood there embracing. It was like neither one of us wanted to let go. I didn't care that my fingers were frozen from the cold air, and that my tears were dried to my cheeks. I had Aiden and I was closer to the surface than I'd ever been before.

Chapter Seven: World A. and World B.

I sat impatiently –like I did every week as she read my diary. My legs crossed as my foot tapped the front of the couch in a quick and rapid pattern. I looked out of the window with my arms crossed over my torso, it was raining –still no snow. I sighed.

I heard her close it then place the diary on her lap.

"You've been spending a lot of time with Aiden." Dr. Gleasyn stated.

I nodded. I could feel the acid producing in my mouth. My own therapist was going to call me a whore. I could feel it coming, with my history of getting pregnant that one time of course I'm a sexed crazed teen.

"I like that, that's really good."

I looked at her skeptically. "It is?" I made it a habit to never ask her direct questions but she caught me off guard, the words left my lips without a thought process.

"Yes." She stated simply. She was messing with me. She knew I needed her to elaborate. She was using reverse psychology to make me speak. She sat patiently with her legs crossed, mirroring mine. My diary was now opened on her lap as she stared at me; she was trying to exude her positive energy onto me. It was so blatant that I wanted to cringe away. It was like she was *willing* the words out of me.

"Why is that good?" I took the damn bait, unable to compete in this particular game of wills.

She placed her notepad on the table between us and uncrossed her legs. "It's healthy for a girl your age to have a boyfriend ..." She trailed off, "I'm correct in assuming he is your boyfriend?"

I nod.

"In the last two months I've seen an improvement in your writing, your energy, and your appearance. I think that this is a healthy relationship for you."

I just looked at her, waiting for the punchline. She wasn't going to criticize me or ask me a million questions about him? She wasn't going to ask if we were being sexually active or not? I was doing something right?

"Oh... thank you." I say. I was so used to villainizing her that it felt weird being cordial.

"You're Welcome, Zoe." She says as she picks her notepad back up. She took her black glasses off of her collar and put them on before continuing. "I want to talk about one of your entries from a few weeks back."

Crap, what did I write? She hadn't really been asking direct questions about my diary entries and because of that I've been writing a *little* more openly. I'm feeling like I made a huge mistake. I should've known it was a trap.

"You said that you and Matt's mother made up and that you wished you could do that with your mom?"

I looked at her and tried to figure out what game she was playing. Why would she bring it up now and not then? I wasn't prepared to answer that question. I'm such an idiot for even writing it down.

"Why can't you do that with your mother?" She clarified.

"I don't know." Old habits die hard.

"Does your mother have a lot of resentment about the pregnancy?"

I swallowed and looked back out of the window. "I don't know." Of course she did, why else would I be sitting here in therapy because of that damn pregnancy. Maybe my mother should be here; she's clearly the one harboring some pent up emotion about *almost* being a grandmother.

My thought pinches an uncomfortable part of my psyche and I blink rapidly trying to assure my eyes that I would not be crying in this office under any circumstance.

Dr. Gleasyn is quiet for a moment while she writes something in her notepad. She pauses, and then continues. "Your mother is married?"

I bit the inside of my cheek. My skin started to crawl and my anger started to spread all over my body.

"Yes."

"How is their relationship?" She questioned.

I'm angry. I'm furious. I want to leave, I'm *going* to leave. In all the sessions I've been to, never once has she asked me about my mother or her husband.

"Great," I answer the question clipped. My aggravation was blatant.

"I know that you've inferred that your relationship with your mother is strained. How is your relationship with your stepfather?"

I finally rip my gaze from the window to glare at her. She knows she is poking a bear. She's staring intently at me, her pen wagging left and right in her hand. "Why does that matter?" I snap.

"It's important that when I start making progress with a patient that I start to learn about their home life."

"Well, I don't want to talk about my home life."

"You're a teenaged girl; your environment is *very* important in guiding me on how to better assess you."

"It's off the table." I shake my head and face out the window again. My foot is tapping so erratically against the couch that the sound is almost echoing in this large and sterile room.

"I'm sorry Zoe, but that isn't something you get to decide." She replies softly.

I stand up immediately grabbing my bag from the floor and hoisting it over my shoulder. I quickly yank my diary off of her lap, her notepad falling to the floor. "Then this is my last session." I storm out of her office with thirty-two minutes left on the clock. *Damn it.*

I did what I do best. I ran.

***

"Well, you tried." Aiden said as he massaged my feet over the white cotton socks I was wearing. We were lying on his bed on the opposite ends of each other.

"Try explaining that to my mom and Matt." I say lying on my back and covering my face with my arms. "They're going to kill me." I grunted.

"You should be able to talk about what you want, isn't that the whole point of therapy?" Aiden asked. My face still covered.

"One would think." I say. I sit up and cross my legs, pulling my foot from his hold. I'm facing him. "Well, one positive thing did come from it." I say with a smile.

"What?"

"Apparently, we have a *healthy relationship*." I air quote with an eye roll.

His beautiful teeth beamed brightly as he sat up to sit directly in front of me. "Oh, so I've been a hot topic at your sessions?" He asked with a raised eyebrow, his curiosity seeping through proudly and expectantly.

"All I said is that there was some kid I couldn't shake, that's about it."

"Oh," he smiled, "Is that right?" He leaned forward to kiss me.

"Mmm hmm," I mumbled against his lips. This quickly turned into a make out session. I loved the way he tasted. I loved the way he felt against me. I was lucky; I never thought I would ever be able to say that. I was lying on my back again with him hovered over me, my hands were in his hair, his hands in mine.

"Okay." He said, reluctantly pulling away from me.

"No." I say sternly pulling his shirt and bringing his lips back down to mine –gripping the sides of his face firmly with my hands. He kissed me back for a moment but I could feel him slowly trying to inch away.

"Zoe." He stated regretfully against my lips. My, how the tables have turned, a month ago I was running out of his room because I thought we were moving too fast. Now he was pushing the breaks, every time it got intense *he* pushed the breaks.

"Just because sex isn't on the table yet doesn't mean there aren't *other* things we can do?" I say rubbing his arm.

"Yea…" he looked me up and down then shook his head. "I know that but I'm going to combust if we keep testing the limits." He sat completely up sitting on the side of the bed while I laid there breathless and disappointed.

I sighed.

"Let's watch a movie?" He suggested.

I stared at my boyfriend and tried to figure out in what universe should I be allowed to have him? It just didn't make sense for him to exist here at the same moment in time with me. I couldn't have created a better person to share my days with. It was idiotic of me to even think about my future in such depth at my age but I knew I couldn't have one that Aiden wasn't in. We were too intertwined, our spirits were intermingled. Our love for each other was palpable. A year ago, hell three months ago, I would've judged someone who spoke like this about another person and I would've been wrong.

To be seen and heard, to *be* love, and to be *loved* were things I could've only wished to experience in my life. I was living it.

I wished I were ready to share that part of myself with him, but I wasn't and I hated myself for it. I knew that he loved me for reasons I will never know or understand and only God knows how much I love him but I was road blocked. My real life nightmares were haunting me every single time Aiden and I got closer and it wasn't fair. I had to bury pieces of myself over a year ago and now emotions have brought those demons to light.

"You pick." I say.

"You okay?" He asked me. He could tell that I was distracted, that I wasn't fully in the room.

"You know I love you, right?" I say abruptly sitting up on his bed.

"Umm, yes. Nothing has changed in the fine print has it?" He answered with a smile.

"No, I'm serious. I love you so much. And it's scary and I'm angry." I confess. No tears, just words.

"You're angry that you love me?" He questioned. "What's going on Zo?" He's staring at me like he's confused and like I'd lost my mind. Maybe that was true. I never quite knew what was going on in there anyways. If I lost it I probably wouldn't notice it was gone.

"I'm angry that we crossed paths and that something in the universe made us love each other because you loving me isn't fair to you." I am reading his face and I can tell he is upset at my words. I wasn't explaining this right. "I don't regret meeting you Aiden, the day you walked into my life my world changed…but there are things I wish I could share, there are things I wish we could *do* and because I am the way I am –we cant."

Aiden is staring at me. I knew him so well, he was pissed and he was going to tell me to stop self-depreciating, but I couldn't help it. He was too good to be true, he was missing out on so much, he needed to know.

"So." He said with a shrug. I stared at him, waiting for him to finish his sentence but he got up and went to look for a DVD.

"So?" I repeat to him as confusion conquered me.

"Yes, Zoe *so…* " he turned around with the most unamused look on his face as if he had absolutely no energy to have this conversation. "What if that's all true? So what? What does that change?"

I'm just looking at him because this is not the direction I saw this conversation going.

"I don't care about all of that extra stuff, I love you and you love me. Last time I checked that was enough."

"What if it's a long time before I'm ready to …"I pause, "ready to have sex…" my voice lower, almost like I was embarrassed to say the word sex out loud or something.

He smirked and chuckled confusingly, then sat back down on the bed next to me. "Is that what this whole thing is about?"

I nodded and suddenly I felt stupid. I always get caught up in my own thoughts –my jumbled and toxic thoughts. Words were words but actions rang true, Aiden has done nothing but prove to me that he is all in and yet I continue to search for outs for him. I knew at this point I could never be the one to let *him* go it would have to be the other way around. I just never wanted him to miss out on anything on the account of me.

"Can we let this be the last time I say this?" He says putting his arm around me. "When you are ready we can have this conversation, okay?"

I nod and kiss him on the cheek. It's quiet for a moment as I sit there in his arms. I used to hate this warm and tingly feeling I would get when he made me blush or held my hand. It felt so weird being that way with someone. I remember wanting to trip girls in the hallway at school who would walk around all goo-goo eyed and in love. I was one of those girls now and honestly I didn't give a damn who judged me.

"I wanna ask you something and you can say no if you want." Aiden said out of the blue.

"If you're proposing you need to get down on one knee and actually have a ring." I say jokingly. "Not half assed, I want a spectacle –an elaborate thought out plan. I want friend's involved and video footage of my reaction." I eye him accusingly.

He laughed and hugged me tighter to him. "Not proposing yet. Give me a couple years." He laughed. My stomach felt warm and started to flutter with butterflies at his response. *Not yet give me a couple years.* He said it so casually and though I was obviously joking his reply thoroughly caught me off guard. I inhaled slowly trying to bring myself down so I can hear what he had to ask me.

"I'm going to Nebraska this summer to visit my mom and I want you to come with me."

I pulled away from his hold so I could better see his face. "The *entire* summer?" I ask. He nods.

My options were to either stay here and spend three months away from my boyfriend, my boyfriend whom I see every single day *or* go to Nebraska with him and be out of that house? Detach myself completely from all my stress here at home for three full months?

"Yes!" I say with a little too much enthusiasm. The smile that spreads across his face is so radiant that it fills me with pure joy. He leans over to hug me and it's just now hitting me that I have to figure out how to tell my mother this. I was still seventeen; she wasn't going to let me leave for three months with a boy… with someone who is a stranger to her.

Shit. She doesn't know Aiden even exists.

Still hugging I say, "Aiden, I haven't told my mom about us."

He pulled away and the look on his face is a complete 180 from how he looked just seconds ago. "It has nothing to do with you and *everything* to do with me." I say grabbing his hand. "I've told you that my mother and I don't have a great relationship and a lot of that animosity stemmed from that pregnancy…her knowing I have a boyfriend –she would just assume that…"

"No. I get it, its fine." He says as he gets up and walks back over to the DVDs. I feel horrible. I'd been so successful keeping my worlds separate that I forgot one important part. I didn't think about how this would make him feel. Again, my capabilities of messing things up were infinite.

"Please don't be mad." I say. "Come over for dinner tomorrow?" I blurt the words out. As soon as they left my lips I wished I could reach out and grab them back before they could reach his ears. He turned around and looked at me.

"Are you sure, Zoe?" He asked skeptically.

"Yes, she can think whatever she wants to think." At this point I didn't care what she thought –at least that's what I was telling myself. I didn't want Oscar to be there. I didn't want my world with Aiden to collide with him in anyway. "I'll talk to her about it tonight."

"Okay." He smiled and I could tell he was relieved. I wonder if he sensed the panic rippling through my entire body, the fear working its way from my toes to my scalp.

I exhale slowly still buried in his arms. What did I do?

Chapter Eight: "Red."

I walked through the front door and I could hear my mother in the kitchen. I took in a deep breath before walking in. "Hey mom, can we…" I stop midsentence as I round the corner and see Oscar digging through the fridge. He looked up and smiled. I looked away and went to dart up the stairs but ran right into my mother as she was turning the corner to walk into the kitchen. I exhaled.

"Hey!" She said grabbing my arms to keep me balanced, "In a hurry?"

"Sorry," I say. I'm out of breath and I hadn't even gotten far. "Actually, I was looking for you. I wanted to talk to you." I can sense Oscar standing behind me and I try not to cringe "…*privately.*" I add lowly.

"Anything you need to say to my wife you can say in front of me." Oscar says, his deep voice vibrating my chest. I step forward closer to my mother. My back is still to him, I exhale before turning around. "She may be your wife but she is *my* mother and I need to speak to *her* not you." The acid ran through my veins. When I looked at him I saw red.

"You guys," my mother said, "that's enough."

"I pay the bills in this damn house you better learn how to respect me!" He barked taking a step closer.

"You don't deserve my respect!" I yell back, surprising myself. I'd never raised my voice to him. I'd never stood up to him in any capacity. I've never challenged him like this before, but today I did. I didn't know why, but I felt like I was on edge and he was scarily close to pushing me off of it. I wasn't going to let him intimidate me right now. *Today* I had a voice and today it was loud and clear and he was going to hear me. He would hear me *this* time.

"Stop it!" My mother stepped in between us, her back towards me as she faced him. "Let me talk to Zoe." She said calmly.

"Un-fucking believable!" He barked angrily. "You let her run this damn place!" He threw his beer bottle violently into the sink glass shards flying everywhere before he stormed out.

"Oscar!" My mother called after him. "Oscar, wait!" She huffed then turned to face me. "Why do you provoke him?" She said with frustration in her voice.

I just stared at her, trying to remember the moment I lost her. Trying to remember the last day she was *my mother*. I wanted to turn around and walk away, I wanted to yell at her, I wanted to shake her until she saw how idiotic she was to be married to that man, but I was on a mission. I'd made a promise to my boyfriend and I wasn't going to let the dysfunction of this household ruin it.

"Can I just talk to you please?" I say completely ignoring her comment. She nodded I could still see the frustration on her face.

"Okay, I'm just going to say it. I have a boyfriend, his name is Aiden and I want you to meet him tomorrow night."

Many emotions crossed her face as she watched the cluster of my words spill out.

"A boyfriend. How long?"

"A little over two months," I answer quickly.

"And you want *me* to meet him?"

I nod. She is just standing there, I knew what she was thinking but I was placing bets in my head on if she'd actually ask.

"Okay," she says, "I would love to meet him."

"Oscar cannot be here." I say, she goes to open her mouth. "I'm *letting you in*, but I can't do that if he is involved." My choice of wording was deliberate. All everyone in my life wants is for me to *let them in*. I stare at my mother for a few exaggerated seconds.

She nods. "He works late tomorrow night." She added.

"Okay."

"Okay."

We are just standing there in the uncomfortable silence and though it's none of her business I say the words anyway. "He's not the father and we haven't had sex." I turn around, run up to my room, and lock the door behind me.

***

"Calm down." Matt says.

"Have you met my mother?" I say as I pace back and forth in his basement. Alicia is sitting on the floor laughing.

"Yea and I think you're over reacting." He amends. I roll my eyes.

"Aren't you gonna be late?" Alicia said, "Its 6:30pm."

108

"Ugh!" I say, "he's gonna show up and I'm not going to be there and my mother is going to eat him alive, literally boil him on the stove." I shake my head. "This was a bad idea, I screwed up. Shit."

"Dude," Matt said, "this is hilarious!"

I stopped and scowled at him.

"It's just funny seeing you care about something, is what I meant."

I roll my eyes again. I grab my bag and head for the door. "Thank you both for nothing."

They're both still laughing. "Let me drive you." Alicia offers.

"No thanks, I need to walk it helps with the paralyzing and mind numbing anxiety."

I didn't stay to hear them laugh more at me. I came over there to vent about how this was a terrible idea, that I should've continued to keep my worlds separate, but in true Zoe fashion I had to find a new creative way to make my life even more difficult.

I ran through my front door and the first thing I smelled was food. I didn't know what she was cooking but it was the first time in months my mother cooked and it smelled wonderful.

"Hey baby girl," my mother had on a soft pink blouse and a tan pencil skirt that cut off right above her knees. Her hair was pulled back in a neat ponytail and she looked like she'd gotten eight hours of sleep. Who the hell was this woman?

"Mom..." I say astonished. "You look great."

"Wow you say that with such surprise!"

"No, I mean..." I paused then smiled. "Thank you for taking this seriously, for taking *me* seriously."

She smiled and nodded. I stood there and watched her pull dinner rolls out of the oven and place them on the countertop.

"So when will Aiden be here?" She asked.

"He just texted me, he will be here in ten minutes."

"Okay, well finish setting up the table." She orders. I'm fighting back another smile because I'm seeing glimpses of the mother I used to know, the mother who I could sit and talk to for hours. I was going to try my hardest to enjoy this night. I was basking in this temporary feeling as I placed the steak knives and forks onto light blue napkins.

I hear knocking at the front door –he's early of course –I take a deep breath in. This wasn't going to be so bad. *Just keep the positive thinking going* I prompted myself.

I opened the door and there stood the love of my life. Gag me. But it was true, every time I saw him my mood changed, every time he touched me my body chemistry changed, every time he said he loved me my entire *being* changed.

"Hey." I say with a smile.

"Hey." He says handing me a teddy bear. "I got your mom flowers and since you hate everything I got you a bear and named it *Aiden* so it would be much harder for you to hate."

I laughed and rolled my eyes. "Yea, I kind of don't hate you or whatever." I say as I slowly go in for a kiss.

"Hello, I'm Kim." I hear my mother say as she comes out of the kitchen with her hand already extended. I step back, a little sad that I didn't get my kiss. "It's nice to finally meet you, Aiden."

"Nice to meet you too, Miss Oakley." He shakes her hand and hands her the flowers.

110

"It's actually *Mrs.* Doyle." She corrects him. "Thank you so much for the flowers, they're beautiful." She smiled genuinely. "Well come in, let's eat. I hope you like steak?"

"It's my favorite." He answers as he steps into the foyer winking at me.

I exhale.

Dinner was going by without a glitch. I couldn't believe that I was actually sitting here quietly as my mother and boyfriend converse over vast topics, from sports, to the midterm elections, to classes, and his home in Nebraska. All the nerves and anxiety that I experienced for twenty four hours were unwarranted. My mother was on her best behavior and Aiden –well he was just being himself which was basically the perfect human.

"Can I get you something else to drink?" My mother offered.

"No, I'm fine. Thank you." Aiden answered with his beautiful – damn near blinding smile. I wonder if this is how he won me over. I do remember noting his smile the second day I saw him. Looking from the outside in it was almost sickening how charming he was.

"So you will be a senior next year, any plans for college?" My mom asked as she poured more A1 sauce on her medium rare steak.

"Yes. There are a few colleges I've been looking at." He took a sip of his water before continuing. "I got early acceptance to MSU but I'm not really sure what my concrete plans are. Who knows what the next year could bring." I sensed Aiden quickly dart his eyes towards me and had I not been already so attentive to his every word I wouldn't have caught it.

When Aiden got the early acceptance letter two weeks ago I remember feeling an emotion I'd never experienced before. I was happy for him, *of course* I was, but the thought of him being over four hours away almost sent me into a panic. Though I congratulated him and tried to be the *supportive girlfriend* Aiden knew me too well he saw the sadness, panic, and fear flit across my eyes. He told me he'd applied before he met me and that this wasn't his only option.

As much as the words stung coming out I told him he could not base his college career off of us, that whatever was decided on his part and my part we would know what to do and we would work it out. I didn't want him to base a huge life choice on me –even though deep down I knew that I would just go wherever he went. My grades were good, not *Aiden honors classes on my transcript* good, but I was sure I would get into a decent college. I applied to MSU last week, that's how *I* was going to *work it out.*

I was pulled out of my thought when I heard keys rattling at the side door in the kitchen. My heart dropped as I looked at my mother.

The look of panic flitted across her face easily mirroring mine before she excused herself from the table.

"What's wrong?" My perceptive boyfriend asked, but I couldn't speak. "Zoe?"

"My mother's husband," I finally say, "I think we should go." I say getting up from the table, Aiden stood up as well but Oscars booming voice stopped us in our tracks.

"Where are you all going? I'm gonna pull up a chair a join the party."

I was fighting back tears. It was a powerful feeling, hating someone so deeply. I looked at my mother, she was saying sorry with her eyes.

Aiden cleared his throat and extended his hand to Oscar. "Hello Mr. Doyle, I'm Aiden."

Oscar stared at his hand and then looked at my mother. "Why do I need to know who he is?" He said pointing to Aiden, his hand still extended.

"This is Zoe's lovely boyfriend." She answered.

He looked at him then laughed. I wanted to spit in his face. I wanted to kill him.

Aiden looked at me and lowered his hand. "Mom," I say, "we're gonna go."

"No," Oscar says, "stay and finish the meal your mother slaved over for hours to make." He looked at Aiden. "Sorry about that son," he put his hand out to shake Aiden's, "we get a tad overprotective when it comes to our little girl."

His words sent rage through every nerve ending in my body. *Our little girl?*

"No problem, Sir." I wish Aiden knew that Oscar didn't deserve that level of politeness.

"Call me Oscar," he said, "now, everyone sit, sit."

I hesitated as I looked my mother in the eyes, she nodded slightly. Aiden saw this exchange and we all sat down.

My nightmare was coming true. My two worlds couldn't coexist, and they were to never cross paths. I felt so bad for Aiden, he shouldn't have to be subjected to whatever mind games Oscar was playing. I was an idiot to think this night would be perfect and drama free. It was *my life* it only made sense for it to be going in this direction.

I sat silently as Oscar asked Aiden a million questions. I detached myself from the world. None of the questions he asked were *that* inappropriate, but I could tell he wanted Aiden to feel uncomfortable. I needed this night to be over. I felt sick. I needed these worlds to be separate again.

"Have you both talked about her baby?" Oscar's words yanked me out of my trance. Had I just heard him correctly?

"Oscar!" My mother said with complete shock in her voice, "stop."

"What? That's a legitimate question."

I stared off into space, it was all I could do to keep myself from crying, from yelling, from jumping across this table and stabbing him in the jugular with my steak knife. What if Aiden hadn't known? He wanted me to remain miserable forever. He was hoping that he dropped a bombshell and that Aiden would leave me? He wanted to keep power over me.

Hearing Oscar even mention that baby sent the feeling of nauseas to my stomach. I couldn't identify what hate, rage, anger, and sadness all clumped into one encompassing emotion would be –I didn't know what that word or emotion was but it filled me completely.

"Yes, I know about the adoption." Aiden answered curtly. I could see he was angry, but he was trying to be respectful. Aiden glanced over to me for a quick moment, I knew him so well. He probably wanted to punch him. I wish he could.

"I'm gonna go get something else to drink. I'll take the plates in." I say getting up from the table.

"Good idea," my mother said, rising up from the table as well, "…why don't we move this into the living room. Aiden, I have some baby photos of Zoe I want to show you!" She smiled, trying desperately to diffuse the tension in the room caused by her husband, "Zoe, can you bring out the cake?"

I nod as I grab the plates to put in the sink. Aiden looks at me before getting up from the table as if to say *are you okay?* I smile and nod again before walking away.

I'm in the kitchen alone, my hands clutching the counter. I will not cry, I will not cry. *I will not cry.*

I hear someone walk in, I turn around and of course it's Oscar. I turn back facing the sink and inhale.

He clears his throat and opens the fridge which is not too far from me. I can sense him walking out and I exhale, closing my eyes. I stood there for a moment trying to regather my thoughts, trying to tell myself if I just stay calm and detached that this night would be over soon and I would go back to having two separate worlds. I was suddenly startled out of my thoughts when I heard footsteps then Oscar's deep voice in my ear before I could even turn around.

"No matter what your little boyfriend does to you," he whispers in my ear, his warm breath pinching my neck, the smell of alcohol permeating my senses. "*I* was there first."

The tears immediately splashed to my shirt. My heart felt restricted, my breathing was erratic.

"When he kisses you, he tastes me. Does he know that?"

The room was spinning, I was nauseated. I could feel his body heat hovering around the back of me. I was sick, I was drowning, where was I?

He leaned in even closer, his lips almost touching my ear. "You think putting that lock on your door will stop me?" He swooped his arm around me and grabbed the front of my upper thigh. He squeezed it tightly pulling me back towards him as he pressed *all* of himself to the back of me.

"When he's done with you tonight, I think I'll have at it again." His lips pressing onto my earlobe, "I gave you more than enough time to heal from your delivery. What do you say, Zoe? Gonna save some for me?" His tongue slowly licking the inside of my earlobe as his hand moved from my thigh to between my legs.

My mother and my boyfriend were in the next room. Only feet away, and he was doing this. Drunk or not he was doing this. I wasn't even safe out in the open in a house full of people. I'd kept fooling myself, telling myself this was over every single time after he'd threaten me or hit on me or touch me. I thought I would never have to deal with this again because I would be smart and never be home alone with him, but right now I realize it didn't matter. I was never going to escape this. He would *always* have power over me.

And like a tidal wave, calmness washed over me. It was surreal. Every emotion I'd ever experienced was vacant from my body. I was numb and I was vividly aware at the same time. The room was still spinning but my thoughts were not jumbled. I was thinking clearly, I was in the moment. I was going to be heard.

I wasn't going to drown anymore.

As soon as the thought flitted across my mind, my hand was in the sink, my fingers were clasping around the handle of a large knife. I turned around and I screamed as my arm flailed back then forward, landing in his flesh. I pulled it back, more screams as I jammed the knife into him again and again.

The tears, the blood, the screams, I was being heard, I wasn't invisible. He would *never* drown me again.

I hear other voices screaming now, Oscar is on the ground and my faded converses are splattered with his blood. I can't see. Everything is red.

"Zoe!" I hear Aiden yell but I can't see him, all I see is red. "Put down the knife, baby please just put down the knife!" He pleaded.

I could still hear screaming, it was my mother. I knew her voice but I couldn't see her. All I see is red. I was shaking, I couldn't control the shaking, the knife was out of my hand, and somehow I ended up on the floor. I felt someone holding me, they were telling me to breathe. They were trying to stop me from shaking. They were wiping tears off of my face.

It was Aiden. I loved him so much.

He was saying *shhhh* repeatedly as he tried to stop the shaking only then did I realize I was still screaming too. I couldn't stop. I was being heard, I wasn't invisible, and Oscar couldn't drown me anymore.

So I kept screaming. I kept screaming until my voice couldn't handle the strain anymore.

After a few minutes the red started to slowly fade. The voices were becoming clearer, and the screams from my mother were actually resonating. I was coming back down to the earth. The fog was being lifted. I'm not on the outside looking in anymore, I am in the moment. I turn to look at Aiden and the fear in his eyes was enough to paralyze me.

What had I done? I look in front of me to see the splotches of blood covering my shoes and pants. My mother was on her cell phone screaming hysterically on her knees as she hovered over Oscar's body. He was covered in blood. I did that? I try to smile, I'm not sure if I did or not.

"Zoe?" Aiden said, "Zoe!" He repeated. I don't know if this was the right word to use but I think he could tell that I was lucid. My screaming had stopped, I was absorbing my surroundings. I was *me,* in some form at least.

As realization swam through me my tears dried up. I did not feel remorse. Was I a sociopath? Was I clinically insane? Was I going to spend the rest of my life in jail? I did not care that Oscar was laying there in a pool of his own blood that I had taken him down on my own. I didn't care that his blood covered my hands.

And yet, as he laid there grasping for his life he still had power over me. How was that possible? *He* was the weak one now, *he* was afraid, *he* was the victim now, but *he* still had all the power. I couldn't let him rule me like this anymore.

"He's the father." My voice is hoarse and nearly gone from all of the screaming.

"What?" Aiden asks. "Zoe, look at me. Zoe?" He gently grabs my face and tries to turn me to face him but I don't budge. My eyes are locked on Oscar's bloodied body.

"He..." I blink slowly, "...he's the father." I repeat methodically.

"Wait, what are you talking about Zoe?" Aiden begged. His arms are back around me as he holds me close to him. He really loved me? He shouldn't be here. He should've run away the second he saw what was happening. He should be terrified. I was so damaged. I was completely done. There was nothing within me left to salvage.

"He's the father of the baby." I whisper. It was the first time I'd ever said those words out loud. The bricks that'd been sitting on my chest and back for a little over a year were slowly being lifted one by one. The cement blocks that had been pulling me to the ocean floor were finally gone.

"Oh my God!" The torment in Aiden's voice shook my foundation, but I had to keep talking. It didn't matter anymore if my words fell into oblivion, it didn't matter if once I said them I could never get them back. Oscar couldn't have power over me anymore. That's all I cared about and that's all that mattered. I was free. The invisible muzzle was removed.

"He raped me." I stated, no tears, just words as I looked straight ahead now staring at nothing in particular. "Last February and I got pregnant. He's the father." I said the words as if I were reading them off of a handwritten list. My voice was controlled and nearly robotic.

My mother was still screaming on the phone as she told the paramedics the address, she didn't hear anything I was saying.

"He raped you?" Aiden repeated. The anger in his voice was terrifying. It was as if what I did to Oscar was nothing compared to what Aiden wanted to do to him.

118

"Yes." I answered as confirmation. I'm looking at Oscar again as he suffocates on his own blood. I found pleasure in this. It was morbid, this I knew, but I didn't care. "I was a virgin before, he…" I trail off as one stray tear falls from my eye. Glimpses of that night flit across my memory in angry spirts. I try to blink them away.

I can hear and feel Aiden's heavy breathing; his body is trembling as much as mine.

"Stop fucking screaming!" He yells at my mother. His voice booming, completely drowning out my mother's cries and Oscars moans. "He raped her!" His voice cracking over the words, I could hear the sob in his throat that he almost choked over. Another tear drops from my eye.

"Wha –," my mother looked up –her makeup running down her face as she knelt beside Oscar's bloodied body, her soft pink blouse was ruined. She hadn't once checked on me or asked how I was. "What?" She was finally able to mutter out.

"Your husband raped her! Where the hell were you? That baby was his!" Aiden is still holding onto me but I feel like I'm more of an anchor to *him*, his anger and hatred is overflowing out of his aura. "You should've protected her! You should've fucking protected her!"

"No," she said confusingly as the color left her face, "Zoe?" She looked at me and I didn't respond. I already said all I was ever going to say about it. "No…baby girl," she sobbed. "No! no, no!" She screamed and it was as if I could actually pinpoint the moment she realized what Aiden was saying to her. I saw it in her eyes the instant she knew she was responsible for bringing that monster here.

She dropped her cell phone onto the kitchen floor and started hitting Oscar with closed fists. Her screams were so loud that I had to close my eyes. I was too physically and mentally exhausted to raise my hands to cover my ears like I wanted to.

I exhaled.

Then, I took in a slow steady stream of air and held it for a moment. It felt like the first breath I'd taken in over a year. It was the first time in over a year my lungs were full to capacity – I was no longer suffocating. I exhale again but this time slowly, enjoying every second of that release, the pressure and the tightness I'd been walking around with was completely gone.

And I think I try to smile, again.

I was heard. I wasn't invisible. He couldn't drown me anymore.

***

June 2014

Dear Diary,

I remember sitting in Matt's basement watching movies all day with him and Alicia. It was a very hot day that day. They wanted to go to the beach but I didn't feel well. I knew being in the heat would make it worse so we decided to buy a bunch of junk food and watch as many movies as we could before falling asleep. I remember just sitting on the couch and then suddenly feeling dizzy. I honestly thought I was going to pass out. Matt asked me if I wanted Tylenol but I refused. I sat there for another fifteen minutes thinking I could coax the dizziness away but it only got worse. I felt nauseas and weak coupled with the fact that I was exhausted. I told them I had to go home.

Once I got home I made it upstairs just in time to run to the bathroom, releasing the contents of my stomach into the toilet. I remember cradling my stomach with both hands as the room spun around leaving me off centered. I'd gotten sick a couple times that summer but this was different, I was convinced I had the flu. As my hands cupped my stomach as if to prevent more vomiting it hit me like a ton of bricks, like a truck had crashed right into my chest.

When was my last period?

Realization crept over me at once as tears swelled in my eyes. I remember thinking there was no way, I was overreacting, it had been five months, there was absolutely no conceivable way this was possible. I tried to remember my last period and I couldn't –just some spotting but I played sports, I was used to having irregular periods. I'd gained some weight but nothing significant enough to be alarmed. I started breathing heavily, panic conquering my entire body. I had to calm myself down; I had to tell myself that it was just the flu, that I was losing my mind to think I could be five months pregnant. The idea was so absurd. The more I thought about it, the quicker I was able to catch my breath and calm my nerves.

I decided to be on the safer side and take a pregnancy test, just so I could fully erase the thought from my mind. I remember being so embarrassed having to watch this older woman ring me out. I could feel the judgement in her eyes, I diverted eye contact as she handed me my change. I rushed home, thankful that my mother would not be home until later that evening.

I stood at the bathroom door – my eyes nearly burning a hole through the test as I waited for the results. Before the timer even went off two dark blue lines appeared and it was as if my entire world had stopped. I stared at the test for so long before I could react. Somewhere deep down I thought if I looked at it long enough one of the lines would disappear.

I was pregnant? I was five months pregnant with Oscar's baby, my mother's husband? I remember coughing out a loud blood curdling scream, followed by my sobbing. The truth of what was happening was crashing down on me all at once. I fell to the bathroom floor crying so loudly that my voice would end up being hoarse for two days. I was choking and coughing as I yelled at God as I begged him to give me answers. I didn't understand what I'd done to deserve any of what was happening to me.

That night in February when Oscar raped me was never going to go away? What was I supposed to do? How was I going to tell my mother? I couldn't break her heart like that. I couldn't ruin her life and her happiness. The tears were still pouring out of my eyes when I managed to finally get up. I walked over to the medicine cabinet and grabbed five random pill bottles and took them into my room closing the door behind me. I sat on the floor with my back against the wall and opened each pill bottle. This felt like the only logical option for me at this point.

For those five months I had to force myself to still be me. I had to pretend and smile and be the Zoe everyone loved while I was dying inside. Chunks of me were being burned away every single morning that I woke up. I was so tired of being me and of keeping this secret and still having to see his face. I could not have his offspring living inside of me, depending on me for survival. I felt disgusting, I was angry that even after all that time my body still wasn't mine. Oscar had taken possession of it when he raped me and I was realizing it was never going to be mine again.

I remember grabbing the first pill bottle and reading the label, it was my mother's pain killers from a surgery she had a few months prior. I emptied the entire bottle in my hand –about twelve pills. I stared at the pills in my palm for an eternity. I couldn't help but think about the people I would hurt if I did this, but also the hurt I was feeling at this very moment and for the last five months was unbearable. I wasn't sure how I was supposed to continue on.

After a few more exaggerated moments I let my hand drop, the pills hitting the floor and scattering everywhere. I sat my head back against the wall as one tear fell from my cheek. My hysterics were finally over. For some reason I was okay with the thought of ending my own life, but I couldn't picture ending this babies life in the process –not this way. I hated it. I had to hate it, right? It was his baby –not mine. But, I couldn't bring myself to do it.

I was pissed at myself for even having an ounce of remorse for the thing that was growing inside of me, but I had to think of a plan. Would I be able to have an abortion? Would I be able to go through labor and give the baby up for adoption? I sat there for an hour. I did not move one inch as I let the truth of what my life had become devour me wholly.

I didn't have any more tears, the well was dry. I was suffocating, I was numb. I was lonely, I was drowning, I was empty –all of the things I'd been feeling for the last five months and now I was pregnant too.

"Miss Oakley?" I hear someone say, startling me and snapping me out of my trance. I closed my diary and placed the pen on top. "Are you all ready? Mr. Jordan is in the hallway."

I smiled. "Yes, I'm ready. You can send him in."

Nurse Letecky nodded and walked out of the room. I put my butterfly diary into my duffle bag then placed that bag on my suitcase.

"Hey," he said with a bright smile as he rounded the corner. He walked right up to me and squeezed me tightly. "I missed you so much."

"You saw me two days ago." I say into his ear. I missed him too.

"It was two *very* long days." He said as he placed his lips gently on mine. "Are you excited that I'm breaking you out of here?" He arched an eyebrow and I had to stifle a laugh.

"If that's what you want to call my *scheduled* release."

After a handful of psyche evaluations and court appearances I was ordered to spend a month at this facility. Apparently, my level of emotional damage and baggage was so hefty that multiple hour long

123

sessions per week weren't enough –I needed twenty four hour surveillance.

"You have to admit you're a little excited about going to Nebraska?" He was abnormally chipper today and I knew it was because he knew I was freaking out about meeting his mother. He read my face then smiled grabbing my hand. "She already loves you, meeting you is going to be the cherry on top."

"She loves the *me* that *you* have created. If she truly knew me she wouldn't want me anywhere near her son." I roll my eyes pulling my hand from his as I grabbed my duffle bag to hand to him. I grabbed my suitcase and started pulling it towards the door.

"Wait," Aiden said as he grabbed my arm placing the bag on the floor. "I haven't *created* a Zoe specifically for my mom. I love all the pieces of you and she will too. Your private business isn't anyone's place to discuss. My mother knows that you make me happy, you make me laugh, and that I love you. That is all she cares about, okay?"

Damn, he was so good at yanking me back in when I let my thoughts spiral. I exhaled and grabbed his hand again, squeezing it then plastering a cartoon like smile on my face. "I'm ready and super excited, let's go! Nebraska here we come!" I beamed playfully, my sarcasm too blatant to be missed. He laughed and kissed my cheek. "Now that is the spirit." He whispered in my ear.

Nebraska was nice, I liked it here. It honestly didn't feel too different than Ohio. It was actually pretty mild outside to be so close to July. The night air was so crisp and refreshing. I kept taking deep calculated breaths. I sat on Aiden's mother's porch as I counted the stars; it was so clear I felt like I could see every star in the galaxy if I concentrated hard enough.

It was a billion miles from home for all I cared. Here, I felt like I didn't have a cloud hanging over my head. Only Aiden knew the baggage that rested heavily on my shoulders –no one else knew. I loved being around his childhood friends and family members who saw me as just a girl from Ohio who fell in love with their Aiden. Nothing more and nothing less, there were no opinions or conclusions to be drawn based off of that simple fact.

"Hey," Aiden said lowly, snapping me out of my thought, "I was wondering where you snuck off to. I thought you'd chartered a flight back to Ohio or something."

I smiled, scooting over on the steps so he could sit next to me. "Surprisingly, I like it here –a *lot*." I say staring off into the blackened night as he sat down next to me, "thank you for inviting me."

He put his arm around me and I reflexively nuzzle my head on to his shoulder. "Of course," He said. I didn't have to see him to know he was smiling.

"I almost don't want to go back." I nearly whisper. The only sounds you could hear were crickets in the distance. It was like everything was unmoving until the morning. It was beautiful.

"It was like pulling teeth to get you here and now you don't want to leave?" He questioned with humor in his voice.

"It's no secret, I'm a complicated girl," I shrugged. He squeezed me tighter, pulling me even closer to him. Maybe it wasn't the fact that I wanted to stay in Nebraska, it was the fact that I was with Aiden. Of course there were things I would love to run away from back in Ohio but everything always seemed a little bit better, a little bit easier when Aiden was around. I could sit like this in his arms for the rest of my life and it wouldn't matter what part of the continent we were on.

"I like your friends." I say with a smile.

"You like the fact that they pride themselves in embarrassing me in front of you." He corrects.

"That could be a huge factor," I shrug. "My favorite part was hearing about you getting suspended for vandalizing the school. You weren't kidding when you told me you had a reputation to uphold?"

He laughed and shook his head, "I vandalized the school on *accident*. Who would've thought pulling the fire alarm would make the sprinklers go off in the hallway?"

I laughed at his attempt at being innocent, "You want me to believe you had *no clue* the sprinklers would go off?"

He paused while staring at me then smiled, "I never ever want to lie to you but I also cannot incriminate myself so I plead the fifth."

"Wow!" I say trying to hold in another loud laugh, "all this time I thought you were so pure and innocent and you're a criminal. We really do belong together."

The humor left the air as he held me tighter to him.

"Zoe, you're not a …"

"Not here," I interrupt, "let's just enjoy *this* and each other, okay?"

He nodded and gave me a kiss on the forehead. I wanted to enjoy this bubble he and I created over the last two weeks here. I didn't want to taint it with real life issues. I was thankful Aiden still insisted on this trip, it was exactly what I needed.

"I love you." I say lightly, turning my head so I could kiss his neck. He smelled so good it was inebriating.

"I love you too, Zoe." He kissed the top of my hair. "More than you will ever possibly know."

We sat in comfortable silence for a while, listening to the crickets – an occasional owl would make its presence known. I looked back up at the stars, my body still pressed against Aiden.

126

"Counting?" Aiden asked. I could feel a light chuckle vibrate from his chest.

"How'd you know?" I questioned suspiciously. I always counted in my head, never out loud.

"You count things when you're trying to distract yourself from something or avoid something. I noticed that, sometimes you even mouth the numbers." I was going to laugh but Aiden sat up straight, I followed suit –before he continued. "What are you trying to distract yourself from right now?" He looked me in the eyes. "I already know what you're avoiding but we aren't going to talk about that here." He adds.

It was so weird seeing how you reflect off of someone else. At this point in my life no one knew me better than Aiden. He loved me wholly and cared about me completely. To be able to see in someone's eyes how much they cared about you was overwhelming.

"Home," I say, "anything that doesn't have to do with us in Nebraska at this moment is a distraction. I don't want to think about anything or anyone outside of this moment here with you." I answered honestly and laid my head back on his shoulder, my eyes darting right back up to the dark sky. I felt safe and for the first time in a very long time I felt genuinely happy –I was lost in the beauty of both feelings.

Aiden was quiet for a moment; I could feel him staring at me as I continued to gaze up appreciatively.

"What's on your mind?" I asked, sensing that he had something to say but was deciding against it.

He paused for a moment longer, then started rubbing my back up and down. "Nothing, you're right. I don't want to think of anything outside of this moment either."

As we sat here in comfortable silence I started thinking about the last two weeks, how welcoming his mother was, how hilarious is Uncle Will was, how insane and rowdy his high school buddies were. I was getting to look at a completely different Aiden through the eyes of others.

He was a beautiful spirit in every lens.

"Hey, those pictures above the fire place. Who's that girl?" I ask randomly, remembering when his mother was giving me a tour of their house. I'd noticed the girl and thought she was beautiful. I didn't get a chance to ask his mom who it was at the time because five of his friends ran through the living room door screaming and yelling at Aiden with excitement.

"My younger sister, Lillian." He answered simply. His voice was low and reserved. I dislodged myself from him so I could look directly at him.

"Your *sister*?" I say stunned and confused. "You never told me you had a sister?" A part of me is a little frustrated. As much time as we spend together, as much as we talk about any and everything he never once mentioned he wasn't an only child. Granted, I'd never asked but I assumed. There weren't any pictures of her at his dad's house.

"She died almost two years ago."

I let his words just sit in the air before I was capable of responding. I had a plethora of questions to ask him. There was so much I wanted to know but I opted to lay my head back on his shoulder and squeeze his arm. "Aiden, I'm so sorry."

He didn't respond and it made my stomach feel hollow. Clearly this was a touchy subject, clearly it was difficult for him to talk about but was I being a bad girlfriend by not asking for details? Would I be a bad girlfriend if I *did* ask for details? Wouldn't that be intrusive? I was surely no advocate when it came to speaking about things you didn't want to speak about, but right now I want nothing more than for my boyfriend to tell me every single thought in his mind.

"Go ahead." He said after a few moments of complete silence.

"What?"

"You have questions, go ahead," he said softly. I sat up and faced his profile; he was looking off into the night.

I swallowed, "How?"

"She killed herself when she was fourteen." I tried to manage my reaction but I wanted to gasp. Suicide? At fourteen? I felt a knot grow in my throat.

"Why?" My voice is low. My attention was still on Aiden's profile trying to read his energy. He was calm and stoic.

"She had a lot of mental and behavioral issues that basically went uncared for. Her father and our mother used to be alcoholics –" he pauses, and then inhales. "It was pretty bad for a while –living in that house. We were on our own a lot, all we had was each other. I was the only person she could talk to."

I cannot hide the disbelief from my face. I had absolutely no clue, not even an inkling about any of this. His mother was an alcoholic? Not the woman I've been around the last two weeks. She was warm and funny. Her gracious presence showed me right away where Aiden got his charm from. My mind was spiraling trying to piece all of this so that it made sense.

"*Her* father?" My voice is almost stuck in my throat as I listen to his words.

"Yea, we have different fathers," he answers lowly. He paused for a moment as if he were gathering his thoughts. "She would threaten to kill herself all of the time. I used to have to literally talk her off of the ledge a few times a month," he shook his head before continuing.

129

"She sent me a text one night when I was at work saying she couldn't take it anymore. That she was going to kill herself and I ignored it." He looked down and my heart stopped. I wrapped my arms around him, tears streaming out of my eyes.

He cleared his throat and continued, "I ignored it because she did this all of the time and I was busy at work. I couldn't leave because I knew I'd get fired. We needed the extra money because her father had just gotten laid off. I told myself I would talk to her when I got home because I knew it would be no different than any other time."

He took in a deep breath and clamped his hands together tightly. "I was the one that found her in her room," his voice was barely a whisper.

"Aiden…" His name struggles to leave my lips as a sob tries to escape. I hold it in as best I could.

"She shot herself with her father's gun." His lips contorted in an odd way, he was trying not to cry. "Had I left work or responded to her text she'd still be here."

"There's no way of knowing that. You can't blame yourself." I say. I felt sick, I felt helpless. The love of my life had been sitting with this and there was nothing I could do to help him. I didn't know how to comfort him because he was the one always comforting me. I didn't even know if he *wanted* to be comforted.

I was realizing that our entire relationship has been about me, my problems, *my* life. I couldn't comprehend what he was telling me because he was so happy and bright eyed. My sunny and shiny Aiden had skeletons too.

I felt selfish.

"I'm sorry," he said shaking his head and kissing my cheek, his demeanor almost changing completely, "that probably wasn't the best thing to talk about our last night here."

"Why didn't you tell me this?" I immediately felt like the biggest hypocrite seeing as though I wasn't exactly the best communicator in the world. I'd kept a lot from him too.

"A dead sister isn't really a conversation starter or something you can just bring up randomly after dessert."

"Aiden, I don't want to joke about this," I say trying to make eye contact with him and failing. "I'm sorry that this relationship hasn't been a two way street…"

"What?" He interrupts finally looking at me, "Zoe, I'm fine. I told you in the beginning I was good with complicated."

Suddenly my mind flits back to when I'd yelled at him in that classroom in the very beginning of our relationship. After I calmed down I told him I was complicated and the way he looked at me and how he responded let me know then that he too had baggage. I selfishly never asked about his issues. I never once assumed he'd have any because he was such a ray of positive energy in this world, in *my world.*

In this moment I'm realizing why he and I connected the way we did so early on, why we were orbiting each other the way we were. We both had *hurt* we were concealing from the world –he was just so much better at it than I. We were both burying things in our lives and trying to look forward and beyond what we were afraid to become. So many times he should've run for the hills but he didn't. He stayed and he loved me harder each time a new layer of myself was revealed. He continued to love me more than what I ever thought I could deserve.

It all made sense; it was all adding up in a very sad but true way.

We were the damaged loving the damaged.

"How are you able to…" I try to find the right word, what word would I use to describe *recovery*? "…cope." Is what I decided on, "you're so happy and so…"

"I can't let it devour me." He said looking directly into my eyes. "If I internalize every single thought I have about Lillian or that day or the blame I'll have to carry for the rest of my life, I wouldn't be able to function. I have no choice but to *cope.*"

I couldn't help but hear the double meaning in his words. It was the oddest conversation to have this feeling but I couldn't love him anymore than I did right now. He was strong and positive and there for me when I was too broken to even realize he needed someone to be there for him.

"Is that why you came to Ohio?"

He nodded. "My mom got her act together and divorced Lillian's dad. He was abusive and a complete enabler. She got a great job and she hasn't drank since the week after Lil's funeral but she has a lot of problems still and if I stayed here I felt like I would know nothing else but regret. I needed a fresh start."

I don't know what to say, I was still walking through the fog and shock of it all.

"The key is finding the bright spots." He said out of the blue, I listened intently. "You just have to look for those moments, those *people.*" He put his arm around me and squeezed tightly. "*Why* I came to Ohio sucks but what I found?" He kissed my forehead and I exhaled. "You see what I mean? You have to always have your eyes open for the bright spots. There will always be a light in *every* situation, Zoe." He emphasized the words as he repeated them.

I let those words wrap around me solidly. I'd learned so much. I still had so many questions for Aiden now that I was sitting next to a different layer of him a layer I would've never thought existed in a million years.

His words were searing into my being. I wasn't mad at him for not telling me this, I was sad that he'd carried it with him and I was too blind in my world to uncover it like he'd did for me. He'd been there for me in every conceivable way and I didn't even open the door for him to tell me anything.

He sighed. "I know you, Zoe." He shook his head. "We are not comparing scars here. You know everything about me now and I know everything about you. We can be happy and fucked up together okay?"

I truly hated and at the same time loved his innate ability to turn any situation into lighthearted banter –I couldn't help but smile. I sighed.

"I kiss your scars and you kiss mine?" I say impishly. He smiled and almost like a light switch the Aiden I was used to emerged beautifully. He kissed my lips and I wished I had the power to cement us in this moment forever. Our layers were exposed like livewires. I didn't want to be clueless to any area of his world as he was already submersed in mine.

For the next few hours we sat on that porch talking about the most frivolous things. His mother came outside to see if we were okay around midnight, we didn't realize how late it had gotten. Aiden grabbed my hand to help me up from the steps then we walked inside to just sit on the couch and talk for a couple more hours.

I was sad that this was our last night here but I was happy that I got hours to talk to Aiden about the good parts of life, the *great* parts of life that involved him.

Our demons were still peeking around the corner, our skeletons were jiggling the door knob of the closet we'd nailed shut –they were waiting for us to slip so they could come out and drown us again, but at this moment they didn't exist. They could not get to us right now no matter how hard they tried.

There was only Aiden and Zoe. My heart was full and my thoughts were of him only.

Chapter Nine: Big Step

Oscar didn't die.

My lawyer and my new psychiatrist seemed to think that was good news. It had been a year and a half since the *incident* in the kitchen and I still can't help but think if I would've just stabbed him one more time maybe he would be in hell right now where he belonged.

I sat in my lawyer's office next to Aiden. He held my hand tightly, *protectively.* Almost as if he thought he could shield me from all of the bad things in the world. Though I wanted him here, a part of me wanted him to leave. He was already too involved in this and I didn't want him in *this* part of my world. He was *still* my sunny and shiny Aiden and no matter how much I'd improved mentally over this last year and a half I still didn't want to leave any smudges on him.

"This man took her virginity, got her pregnant, and then sexually harassed her for over a year in her own home! What do you expect?" My lawyer yelled on the phone. She paused for a moment then said, "It was self-defense and your client knows it. That's why no charges have been filed. She was a *minor*; you're walking on thin ice!"

I can feel Aiden's hand clench around my hand even tighter, her words stinging him. I felt nothing and not in an emo numbing sense. I felt nothing because she listed facts. These were things that he did. These were things that happened to me. Oscar did not have that to hold over me anymore, he was powerless against me now. I had nothing to fear, I experienced the worst thing that could happen to me and I survived it. *Barely* –but I'm still standing nonetheless. My lawyer's words did not hurt me in anyway.

"I will speak with my client. Goodbye." She hung up the phone and sat down. She looked directly at me; her light eyes were prominent when contrasted with her deep russet skin. She sighs and clears her throat. "Well," she says with a stoic look on her face.

I looked at Aiden, his eyes were already on me, and they were always on me. It was like he feared if I wasn't in his sight I would get hurt again, that I would disappear in the blink of an eye. This was exactly the burden I didn't want him to carry. His love for me was overpowering the fact that I came with too much to carry, too much for both of us to carry.

"I have a deal that I proposed via email that they are considering and I think it's as good as we will get, considering the circumstances." She says looking directly in my eyes.

If the deal was anything shy of him rotting in prison I didn't want it. If I couldn't send him to hell I wanted to make sure he spent the rest of his life in hell on earth. I never wanted him to see the light of day again. I was a prisoner in my own home for over a year, a prisoner in my own *body*. Being in jail would only be a tenth of what I experienced and a tenth of what he actually deserved.

I nodded at my lawyer –Mrs. Pierce – signaling her to continue.

"If we settle out of court he will plead not guilty to the sexual assault charge but plead guilty to the sexual harassment charge. He will be on three years' probation, with 1800 hours of community service. You have to continue psychiatric evaluations and anger management courses for the next eighteen months."

I looked at her like she was speaking another language. Her words strung together in that order made a complete sentences, but when they washed over me they had no meaning. I was stuck in quicksand trying to fully understand what she'd just said to me.

"Wait…" Aiden said letting go of my hand and leaning forward, "what do you mean not guilty?" The frustration blatant in his voice was exactly how I was feeling. I just couldn't express it with words yet. "He *is* guilty? There's a fucking baby out there somewhere as proof? No jail time, this doesn't fucking make sense!"

"Mr. Jordan," my lawyer says calmly, "the *not guilty* is all legal jargon, look at it as a technicality. At this point it's just words."

It's *just words* she'd said. Before that night I'd spent over a year keeping my words in. I let them soil my spirit, rot my foundation, invade my mind. Those words that I buried so deep within me finally boiled over and encompassed my entire body. All the words I refused to say, all the words I refused to share, and all the words that would've lifted the steal tons off of my chest viciously came out in a flurry of stab wounds in Oscar's body.

"They're not just words," I said lowly and confidently, "it either *is* or *isn't*. He *is* guilty of raping me, I know it, you know it, his lawyers know it, and he knows it. I'm not agreeing to this deal, I want to go to court."

My lawyer sighed and uncrossed her arms. "Look, I know what happened to you and it's horrible and I feel for you 100%, but you are my client and I have to do what is best for you and this case." She looked me square in the eyes.

"You didn't tell anyone about the rape, you didn't go to the police, there's no rape kit or any physical records or documentation to prove you were raped. The only witness to the sexual harassment in that kitchen was your boyfriend. The only thing I know and that's only because I believe you –is that you both had sexual relations that resulted in a child –a child who was given up for adoption. Oscars name was not on the birth certificate or identified as the father during the adoption process. There's no DNA evidence that he is even the father thus almost erasing any proof of sexual contact to the courts. If this goes to court, they *will* attack you. They will treat you like you are not the victim, it will be painful and grueling and he could get off scot-free with the evidence we have to work with."

She stood up adjusting her deep red blazer and walked around her desk standing directly in front of me, she grabbed my hand. "Off the record, if it were up to me I'd give you a gun and put you and Oscar in a room together with no witnesses. He is scum, I understand that *but* my job is to protect you. It's easier said than done but we have to leave emotions out of it."

I looked into her eyes, and I could feel the sincerity. I wiped away a tear and nodded.

"We could get lucky and get jurors who are sympathetic to your story, or we could get a judge that looks at the facts alone… we could fight this head on for the next two years in court if that is what you truly want, but with the circumstances in this particular case I don't feel confident enough in landing him in jail and keeping you out for the assault. There are just too many gray areas."

I inhale and exhale slowly, frustrated that her words were making total sense. Frustrated that with everything that transpired Oscar was barely going to get a slap on the wrist while I have to continue ridiculous psyche evaluations.

"I'm going to fight to get his name added to the sex offenders list, if it's the last thing I do. We have to make this deal if we want *any* justice served." She said softly, she looked over at Aiden and his eyes were red. He was livid but he knew that we had to do this.

"Okay." I finally said softly. "Make the deal." I added. I looked over at Aiden and his eyes were already on me. They were sad and angry but even through the fury I could still see the love he had for me blaring loudly. I grabbed his hand and squeezed it tightly, letting him know I was okay and in that second as I was locked with his gaze, I truly was okay.

***

"You're not speaking." I say to Aiden as we sit in a restaurant waiting for our order. He didn't say much when we left Mrs. Pierces office and he hadn't said a word on the entire drive to the restaurant.

"Just tired," he answers lowly.

I stare at him as he stares at his cell phone, scrolling mindlessly. I sigh and look out of the window, taking a deep breath in. I had to confront him about this pattern of his.

"This happens every single time," I say looking back in his direction, he furrowed his eyebrows.

"What?" He said putting his phone down. I just look at him and its crazy how I can actually physically feel his love. I always thought love was a concept, a thought, an idea but when I look at him his love covers me completely. It's tangible –so much so I feel like I could literally reach out into the thin air and feel it with my palms. It's like a warm blanket that feels safe, it feels like home.

"Before this court stuff…" I trail off. "We were Aiden and Zoe and it's like any time the case or Oscar is brought up, or I have to go to evaluations, or meetings with Mrs. Pierce you disappear from me."

"Disappear?" He said angrily, "I'm always with you Zoe, I *want* to be there."

"Yes you're there physically, and you will never know how grateful I am and how indebted I am," I say wiping a tear, "I'm saying…" I trail off again.

"What are you saying?" He begs. His voice was still defensive.

"I'm saying we don't have to change because of what happened in my past. You don't have to tip toe around me, guard me. You don't have to feel like I'm this fragile object –that I'm going to break the second you look away." I said the words in one quick blur.

"You can't shut down every time this is brought up. It's a part of me in a very integral way unfortunately. You once said you loved all the pieces of me, well this is a major piece and every time I have to deal with it I don't want you to feel like you have to carry the burden or the heaviness of the situation. I just want you to be *my Aiden*; nothing else is required from you."

He is just staring at me. I can't figure out what emotion he is feeling but it isn't anger anymore. I can see that he at least understands what I was trying to say.

"I snapped," I say, "a year and a half ago I snapped and I almost killed the man who raped me. That is the elephant in the room." I added. The words have been spoken plenty of times at this point but I needed to strip those words of their power over Aiden. "When he did that to me I should've handled things differently and I didn't and because of that I let it rule my life. It doesn't rule my life anymore and it shouldn't rule yours. You told me that you can't let the bad devour you. Well I can't and you can't let this devour you either. So please don't disappear, because I promise I am not going to."

Aiden has yet to say anything. I knew he comprehended that I was speaking figuratively, but I meant that literally as well.

"I love you so much and you have stood by my side but I'm not broken like that anymore. No, I'm not completely fixed and I can't say that I ever will be but I'm in a better place right now than I ever have been before and in most part it is because of you," I smile softly, reaching across the table to grab his hand. "Don't let this situation take anything else from you. It can't take anything else from me."

Finally, the serious and focused exterior Aiden had plastered on his face since we walked into my lawyers office this morning was now gone. He was calmer, more relaxed, I could detect a faint smile whispering across his lips as he stared at me placing his other hand on top of our already connected hands.

"Move in with me." He says out of the blue. I froze, replaying the question in my head ten times before I was able to thaw out. I was completely caught off guard.

"Wait, what?" I say almost stuttering over my words, I knew what he asked. I heard it clear as day and it was still playing back in my mind on repeat. I just needed to buy more time to actually process the words.

"Move in with me." He repeats – his tone was much more serious but I could hear a slight note of anticipation and excitement in his voice. "You know I'm getting an apartment off campus at the beginning of next semester…"

"Wow," I say flabbergasted. He was almost done with his first semester of college. He would never admit it to me but I know he decided to go to an in state college in order to stay near me. After we graduated high school I decided I didn't want to go off to college right away. I wanted more time to actually figure out *who* and *what* I wanted to be before going to school. The years that teens usually spent deciding what colleges they were going to go to or what majors they would choose I was busy giving birth and going through therapists, psyche evaluations, and court.

"I…" I stutter, "I, yea…okay." I say the words in an excited blur. Nothing about Aiden and I had ever been customary. We met randomly, we liked each other instantly, we loved each other quickly, and he learned about my demons much sooner than I'd hoped. I learned about his too. He just turned 19 and I was 18 and to some it would seem like we were too young for a step like this but with what we'd been through and how we've stuck by each other, everything that happens with us feels natural, nothing feels rushed.

"Yea?" He said excitedly. I nodded with a huge smile on my face. "I love you." He whispered.

"Clearly," I answer with a smile. I'd been living in Matt's basement all of this time while he and Alicia were out of state away at college. Mrs. Hunter took me in and treated me as if I were her blood daughter. I couldn't stay in my house any longer. Too many real life nightmares existed there.

"I have one condition," I say, I looked at him sternly. He looks at me incredulously before nodding. "I want full reign on decorating the living room and bedroom, I've seen your dorm. I can't live in that."

He smiled genuinely, "Deal."

Our food came and we spent the rest of the time planning and navigating through our future together. That was the best part about being with Aiden. We could argue, be honest, be angry at each other, and joke because we knew what we had was real. We didn't have to prove ourselves to anyone. I would never be loved again as intensely as he loved me and that alone was enough to get me through anything.

Chapter Ten: Trust

I sat there quietly looking straight ahead. My mother was on the opposite end of the couch staring at the therapist. This was our third joint session and not much had been accomplished and for once it wasn't on my end. I did not want to be here but my mother fought tooth and nail to make it mandatory within my court ordered evaluations since I was a minor when everything transpired.

"Mrs. Doyle," the therapist said. I cringed at the name; she was still married to him. After all this time she still had his last name. "I want you to tell your daughter why you're hurt."

I try not to roll my eyes and I try not to snort in annoyance. I'm trying to understand in what world should *she* be the hurt one? She wasn't the victim in this scenario but somehow she'd made it about her, she'd managed to drain out crocodile tears throughout these sessions as I sat there unmoved and unbothered waiting for the clock to wind down on our required hour.

"Zoe," she says facing me. I take a deep breath in before facing her direction. "You cut me out of your life completely. You moved out and I had to find out through someone else, you don't call or try to communicate with me in anyway. I feel like…I feel like you blame me."

"I *do* blame you," I answered honestly. The hurt that rippled across her features did not faze me. I was no longer able to put the feelings of others in front of my own. When he raped me I was so stupid and so blinded by the fear of it hurting my mother that I said and did nothing. I sat and lived in my hurt all of that time –not once thinking about me, only thinking about her.

When I found out I was pregnant I acted as if I had no clue who the father was. I was called a whore and a slut and only God knows what people were thinking when they looked at me, but I went through all of that to protect my mother. I didn't care that who I was, was now destroyed, that pieces of me were shattered and fading away. I knew how happy she was, I knew how in love she'd fallen. She made him her entire world while she gave me –her only child –scraps. I couldn't be the one to take her whole world away from her –I didn't want her to secretly resent me.

I kept my mouth closed so she could remain happy. I was young and it was a stupid decision but I did it all for her, at least that's what I told myself.

My therapist looked at me and wrote in her notepad. "Why do you blame your mother for Oscar's actions?"

"Obviously I don't blame her for everything that occurred," I say, "I blame her for ignoring me before it happened, I blame her for bringing him into our world even when I told her I didn't have a good feeling about him, I blame her for *still* having his last name."

"It's not like that, Zoe!" she snapped, "its legal stuff that I cannot control."

"How many times have you spoken to him or visited him in the last year and a half?" I ask angrily. She just stared at me. That's all the answers I needed. I didn't cry or fall apart like I imagined I would. I actually started laughing. The idiocy of it all was baffling to me.

"You know, I actually felt bad at first, like maybe somehow all of this was to bring us closer together. I figured we could find each other again because we'd lost each other there for a while," a tear manages to escape my eye but the disbelieving smile was still there.

142

"Your husband raped your daughter, got her pregnant, and sexually harassed her every single chance he got –right under your roof. I was so happy when he got that job as a truck driver because he would be gone for weeks or months at a time and I could finally feel safe. I didn't have a nagging fear that he would pick the lock to my bedroom door or that you'd pickup an extra shift and I'd be home alone with him. I lived in fear for over a year, cried myself to sleep too many times to count."

I shook my head still trying to fathom how this was even possible, how she couldn't see her wrong doing in this at all. It was crazy how I was able to say the words so casually, the same words I couldn't even let surface to my memory for so long.

"That night when I stabbed him do you know that he didn't just grab me, he asked if Aiden knew that he'd *been there* first?" My mother's tears pooling out of her eyes, she turns from me to look down at her lap. I continued, "He told me that the lock on my door wouldn't stop him, that he'd given me more than enough time to heal after giving birth. He said that after Aiden was done with me he would *have at it again.* He said those words as he pressed himself against me, with you –his wife –in the next room." I took a deep breath in, "…and you *still* love him." It was an unbelievable thought. "You are able to love a monster but you are unable to love me."

"Zoe," she cried facing towards me once again, "I do love you, more than you will ever possibly know."

"I know that, but there are different kinds of love. You love me because I came from you; it's in the stars for you to feel connected to me in some way because I was once a part of you, but *Kim* loving *Zoe*? You don't. You would feel the hurt and see the scars and understand how your actions have proved otherwise." I got up grabbing my bag as I looked at the therapist.

"I'm so sorry," I said sincerely, "I have to meet my boyfriend to sign our lease. I can't be late."

She nods.

"Zoe!" my mother calls out as I walk out of the room. I wipe the last of my tears and head towards the elevators. I couldn't wait to see Aiden.

***

"I can't unpack another box!" I yell while sprawling myself across our new living room floor, the plush tan carpet comfortable under my tired body. "If I see another box, I'm throwing it out of the window."

I hear Aiden laughing in the kitchen as he walks into the living room to lie down next to me. We are both on our backs staring at the ceiling, he grabs my hand.

"We did it," he said, I could hear the smile in his voice. "We're grownups!" he laughed.

"Kind of feels like it doesn't it?" I laugh as well. I think about where my life was a little over two years ago, never would I have imagined I would be here. I didn't think people like me were ever allowed to feel this way. I remember conversations I had with Matt and with my mother, on separate occasions they'd both said they wanted me to be happy and I told them that happiness wasn't meant for everyone. I remember how sad those words had made me feel, how lonely and vulnerable accepting sadness had felt.

In the very beginning of our relationship Aiden asked me confusingly why I was so okay with being unhappy and I remember how angry his words made me. Looking back at it now and seeing the entire picture of what I'd gone through I wasn't mad at his words I was mad at the fact that they were true and that I was doing nothing at the time to combat its truth.

I turned to Aiden to just stare at him. I'd told him before, but he would never truly know how he saved me in a sense –that he'd come into my life at precisely the right time. His unmoving presence was a

144

constant reminder of the good that did exist in the world. Knowing that someone could love me so unapologetically gave me strength. It made me brave.

He faced me and smiled, "What?"

"I trust you." I say to him. He smiles and squeezes my hand tighter.

"I trust you too." He said as his smile lit up our dark living room.

"That's stronger than love to me," I say softly, feeling the meaning of my words swirl inside of my chest, "I could love you forever and I *will* but to trust someone the way I trust you…" I trail off.

"Zoe, are you okay?" He said as he turned his body slightly towards me, placing his hand on my cheek. I leaned in and kissed him. I pulled him as close to my body as I could physically allow.

"I'm ready." I whisper against his lips, my voice shaky but the meaning unwavering.

"What?" He says as he pulls away from my lips slowly to stare into my eyes.

I smiled as the nerves cascaded through my entire body. "I'm *ready.*" I say the words more deliberately.

Understanding read clear across his features.

I had no words to describe how patient and understanding Aiden had been. My demons, my fears, my anxiety, and my lack of confidence wouldn't allow me to give that part of myself to Aiden. We'd been together just shy of two years and hadn't had sex as unbelievable and crazy as it sounded. He never complained, he never made me feel pressure, he never made me feel less than. He knew the internal issues I was going through and working through and he was there beside me every second never faltering once. Constantly reminding me he loved me no matter what.

"Zoe," he said as he tried to read my face.

I was sure. I was scared and terrified, but I was sure about Aiden.

I nodded and placed my lips back on his, we kissed gently. Delicately, we'd never kissed like this before. Aiden was taking his time. I knew him; he was waiting for me to change my mind. He was waiting for me to push him away; he was waiting for my fears to overrule my wants like they had so many times before in our relationship. For once I wanted the love of my life to stop thinking about me and to start thinking about himself.

"Aiden," I say placing both of my hands on either side of his face. "I love you, I trust you, and I am ready." I said the words with confidence and with desire. The fire in his eyes blazed so brightly. He kissed me passionately.

Aiden knew parts of my being that I never could imagine anyone else in the world knowing, he'd seen me at my lowest and darkest point. I wanted him to know *this* part as well. I wanted to share this part of me with him and only him for the rest of my life. I didn't want to have anything left in between us that either of us was unfamiliar with or hadn't experienced.

I remember when we got into the biggest argument we've had to date. It was after he found out about the adoption. We were screaming at each other, yelling like we were the only two people in the entire world with ears. It was the first time he said he loved me, I remember thinking about how the world kept spinning and birds were still flying and people apart from us were still living their lives, but how in that moment my only focus was him and the truth of his words.

Right now the opposite was happening. I was succumbed and blinded by the energies passing through both of us. Time stopped. The world was not spinning on its axis. Everything from this moment in my life was nonexistent if it didn't involve Aiden and the exhilaration I was experiencing for the first time with him.

"I love you," I say in his ear, barley able to get the words out. But I did, I loved him fervently and unabashedly. I would never stop loving the man who helped save me from drowning, the man who helped me find who I truly was outside of my anger and unhappiness. As we made love I found solace and peace within myself. I explored ecstasy on levels I never knew could exist. There was no other thought in my mind as these moments of love overpowered every nerve ending in my entire body.

I was one with the man I would spend the rest of my life with and now I'd shared *every* part of my being with him.

Chapter Eleven: Post Traumatic Stress

I woke up suddenly, a sob escaping my throat. I sat up and tried to catch my breath.

"Baby," I hear Aiden pop up next to me, immediately putting his arm around me and pulling me close to him. "What's wrong?"

"It was just a dream, I'm sorry," I sniffle wiping my tears, "I didn't mean to wake you. I know you have to be up early."

"Was it about …"

He didn't finish the question because he knew what the answer would be. I'd been having this reoccurring dream about Oscar, about him breaking into the apartment and attacking me. I was livid that he had managed to immerse himself into my subconscious.

"Zoe, this is happening because of court next week." He said. I knew that. Monday would be the first time I saw Oscar since that night. I would have to stand in the same room with him for the first time in two years. I wasn't scared, I wasn't nervous, I was angry. Because he was a stubborn and a bitter man he wanted to refute my deposition that I'd given in order to solidify the deal our lawyers made. This, already long process would now be even longer.

Unfortunately, I knew him. He was a weak minded person his only way to feel like a man was to feel like he had control. So it pissed me off that though I do not feel threatened by him –in my dreams I'm that sixteen year old girl too weak and too afraid to fight back. I wasn't her anymore. She and I were two completely different people.

"I'm fine," I say. "Seriously, you need to go to sleep because you have a final and I will not let you blame me if you're sleep deprived tomorrow." I kissed him on his cheek and wiggled out of his hold, turning my back to him.

"Zo," he said, grabbing my shoulder.

"Goodnight, love you." I say overriding his voice. I hear him sigh and about two minutes later I hear his light snore. I smile and exhale. I waited a few more minutes to make sure he was actually sleeping so as to not wake him when I got out of the bed. I looked behind me to see that he was completely knocked out before slowly inching my way out of our room.

I quietly walked to our living room closet. I dug out two boxes that we still hadn't unpacked. I sat on the floor and searched through both boxes frustrated that I couldn't find what I was looking for. Though it had been over a year and a half since the last time I'd seen or written in it I wanted my butterfly diary. Things were starting to spin wildly in my thoughts, so much so that it was following me into my sleep. I was still unable to *open up* to therapists and psychiatrist and I knew I could talk to Aiden about anything but I just couldn't burden him with the thoughts that had been going through my mind as of late. I didn't want to scare him.

I put the boxes back into the closet then walked over to Aiden's desk to grab a few sheets of paper and a pen. I sat at our kitchen table just staring at the first blank white sheet, it didn't feel right. I had words that needed to be let out, but this random piece of paper was not the same. I felt like my words wouldn't be safe floating aimlessly outside of my butterfly diary.

I laid my forehead on the table and sighed; trying to convince myself I was crazy for overanalyzing something as tiny as a piece of paper. After a few moments I sat up and inhaled deeply. The rape, the pregnancy, the lying, and the aftermath of everything were obviously painful things to go through but something I never talked about, never discussed openly was the pain of telling my mother I was pregnant. For some reason that day in July was playing over and over in my mind and I knew the only way to stop the images and voices from looping in my thoughts would be to write them down.

I bit my lip, and then pressed the pen to the loose paper. As soon as I wrote the first word I was immediately able to place myself right back at that time. I was able to feel the fear, embarrassment, and isolation I felt.

Dear "Diary"

My heart felt like it was going to beat right out of my chest, I was sweating and I felt nauseated and for the first time in a week the nausea wasn't because of this pregnancy it was because I knew everything in my life was about to be burned to the ground.

I texted my mother and told her that it was an emergency and that I needed to speak to her as soon as she got home. I remember her texting back asking if I were okay and the honest to God's truth would've been to say no I am not okay but I didn't want to panic her. I just didn't reply. I sat on the couch staring at the door, every time a car drove by I jumped or flinched thinking it was her.

I'd found out a week prior that I was pregnant and already five months pregnant at that I knew I couldn't hide it any longer and there was no way to avoid the inevitable.

The front door opened and the room started spinning immediately. How was I supposed to do this? I felt the panic creeping through me. I'd already made the decision that she could not know it was Oscar's baby. I couldn't even allow my thoughts to even think about it long enough to oppose that decision.

"Zoe?" She yells out before she even closes the door behind her.

"I'm in the living room." I remember my voice cracking when I called out to her. She came around the corner with nothing but concern on her face. She put her purse on the coffee table and sat down on the love seat across from the couch where I was sitting.

"What is going on? Why didn't you text me back?" She rattled off quickly. "You don't text your mother –it's an emergency, please come straight home – and then not elaborate!" The concern on her face was quickly turning into frustration.

I stared at her and at that moment I thought that maybe my mother wouldn't react the way that I feared. Maybe she'd comfort me. Maybe she'd help me not be so scared. Of course she would be disappointed but maybe just maybe she could help me through this because she was all that I had. I decided not to waste any more time. The anxiety I experienced for the last week was eating me alive, I didn't want to feel that anymore.

"Mom," I say and as soon as I opened my mouth streams of tears fell against my control. The fear and sadness that crossed her face made me feel guilty but appreciative of her compassion. She got up and sat next to me wrapping her arm around me tightly –slowly rocking me back and forth.

"Baby girl," she crooned, "what is wrong? Please talk to me."

"I'm pregnant."

The Band- Aid was ripped, the truth was out –the words were floating intensely around both of us. The rocking stopped suddenly, her arm still around me.

"What?" There was no anger. There was just pure confusion at this point.

"I found out last week that I'm pregnant." My voice cracked each time I said the word pregnant. It was still so unreal, I was telling her this and I still hadn't fully comprehended it myself. She moved her arm from around me.

"I ..." She began but then stopped to wipe a tear from her cheek. I felt my heart break. *"I don't understand ..."*

I sat quietly letting her process my words as I stared at the floor.

"You're sixteen. You're a baby!" She said this almost to herself. I could hear anger starting to find a place in her words. *"How... how could you be so irresponsible? I didn't even know you were sexually active...I don't ...I don't understand this?"*

Her words were running together as the truth was finally starting to settle in for her. I said nothing because there was nothing I could say.

"I didn't even know you were dating!" She said angered. *"You have never mentioned a single boy other than Matt..."* She trailed off and I could see where her thought was going.

"It's not Matt's." I said quickly before she could come to that conclusion. I wiped a tear away.

"Then whose is it?"

This is what I feared. This was the question that I knew would haunt me for the rest of my life. I swallowed and with everything in me I lied through my teeth.

"I don't know."

"What?" The pure disgust and befuddlement in her voice made me feel small.

"I don't know who the father is." I say the words clearly.

151

"There is more than one possibility?" She questioned, I nodded. "Fine," she said with so much anger and force that I jumped, "tell me the two names and we will go from there."

"I can't give you two names." I say lowly, realizing that I didn't think this through. In my head I would tell her I didn't know and we would move on. Last week I considered telling her I was raped by a stranger but I didn't want to file a false police report, I didn't want to give a fake description and have innocent men dragged in for line ups all so I could say no that's not the guy every single time. My mind didn't think about how specific things would get.

"Oh my God," and for the first time in my life I saw my mother sob. I've seen her cry before but she started sobbing uncontrollably and I felt helpless and hopeless wishing that my words weren't the thing causing her this pain.

"I did not raise you this way!" She yelled through tears. "You just ruined your life!" She screeched and I felt faint. She was right, my life was completely ruined. That I knew for sure. "Do you have any respect for yourself or any self-control? I don't even know who you are right now. I can't even look at you." Her voice was repulsed. "I'm ashamed to be your mother." She spat out angrily then got up to storm out of the living room.

I'm ashamed to be your mother.

I replayed those words in my mind over and over again until they didn't even sound like words anymore.

It felt like she shoved her hand through my chest, ripped my heart out, and stepped on it. This was what I expected in away but deep down maybe I thought that through the initial shock and anger she would want to support me, that she would be my mother. It was hopeful thinking. I sat on the couch sobbing soundlessly unable to move, paralyzed by the stress and shock of it all. I was snapped out of my mind numbing thoughts when the front door opened.

It was Oscar. He hadn't been here for the last three weeks and wasn't supposed to be home for two more days. I felt the bile rise in my mouth as soon as he walked through the foyer, I immediately went to dart up to my room but not before he looked right at me and saw my tear soaked face.

"Oscar!" I heard my mother yell from the kitchen, her voice angered and laced with a sob.

He looked in the direction of the kitchen then back at me and for that split moment I saw fear flit across his features. It was oddly calming knowing that for the next few seconds he would think I told her about what he'd done. I was only able to enjoy his fear for a few moments when like a tsunami it hit me that my mother was about to tell him I was pregnant. I needed to get out of this house. I needed to get out of this life. I remember darting out of the side door and running the entire ten minutes to Matts house.

"What's wrong?!" Matt said panicked as he jumped up from his basement couch to wrap me in his arms. I'd never cried so hard in my entire life, not even when I found out I was pregnant last week. I felt like I was in physical pain, like I was being burned at the stake.

"I'm pregnant." I screeched into his chest, my words mumbled.

"What?" He said with pure shock as he pulled me away to look at my face, my face that was red, swollen, and tear streaked.

"I'm pregnant!" I yell at him, like it was his fault. "Everything is fucked up." I pull myself from his grip and hit the floor. I felt weak, I felt like I couldn't go on another second being Zoe.

"How? Who?" Matt asked confused as he sat on the floor in front of me trying to make eye contact. "When?"

"Matt, please." I beg lowly, trying to catch my breath.

"I don't understand." His voice was in shock, he couldn't wrap his mind around it. Neither could I.

153

"No one does." I snap, covering my face with my hands.

"I'm sorry." He said moving next to me. He wrapped his arms around me and started rocking me and rubbing my back like my mother was doing right before I told her the horrible news. It made me cry more.

"What do you need?" Matt asked sincerely even though he sounded hopeless. *"What can I do?"*

I thought for a moment and there was honestly nothing anyone could do. "Just be here." I finally choke out.

"Okay," he said, still rocking me, *"I'm here. I'll always be here."*

I placed the pen down, realizing that almost two hours had gone by. The paper was wet from my tears, some of the words smudged, but I felt better. There was more I could've written, so much more about sitting with Matt for hours watching movies being able to disconnect myself from reality for a moment. How in all the years I'd known him I appreciated him most at that time because he didn't abandon me. Or I could've written about going home and having my mother scream at me more with Oscar standing right there. With his beady eyes staring directly at me, knowing that he had raped me, knowing that the child I was carrying was his.

But I wrote all I had in me, though I felt better for finally giving these words a place I felt depleted from the details of the memory. I sigh and then tear the two pages I'd just written into little pieces then threw them away. There was no need for the words to exist in the real world anymore. I just needed them off of my chest, I needed them to breathe and see the light of day because they'd been weighing me down.

I walked back into our bedroom and Aiden was awake sitting with his back against our headboard.

"What are you doing up?" I say surprised as I walked towards the bed. "I'm sorry, did I wake you?"

"Were you able to write it all down?" He asked genuinely. "Do you feel any better?"

I stopped walking. "How did you…"

"I got up to check on you when I didn't feel you next to me. I saw you writing and crying so I came back in here I knew whatever you were writing must be what has been bothering you lately."

I smile and wipe a tear, "I love you." I say as I get into the bed and kiss his cheek. "Yes, I feel better."

He wrapped his arms around me. "I love you, too." He whispered. I felt calm. I was able to bring myself back into my new world with Aiden. I'd submersed myself for two hours in the old Zoe's world and it made me feel so weak and scared. I embraced the love of my life tighter when I realized I'd never be who I once was and I was thankful that he was a part of the reason.

＊

Aiden and I got to court early. I hated how it looked, how it smelled. Everything was so stale, old faded wood, deep brown hues –it was depressing. Aiden sat behind me as I sat next to my lawyer while she prepared. She'd warned me that this was just the defenses way of giving us more loops to go through but that everything was precautionary, that everything was still going as planned.

I would turn around and look at Aiden every once so often. He was my rock, knowing he was there made me feel eerily calm. Every time I looked at him he either smiled, or winked, or stuck his tongue out at me. I was happy that through all of this he was the one to show up. And not just to court but in general. He showed up every

155

time. Sometimes words were everything –that much I learned, but being there could be just as powerful.

It was now a few minute before 10 am and people were starting to come into the court room. I did not want to see Oscar, not because I was scared, but what if I snapped again? What if I lost it? I remember everything moving in slow motion when I stabbed him, I didn't black out, I didn't forget what happened I was completely aware of what I was doing. I didn't know I was going to snap, that's the point of its meaning. What if I reached over my lawyer grabbed the glass pitcher of water, broke it, and went to stab him again?

I turned to look behind me at Aiden again to settle my nerves, when I saw the courtroom doors open and a huge smile spread across my face. It was Matt and Alicia. I had no idea they were coming. I looked at Aiden as a tear fell down my cheek I wiped it quickly. I looked at Matt and he rolled his eyes then smiled. He was laughing at the fact that this surprise made me cry. They sat down next to Aiden.

A few moments later Mrs. Hunter walked in. I smiled at her as I watched her sit next to Matt. It felt so weird, looking at the situation for me to feel this jubilant. I didn't just have Aiden in my corner I had a small tribe of people here to support me. I didn't ask them to come and I never wanted them to feel obligated to, but there they were.

The doors opened again and I paused. I stopped thinking for a moment as I saw my mother walk in. I hadn't spoken to her in two months. The only way she would've known about the hearing would be through Oscar. My heart sank. With my own eyes I was going to watch my mother go sit on his side of the courtroom. She was going to openly and blatantly choose this man over me like she'd done time and time before.

I saw her walk forward as she looked around the room, we made eye contact briefly. I saw sadness in her eyes, I had to look away. I wasn't going to let her make this about her again. I watched her slowly walk towards the seats; she paused then sat down next to

Mrs. Hunter. I looked at her with my mouth gaping open. She was here to support me? She was here for me and not for Oscar? I looked at Aiden and he nodded as if he were reading my thoughts. *He* did this, he is the one who contacted everyone to come and support me today. He wanted me to know that I would never be alone in this.

I didn't think I could possibly love him more than I already did, but I felt like my heart was going to explode.

I was quickly yanked out of my positive space when the door opened again and this time it was Oscar. He was walking in with a cane, deep scars on the side of his face. I wondered if those marks were from me. I didn't know where I stabbed him or the extent of his injuries. The feelings I thought I would have when seeing him weren't the feelings I was experiencing. I felt relief. I think I'd built this moment up in my mind that now that it's here I feel nothing. I still hate him, I will always hate him but it's not encompassing like it was two years ago. When I could feel the hate I had for him in my bones, deep within my being.

I'd moved on with my life and watching him walk into the courtroom with that same evil scowl on his face, knowing he wanted this hearing to prolong the judicial process all proves that he's stuck in that space of time. He has not learned or grown in any capacity. He was pathetic and in a way it was cathartic to see.

"All rise." The words were spoken aloud as the judge walked in.

"Please, be seated." Judge Waldron ordered.

As soon as the trial started Oscar's lawyers stood up and said a bunch of things that confused me. I looked at my lawyer but it was as if she were purposely avoiding looking in my direction.

"We would like to motion new information into evidence, your honor." His lawyer stated.

"Objection!" My lawyer Mrs. Pierce said. "Under what grounds? This is preliminary, the only evidence in either case are the plaintiff and defendant."

"And their child," his lawyer said. Hearing him say *their child* sent a shock wave through my body. It was disgusting to think that I'd had a child with that man. I was so happy that the one thing I could do for that baby was give it a life away from that house and him. I couldn't be its mother but at least I could protect it in my own way.

"Overruled." The judge said.

"Miss. Oakley gave birth to a child November 8, 2013. In the state of Ohio you must have both the birth mother and the biological father's signature in order to release custody to the state." His lawyer placed a folder in front of Mrs. Pierce and handed the bailiff a matching folder to give to the judge.

His words reminded me of when Erica told this to Aiden at the pep rally with the hopes of ruining our relationship. She wanted to out me as a teen mother but most importantly she wanted to make it look like I was a whore who didn't know the father of her child. With that thought my stomach felt tight and my heart began to race. I was praying they weren't going to say what it felt like they were going to say.

"Miss. Oakley declared to the state of Ohio that she did not know the paternity."

"Objection!" My lawyer stood up, slamming the folder down.

"I'll allow it." The judge answered as he looked through the folder. I wanted to know what was in there. I turned to face Aiden and of course his eyes were already on me he nodded and mouthed *everything is going to be okay* I took a deep breath in and turned back around.

"Miss. Oakley's claim that Mr. Doyle sexually assaulted her which led to her pregnancy is either false or she *knowingly* falsified

158

documents." He placed a white sheet of paper on my lawyer's desk. "We would like to request a DNA test, if the child is indeed Mr. Doyle's his rights as a father have not been legally relinquished and her rights that she relinquished would be reinstated. Therefore my client will be suing Miss. Oakley and the state of Ohio for sole custody of the child in question and I believe criminal charges should be pressed against Miss. Oakley for filing false documentation."

I heard the words but the way they were strung together didn't quite make sense, I was unable to comprehend. I heard gasps, and angry growls from behind me, I heard my lawyer yell objection. I heard the bailiff clear his throat. But I was stuck. I was submerged in a deep hole of shock. It was as if I were on a delay, once the words started to make sense it was like a crescendo. The anger and rage devoured me. I was seeing red again and angry at myself for not thinking clearly enough to stab him in his heart when I had the chance to two years ago.

"Your honor," I heard Mrs. Pierce say, "if we allow this you are essentially allowing a rape victims attacker to dictate these proceedings." She said angrily. "She told the state what she had to tell the state in order to protect her family and her child. She was not malicious; she is not the one on trial here. The defendant does not want to be a parent to that child he is using this unique situation to prolong his court date and sentencing."

"He *allegedly* sexually assaulted her," his lawyer rebutted, "with the evidence presented this could have very well been consensual."

I could hear the angry snares from my loved ones behind me. I couldn't wrap my mind around what was happening.

"She was sixteen years old, your honor!" My lawyer pressed. "She was a child! This man deserves to be in jail and on the sex offenders list!"

"My client was under the impression she was eighteen at the time of the sexual contact." His lawyer countered.

I could feel my heart beating in my fingertips, the tears stinging my eyes nearly blinding me.

"Your honor this is ridiculous!" Mrs. Pierce urged. "That is not a defense!"

"Settle down," Judge Waldron said as he banged his gavel. "This hearing is for the deposition and the motion to add the paternity of the child in question. Now, Mrs. Pierce," Judge Waldron looked directly at her, "though I sympathize with Miss. Oakley, the law is the law. No matter how unfavorable it may be, if the child in question is in fact Mr. Doyle's, not only does he have every right to fight for custody, the parental rights that Miss. Oakley relinquished will be reinstated until a custody hearing is scheduled."

I'd asked for a closed adoption. I never wanted that child to know I existed. I didn't hold it, I looked at it once. I don't even know its name. Not because I just hated it, not because I blamed it, but because I knew I would love it and I didn't want to. I didn't want to love anything that was associated with that man. I knew I would want that baby no matter how idiotic that sounded. It took me a long time to realize that even though that baby was a product of the worst moment in my life it was still a part of me in some sick twist of fate kind of way. It shouldn't hold the blame for what that monster did to me.

Now the judge is telling me that I have parental rights, rights that I thought I'd relinquished, rights that I never wanted from the very beginning. Oscar is going to snatch this innocent child from a home it has been in for over two years in order to hurt me. He already ruined one family now he was on the verge of ruining another. The acid stung my lips, the anger encroached itself around my entire body.

"Why are you doing this?" I said turning towards him. I didn't yell. My voice was almost a whisper. He looked at me as anger rippled across his aging features.

"Miss. Oakley you are out of order." Judge Waldron banged his gavel. I was still looking at Oscar in the eyes, I was not intimidated. He could not and would not scare me, he had no power over me anymore and I could see that it infuriated him. That's why he was doing all of this.

"You hate that you can't control me anymore. You're powerless and feeble and desperate. Does this make you feel like a man?" My voice was a little louder now as the anger sat at the base of my throat.

"Zoe, enough," my lawyer says sternly grabbing my wrist.

"You're a sad miserable excuse of a human and you're going to rot in hell." my voice is even louder. I can hear the gavel, I can hear Aiden trying to get my attention, but I'm too far gone.

"Miss. Oakley, I will hold you in contempt!" Judge Waldron ordered.

"You already tried to ruin my life. Now you're going to ruin that child's life!" I'm trembling. I can feel the anger and sadness wrap itself around me tightly. My words were spilling out at once and I can't control it.

"She has a home. You can't snatch her from it!" Now I'm yelling. I didn't know how it happened but the more I spoke directly to him the smaller he looked, the weaker he became, the more real *she* became. "If you think I'm going to let you anywhere near my daughter!" I shouted, surely my veins were popping out of my neck.

"Enough! Mrs. Pierce, control your client or she will be in handcuffs!" Judge Waldron demanded.

"Fifteen minute recess your honor?" Mrs. Pierce asked as she stood grabbing my arm. My eyes were still blazing, the tears that fell down my cheeks weren't from sadness or fear they were from hate and anger. I realized in that moment that I didn't say *that child,* that I didn't call her *it*... I'd called that little girl *my daughter* and that thought sent me through a completely different spiral of emotions.

161

"Fifteen minutes." Judge Waldron banged the gavel

I was already rushing out of the courtroom before he dismissed us. I could feel Aiden right behind me. I couldn't catch my breath. It was like the anger was caught in my throat, manifesting itself in different areas of my body.

"Zoe!" I hear Aiden as he runs up to me immediately bear hugging me. "Fuck," he said lowly into my ear.

"Fuck." I repeated through sobs. We just stood there outside of the courthouse holding each other until I was able to eventually catch my breath.

"Are you okay?" He whispered in my ear.

"I'm so scared." I say honestly. I was terrified.

"I know baby, but he can't hurt you anymore." He held me closer.

"I'm not scared for *me* or of him. I'm scared for my daughter." My tears splashed out of my eyes. "I didn't give her up because I didn't want her, I didn't give her up because I was seventeen, I didn't give her up because I hated her, I gave her up because I didn't want her to be anywhere near him, anywhere near that house. I didn't want her to know that she was related to a monster. I wanted her to have a better life and he is trying to take that away from her."

I'm sobbing again because I honestly didn't know how much I cared. This was the first time I'd actually said these things aloud. "It was the *one* thing I could do as her biological parent and now I can't even do that."

I feel so horrible dumping all of that out on Aiden, how was he supposed to respond to that?

"We are going to fight this every step of the way." He says as he rests his chin on the top of my head. So much happened in the

162

courtroom I couldn't retain it all. I was the victim and now *I* was being sued? I was being told I consented to having sex with my mother's husband? I was sick to my stomach. I could feel the bile erupting in my throat again. I pushed away from Aiden and ran to the nearest bush to throw up.

"It's okay." He rushed over to me rubbing my back. "It's going to be okay, I promise." He held my hair back as I emptied the contents of my stomach. I was finally able to breathe, sweat coating my forehead. "I'm going to get you some water and a paper towel." I could hear the pain in his voice; I knew it was killing Aiden to see me like this. It was killing him to see me have a problem that he was unable to help or fix in anyway. I truly hated what my baggage was doing to him.

I nodded and sat down on a bench. He kissed my forehead then walked back into the courthouse. I sat there with my eyes closed wishing I could go back in time and do things differently. I would go back to three years ago and beg my mother to not pick up that extra night shift. I would be honest with her and tell her I didn't feel comfortable being alone in the house with Oscar. I would've locked my bedroom door that night…

"Zoe," I hear a familiar voice pull me back to earth. It was my mother, her face was tear soaked. She looked like she hadn't slept in days. "Can I sit?"

I nod.

We are just sitting there quietly. There's no tension –just silence.

"I'm sorry." She said abruptly. "This entire time, I never said *sorry*. I never said it once."

I turned to look at her.

"I was feeling guilty for myself. I hated that this happened to you but my anger and my sadness was from my embarrassment, I was selfish. I let you down." She wiped away a tear, "I let my baby girl

163

down. And then after everything I chose him over you." She shook her head. "What's sad is that I didn't even know I was doing it. I…I just wanted to be loved."

Tears were streaming down my face. My mother had never been so honest and open to me in her entire life. I grabbed her hand as I wiped my tears away with my other hand.

"I wanted to be loved and forgot that the most important love I could ever experience was the love between us, the love between a mother and a daughter." She squeezed my hand.

"I want my daughter back and you can decide to never say another word to me again and I would understand but I will *still* be here. Every hearing, every birthday…I'm going to do something I wasn't able to do for you these last few years. I'm going to show up and be there for you."

My face was probably unrecognizable; the tears were running down my neck, my makeup was most likely gone. In that same moment Aiden walked up with a cup of water and some tissue. My mother and I stood up, our hands disconnecting.

"It's good seeing you, Aiden," my mother said as she touched his shoulder, "thank you for reaching out to me…thank you for taking care of my baby girl."

He smiled slightly then nodded, "of course Mrs. Doyle."

"Oakley," she corrected, "Miss. Oakley." She looked at me then walked back into the courthouse. I just stood there watching her walk away.

"Are you okay?" Aiden asked. "What was that all about?"

I bit my lip and shook my head, taking a deep breath in, "I think I just got my mom back."

Chapter Twelve: Charades

"So…" I say bumping Matt's arm with my shoulder looking at him accusingly, raising one eyebrow.

"What?"

"When are you going to pop the question?" I ask excitedly.

"Shhh!" He said looking over my shoulder to make sure no one heard me. We were in my kitchen getting the snacks and drinks ready for our couple's game night.

"I'm just saying…" I whispered, "You sent me a pic of the ring weeks ago."

"I'm waiting for the right time." He shrugs. He was avoiding eye contact as he poured chips into a bowl. I studied his face for a moment trying to force eye contact. If it's one thing I knew in life, it was my best friend Matt.

"What?" He said again, but this time he was annoyed.

"You're scared?" I accuse, "…of what? You two are perfect for each other. Do you think she is going to say no? Because I can tell you she will *definitely* say yes."

"No," he rolled his eyes, "I'm not scared. I just don't want to rush things. We've been together a long time but we are young. *Super young.*"

"Okay?" I say looking at him like he was crazy, "…and?"

"It's just…how did you know with Aiden?" He asked me as he grabbed cups out of my cupboard.

"Me and Aiden aren't engaged." I corrected.

"You guys have been engaged since your first date who are we kidding?" He nudged my shoulder. "I mean, you guys are living together how'd you know you were ready for that? That it was serious?"

"I don't know. I don't think I was ready." I answered honestly. I thought about the day Aiden and I met how he invited himself to sit at my table and shared his burger with me. I saw how caring he was just by looking into his eyes, I knew immediately that he was one of the good ones. "I don't think anyone is ever ready... I think you just know that it's real and go from there." That probably wasn't the best advice to give but I think somewhere in me I knew I would be with Aiden, he knew it too.

"Also," I said trying to stop myself from getting emotional, "once someone pries a bloody knife out of your hand after you try to kill someone it kind of cements an unbroken bond."

I was trying to be funny but Matt scowled, not laughing at my joke. "Come on..."

"No," Matt interrupted angrily. "We can joke about a lot of things but I can't joke about how I wasn't there to protect you from that piece of..."

"Stop it," I grab his clenched fist. "We are *not* doing this tonight, okay?" I smile and force him to look in my eyes. "I'm good. *We're good.*" He pauses then inhales –*finally* relaxing his hand. He sighs then turns to hug me.

The night I stabbed Oscar, Matt came to the hospital to visit me. The nurses were checking to see if I had any injuries, I guess it was protocol. They'd asked me questions, so did the police, but I was unable to speak. I'd confessed everything that happened over that year to Aiden. There was no more need for words. It had been hours and I was still in some kind of trance, my tears had stopped completely. My thoughts were clear and fluid, but all I could

166

remember was thinking *I hope I killed him* my thoughts were obsessive and if anyone had the ability to shine a light on my thoughts they would've been terrified at what they found.

I remember sitting up in the bed just staring at the wall. Aiden was taken away to give a police report. Apparently, he'd walked in right as Oscar grabbed me. He'd stormed in and yelled something but I hadn't noticed him, my attention was on the knife in the sink and wanting to put that knife in Oscar's body *–repeatedly*. I didn't remember Aiden being there until he was on the floor cradling me, trying to get me to stop screaming and shaking. My mother hadn't come to see me yet, I wasn't sure if she were with the police or with Oscar.

I remember Matt walking in. I looked at him then looked back at the wall I was staring at. No emotion on my face. He didn't say anything; he just walked in and sat in the chair across from me. I kept my focus on the wall, again my only thought was *I hope I killed him* I didn't care about what could happen to me or to my mother or to my relationships with anyone. I just wanted Oscar dead the *need* for it was overwhelming.

About fifteen minutes of complete silence went by when in my peripheral vision I saw Matt slam his head into his palms –his shoulders bouncing up and down slightly. It was then that I realized he was crying. In that moment it was the first time I *felt* anything since sitting on my blood covered kitchen floor. My heart reappeared, my stomach lurched, but my tears were gone I didn't have a single drop left.

I heard him sniffle as he lifted his head up, he was livid the anger on his face is something I'd never seen on him before. He got up and walked to my bedside. "Scoot over." He ordered. His voice was low and grainy. I moved over as far as I could, his large football frame barely able to fit but he managed. He put his arm around me and we sat like that for a few more minutes before he said anything.

"I'm here. I'll *always* be here."

The words struck a nerve. I remember a flood of flashbacks flitted across my mind almost dizzying me. I thought back to when I told Matt I was pregnant, how I'd fallen to his basement floor sobbing unable to comprehend what my life had become. His exact words to me were *I'm here. I'll always be here.* I remember it vividly because it was the only thing during that entire time that made me feel comforted; that made me think I wasn't completely alone in the world.

I started sobbing leaning my head against his chest because it was true. He'd never left my side, just like he declared and I'd took his friendship for granted the entire time I was going through hell. I was going through it alone and I didn't have to.

"Zoe," he said painfully, as he tried to calm me down. Reality was finally crashing down on me. The trance was broken. "I'm sorry, I'm so sorry for everything. I should've known, or been there or stopped it…"

I was still unable to form complete sentences. My mind was shredded with anger, grief, and shock for what I'd done and for what I'd been through over that year. I just shook my head. No one was to blame for my actions but Oscar.

"I'm going to kill him." He states through his teeth, I could almost feel his chest vibrating from the rage.

I sighed and looked directly at him, "I hope I killed him." My voice is gone but the words were clear, they were the first words I'd said in hours. Matt sighed and held me tighter.

"Me too."

I quickly snapped myself out of that memory from over two years ago, as I stood in my kitchen hugging my immovable best friend.

"Thank you for being here," I say as I squeeze him tighter. "Thank you for *always* being here." I whisper.

He chuckled lightly, "Of course," he paused then continued. "I'm happy you found Aiden or that he found you." He said lowly in my ear, "I know I said he wasn't good enough for you..." he paused again, "...and I *still* don't think he is." I pulled away and punched him on his shoulder. Matt was great at ruining a moment.

"There's a *but*! Let me finish," he smiled. "But he is a good guy and he truly loves you. I'm glad he makes you happy. That's all I've ever wanted for you."

"Thank you?" I looked at him suspiciously, though I knew he meant it –it was just super random for him to say. "What's wrong, are you dying? Am *I* dying?"

He smiled, "Nope! I can just feel the love in the air."

"You're being weird." I would've interrogated him further but I hear Alicia yell out "What the hell? Where are my chips?!" Then quickly after I hear Aiden say, "I want my popcorn, now!" Matt and I grab everything and bring it into the living room.

"Okay, people," Matt says in his most football quarterback-y voice, "you know the rules of the game, Men vs Women. Charades, ladies prepare to get your asses handed to you."

Alicia and I flip them both off as we go to sit on our side of the couch. I loved that though they both attended MSU out of state they still made sure to come visit Aiden and I *at least* once a month.

"Gentlemen first," Matt says with a smirk as he sticks his hand in the hat to pick a homemade card.

"Four words," Aiden yells after reading Matt's fingers. Matt starts jumping around the room like a crazy person. Alicia and I are cracking up. There was no way Aiden was going to guess what he was saying. He looked like he was having a seizure.

"A phrase?" Aiden guessed. Matt nodded enthusiastically. The time was starting to run out on the clock.

"Thirty seconds!" I warn them. I could tell that this would be another easy win for the ladies. The boys sucked at the games we chose. They always wanted to play battleship and video games. Alicia and I had to veto those games from being allowed on game nights.

Matt pointed at Aiden, jabbing his finger at him as if the words were going to fly out the end of his index. "You?" Aiden guessed. Matt nodded and started pointing towards where Alicia and I were sitting.

"Girls?" Aiden guessed. Matt shook his head to indicate *no*.

"Ten seconds!" I yell.

"Will you?" Aiden guesses correctly and randomly. At this point I'm convinced they're cheating. There was no way Aiden should've been able to guess that from what Matt was doing. Aiden stands up and Matt nods again pointing directly at me.

"Will you marry me?" Aiden yells and then Matt screams, "That's it!"

"Times up!" I yell at the same time. Aiden falls to the floor in defeat directly in front of me then grabs my hand. "Will you?" He asks.

Alicia gets off of the couch, I hadn't noticed but her cellphone was out, she had tears in her eyes. Matt was standing there staring and I could see pure joy on his face. Aiden was on one knee. I was confused. It's like I knew what was happening but my brain wasn't processing it quickly enough.

"What?" I was stunned. I was trembling and my heart was pounding so hard I thought I was going to go into cardiac arrest.

"Zoe Grace Oakley, will you marry me?" Aiden spoke clearly and confidently I was so lost in his eyes that I hadn't even noticed the ring box in his hand. When I looked at Aiden I felt whole, I felt like I was supposed to know him, that he and I were put on this earth to love each other. My answer was obvious. I didn't need to think about it. I knew wherever Aiden was, was where I needed to be. Anywhere he was –was home.

I nod, almost frantically, "Yes!" I immediately hug him so close to me that we could be one person. I hear Alicia and Matt yelling and clapping behind us. It was surreal. It wasn't like I didn't know that at some point this would happen. We'd talked about marriage before multiple times but it was always in a hypothetical sense. It was always far in the future in my mind.

Aiden pulled away from me and grabbed my hand placing the ring on my ring finger and understanding crept over me.

"Wait…" I say as I realize where I'd seen this ring before.

"Yea," Aiden said. "I had Matt show you the ring to make sure you liked it. You and Alicia kind of have the same taste when it comes to that kind of stuff."

"You guys were in on this?" I say through tears.

"Yep!" Alicia smiles, before taking another picture.

"You're so damn picky and you hate everything he was paranoid you weren't gonna like it," Matt added.

I was still staring at the ring. It was beautiful, way more than I knew Aiden and I could afford, but I was too happy and overwhelmed to focus on that right now. "I love you," I say kissing him on the lips.

"I love you too," he says against my lips, "so much."

***

"You have to let me coordinate this!" My mother was almost bouncing out of her chair. When I told her Aiden proposed I actually think she had I better reaction than I did, she certainly had more tears.

"There won't be anything to coordinate." I say trying to placate her enthusiasm.

"What if we kept it small? Like seventy five people?" She tried to bargain. I loved how enthused she was but Aiden and I had so much going on, I couldn't fathom putting energy into throwing a wedding. It seemed impossible.

"I was thinking a *little* smaller." I say as I take a sip of my tea avoiding eye contact with her.

"*How* much smaller, Zoe?" She asked the question as if she were scared of my answer.

"Umm, besides me and Aiden…" I took another sip, "You, his parents, Mrs. Hunter, Matt, Alicia and Aiden's friend Dante and maybe his Uncle Will."

"Zoe!" Her voice too loud for the small café we were sitting in. "You might as well get married at city hall!"

I gulped and avoided eye contact again.

"Wait, you're going to get married at city hall?!" The shock and disgust in her voice was laughable.

"Aiden's fall semester starts, and I start my fall courses, and we keep appealing the paternity hearing. There's just too much going on to focus on a wedding. I'm sorry to disappoint."

My mother sat quietly, I felt a little bad. It's probably every mothers dream to help plan their daughter's wedding but our circumstances weren't as simple as other peoples.

"Are you prepared?" She asked, her voice taking on a completely new tone.

"Yea, you can help me pick a nice summer dress and…"

"No," she interrupted. "I meant are you prepared for this appeal, it's the last one before they bring her in."

There was no way to prepare for ripping my daughter from the only home she's known for over two years. My legal team had been using every tactic they knew to halt bringing her in for the DNA testing. She would be in the system until custody was figured out. I couldn't fathom what her parents were going through right now with all of this going on. None of this made any sense to me. Mrs. Pierce told me the family could possibly skip town with her to avoid having her being taken away. That's why the state would have to take her.

I wouldn't blame them if the thought crossed their minds, I would contemplate it too. I would do anything to protect her from him.

I shook my head. It was hard to talk about. I learned not to keep things bottled up, but it made me sick to my stomach every time I thought about that family and how all of this could ruin her life..

"I didn't mean to bring it up."

"No, mom," I smile. "It's okay…I just want her to be happy and safe. He can't have her. I won't allow it." The waiter comes with our food, "Thank you." I say before I continue speaking.

"I'm going to fight for her family, she deserves a good home."

I picked up my sandwich and took a bite, when I looked back up my mother's eyes were bloodshot red.

"Mom?"

"Oh," she wiped her tears quickly. "I'm sorry. I just…*you* deserved a good home too and now my mistakes are making it so my granddaughter can't have a good home either. It's like a domino effect. I can't stop the pieces from falling."

I listened to her words and took a deep breath in. "Your granddaughter?" I said trying to prevent my voice from cracking. "You see her as your granddaughter?"

She sniffled and dabbed under her eye with a napkin. "She's apart of you Zoe. Of course I see her that way." She answered simply looking at me directly in the eyes.

I'd said that to Aiden weeks ago, that she was a part of me even though the circumstances sucked. It was different and weird hearing my mother say the words. I cleared my throat and took another sip of my tea. I needed to speak to Aiden tonight.

Chapter Thirteen: Lana Elizabeth Hill

My foot wouldn't stop shaking. I kept looking behind me at the courtroom doors waiting for them to open. As predicted we lost our last appeal to prevent the paternity hearing. My daughter was taken last week from her family. It broke my heart, I wished there was a way I could reach out to them. To tell them that I was going to fight tooth and nail to make sure Oscar never even holds her let alone gets custody. They were her parents. They are who she knew.

I looked at Aiden and he nodded to reassure me. It would be the first time since the day she was born that I would see her. I had a panic attack this morning, I was terrified of what I would feel when I saw her face. The last time I saw her she was being carried out of my hospital room. I told myself I didn't want to see her, I didn't want to look at her and see Oscar's features.

I think that was my fear now, would my determination to protect her from him be waivered if I see her face and feel animosity? I hated thinking like this but I couldn't predict how I would react.

Everything about this situation was traumatic and difficult; there was absolutely no way to prepare.

I heard the doors open and I turned around immediately to see a woman in a dark brown pant suit with big curly natural hair walk in. And next to her walking in was a tiny little girl. She had brown curly hair, big brown eyes and dimples. Her eyelashes were thick and long, curling over at the top. Her cheeks were chunky and tinted with a soft rose color. She looked so scared, she looked confused. She waddled next to the woman as her eyes scanned the room.

The air was caught in my throat. She looked just like me, from her tawny complexion, to the slant of her forehead, to her button nose, to her full lips. She was my carbon copy. A tear fell and I didn't even bother to wipe it. I heard my mother gasp and it made the little girl look in her direction. My mother smiled through tears as she discreetly waved at her.

I couldn't keep my eyes off of her. Her energy was literally painting the room. I'd given birth to her. I'd helped her become a part of this world. It was phenomenal. I was forgetting how to breathe.

"All rise," the bailiff said. I was in a trance unable to rip my eyes from this magical little girl who'd just walked into the room. My lawyer tapped my arm and finally I was able to reluctantly tear my eyes from her and stand up. I took a deep breath in, my lungs not remembering the pleasures of oxygen.

"You all may be seated." Judge Waldron ordered. As soon as I sat down I turned back around to look at her. I felt like I could look at her forever, I *wanted* to look at her forever. She was sitting next to the social worker playing with a red and white teddy bear and like a pile of bricks crashing down on me I realized it was the same teddy bear Alicia had brought to the hospital for her.

I remember holding that teddy bear and staring at it for a long time. I'd already given birth and knew I would never see her again. Alicia told me to keep it; she was unaware that the baby would not be back in the room again. When I was discharged I placed the bear on the hospital bed with a note that read *for the baby*. I remember thinking I was crazy and that there was no way of knowing if she would get it.

At that memory, I had to look away from her as another tear fell. All this time she'd had a little piece of my world with her in some form. The most intense feeling conquered my entire body realizing that fact.

"We've prolonged this long enough. I have the results of the paternity right here." Judge Waldron said. "In the case of two year old Lana Elizabeth Hill, with 99.98% accuracy Oscar Vincent Montello Doyle is the father."

This news was not shocking to me because I knew the truth; the news was not shocking to Oscar because he knew the truth. All of this was to make me look bad, to prove that I lied to the state.

What this meant was legally this little girl no longer had a family. The family that cared for her no longer had any rights to her. She had no clue that her life had just been shattered.

"With this information," Oscar's lawyers said, "we would like to petition the court for full custody."

My lawyer warned me that this would happen as soon as the results were read. She told me that though he can petition for full custody he would not be granted custody until the trial because his name was not on the birth certificate. If I contested it I would be obliging to my reinstated parental rights and she would be released into my custody instead of staying in the system then possibly being transferred to his custody during the trial. I discussed this with Aiden; I only wanted to use my parental rights in order to give her back to her real family. We all agreed that I would not contest. I would *not* hold temporary custody.

"No." I say the word, my lawyer looks at me.

"Zoe, I told you this is protocol." She whispered to me. Though I knew this, I couldn't stop the words from coming out of my mouth.

176

"I contest." I say clearly.

"Miss. Oakley you do understand that by contesting his petition you are reinstating your parental rights. She will be released into your custody within forty eight hours and will remain in your custody for the duration of the trial?"

I swallowed. I didn't want this. I never wanted this, but I couldn't let my daughter stay in the system and then possibly end up with Oscar during the trial. I hated that she couldn't just stay with the Hills until this was sorted out. Only God knows how long a trial like this could be. I abandoned her once. I couldn't do it again. I would never let him near her.

"Yes, your honor. I am fully aware." I speak the words as if they are a declaration. I had no idea what I was doing or what I was saying, but as I looked at that little girl in her eyes I couldn't be the one to ruin her life and I would be damned if I let Oscar ruin it any further.

"Okay, I will give you forty eight hours to reverse your motion. I'll send Miss. Ramsey to observe and evaluate your living space. After forty eight hours Lana Elizabeth Hill will be released into your custody." Judge Waldron banged his gavel. "Court is adjourned."

I let out a deep shaky breath and turned to face her. She had no idea what was going on around her. Her only concern was the red and white teddy bear in her arms. She was so innocent. I hated Oscar for doing this to her, destroying lives just to get back at me. I looked at him and for a brief moment we made eye contact. He winked.

I wouldn't let him get to me. I looked away and looked at my fiancé and for the first time in our relationship the anger on his face is so blatant I had to look away.

I fucked up.

***

177

We sat at our kitchen table directly in front of each other. He was so mad that he didn't say a single word to me on the drive home. He couldn't even look at me now.

"Can we talk about this?"

"Oh," he laughs sarcastically, "*now* you want to talk about this?"

"Aiden…"

"No Zoe," he interrupted, "we *already* talked about this in detail for days. We made a decision and then you go and do that? I'm about to be your husband, we live in a crappy two bedroom apartment in a shitty neighborhood and you want to bring a kid here?" He snapped.

I didn't say anything, if there was one thing I knew about Aiden it was that I had to let him get everything out. I wanted him to let every feeling he was having out before I spoke.

"Did you even think about me when you made this decision for us?" He questioned, "Did you stop for two seconds and think about how I would feel to have to…" he trailed off. His eyes were red; his anger was making his hands tremble.

"… to have to *what* Aiden?" I wipe a tear away because I knew what he was going to say.

"To have to look at that bastard's child every morning for God knows how long?" He said through his teeth. A tear fell from his eye and he looked away from me. I took a deep breath in, his words cutting me, his pain crushing me.

"She is mine too." My voice is shaky.

"He raped you, Zoe!" I feel like he is about to erupt. I'd never seen this level of fury in him before. I didn't even know he could get like this. The hate he has for Oscar is radiating off of him. I didn't recognize this person. "He fucking taunted and harassed you for a year!"

178

"Aiden, I know." I cried. I wished he could understand. I wish he knew how absurd it was for me too. I didn't know I was going to contest the petition. I didn't know I was going to want temporary custody of her, but when I saw her face, when I felt her aura, when I saw her holding that teddy bear something in me clicked. I was connected to that little girl, no matter how horrible the circumstances were. "Did you see her, Aiden? I mean, really look at her? She looks just like me…she has so much of me."

"So what!" He yelled. "You want me to play daddy to her? I can't do that!"

"I'm not asking you to!" I finally yell back. "I'm sorry okay, I fucked up. I let my instincts take over, but I can't change it now. I have to protect her as best I can. It's not permanent…"

"Give me a break Zoe, I saw you looking at her. You want her and you didn't calculate me into the equation." He's breathing heavily. "If something happens and he's granted full custody you know damn well you will want her. Then what?"

I just stared at him. I didn't know what to say because maybe he was right. I don't know. I was confused. I was fighting for the Hills, this wasn't *my* battle. It was theirs. There was no way Oscar was going to get her. It wouldn't come down to that.

"You say you can't change it, well the judge said you had forty eight hours to reverse your motion." His voice is much calmer. I look at him then look down, more tears coming out of my eyes like a waterfall.

"I'm not going to reverse the motion," I said softly.

Aiden just sat there looking out of the window. We sat there in silence for what felt like an eternity. I wanted to reach across the table and hold his hand. I felt like I was breaking apart because my foundation – *Aiden* – was wavering. He finally got up and walked towards the door.

"Aiden, where are you going?" I say through tears.

He stopped, his back was to me. I could see him breathing heavily before he turned around. "I can't play house with that kid, a kid that resulted from you being brutally raped when you were a kid yourself." He grabbed his keys. "I've put up with a lot of shit in this relationship, but this…"

"What are you saying?" I cry, interrupting him as he trailed off. I wish I could just stop doing what I was doing and just keep Aiden near me for as long as I possibly could.

"I can't do this, that's what I'm saying," his face broke as he tried to fight back tears. "I can't live here with a constant reminder of the darkest day of your life and try to act like it's some kind of blessing," his words were like bullets to me, "you're not thinking far enough ahead, Zoe. This isn't what you want. You are going to set all of your healing back. You're going to relive that moment every single time you look at her."

His words stung, they burned a hole right through my core. I stood, the anger pouring out of every inch of my body. "*I'm* the constant reminder, Aiden!" I yell. "Every single day I look in the mirror and I think about that night. I see Oscar hovering over me and I scream inside, I die inside, I relive it…I live *in* it." I'm trembling as I say the words.

"Just because I don't talk about it every day to you, just because I don't hide in a dark corner cowering out of fear, doesn't mean that I am healed. I don't think I am capable of healing. I am coping, that is it. After what happened to me *I* am living breathing proof that evil does walk on this earth, but that little girl?" I say angrily through a flood of tears, "*my* daughter is a reminder that light can still exist!" I yell the words. They were weighing so heavily on my chest.

"*You* told me to always look for the bright spots. *You* said there will always be a light in *every* situation. Well, maybe it's her Aiden?" My voice cracked over his name. "Maybe she is that one thing from all of this darkness that isn't meant to carry hate, fear, and anger? She did not ask for this, she doesn't know what's going on around her, and my hate for him cannot and does not eclipse my wanting to protect her and care for her. I'm doing the right thing, you have to see that."

Aiden just stared at me. His eyes were glossed over and red. We stood there in silence. We both laid everything on the table, we were both brutally honest about our feelings, still through all the anger and rage I wanted to reach out to him. I wanted to feel his love; I wanted him to feel mine. In the core of our darkest moments, I needed us to still be *Aiden and Zoe*. I needed us to still have our bond to keep us centered.

"I'm sorry," he said softly, "I can't see it that way." He turned around and walked out of the apartment.

"Aiden!" I yelled but it was not answered. For the first time in our relationship we didn't find our way back. I felt weak, what was I doing? Was I truly jeopardizing my life with Aiden for this little girl? He and I never got into an argument like this. It was a new kind of pain, an unfathomable type of pain. This made me despise Oscar even more. He didn't want me to have peace or solace in any aspect of my life.

Aiden had been there for me every step of the way going above and beyond to make sure I was okay. He dealt with things that he didn't have to in order to protect me, in order to love me, and in one moment I decided to turn my back on him. I blindsided him. Maybe this was the straw that broke the camel's back. I'd finally asked too much of him.

Of course I could see it from his point of view but when I looked into Lana's eyes I didn't see Oscar, I didn't think about the night he attacked me. All I saw was a beautiful child that I'd given birth to. A child that no matter how hard I tried to avoid and *pretend* just to get through the process of giving her up, –I cared about her. It was probably insane but she was a part of me. I wished Aiden could understand that, but I could barely understand it myself.

181

I was at peace with my decision, I had to be, but I was wrecked and broken inside from the outcome of my decision. I had to have faith that Aiden and I could figure this out. He and I *had* to figure this out.

Chapter Fourteen: Home

It had been forty eight hours.

I sat in the courtroom, depleted. I hadn't heard from or seen Aiden in those two days and I was sick. In our entire relationship I hadn't gone longer than a few hours without having some type of contact with him. I sat there wondering was this all even worth it? I could possibly lose everything if he and I didn't figure this out. I turned to see my mother sitting there and it oddly gave me comfort. She wasn't lying when she said she would *show up* and *be here.* She's been to every hearing and has made sure to be readily available whenever I needed her, even when I didn't think I needed her she was there.

She came over and helped me set up the extra room for Lana. I told her she spent way too much money, but she didn't want to hear it. She stayed when Miss. Ramsey came to evaluate the apartment and told me she would stay as long as I needed her to stay in order to help with Lana. I'd really never been around children other than younger cousins. I honestly didn't know what I was getting myself into. All I knew was that I wanted this little girl safe and I wanted her as far away from Oscar as possible.

Lana walked in with the social worker and again her presence was all consuming. She had a yellow bow in her hair holding her curls out of her face. I smiled at her and she smiled back, it was like the gates to heaven opened up, it was like the first time seeing the sun. It was like the first time witnessing a shooting star flit across the sky on a clear night.

It was worth it.

Right?

My mind drifted to Aiden. I imagined him and I breaking up over this and I had to stop the thought immediately because I knew I'd collapse and burst into tears in this courtroom. I regathered my thoughts and kept my eyes on Lana.

The judge made it clear that this was not a hearing. I didn't need to sign anything further because all of the paperwork I'd signed when she was born was now null and void.

"Everything checked out during your evaluation, you are free to go." The judge ordered after a few moments of glancing over some documents and speaking to my lawyer. "She is released into your temporary custody."

I took a deep breath and slowly breathed out as the social worker walked Lana over to me. My lawyer leaned over to whisper in my ear. "She looks just like you. It's uncanny."

I smiled nervously, trying not to let these tears fall. I didn't want to scare her. I squatted down in front of her trying to smile and trying to be as welcoming as possible. "Hi Lana," I said softly, "you're going to stay with me for a bit, okay?"

She just looked around the room, clutching her red and white teddy bear. "My name is Zoe." I add bringing her attention back to me.

"Zoweee?" She said and I thought my chest was going to explode.

"Yes, Zoe." I smiled and bit my lip. Do not cry in front of her. Do *not* cry in front of her.

"Mom?" I say asking her to come over. "This is my mom, Miss. Kim. She is going to hang out with us." I say to Lana as she stares up at my mother curiously.

"Hello precious little girl." My mother was a blubbering mess. Lana looked at her and then looked at me as if to ask *what her problem was*. I smiled.

"She is really happy about getting to know you. I am too."

Our social worker handed me a bag and some paperwork. "Everything you will need. She's a really good girl," she added. "You shouldn't have any problems getting her acclimated. Here is my cell if you have any questions or need any help with anything." She handed me a piece of paper, then said goodbye to Lana. She smiled brightly at her before she walked away.

And just like that, she was mine –for now. It was an unreal moment; a moment that two and a half years ago I didn't think would ever happen or even be a possibility, but here I was.

"Okay," I say taking another deep breath, "let's get going. Mrs. Pierce, do I need to be present in two weeks when they set the trial date?"

"No," she smiled, "I will email you when we get a trial date. Until then, have fun." She patted Lana on the head. "Goodbye sweetheart."

I exhaled and the air left my lungs raggedly, the nerves trying to fight their way to the surface. I looked back down at Lana and couldn't help but smile again. *Off to this new adventure*, I thought to myself trying to be more positive in this moment than I had ever been in my entire life.

We walked out of the courthouse hand in hand. I was so nervous that she would shy away from me, or scream, or immediately start begging for her parents. No one had instructed me on what to do or say if and when this was to happen. This little girl had no idea the craziness that was involving her. She was so calm and so peaceful, while the world was set ablaze around her.

We got to the car and standing there was Aiden. He was leaning against the car with his hands behind his back. I could no longer hold in the tears, God I loved him –but I was so angry with him, I was livid. I don't think I'd ever been this mad at him, he'd never been this mad at me that was for sure. I walked up to him with Lana still holding my hand.

"Hey." I said.

"Hey." He said back. He looked at my mother and said *hello* to her then looked down at Lana and smiled softly at her, he knelt down in front of her before he spoke.

"Hi Lana, I'm Aiden," he said serenely, his voice easy and warm. "I have something for you." He handed her a stuffed giraffe and her face lit up. She looked at it for a moment squeezed it then looked back up at Aiden with a radiant smile on her face.

"Take yew!" She said as she held her red and white teddy bear next to her new giraffe.

"You're welcome," he said. "I have to tell you something…" he whispered to her. She looked at him with anticipation in her eyes. "This lady holding your hand…"

"Zoweee," she interrupted with a smile on her face.

Aiden smiled and nodded. "Yes, Zoe…I wanted to tell you she's the coolest and funniest person in the world. You're going to have so much fun with her!" He winked and she smiled.

He stood up and stared at me for a moment. Though, I was anxious to get Lana to the apartment and settled in I was wishing Aiden and I were alone right now because I felt like I was seconds away from having a complete meltdown. He reached his hand out to me and handed me a large Kit Kat bar. I smiled gently and shook my head, trying tirelessly to coax these slow building tears from falling.

"Thank you." I said quietly.

"Can we talk?" He asked.

"Hey Lana," my perceptive mother said immediately grabbing Lana's hand from mine, "let's go look at the flowers, there are so many different colors!"

I looked at them as they walked over to the courtyard garden. I turned back around to face Aiden.

We just stood there. We had so many things to say to one another that we didn't know where to start.

"Two full days," I say, I couldn't hide the anger in my voice. No matter what we were going through I couldn't believe he'd actually left for two days. That I didn't know where he was, if he were safe, how long he'd be gone. That hurt me so deeply.

"I was at my dad's." He answered quickly. "I just needed to clear my head…and think about what you said."

I nodded. I hated how this felt, I never felt a disconnect with Aiden, but my emotions were battling with wanting to be mad at him, wanting to hug him and act like nothing happened, and wanting to hit him and scream at him for walking away.

"Look, you made a decision for the both of us and I was pissed and confused." He said. "You can't honestly say you don't see why I was mad? This is a lot to take on, Zoe."

"It got hard, and it got tricky and you disappeared." I said calmly. "The one thing we said we would never do was desert each other and that's what you did. I used to run from you in the beginning. Every time it got rough I'd bolt and *you* would tell me over and over again to stay and talk, to not disappear."

He didn't say anything at first, but I could see the anger in his eyes mixed with regret as he exhaled. "We also promised to make decisions *together*, to include the other person. To not ever choose

186

something over the other person. You did all of those things in one swoop. I think I'm allowed to process those emotions in whatever way helps me not lose it completely."

I could feel the wall, there were so many bricks piled up between us. I hated it. I never ever wanted to feel this far away from Aiden.

"I apologized for that," I say. "I can admit that I was wrong, I shouldn't have made a decision that affects us both without talking to you. But, I have her now and I can't turn back and I don't want to turn back. I have to protect her and this is the only way I…"

"I didn't come here to argue, Zoe." He interrupted as he looked over my shoulder at Lana. "We obviously have a lot to work through when it comes to communication, but even so, it doesn't stop me from loving you. *Nothing* is capable of doing that."

He exhaled and took a step closer to me. "This is some heavy stuff and we both didn't handle things the way we should have. With everything going on the one cemented and concrete thing that will never change no matter the circumstances is that I'm never going anywhere. I'll always want you, I'll always need you."

He's looking into my eyes, "I told you *very* early into this relationship that I knew what I couldn't live without. I'm not going to let this tear us apart or anything. I looked into that littles girls eyes and the anger and the animosity I thought I would feel wasn't there. I expected it, I prepared for it," he grabbed my hand, "but I saw *you* Zoe and it's a little overwhelming how much of your essence I see in her. I heard your words replay in my thoughts for the last forty eight hours and at the end of the day you birthed her. You have a connection to her and it's not for me to understand or not understand. You did what you felt was right and what you thought was necessary to protect her and as your soon to be husband I have to support that, I have to support you. If this is what you want then this is what *we* want."

Again, I didn't know how or why this man existed at the same time as me. He sacrificed so much for me and sacrificed so much to be with me. I was consumed by how much I loved him. I hugged him as tightly as I could. My foundation, my Aiden.

"I missed you." I say in his ear. He squeezed me tighter. I could stand here forever. "I'm still so pissed at you." I mumble against his neck.

"I know." He said lowly. "I'm still pissed at you too."

I squeeze him tighter and exhale finally we were able to disconnect from one another. "We can't ever walk away from each other. No matter how bad it gets, no matter how angry we are, we have to stay. We have to talk it through until we fix it." I said as I wiped a stray tear from my eye. "…and we have to communicate everything to one another. No more decisions will be made without the both of us coming to a conclusion."

He looked at me and a soft smile rested on his face. "I can agree to that." He said as he kissed my forehead. I smiled and knew if I never did anything else right in my life again, being with Aiden was the best decision I'd ever made.

"Mom?" I call out. I watch her walk over hand in hand with Lana and it made my chest feel warm inside. I grabbed Aiden's hand tightly and securely, as if I were incapable of ever letting go. Why would I ever want to? I smiled almost triumphantly and looked right at Aiden.

"Let's go home."

***

It had been a month since I was granted temporary custody of Lana. Everything I expected was completely untrue when it came to this little girl. I expected her to cry for her parents, I expected her to be scared or throw tantrums but nothing. She was so calmly tempered and just a breath of fresh air. I was trying so hard to push against it, but you couldn't help but fall completely for her, she was amazing. Aiden was even beginning to have a little soft spot for her.

I have to keep telling myself that this is only temporary that I have custody of her only to keep her out of the system and out of Oscar's custody. My fight would be for the Hills. I cried every single night the first week Lana was here because I kept imagining what the Hills must be going through. It bothered me that they had no say, no rights, and no contact with a child they'd raised from birth. It didn't make sense at all to me.

Almost a week ago I sat down at Aiden's desk and wrote a three page letter to the Hills, with much pleading and begging I was able to convince the social worker to pass the letter along. Miss. Ramsey said she would give them the letter only because the circumstances were so outrageous and unprecedented. And they were. I wonder if anything like this has ever happened before. The rapist sues for custody of a child who has been with an adoptive family for two years. It was absurd.

In the letter I apologized for falsifying documents, wishing that I had just been honest from the very beginning. I told them exactly what Lana had been doing. I told them how my fiancé and I take her to the museum or the park and nature walks every single day. That we work on numbers and the alphabet throughout the entire day. I told them that my mother has been over every day since the day Lana got here, cooking and doing her hair. I told them how Lana made up a cute song for her new giraffe friend that Aiden had gotten her. I put three photos of Lana in the letter —one for each week she'd been with us. I just wanted them to know that I felt horrible that this was happening to them, but hoped they could find comfort in knowing she was safe and cared for.

I ended the letter with saying I was going to *fight for them.*

It stung when I wrote the words because I knew fighting for them meant that Lana would have to leave. It made my stomach feel uneasy. It would be the second time I had to give her away, I couldn't think about it without my eyes watering. It was a ridiculous reaction to have, I knew it would never make sense for her to stay here even if given the option, but still at the core of me it hurt to imagine at this point.

Miss. Ramsey came by an hour ago to hand me a letter from the Hills. I hadn't expected such a quick response. Aiden was at work and Lana was taking a nap as I sat on the couch staring at the unopened letter. I was afraid to open it. For some reason this letter made them real. It was almost easier to handle everything that was going on when the Hills were just a name I'd heard a few times in court, but to know that true feelings and personalities were going to put a theoretical face to those names made me feel uncomfortable.

I picked up the letter and held it in my hand for ten minutes before I was finally able to convince myself to rip the Band-Aid. It was one sheet of paper with barely a paragraph written:

Zoe Oakley,

Thank you for reaching out to us. We both appreciate the photos. It's very difficult for me to be writing you. I don't know your entire story, but know that the second we saw Lana we knew she was our daughter. I haven't the words to describe the pain and grief we are feeling without her here with us, but in some small way knowing that you and your family care about her brings me comfort. I would like to meet with you. I am not asking for you to bring Lana as I know it would go against the court orders, but I am still her mother and no matter the outcome of this situation she will always be my daughter. I would like to meet the woman who is taking care of Lana. I understand if this is something you do not feel comfortable with. I just need to see you face to face to truly feel like she is safe. I hope to hear from you soon.

Emilia Hill

I exhaled and wiped a tear from my cheek. I had to meet her. I had to let her see that I was a good person. For all that she was going through it would be the least I could do. There was no way I was going to tell my lawyer Mrs. Pierce. I knew this wasn't the best idea

190

in the world, but she deserved to know who was taking care of her daughter.

I was snapped out of my trance when the front door opened.

"Is she sleeping?" My mom said as she came in immediately looking at the floor for Lana.

"Hello to you, too," I say placing the letter on the coffee table, quickly wiping another tear.

"Oh, hi sweetie," she closed the door then walked over to kiss my forehead.

"You know that key was given to you for emergency purposes?" I say with a raised eyebrow as she sits down on the couch next to me.

"This is an emergency," she answered quickly. "I wanted to take Lana to the mall before I go back to work. There is a sale on toddler shoes and it ends today."

I'm trying to stifle my laugh. "We have to have a sit down on what constitutes an *emergency*."

"Sweetheart, I know you are not too familiar with children, but they grow like weeds. The few pairs of shoes she has now may not fit her in a couple of months. Six months from now you will be in a hurry to get her dressed and then you're going to realize the shoes you've had are too small. You'll be thankful you had a mother who thought ahead."

My stomach lurched and I looked away from my mother and wiped yet another tear from my cheek.

"Zoe?" She said grabbing my knee. "What's wrong?"

"Six months from now she won't be here." I was realizing the longer Lana was here the harder it was going to be to give her away. My mother was being sweet, there was nothing malicious in her words, but they struck a chord.

"Baby," she says lowly, "I'm so sorry. I didn't even think about the…"

"It's okay," I interrupt. "You didn't do anything, it's just …" I trail off as I picked up the letter and handed it to her. I sat silently as I watched her read it.

"Hill? This is…"

"Yes," I say. "I wrote them last week to let them know Lana was safe and being taken care of. I *have* to meet her," I say. "I mean, right?"

My mother didn't answer immediately as she read over the letter again.

"What does Aiden think?" She finally asked. Her eyes were still on the letter.

"He doesn't know," I shrug. "He doesn't even know I sent a letter."

My mother looked up at me as she folded the letter and placed it back on the table. "You and Aiden are going to be married soon. You shouldn't have kept this from him." Her voice was soft, but concerned.

"It's not that I kept it from him spitefully. I just knew he'd talk me out of it and no matter how I feel about Lana her parents deserve to know what is going on with her." I'm not even bothering to wipe my tears now. My emotions were sitting on my chest in a giant ball. My anger and my frustration about this entire ordeal were all catching up with me at this very moment.

"Why is this so messed up?" I nearly sob, before I could finish my question my mother had me wrapped in her arms. "None of this makes sense." I choke out painfully.

"I'm so sorry, baby girl." She cried along with me. "*I'm* so sorry." We sat like this for a few minutes.

"I didn't want her," I say lowly, finally breaking the silence. My tears slowing down as I laid my head on my mother's chest. "I gave her away and now the thought of never seeing her again after this trial…" I can't find the words. "I love her and I swear to God I hate that I do and I wish that I didn't." I say honestly to her, the words were swirling around the room with a heavy presence. She doesn't say anything, she just squeezes me tighter.

"Zoweee!" I hear Lana croon from her bedroom. I pull myself from my mother and immediately jump up to go into her room. She is sitting up in her pink princess bed staring at the door like she'd had a bad dream.

"Hey little one," I say. I sit on the floor next to her bed. "How was your nap?" Her room was very dimly lit so I was sure she couldn't see how drained my face looked from crying. She didn't answer as she climbed out of her bed and curled into my lap, laying her head down on my stomach and closing her eyes. I inhaled and massaged her hair back as she slowly fell back to sleep.

I smiled and looked down at her knowing that Aiden was right about what he said when we'd gotten into that argument about the custody. I *did* want her. At this very moment I didn't care about the hearings, or the Hills, or the strain keeping her would put on my relationship with Aiden. I just wanted Lana here with me and that was it –no further explanation needed. It was an intense overwhelming feeling of possession and devotion that I'd never experienced before.

I sniffled as the realization of knowing my *wants* would never be enough. I was going to have to walk away from her again, but this time the pain would be louder and more cemented in me.

"I love you." I whisper to her for the first time out loud. I exhale and close my eyes, internalizing and embracing this moment.

Chapter Fifteen: If the World were a Perfect Place

I sat impatiently staring at the café doors obsessively for the last twenty minutes; I'd gotten here way too early. Every time the glass doors opened I would tense up, my hands would begin to sweat, my heart would lose its mind, and then I'd calm down when I realized the person walking in was just there to get coffee. I had no clue what Emilia looked like, I had no idea what to expect.

When I told Aiden I'd written a letter and that I was planning on meeting the Hills he was upset that I didn't tell him and he had every right to be. I'd just promised him a month prior that I would be more communicative, but it honestly was not my strong suit. I knew I had to do better and I was going to try so hard to do better *for him*.

We sat down and discussed it and came to the agreement that we would meet the Hills, that if we were in their shoes we'd want the same opportunity. Aiden wanted to come, but was called into work last minute and with our bills and now an extra mouth to feed we couldn't afford for him to turn down the extra hours. It made him nervous that I was meeting strangers by myself so he gave me mace which I thought was absurdly ridiculous, but I did bring it.

"Zoe Oakley?" I hear from behind me, snapping me out of my thought. I turned around and stood up immediately.

"Yes." I say, my voice is low and uneven as I stare at the tall brunette in front of me.

"I'm Emilia." She extended her hand for me to shake. "My husband couldn't make it."

"It's nice to meet you," I say as I nervously shook her hand. "My fiancé couldn't make it either." I clear my throat. "Have a seat."

We sat in awkward silence for a few exaggerated seconds before she spoke. "Thank you for agreeing to meet with me. I know this is…"

"Uncomfortable?" I finish her sentence, she exhales slowly and nods.

"…and unbelievable," she added softly. She was very prim and proper I noticed already just from these few moments in her presence. She was wearing a collared button up with a baby blue sweater over it. Her hair was neatly pinned back into a tight ponytail. She was probably in her late twenties to early thirties. She looked like a mom; she looked like someone who'd planned on being a mom since they were a little girl. I swallow trying to rid the lump and dryness in my throat.

"I'm sorry," I say abruptly. "I'm sorry that I lied and that my messed up life is affecting yours." I try to compose myself before I continue because I can feel my words coming out at a mile a minute. "Never in a million years did I imagine this would happen."

She exhaled slowly and folded her hands in front of her onto the table.
"Why did you lie?" She asked. I could see the pain in her eyes. I bit my lip, realizing that in the letter she'd written me she said she didn't know my whole story. "You and I both wanted a closed adoption. I don't understand how any of this is happening, how it's even legal."

"How much do you know about my…" I paused and looked down at my tea before looking back into her direction, "*situation?*"

She inhaled, "That you got pregnant at sixteen and wanted a closed adoption."

I blinked, and it was hard to open my eyes back up. I decided in that moment I would tell her the truth, she needed to know that though I should not have falsified documents –that my intent was to protect not only myself, but my mother and Lana especially.

195

"I was raped." I say the words and I will never get used to the acidic taste that word left in my mouth. "My mother's husband is Lana's biological father." It burned my throat to say that truth. The sadness and remorse that covered Emilia's face made me want to cry. She was going through the worst possible thing a mother could go through, but still managed to find compassion for me.

"I was naïve and afraid for anyone to ever know what he'd done so when it was time to file the paperwork I said I didn't know who the father could be." I can feel my cheeks getting hot and my eyes starting to prickle, but I did not want to cry in front of Emilia. I did not want or need her sympathy. It was my fault she was even in this situation. I had no right to make her feel guilty. I just wanted her to know the truth.

"I'm so sorry you had to go…"

"Please no," I interrupt softly. "This isn't about me anymore. I just wanted you to know that something like this happening never crossed my mind. I never knew it was possible. He is just …"

"*He*," she says quizzically, "your mother's husband?"

"Yes. Oscar, Lana's biological father is why we are in court." I can feel the anger rising in my chest. "He is a very angry man and he realized that wanting and asking for custody would not only hurt me in some way, but it would help his case. That's what my lawyer told me at least."

I bite the inside of my lip as I force the words out. "He's trying to say that he did not rape me and had he known Lana was his he would've taken responsibility." I shake my head "The details don't matter, but that is why she is here with me. He's a monster and the courts would've put Lana in the system during the duration of the hearing or in Oscar's custody and I couldn't allow it. She can't be anywhere near him."

Emilia's eyes are bloodshot red, a tear finally falling. I wondered how much she'd cried over the last few weeks. "Thank you," her voice is shaky, "…for standing up for her when the legal system didn't. When I was powerless," her words made the tears that were holding on for dear life finally fall down my cheeks.

"Thank you for raising Lana to be such a magical little girl." I say softly my voice cracking throughout.

She smiles through tears, "How…" she started to say, but then her face broke into a full blown cry, her shoulders shaking slightly as she looked down at her lap. "How is she doing?" She managed to say through her sob.

Reflexively I reached over the small table and rested my hand on top of hers. My heart was breaking, I couldn't imagine going through this pain. As I thought the words I realized that soon I *would* be going through a similar agony. I had to block that thought out of my head before I completely lost it too.

"She's everything you've raised her to be," I am finally able to say. "She's funny, smart, beautiful… *messy.*"

Emilia smiled lifting her free hand to wipe multiple tears. "I'm sorry," she said moving her hand from under my hand to wipe more tears. "I'm being so inappropriate. I promised myself I wouldn't do this. I just wanted to know more about you and your story so I could sleep better at night. I had to see you face to face."

"Please don't apologize. I understand."

"I didn't know if you were aware, but we have filed a suit against the state of Ohio and we will be appealing the ruling when custody is awarded to whomever. I don't want you to be blindsided like we were, but we are fighting for her, we are never going to stop fighting for her."

Though I expected this, and who would not have expected this, my stomach and chest felt like they were set on fire. I knew Lana couldn't stay with me, in no realm would that even make sense, but knowing that and *accepting* that were two completely different emotions. "I know. I'm fighting for you too." My voice wavering but she could have easily interpreted it as my crying.

She sighed and picked her purse up from the floor. "Thank you. I have to be leaving I have an appointment at 3pm on the other side of town." She smiled serenely as if she were actively trying to reserve herself. She stood up with her hand extended and I followed suit. "It was very nice to meet you, thank you for sharing your story when you didn't have to."

I shook her hand and nodded unable to speak, my thoughts circling Lana and her ever presence in my home with Aiden.

She started to walk away. "Wait!" I say a little too loudly for the size of this small café. She stopped and looked right at me her eyes are so red that I can't look directly at her. I reach into my purse to grab a scrap piece of paper and a pen. I scribble on it quickly and walk over to her.

"In case you want to hear her voice." I say softly as I place my cell phone number in her hand. She looked down at it and another low sob escaped from her throat, she immediately had her arms around me hugging me tightly, appreciatively.

"Thank you, Zoe. Thank you so much." She whispered as her voice broke. I didn't say anything as I hugged her back because I was too focused on controlling myself from my own breakdown. I was breaking every conceivable rule possible during this custody battle, but I didn't care. What was happening to Lana and to her family wasn't fair. It wasn't fair to any of us.

Emilia let go of me, readjusting her sweater, and wiping the tears from her cheeks. She folded the number neatly and placed it into her purse before exhaling and looking back up at me. "Thank you." she said again calmly her face still tear soaked, but her demeanor trying idly to fall back into being reserved. I nodded wiping a stray tear from my cheek then she walked out of the café.

I felt depleted after that. There were so many different emotions cascading up and down my body –grief being the most dominant one. I grabbed my bag and walked out of the café the urge to get home to Aiden and Lana was overwhelming. I needed to enjoy every moment I had left with my little temporary family.

***

"Crap! Crap!" I say barging into our bedroom as I hung up my cell phone and placed it in my pocket. I head to our bedroom closet, immediately shrugging out of my lazy/hanging around the house clothes.

"What's wrong?" Aiden sat up slightly from the bed. He'd just gotten home from a fourteen hour work shift twenty minutes ago and I was realizing at that moment that I just woke him up from a nap.

"Crap!" I whisper looking at him, "I didn't mean to wake you. Go back to sleep."

"Zoe," he sat completely up this time, rubbing his eyes. My poor baby was so exhausted. "Why are you hopping around half naked and panicked?"

I begin to ramble quickly, "Work called and said they had an extra shift for me and you know we need the money, but since Lana had a temperature yesterday at pick up she can't go to daycare for twenty four hours so I made her an appointment for 11am today *before* I knew I had to work at 10am. So, now I have to drive Lana all the way to my mom's so she can take her to the appointment, but my mom has to be at work at noon and it's cutting it so close." My words are coming out in a flurry my thoughts running rapidly through my mind trying to figure everything out as I go.

"She said she would call off," I continued, "…but I could not let her do that. As of now either my mom is going to drop her off at your dads house or I'm going to leave work to pick her up from my mom then drop her off at your dads then head back to work." I say

199

breathlessly. I was trying to put on my pants without falling over into the wall and killing myself.

"I was calling your dad back to see if he can watch her until 6:30 pm instead of 4:30 pm, but he isn't answering the phone. Oh and Lana is refusing to put her shoes on."

Aiden is just staring at me as I struggle to get my shirt over my head. "Zoe, why are you doing all of this?" He finally says.

"Huh?" I said confusingly. I'm trying to figure out where my phone is so I could call his dad *again*, then text my mom the tentative plan.

"Just go to work, I'll take her to the appointment and stay with her today." He said simply as he yawned and got out of the bed.

I finally stopped and was able to catch my breath. "Aiden, I can't let you do that. You just got home. I don't want you to feel obligated to do anything and you're exhausted."

"…and so are you." He countered stretching his arms and yawning. "There is no need for you to be running around like a chicken with its head cut off. And *obligated?* We are a team. I told you *we* were doing this together."

I just stared at my fiancé –my heart too full to explain in words. The urgency I felt to become his wife at this very second was overpowering.

"What would I do without you?" I say. I was able to finally exhale, seeing the stress of what my day would've become dissipate.

"Let's pray we both never have to find out." He walked over kissing my lips lightly. "I'm going to take a shower, leave the appointment address and tell your mom she can join Lana and I for breakfast before the appointment if she wants." He walked out of the room into the bathroom.

I nodded, though he didn't see me, a soft smile rested happily on my lips. I pulled my phone out and texted my mother, she replied immediately.

I just love my future son-in-law she texted with a smiley face.

I smiled to myself; I loved him too, so much.

My shift was long and agonizing, but it was finally 6:00pm. I was surprised I didn't get a ticket for how fast I was driving. I was anxious to get home to them. I walked through the door to hear children's music playing in the kitchen. "I'm home." I say as I closed the door placing my bag on the ottoman.

"Hey!" Aiden called out. I walked into the kitchen to see two candles lit, a lilac table cloth I'd never seen before, and Lana sitting in her booster seat. "Dinner is served!" Aiden smiled.

"What is this?" I say sitting down right next to Lana. "Hey," I whispered to her placing a light kiss on top of her hair.

"Well," he said as he walked over to me and placed a napkin on my lap, kissing my cheek on his way up. "I had this big idea to cook you an elaborate dinner, but Lana and I agreed that we didn't want to risk accidently poisoning you or burning the apartment down." He turned around and opened the stove pulling out two large pizza boxes.

"So, we got your favorite pizza instead." He shrugged. I smiled brightly and humorously.

"The quickest way to my heart, thank you."

As we ate I realized that this was technically our first dinner together at this table. Usually Aiden was at work, or it was my mom, or we were all crashed out on the couch in front of the television. It made me happy, but the feeling was fleeting just like I knew these moments would be. They would be coming to an end soon.

"So how was your day? What did the doctor say?" I say trying to distract myself from my thoughts that I knew would soon make me cry if I let them swirl around in my head too long.

"She's fine, just a little hay fever. Keep her hydrated and that's about it." He said as he looked at her with a smile. He looked back at me, "We had breakfast with your mom beforehand then went to the park with my dad afterwards." He took a sip of his pop before continuing, "then I took her to get ice cream and to that toddler puppet show at the library, but it freaked her out so we left."

I observed how his eyes lit up talking about their day, how I knew he was exhausted but he did all of this with her and actually enjoyed it. It made my heart swell.

"Sounds like you guys had an amazing day?" I say looking at her.

"I don't like the puppets." She said with big eyes shaking her head back and forth.

"No more puppets!" I say as I imitate her distaste. "Right, Aiden?"

"Right!" He agreed, looking at her with mock horror on his face as well. We made eye contact again and I smiled warmly, mouthing *thank you.* He rolled his eyes and I laughed. I was beginning to love these moments much too much. I had to start preparing mentally for the inevitable.

***

I sat on the floor across from Lana and Aiden as she played in Aiden's hair. He had pink butterfly clips, rubber bands, and two headbands on him. He looked ridiculous so of course I took a million pictures.

"You're enjoying this too much." He says as he glares at my phone. I take two more pictures before responding.

"It's actually my favorite thing ever." I say with a serious tone, taking one more picture "Can you at least smile?" He shows his bright teeth sarcastically and I laugh. "I told you that you needed a haircut, this is what happens when people don't listen to Zoe." I winked and put my phone back in my pocket.

"Hey Lana," Aiden says ignoring me all together. "I think we should do Zoe's makeup?" She was still hovering over his head. He wasn't showing it, but the way she was pulling at his hair looked painful.

"Umm," I say. Lana's face lit up, I knew then that my face was going to be painted and I would have to endure it. Luckily, I only wore makeup on special occasions so I had a lot of basic neutral colors. She wouldn't be able to make me look like Ronald McDonald. "Sure," I say squinting at Aiden incredulously. He smirked and pointed to his wild hair.

"All is fair in love and makeovers."

I rolled my eyes, getting up from the floor to go dig through our bathroom drawers for the little bit of makeup I had. Once I got into the bathroom my phone started buzzing –it was Mrs. Pierce.

My heart dropped.

I was dreading when she called because I knew that meant a court date had finally been set. It kept getting pushed back we were nearing two months when it should've only been two weeks.

"Hello," I answer. My nerves were making my voice shaky.

"Zoe," her voice sounded sad and concerned, "I have some very difficult news."

It felt like the blood in my veins froze, I was afraid to breathe. The very first thing that popped into my head was that Oscar was going to get Lana or something along those lines. My heart started racing at an unhealthy pace. At that moment I realized they would have to pry her from my dead body before he was allowed anywhere near her.

"Oscar is not getting her!" I yelled into my phone. "I'll leave the state, he…"

"No Zoe," she interrupted. "Nothing directly related to Oscar." She paused and took a deep breath in. "I just got off the phone with Miss. Ramsey and judge Waldron, Lana's adoptive mother Emilia Hill was in a terrible car accident and died yesterday morning."

It was like the air had been kicked out of me. This couldn't be real, I had to be dreaming. I didn't make a sound as tears began to flow recklessly down my cheeks, finally the weight of her words started to make sense. I covered my mouth with my hand as to hold the sob that was trying to escape from my throat.

Aiden was standing behind me; he'd heard me yell about Oscar.

"Zoe?" He said grabbing my shoulder. I could feel the panic in his touch and hear it in his voice.

"I don't understand. I just…" I say into the phone. I had to stop myself because I was about to say I'd just met the sweet woman two weeks ago, that I'd given her my cell phone number, that she called four times and listened to Lana play and sing in the background while I put the phone on speaker. I couldn't tell Mrs. Pierce that I'd disobeyed direct court orders blatantly and excessively.

"It gets a little more complicated," she said lowly. "Darren Hill, Lana's adoptive father has decided to drop the suit and will not be appealing."

"What does that mean?" I wasn't fully focused on Mrs. Pierce's words I was focused on Lana, how this would affect her. She was taken from that home not knowing she would never see her *mother* again. I wiped a tear. Aiden walked all the way into the bathroom, putting the toilet lid down, and sitting on top of it. Fear and sadness crossed his face as he tried to decipher what was making me so emotional.

"It means that he has removed himself from fighting for custody."

I let her words sink in; I slowly understood what she was saying. My eyes bugged out and I looked at Aiden. I could see that it was killing him that he had no idea what was going on, but my brain couldn't process this information, it couldn't process talking to Mrs. Pierce and then having to explain it to Aiden all at once –I was in quicksand.

"Zoe, are you still there?" She said.

"Yes," I manage to choke out. "I'm here."

"Do you understand what this means?" She questioned. There was urgency in her voice. "This custody battle is now you against Oscar, unless you opt to relinquish your rights. Is this something you are prepared for?"

Since getting Lana I dreaded the day I would have to give her back, but I knew it would be what was best for her. I knew that was the most logical thing to do. I always knew that though it would hurt me more than anything had hurt me in my entire life –I always knew she wouldn't be here for long. I was prepared and had somewhat accepted the fact that it would be absurd to want to keep her and now I'm being told that I am going to court to fight for full custody against my rapist and if I didn't go to court and decided to relinquish my rights to her my rapist would receive full custody.

It was insane, it was such an unreal notion to try and digest. How was this real life? How was any of this happening right now?

My gut immediately wanted to say *yes* I will fight to keep her as impractical and unbelievable as it sounded, but I looked at my fiancé. I was not going to answer *for* us like I had before. It almost broke us when I did the last time. I had to have a conversation with him first.

"I have to speak with Aiden," I say exasperatedly. "Can I call you back?"

"Yes," she said solemnly. "I know this is a very difficult situation. Take your time."

I hung up the phone and placed it back in my pocket.

"What's going on?" Aiden said, walking to me instantly.

"Where is Lana?" I ask. Wanting to make sure she wasn't in hearing range.

"On the couch watching her show," he said quickly. "What's going on, Zoe?" He urged "Is it Oscar? What did he do?"

I exhaled and let more tears fall, "Emilia died in a car crash yesterday." It didn't feel real as I said the words.

"Oh my God," Aiden's shocked face made me cry more. I took a deep breath before continuing.

"Her father dropped the suit and won't appeal. He doesn't want to fight for custody anymore."

Aiden is just staring at me with shock in his eyes. I didn't know if he'd put the puzzle pieces together or if he were still reeling off of the fact that Emilia had died. Though I'd met her once, in that short time I knew she was a good person. I look at Lana every day and can tell she was a great mother. The proof was right there. It was hard to fathom that she was no longer here. That she died without being able to see her daughter for the last weeks of her life. I wondered how many times my heart could break; the pieces were starting to crumble.

"What does this mean for Lana?" Aiden asked. The pain in his voice made me even sadder which I didn't know was possible at this point. I'd seen Aiden grow closer and closer at his own pace with Lana. He cared about her too. He worried about her happiness and wellbeing just as much as I did.

"It means that she will be in Oscar's custody or back in the system if we don't fight for her." My grasp on reality finally broke. I broke down completely. I didn't have time to acknowledge Aiden's reaction because he quickly had me in his arms bear hugging me.

"What am I going to do?" I mumble into his chest. Aiden and I had the biggest fight we'd ever had over Lana. I knew that this was not how we imagined our young adult lives to be. I had no right to force him to be a father figure to this child he thought would never be in the picture, but here I was desperately praying inside that I could keep her with me.

"Oscar isn't getting her, Zoe," he said intensely as he squeezed me tighter. "*We* have to fight for her, right?" It was almost as if he were speaking to himself.

I pulled myself away from him to look in his eyes. My vision was blurry, but I needed to stare the love of my life directly in his eyes to truly comprehend what he'd just said. "What?"

"We don't have another option. We have to." He said lowly, he said the words as if he were trying to convince me. I didn't need any convincing.

"No, Aiden, I mean you're okay with this? She would be ours…" I pause staring my beautiful fiancé in the eyes, "forever." I add.

It was heavy, the word *forever,* but it wasn't as intimidating as I thought it would be, as it actually should be.

He let go of me and sat back down on the lid of the toilet, putting his face into his hands. I stood there scared, for a moment I thought he truly wanted her, but now I see that he feels like it is an obligation or maybe he knows that I want her and he fears it will tear us apart like it almost did before. My heart sinks and I wipe another tear before moving towards him, "Aiden."

"We can't let anything happen to her," he interrupts lowly. When he looks up at me his eyes are glossed.

"Aiden," I cry out softly sitting on the bathroom floor in front of him. "What are you saying? What are you thinking?" I'm almost sobbing, my words gargled and whispered. I was so confused. His words were contradicting his demeanor.

"I know this is so much to take on, but I don't want you to agree to this or feel obligated because you know it's what I want..." oh God, how would we survive this impasse? If he truly doesn't want her and I want her with my whole heart? How could we possibly make it? I felt sick and numb. I was terrified for the direction this conversation could take.

"Zoe, we are getting married we have to be on the same page especially something this huge and life changing, but I'm not agreeing to this solely because I think it's what you want and I don't feel obligated. We are young, *so* young and we have so much we have yet to do in our lives. Financially we are barely getting by and now we're going to be parents? Permanently? So I'm not upset, or angry, or frustrated because you think I feel like I don't have a choice," he pauses, closing his eyes and exhaling slowly. "I'm scared, Zoe." His voice is so low. "I'm scared that we are not ready and that crippling fear means absolutely *nothing* because in my eyes she is already as good as ours."

I'd never heard him say the words *I'm scared* before and through all of this drama I was realizing that I hadn't truly acknowledged the fact that I was scared too. Everything Aiden was saying was true, we were so young, there was so much we hadn't experienced, but Lana was more important than all of that.

She is already as good as ours. I couldn't stop these tears from falling if I tried.

208

"I'm scared too," I say softly. "I'm terrified."

We are quiet for a moment as I rest my head on his knee. He's caressing my hair before he breaks the silence.

"We can handle this?" He asks me quietly. I sit up and stare him directly in the eyes. "We can do this." He adds, but this time it wasn't a question.

"Yes," I say. "We can do this." I agree. He exhales again then leans forward to hug me.

"Okay," he says against my hair, "we are fighting for her."

There have been many moments in the time I'd been with Aiden that I said the phrase *"I didn't think I could love him anymore than I already do now, but..."* this was one of those times. My heart was full nearly ready to explode with how much he meant to me. I felt so undeserving of his love.

I didn't say a word. I just hugged him and exhaled. I remember being afraid that my dark and black storm cloud would leave smudges all over my shiny and sunny Aiden. I was beginning to realize that his shiny armor was impenetrable. All this time I'd been worried about tainting *him,* he was actually leaving his light and positive rays all around for me to trip over. He'd been slowly turning my storm cloud into a rainbow and I hadn't realized it until this very moment.

"I love you." I breathe, squeezing him closer to me.

Chapter Sixteen: The Special Things

"What are you doing out here?" Aiden walked out of our bedroom wiping his eyes "It's three in the morning?"

I was sitting on the floor in front of Lana's cracked bedroom door. "I thought I heard her crying." I yawn and stretch my arms reaching my arms towards him so he would sit down next to me.

"How long have you been sitting here?"

"Since 1:45am."

"Baby," Aiden says as he sits next to me.

"I know," I say laying my head on his shoulder. "I keep thinking she's going to freak out. I keep waiting for her to want to leave, for her to hate it here and beg for her parents."

"It's been over three months," he wrapped his arms around me. "I think she is somewhat used to it by now…what's really going on?"

It was scary how well he knew me, though what I said was true. I just left out an important part. "I had a nightmare that Oscar and his Lawyers broke in and took her away and we had no rights. She was just gone and there was nothing we could do about it."

Aiden didn't say anything as he wrapped his arms around my shoulders.

"I know, I'm crazy," I add. "It's just, we still don't have a trial date and the longer we wait the more anxious I get. I don't want to go to court. The fact that it even has to go to court repulses me. She's ours. She belongs here with us." I was so tired of crying. "How can they not see what Oscar is doing?"

"No one is going to let him have custody of her. I know the waiting sucks but she *is* ours. We just have to be patient. She's not going anywhere." Aiden softly massaged my back.

His words were comforting, but it didn't help lessen the fear that I had. What if by some freak of chance Oscar *was* granted custody? I was young, I'd given her up once, I've lied to the courts and state by falsifying documents, I've tried to kill a man, and I've been admitted to a psyche ward before. What if they deemed me unfit? What if they awarded him my daughter because I was crazy not caring that I was crazy because of what Oscar had done to me? How was I supposed to function if this happened? I would be put in jail or in another psyche ward.

I was still trying to fully comprehend the fact the Emilia passed. We have yet to tell Lana and though I'm sure she wouldn't understand anyways it still tore me up inside that she did not know. I knew that one day Lana would ask questions so I decided to go to the funeral. I wanted to pay respects to the woman who raised Lana to be the angel that she is and I wanted to get a program to give to Lana when she was old enough.

I met Darren, Lana's adoptive father and it was probably one of the most difficult conversations I'd ever had to have in my entire life. He told me that he felt like he was a horrible person and that he didn't want me to think that he was, but that his small family was so cemented together that he could not fathom raising Lana without Emilia, that Emilia was the calm in his storm of a life and it wouldn't be fair to Lana to grow up without a mother. He broke down twice during our short conversation and winced every time he said Emilia's name.

I ached for him, obviously not wanting to fight for custody was a very hard decision for him, but I understood it. I understood *exactly* what it felt like to want nothing but the best for Lana all the while knowing you weren't capable of doing it yourself. That's one of the reasons I'd given her up for adoption.

"I love Lana so much," he said as his eyes nearly glossed over. "A day doesn't go by that I don't think about her, but I can't … I just can't raise her on my own. I can't give her the life she deserves –I need my wife. My wife was meant for this, not me …."

"I understand," I said painfully. "You are not a bad person, Mr. Hill."

211

He took a deep breath, "If it ever comes up, please tell her that I love her and that I always will." He handed me a picture of the three of them together. Lana was so tiny cradled in Emilia's arms. "This was the first day we brought her home." He wiped a tear and it felt like my chest was going to cave in. "Give this to her one day if you want."

I nodded, "I will." I say softly then I left. I broke down in my car crying when I read the back of the photo it said, "*I wish I were stronger. I'll love you always, peanut.*" It was all so much to take in. I tried to put myself in his shoes. I couldn't imagine losing Aiden just the thought in a hypothetical sense made me queasy. I'm sure I would figure out how to manage some miserable version of *life* at some point, but I couldn't picture raising Lana without Aiden. I couldn't picture doing most things without him. The agony in Darren's eyes showed me that was exactly how he felt about Emilia.

"Let's go to bed." Aiden whispered in my ear, bringing me out of my trance. I sighed and lifted my head from his shoulder.

"I think I'm going to stay out here a little longer."

He kissed my forehead then got up. I gently laid my back against the wall and stared at the ceiling –counting the paint lines. A few seconds went by and Aiden was back with two pillows and our comforter.

"What are you doing?" I ask

"We're having a sleepover in front of Lana's room." He answered, he handed me a pillow and laid down beside me. I smiled and put my pillow down next to his.

"You don't have to indulge my idiosyncrasies. I know you have to be up early for work tomorrow."

"So, have you picked a dress yet?" He said quickly changing the subject. I smiled and laid my head on my pillow.

"Yea, my mom and I went when you and Lana were at the park."

He moved a few of my curls out of my face and placed them behind my ear. "Can I be honest with you?"

"It's preferred." I say with a smile.

"I would like to wake up early and head right down to city hall, just me, you and Lana."

I'd let my mother talk me into a small church wedding. I never really cared where, when, or how Aiden and I got married. I just wanted to be his wife.

"My mother would lose it," I say staring into his beautiful brown eyes. "Plus, you have to work tomorrow."

"I could go in late or call off. I have fifteen hours of overtime already. We could get married tomorrow and still let her throw the wedding?" He arched an eyebrow. I looked at him incredulously. "I can't wait another six months to make you my wife." He placed his hand on my cheek.

"So you're saying we get married tomorrow, don't tell anyone, and then still have the wedding six months from now?"

He nods with the biggest grin on his face, "Just our little family." He adds.

I thought he was crazy, completely insane, but I guess I was crazy and completely insane as well because it was starting to sound like a good idea. Weddings were always for the family and friends more so than they were for the bride and groom. I didn't care about that stuff. Aiden could be my husband now and we could still have the party and take pictures with our loved ones in a few months.

I sigh then bite my lip, he hugged me immediately. He took my silence as a *yes.*

"So tomorrow I will be your wife?"

"Officially, Mrs. Jordan," he says with a triumphant smile.

I kissed him softly and gently. "You're the worst." I said to him between kisses. He smiled and kissed me one more time before we both eventually drifted off to sleep cuddled with each other on the hallway floor.

***

I always imagined being nervous. Not being able to concentrate, wanting to run for the hills just like the runaway bride, but I was calm and honestly just excited to become Zoe Jordan. I took Lana to the mall and got her a cute yellow sundress with white flowers. I wore a sundress that I'd had for a couple years. It was the fanciest thing I owned.

I look over at Aiden and he looks like it's just another day. He's so at ease, not a single nerve about the fact we were about to get married. He senses me smiling at him.

"What?" He says returning a smile.

"We're nineteen and I feel like we've already been married for ten years." I say grabbing his hand.

"I hope that's a good thing?"

I laughed, "It's a great thing, this doesn't feel as scary as it probably should feel," I shrug.

"Yea, never in a million years would I have imagined getting married," he squeezed my hand. "Not until I met you, then it got scary."

We are standing in line waiting to get the paperwork for our marriage license. Lana is playing with her giraffe and teddy bear next to me.

"It got scary? You gettin' cold feet on me?" I say with a raised eyebrow.

"Walking on lava, baby," he winked. I roll my eyes. "I got scared when I realized that somehow at seventeen I never wanted to go on another first date. I'd only had one other serious girlfriend and gone on a couple dates here and there back in Nebraska. So it was terrifying."

"When did you realize it?" I say as I gaze into his eyes. The way his eyes sparkled when he talked about me made me fall deeper in love with him by the second. He wore his admiration for me blatantly. It was a powerful feeling.

"When did I realize I didn't want to date anyone else?" He said as he turned to face me. "It's kind of a two part story."

"I've got nothing but time."

He puts his arm around my shoulders as I grab Lana's hand to move up in line. He smells like summer and feels warm like it too. All I wanted to do was go straight home after this and lay in his arms. I always felt so safe in his arms, never in my entire life had I felt so whole, even with all of the negative drama going on I was still complete next to him.

"That second day," he said assuredly. "When we ate lunch together outside."

I looked at him incredulously. I remember every moment I've spent with Aiden very specifically. There was no way he knew I was the one then. I was so oblivious to our attraction at that time, not knowing that the warmth I was feeling in my chest was a clear cut sign that I liked him.

"We hadn't even gone on a date yet," I say. "Seriously …"

"Really!" He rebuts adamantly. "I remember looking for you in the cafeteria. After that first day when that teacher interrupted us …"

"Mrs. McCabe," I interject.

"Yea, after that I felt like I had more I wanted to ask you. I needed to know more. That next day when I didn't see you, I honestly felt crushed and then I walked outside and there you were. You were sitting there with your eyes closed, you took a deep breath in and you just looked so…you were the most stunning girl I'd ever laid my eyes on."

I can feel the blush rise up all the way from my feet to my hair follicles on the top of my head.

"Then you opened your eyes and when you saw me, you smiled and at that moment I knew I had to ask you out. I just didn't know how because you seemed so unreal to me. I didn't think I would have a chance." He's holding me so close, I could feel his heartbeat. "Then on top of being gorgeous you were funny and goofy. I just wanted to be around you."

It was amazing hearing his perception of me knowing what I was going through during that time. I remember being scared of the thought of Aiden because I felt like he and I grew close too quickly. I'm glad he didn't let me push him away though I tried so many times in the beginning.

"The second part was our first date." He adds.

"That's when I fell for you too," I agree. "I just remember it being the most intense feeling I'd ever experienced. I specifically remember thinking who the hell were you and what would your significance be in my life." I wiped another tear. "*Damn*, I really love you."

We both start to laugh.

"You felt all that and still tried to break up with me before we even had a second date." He shook his head.

"You scared me," I say simply. "… and I didn't want to taint the good in you with the bad in me."

"That's ridiculous." He said as if I were crazy. "You're the best thing that's ever happened to me. It was early on when I knew I wanted to propose to you too…"

"Zoweee," Lana interrupts before he could finish his sentence.

"Yes?"

"I wanna go." She says, hugging her arms around my leg. I squat down to look at her at eye level.

"Can you keep a secret?" I ask her, she nods. "Aiden and I are getting married today. So a little while longer and we will be home, okay?!"

"What's married?"

I didn't really know how to answer that question in away a toddler would understand. Aiden saw my hesitation and knelt down beside me.

"Lana, marriage is when two people want to be together forever."

Leave it to Aiden to keep it simple and perfect.

"Together, forever?" she repeated.

"Yes." He answered with a smile.

"Can you marry me Zoweee?" Her little voice ruling my world, I couldn't believe how many tears I was able to produce. She wanted to be together forever. My heart was melting out of my chest.

"Mommy and Daddy and Aiden and Miss Kim can marry me too."
She added.

It was the first time she'd truly mentioned her parents. My stomach
was hot and my heart was racing. I looked at Aiden. I couldn't read
his expression, but I knew he was probably feeling what I was
feeling. I tried to discretely wipe away my tears, "Yes, I want to be
together forever too." I say softly. It was all I could say right now.
She smiles and hugs me.

"Next," I hear the woman at the counter say.

"Okay," Aiden says as he takes in a deep breath. We make eye
contact and we both can't help but smile at each other. He places his
hand on the small of my back. "Let's go get married!"

Chapter Seventeen: Burn

"I think I'm going to email Mrs. Pierce." I say. I'm attempting to
make spaghetti. I think cooking something you despise makes it
more difficult to follow the directions. There's sauce everywhere.

"You need to stop freaking out." Aiden says, he's sitting on the
kitchen floor with Lana having a tea party that I wasn't invited to
because according to a two and a half year old, I don't do it right.

"I'm not freaking out." I rebut Aiden looks at me with a raised
eyebrow. I sigh, "Maybe a little, but it's been almost five months, no
trial date? No contact? Maybe *he* gave up?" I refuse to say his name
around her.

"If that were the case don't you think that's something she would've
communicated with you?" Aiden replied.

"Maybe she is busy? Heavy case load?"

"Mrs. Pierce is very thorough."

I sigh and turn back around. Maybe I should put the garlic in now?

"Look, email her, but I think we should just focus on us right now. Admit it, it has felt so good not being in that courtroom all of this time?"

Aiden was right, it did feel good. I was just so nervous. I was so attached to Lana; *we* were so attached to her. The anxiety of knowing a court date was looming was enough to paralyze me. We were initially told two weeks, and then we were told six to eight more weeks we would have a court date. We are nearing six months and Lana *is* our family. I don't want to put her or our little family through this. I just wanted it to be over.

"It has been nice." I say quietly, throwing garlic in the sauce pot.

"Ummm," Aiden says getting up from the floor, "did you call my dad?"

"Yea, why?" I say as I pour pepper into the sauce and stir.

"I'm pretty sure you weren't supposed to put that whole thing in there, just a clove or two." He wrinkles his nose. I just stand there staring at the pot. I feel Aiden walk up behind me, and then he bursts into laughter.

"I hate spaghetti!" I say angrily. "It's not funny, you finish it." I walk out of the kitchen and this only made him laugh harder.

He followed me into the living room and grabbed my hand. "Don't be mad, I don't like spaghetti, you don't like spaghetti why stress out about it?" He says.

"Because, we are married, and we have a child, and can't keep ordering take out, we can't afford it and it's unhealthy." I say matter of fact. "I...*we* need to start cooking more for her. Set an example or whatever."

Aiden looked at me. He wasn't smiling, but there was a smile in his eyes. "What?" I say.

"Nothing," he says then cocks his head to the side. "You're an amazing wife and an amazing mother. I hope you know that." I smile as he kisses my forehead.

Suddenly, I hear a loud scream. It was blood curdling and it radiated throughout the apartment. My heart dropped and fear crept through my entire body. I didn't have time to think or process before my feet were already moving towards the kitchen.

"Lana!" Aiden and I both yell as we run into the kitchen. Her cries are haunting, the pain in her shriek was crippling. It took us all of two seconds to reach the kitchen and see Lana on the floor next to a puddle of steaming water. She'd pulled the pot of boiling water off of the stove.

I'd never experienced a feeling like this before, as I run to her and hold her in my arms I feel like dying. Not even on my worst day had I felt like this. My only job was to protect her and I failed, I failed miserably and she wasn't even officially mine yet. We had to get her to the hospital immediately. I grabbed her; Aiden grabbed the keys and her travel bag. We were at the hospital in less than fifteen minutes. My mother met us there about ten minutes afterwards.

Lana cried and screamed the entire drive. I felt like my soul was being snatched out of me and ran over by an eighteen wheeler. This was my fault. I never wanted her to experience pain, mentally or physically –especially on my watch and here I was watching her scream at octaves I didn't know she could reach.

Thankfully we did not have to wait. They took us to a room and examined her right away. She calmed down a little bit, but she was still visibly shaken. The nurses told us to wait in the room until the doctor came back with more information for us. My impatience was on a completely different level.

"It's going to be okay," I say as I hold her little hand, my tears are blinding me.

Aiden pulled out her giraffe and her red and white teddy bear. He was able to keep her calm while we waited. God, she was in so much pain. I felt sick.

"Okay," the ER doctor finally walked in. "Now, we have good news, the tissue isn't deeply burned. They *are* first degree burns, but this could've been much worse. Be grateful it only got part of her shoulder. I'll give you paperwork on how to take care of a burn like this. She should be fine in a few weeks."

I exhaled.

"She will be sore for a few days, but I'm sure that's nothing a few extra cuddles couldn't cure." He added with a wink towards her before walking out of the room.

I looked at Aiden, and then burst into tears. I had to leave the room. I can hear Aiden asking my mom to keep an eye on Lana while he follows me.

"Zoe," he says.

"This is my fault," I sob. "I shouldn't have walked out of the kitchen. How stupid was I to leave the kitchen with the fucking stove on?" I'm almost convulsing, I'm crying so hard that it's difficult to catch my breath.

"Shhh," Aiden says as he wraps his arms around me. "I shouldn't have left the kitchen either, this isn't just on you."

I didn't respond at first. I just kept replaying the sound of her scream, the tears in her eyes, and what I felt when I saw her on the floor. When traumatic things happen to people they usually say *I saw my whole life flash before my eyes* ... seeing her on that floor all I saw was my life with *her*. The day I gave birth to her I remember hearing her cry it was strong and piercing. The nurse asked me if I wanted to hold her and I shook my head *no*, incapable of using words.

I'd told myself throughout the entire pregnancy that I wouldn't look at her. I didn't want to see Oscar's face. When they took her out of the room and what I thought would be out of my life I looked through the window and saw a glimpse of her face and head full of curly brown hair.

I remember rolling over in the opposite direction sobbing silently into my pillow. I pushed her face and the sound of her cry so far back in my memory that it easily could've been confused as just a dream.

Every detail of that day came flooding back to me when I heard her screaming today.

"What if they take her from us?" I ask, and I choke over the words. That reality seemed unfathomable at this point. "What if Oscar uses this against us?"

"These kinds of accidents happen all of the time," Aiden said. "They're not going to punish us for this."

"You don't know that." I wipe my tears. "Miss. Ramsey is on her way up here. What do we say?"

"We say the truth Zoe, don't over analyze this. They're not taking her from us."

I exhaled again and closed my eyes as he pulled me closer towards him.

***

"Okay, so that's it?" Miss. Ramsey said.

"Yes." I nodded, I was so unbelievably nervous.

"Now, any injuries that occur while on temporary have to be reported." She says as she closes her folder. My heart starts racing and I squeeze Aiden's hand. "…but it's just precaution. I wouldn't worry about this affecting any future proceedings. You'd be surprised how many times accidents like this happen. Just be more careful." She smiled.

I tried to return the smile, but I wasn't sure if my face was doing it. I was so paranoid.

"Okay," Aiden said, realizing that I was frozen. "Thank you." He shook her hand before she walked away.

"Zoe?"

"Yea," I answer looking down at my palms.

"You heard her? Everything is going to be fine."

I nodded. It was quiet for a moment as a tear fell from my eye hitting my hand.

"Talk to me."

I take a deep breath in, "Maybe she should be with a new family, a family that can take good care of her." I say softly. I thought I would be all cried out by now, but I was far from it. The words burned my lips as I said them. I loved Lana. I loved her so much that it hurt. It was a scary kind of love.

When I looked at her it was like my heart, and my spirit, and all the love my body could contain were now a walking, living, breathing, entity existing outside of my body. Of course I wanted her, I never wanted to be away from her ever again, but when you love someone so powerfully you automatically want what's best for them, even if what's best for them isn't you.

I remember having a similar feeling early on in me and Aiden's relationship. I loved him so much but I knew the demons I had. I knew that I couldn't be the person a man like him deserved. I was too weak to walk away because I knew he was keeping me afloat, but I always wanted him to walk away from me. It would hurt but I always felt comforted knowing he would find someone who was better suited for him. Even after all this time I *still* have those thoughts of unworthiness.

"What?" Aiden said angrily.

"We aren't ready for this, you were right before. We are kids ourselves, what was I thinking? To be responsible for her life, responsible for every single thing that ever happens to her? I don't want to ruin her, Aiden. She can still go to a good family that can protect her better, raise her better. They'll have a house and a dog and…"

"Zoe, are you serious right now?" Aiden interrupted me angrily. "You think sending her to some strangers is going to prevent her from ever falling down, from ever having a single problem?"

I didn't say anything. I just wanted her to have the best life. I wanted her to have more than I ever had. I never wanted her to even know a world like the one I lived in could even exist.

"She is *our* daughter and there is no other way to see it," he said. "I know you're sad and angry and you feel like you should carry the blame and the weight of the world on your shoulders, but I'm not going to let you." His words are forceful and full of passion. "You feel like shit right now, I get it. I do too, but we are going to take her home and curl up on the couch and watch her favorite movie and continue to be a family and move on from this."

His words made my body warm all over. I wiped another tear as I continued to look down.

"As for the house, and the dog, and the white picket fence, or whatever, every day when I get up and go to work and go to class it is all in preparation for our future and our future children. We can give her a happy home. We *have* one."

Of course Aiden was right. He was my inner compass. Whenever I got lost in these thoughts, whenever I started drifting, he knew where to find me. He knew how to bring me back. Listening to his words made me love my husband more. I don't like to think about that argument, but nearly six months ago when I decided I wanted Lana and I didn't discuss it with him it almost broke us. It rocked our foundation hard. He said things that hurt me though he didn't know that they would and I did things that hurt him.

So seeing him say these things with passion and love in his eyes made me wish I could marry him all over again. At that thought I was happy that I'd actually be able to in a few weeks.

"I love you." I say, finally looking at him. He kissed me lightly and put my hair behind my ear.

"I love you too," he said with a gentle smile. "Let's go see Lana."

We got to the room and Lana was asleep. I looked over to see my mother's face and she looked like she'd seen a ghost.

"Mom,' I say concerned sitting down next to her. "What's wrong?"

She looked at me and I could see the anger and sadness in her eyes, "Oscar just called me from a private number."

A sharp jolt of acid swam through my veins. I felt like it had enough force to knock me over.

Aiden walked over to my mom. "What the hell did he want?"

"He wanted me to meet him for lunch and he told me to tell you that he wasn't fighting for full custody anymore."

It almost seemed unreal. Those words were the words I could've only dreamt of hearing, but my mother's reaction didn't match how good this news was.

"That's a good thing, mom? What's wrong?"

She took a deep breath in, "He wants joint."

"Over my dead body," Aiden said, his voice raising just enough to cause Lana to stir. Her eyes stayed closed as she gripped her favorite giraffe tighter.

"I hung up," she said. "I can't believe he called. I promise you I haven't spoken to him, Zoe. I'm not meeting him for lunch. I'm going to change my number…"

"It's okay," I interrupt her rant. "We know you haven't spoken to him."

"This isn't happening," Aiden said as he stormed out of the hospital room. I didn't follow after him immediately because I knew he needed to breathe. He needed to get all the anger out. But he was right – this was not going to happen.

I didn't understand what Oscar was up to, but I knew it was coming from a bigger plan. I knew it was coming from hate. Why would he go through all of this? Ripping Lana from her home because he wanted sole custody just to flip and say he wants joint now that I have her, now that I *want* her?

"Can you stay here a little longer while I look for Aiden?" I ask my mother. I'd cried so much today that I think I was officially tapped out.

"Absolutely," She said as she grabbed my hand. "I'm so sorry."

"You don't have anything to apologize for." I kiss her on the cheek then leave the room.

I walked around the halls of the hospital and even went outside, I couldn't find Aiden anywhere. I finally sat down in one of the waiting room chairs, putting my face in my hands, trying to calm my nerves. I was so sick of this, so sick of Oscar toying with my life because he was bitter.

I couldn't continue to wait for court or wait for Mrs. Pierce to try and fix this. I had to take matters into my own hands somehow, I had to end this. He needed to understand that I didn't want this battle anymore that all I wanted was Lana. I would drop the charges –no probation for him, I would turn the other cheek, he could get away with what he did to me and never have to hear another thing about it again. I just wanted my daughter.

In that moment I realized what needed to do. No one would agree with me, but I knew what I had to do in order to protect my family. I got my phone out and texted a classmate of mine, I was sure she could help. I took a deep breath and went back to Lana's hospital room.

I peak into the room to see that Lana has woken up. My mother is lying on the bed next to her reading a book. Never in a million years could I have imagined having a daughter as bright and as beautiful as Lana. Never in a million years would I have imagined being able to be this close with my mother again.

In the middle of this gray war, filled with hate and animosity I'm always reminded of what Aiden said to me on his porch back in Nebraska. He said that there would always be a light, a bright spot in every situation that I would have to focus on through all the murky fog. There were glimmers of joy and peace. Under the gritty sludge of anger and control there was an immaculate flower blooming from nothing. I could see the potential in my future, my family, my life. The fog was going to clear, the grass would be greener, and the water would be crystal clear.

I smiled and walked away, I had a very important phone call to make.

Chapter Eighteen: Team of One

Maybe this was the stupidest thing I'd ever done, but when your back is against the wall you have to make unsavory decisions. I stood in front of this big gray door. I wasn't nervous. Shockingly, not one thing in me made me feel scared. Maybe I should be scared? Maybe I should be nervous? The overwhelming sense to protect my family was overshadowing all doubt or fear I should be having.

I knocked twice. Standing there patiently, I could hear movement before the door finally opened. I clutched my hands around the mace in my purse, just in case.

"What the fuck are you doing here?" The scowl on his face is one I remember vividly.

"Oscar, we need to talk." My voice is calm and clear. I was able to find Oscars address through one of my college classmates whose father does background checks. It was actually scary how easy it was to find him.

"I have nothing to say to you." He nearly spat the words at me.

"But you seem to have a lot to say to everyone else." I am keeping my tone calmly tempered. I couldn't afford for this to go south. If Mrs. Pierce found out I came here she could drop me as I client. I had to play my cards right.

"You come here to shoot me?" The evil smirk on his face made me cringe. It was astonishing how you could literally see the devil in some people. It still baffles my mind that my mother didn't see it.

"No," I say. "You know I'm here about Lana."

He starts laughing and I had to suppress the rage that raced through my limbs.

"Yea, how's *our* little bastard?"

I had to swallow the venom to keep from screaming. His words reaffirming what I knew all along, he didn't want her. *Remain calm,* I told myself. *Think about the bigger picture.*

"Why are you doing this?" I ask him honestly.

"Doing what?"

"Trying to ruin her life?" Saying the words almost made tears fall from my eyes, but I had to stay strong. I had to speak on my little girl's behalf. "You hate *me* and that's okay, that is understandable, but she didn't do anything. You snatched her from one family and now you're trying to …."

"Snatch her from yours?" He interrupted. "You and that boyfriend of yours are still playing house, I see."

"Husband," I correct. And I don't know why I said it. I didn't need or want Oscar knowing anything else about my life. Oscar laughed again, but I couldn't get upset about it. I was here for a reason.

"If you want charges pressed against me for filing false documents, then fine I'll go to court. I'll do whatever, but you and I both know you don't want Lana. Let her have a chance at having a good life and a family who loves her. Relinquish your rights," I say. *"Please,"* I add softly. I hated that I was begging him for my daughter, but I had to do everything I possibly could to keep her with me.

"What do I get out of this?" He says. He takes a small step forward. "You said you'll do *whatever?"* He looks me up and down and suddenly I am transported back to a time in my life where I had to make myself feel small and invisible around him because watching his eyes roam my body made me want to scream, made me want to kill myself. I felt like I was seventeen again, afraid to come home, watching the clock because I couldn't step foot in that house a second before my mother got home.

"Oscar," my voice shakes. I take a step back. My fingers were gripping the mace even tighter. He started to laugh, a deep and dark laugh while finally making eye contact with me.

"Don't flatter yourself. I wouldn't touch your crazy ass with a ten foot pole." He sneers in disgust.

I exhale and quickly wipe a tear that managed to fall. I was realizing that maybe I *was* scared, and nervous, and downright terrified, but I was numb to it on my way here because I was on a mission. Flashes of the night he raped me flood my thoughts in an angry blur and it feels like my heart is trying to detach itself from me. I take deliberate breaths trying to calm myself down.

I was beginning to think this was a mistake, that there was no way what I had to say to Oscar would get through to him.

"You come in here with your puppy dog eyes, crying for that little *mistake* that you didn't even want until I said I wanted her. You tried to kill me in my own home!" He yelled. His booming voice snapped me back into real time. I felt slightly disoriented, hearing his loud voice, smelling him, seeing his face.

The memory of him violently slamming me onto my bed flashes by in a quick blur and almost knocks the wind out of me. I breathe out slowly.

I shouldn't be here.

"…and now you're asking for favors! I should call the police right now. I'm fearful for my life." He smiled ruefully. He was acting as if this were a game.

I took another deep breath in and breathed out slowly. He truly believed he was the victim in all of this. In this moment I'm realizing that he doesn't or can't see what he did to me and the fury is beginning to boil inside of my chest completely extinguishing any other emotion I was experiencing.

"*Why* do you want joint custody Oscar, just tell me why? I need to understand why we have to go through all of this? What's the point?" I can feel myself getting worked up. I was trying so hard to calm myself, but I was going through a myriad of different feelings. He was just looking at me with that disgusting smirk on his face and I wished I could rip it off. I took a deep breath in again.

"You're hopeless," I say exhaustedly. "What is in your brain that can't understand what you did to me? What you did to my family? I'm not here for pity, I'm not here to apologize and I don't want an apology from you. I just want you to go on with your life and leave my daughter alone!" I yell.

I couldn't hold it in anymore. "You won already Oscar, okay? You fucking won. I was weak, and I was quiet, and I let you get away with it. You won, if you want the power fucking take the power, it is yours – I'll drop the harassment charges and you'll never have to see my face again. Just leave my daughter out of this!" The tears that welted in my eyes were from pure anger.

He's still staring at me with that damn smirk on his face. The evil in his eyes are setting an uneasy aura over me. Nothing I am saying is getting through to him and I was an idiot to think it would.

"I want to see you lose everything." He says the words as a declaration, as if the anger was blistering him from the inside out. "I don't want you to experience happiness ever again. I want you miserable every single day until you take your last breath."

In this moment I felt like other than my hatred for him, there wasn't another person in this world who hated someone as much as Oscar hated me. He was wearing this disdain on his face blatantly. I believed every single word he'd just said. I wipe another tear.

"You walked around that house with your short shorts on and tank tops," he continued, "flaunting everything in front of me and then when it came down to it you wanted to play the victim."

I was in complete befuddlement listening to his false perception of what happened.

"Then you went and got pregnant, you should have aborted it, but you wanted to throw it in my face, you wanted something to hold over me. Because of you I've lost my job, my home, my wife, and I'm on disability. I don't give a fuck about you or your bastard kid, but if what I'm doing is enough to make you miserable then I'm going to keep doing it. If having to see my face every single week for the rest of your life brings you pain then I'll gladly do it with a smile on my face. If acting like I give a shit about that kid clears my name in anyway then I'm going to continue to do it. "

I stood there in utter shock and disgust. I felt weak, I was blinded by hate. What had he actually said? Did he truly in his heart and mind believe his words or was he just enjoying new ways to torment me? It hit me like a bus.

"You're a little naïve girl, Zoe. You played right into my hands. I knew that you would see that child and want to raise her and what better way to torture you for the rest of your life than to make you feed, clothe, and *love* the semen I put in you. Remember? I was *inside* of you. You can try and rewrite history and play house with your husband, but that kid is *my* daughter and she always will be." He leaned forward nearly snarling. "I could die tomorrow and for the rest of your life you have to think of me every single time you see her face. Every time she calls you mommy you will be reminded that I am her daddy and I was once yours."

Frozen and depleted. His words circled my thoughts repeatedly before I could breathe. My chest was so tight that I thought in that very moment I was going to collapse. The flood of tears streaming down my face made me feel light headed. What he said is what I feared this entire time, what Aiden said would happen before I got custody of Lana. I love my daughter, but I always had it in the back of my mind the fear of one day looking at her and only seeing what happened to me that night. Then what happens? It almost crippled me thinking that I could ever associate her with the darkest moment in my life.

232

"You…" my lips were trembling. I was trying to hold back the scream that was rumbling inside of me, the ache that his words caused. There was no way to respond, why was I here? What did I think I was going to accomplish. I was stupid and this truly was a mistake.

I didn't finish my sentence. I couldn't find the strength to force the words to come out. Another tear fell from my eye. I felt like I was dreaming, I didn't know what I'd done in a past life to be cursed with meeting this person.

"I'll see you in court." He slammed the door in my face. I was breathing heavily still trying to process what just happened. This entire time I thought this was about power, him wanting to feel like he still had control over me, but it wasn't *just* that. He just truly hated me and he was vengeful, that's all this has ever been.

He said he wanted to see me lose everything, even after death he wanted to feel like he'd ruined my life and if Lana's was ruined in the process it didn't bother him in the least bit. She was just a pawn in his game. This wasn't only about clearing his name, he wanted me to hurt.

My sadness quickly turned into fury, and something snapped inside of me. I banged on his door with both of my fists "Oscar!" I screamed. I was losing it as I kicked and yelled at his door. "You can't hurt me, you fucking bastard! You will *never* be her father!" I shrieked. He didn't answer. I felt so helpless. How did all of this spiral out of control so completely? I finally stopped, still breathing erratically.

I'd made it worse.

***

I unlocked the apartment door and could hear the television before I fully walked in to the living room.

"Look who is home!" Aiden said.

"Zoweee!" Lana said as she jumped off of the couch to hug my leg.

"Hey," I say and my voice cracks. "How does your arm feel?" A tear falls and Aiden is immediately next to me.

"Hey, Lana," he said. "Go sit on the couch. I have to talk to Zoe for a second, okay?"

She turned around and climbed back on the couch. She put the blanket over her and her giraffe and stared at the television.

"Why have you been crying?" His voice was a forceful whisper. "What happened?"

"You're just going to be mad and I can't take anymore yelling today." I try to walk past him but he blocks my way, trying to force eye contact.

"*Anymore* yelling?" He repeated, "Zoe, come on?"

I inhaled, I knew my night was about to get a lot worse. "We can't yell in front of Lana." I whisper back to him. Lana is in her own world watching her favorite cartoon, but I knew once Aiden found out where I'd been he would lose it. He nodded and waited for me to continue.

"I just left Oscars apartment."

I didn't know how to describe the look on my husband's face. I was forever grateful for my daughter being only feet away.

"Did he touch you?" He said through his teeth. I shook my head implying *no*, and quickly wiped a tear away. "Why…" he was having a hard time finding the right words. His hands were unsteady, his whole body nearly vibrating as he tried to contain himself "Why were you there by yourself, Zoe? Why were you there at all?"

234

"I thought that if he knew there wasn't a power struggle that all I wanted was Lana and nothing else that he would leave it alone. I told him I would drop the charges that none of it mattered anymore." Of course I'm crying because it's all I could do.

As I said the words aloud they didn't make as much sense as they had earlier today. "He doesn't see what he did to me, Aiden. He thinks I wanted it, he thinks I asked for it…" my voice was getting a little louder, he held me close to him trying to calm me. "He did all of this because he thinks it will help his case and he knew I would want her, he said he wanted me to be reminded of him every day when I look at her." I sobbed into his chest because that was and always would be my biggest fear.

"It's okay," he whispered in my ear. I can still hear the anger in his voice. "We are going to win this. He doesn't have a solid case, Zoe."

"He wants me to lose everything. He said I ruined his life and that he will keep doing whatever he has to do to make my life miserable. He doesn't care about her at all." My sobs are hard to control at this point. "It's never going to end." I whisper.

Aiden didn't say anything, he just held me and honestly that's all I wanted. There wasn't anything he could say that would actually make me feel better.

"I messed up," I say in his ear. "I know I did. I just needed to *do* something."

"Look at me," Aiden says, he grabs my shoulders and moves me from him so I could see his face. "At the end of the day he is bitter and angry. The judge will see that, you will tell them the truth and his rights will be relinquished. We have to stay positive for her, okay?"

Through his anger and frustration he managed to find words to say to me that were enough to placate the sorrow I was feeling at the moment. I could see the hate Aiden had for Oscar in his eyes. His

235

aura was not matching his words. He was obviously angry with me, but he was trying to support me at the same time. I didn't deserve him, I never have.

"I'm sorry," I say, he nods and doesn't say anything. "We can talk about this more when she is asleep." I add. I knew he had things on his chest he wanted to say, things that I know I needed to hear. Today I'd made a big mistake. I had to face that fact.

"Zoweee!" Lana calls out. "I'm thirsty."

"Okay," I say softly heading into the kitchen.

"Hey," Aiden grabs my arm before I could walk completely by him, "it's going to be okay."

I nod and walk into the kitchen.

I stood there in front of the refrigerator looking blankly off into space. My limbs felt like jelly. I think the adrenalin was finally wearing off. How insane was I? Had I actually gone to my attacker's home? Had I stood there in front of the person that altered my life, a person that I almost killed two years ago, had I actually stood there and demanded to be heard and acknowledged? I had to be certifiable, I felt sick and off balance, my chest was caving in. I grabbed a hold of the kitchen table, but it wasn't enough to stop me from crashing.

I don't remember falling, but I remember the impact. I felt my head slam onto the cold floor. Aiden's voice was muffled and my vision was blurry.

"I'm…" I begin to say, "I'm fine, just sleepy."

Aiden is saying something frantically, but I can't understand him. I just want to sleep. I feel him shake me, but I was finally able to drift off.

Chapter Nineteen: Grown Ups

"Hey," I hear Aiden say calmly.

I fluttered my eyes open, searching around the unfamiliar room. The walls were white, the lights were bright, and they hurt my retinas. I was able to turn my head just enough to see Aiden sitting there staring at me.

"Hey," my voice was groggy. I was so tired, I wanted to go back to sleep.

"How are you feeling?

I yawned and felt the bandage on my forehead move. "Oh God, better than I look, I'm guessing?" I touched the bandages and sighed. "What happened?"

He got up and laid on the hospital bed next to me, "You passed out in the kitchen. Your blood sugar was low."

I didn't say anything, I tried to think back to the last thing I remembered and all I could remember was Lana saying she was thirsty. "Where's…"

"In the cafeteria with your mom," He answered before I could even finish the question. "The doctor said he would be back in a few to tell us more."

Aiden sounded so somber. I could tell there was so much on his mind. I didn't know what to say to him. "I'm sorry." I say because I *was* sorry, for everything. "Lana isn't here. Just say everything you wanted to say. Get it all off of your chest."

"I don't want to do this here." He said lowly.

"Go ahead." I say. It was always better that we were honest with our feelings. I wanted him to say what he was thinking. "I don't want you to feel like you're holding anything in." He's quiet for a moment. I can see the wheels turning as he decides what he wants to say.

"In what world did you think it was logical or rational to go see Oscar? Alone? With no one knowing you were there? Do you know the danger you put yourself in? Do you know what I would do if he ever even *looked* at you the wrong way at this point?"

Aiden is trying so hard to keep his voice leveled, but I can see the fumes. I can taste the anger.

"Zoe, you act on impulse. Now that we have a child you can't do that. You have to consider every aspect of every single decision you make because it directly affects her. This isn't just about me being pissed or trying to prove a point…"

"You're right," I say lowly because he was right. "I really thought that I could fix this."

"I'm *in* this with you." He says as he grabs my hand.

"I know."

"No, you don't know because if you knew you would stop leaving me out. We are a team to the utmost definition of the word. How many times do I have to tell you that? Involve me –we are on the same side. Okay?"

I let his words resonate. He was right. I was so accustom to having to battle everything on my own even when I had people who wanted to be there for me like Matt, Alicia, and even Mrs. McCabe. I'd gotten so used to the bubble I'd created around myself that sometimes I didn't realize it when I reverted back to it.

I didn't get to respond because the doctor walked in.

"How are we doing?" He says as he walks in placing my chart on the counter.

"A little headache but I feel fine." I say. Aiden was still sitting next to me with my hand in his. I loved that even though he was angry with me, that even though we were technically in the middle of a fight, he was still my rock. He was still supporting me. Even though he is my husband, I'm still getting used to someone being there for me unconditionally and me actually allowing them to be.

"Well, we ran some tests to figure out why your blood sugar dropped so suddenly, and it appears that congratulations are in order." He smiled genuinely. His words went over my head. It's like I heard them, but missed the meaning by time my brain tried to process it.

"What?" Aiden said leaning up off of the pillow, his hand still wrapped around mine.

"You're pregnant." He said. The same smile on his face. I was on a delay. He was speaking another language. I was dreaming. Nothing made sense.

"Pregnant." Aiden repeated, shock in his voice, he looked at me but I still wasn't able to compute the information. I was pregnant. I was having another baby. I was having another child? Me?

"Wow," was all I could finally say. I was in wonder. It was all I could process. I didn't know if I was excited or was I supposed to be mad? Would I be able to fit my wedding dress? How would Lana react? What if she thought this new baby would take time away from her? I had too many questions and too many fears and all I could say again, but this time in a soft whisper was, "Wow."

"How far along?" Aiden asked his voice seemed so distant. So did the doctors.

"About seven or eight weeks," he said, "I'll let you two process this and I'll be back shortly." The doctor walked out of the room and

Aiden and I just sat there staring at each other quietly for what felt like forever.

Cosmically, something shifted in the room. In our locked eyes an underbelly of joy and happiness saturated our emotions. At the same time we both burst into cheerful laughter then hugged each other. We stayed like this for a few minutes, my tears drenched his shirt.

"We're gonna have two kids," Aiden says. "We need a bigger place." I can hear the joy in his voice, but he was right. We weren't prepared for another child, we were barely prepared for the one we had. I worked part time and went to school part time. Aiden worked fifty five hour weeks and went to school fulltime. If it weren't for his father and my mother helping us here and there we wouldn't be able to stay afloat.

"What are we going to do?" The logical worries I had couldn't overshadow how happy I was to have created life with Aiden. I loved him so much and to see it manifest into another human being was a breathtaking feeling.

"I don't know what we are going to do." Aiden answered honestly. "The only thing I can guarantee is that I will love all three of you with my entire heart for the rest of my life."

I smiled. I smiled a huge, genuine, and authentic smile.

I talked about the immaculate flower sprouting from nothing, under the sludge, during a gray war. I said that I could still see light despite it all –that the future would be favorable. *This* moment is what I was talking about. Though things are glim, and hurtful, and just downright depressing at times love can pull you out, having faith in the process can keep you on solid ground.

"Hey, how are you feeling?" I hear my mother's voice say as she slowly peeked around the corner with Lana right along with her.

"I'm great, come in!" I have a lot of enthusiasm in my voice for someone whose head is wrapped in bandages. "Lana, come here," I say with a smile. She walked over slowly as if she were afraid to touch me. "It's okay." I persuade.

"Did you hurt your arm too?" She asked me as she climbed up Aiden to get to the bed.

"No, but I do have exciting news," I say. "Mom," I look at her with a huge smile on my face. She looks at me incredulously as she sits down in the chair.

"We're having a baby!"

The look on my mother's face was almost enough to make me start crying again.

"What!" She exclaimed as she walked over to my side of the bed to hug me, and then she hugged Aiden. "This is just... this is wonderful." She happily cried onto Aiden's shoulder.

"Baby?" Lana asked confusingly.

"Yes, there's a baby in my tummy." I take her hand a place it there.

"Oh," she said. A confused look was still on her face. "Hi baby!" She said enthusiastically.

Right now as I sit here with my little girls palm on my stomach I so badly want to tell her that her baby brother or sister is in there, that she is going to be the best big sister in the world, but I can't say the words, not yet. This was one bright spot that was being dimmed.

"We should let Zoe rest," I hear Aiden say. "Let's go get some ice cream!"

"Yay!" She squealed jumping into his arms.

"Ice cream?" I say with a raised eyebrow, "It's like seven at night?"

"We are celebrating!" Aiden says with a smile. "Isn't that right Lana?" Her smile beamed across her face radiantly as she agreed. I sighed and didn't say anything as they left the room.

My mother was sitting back down in the chair, she was so quiet.

"Mom?"

"Yes?" She said distractedly finally bringing her attention to me.

"You okay?" I ask her, carefully positioning myself so I could sit up a little higher.

"Oh, of course," she wasn't being honest. My mother and I have worked hard over the last few months to restore our relationship, because of this I was more in tuned to her emotions and vice versa than previous years.

"Mom," I say with concern in my tone, "what's wrong?"

She stared at me, and then took a deep breath in. "This very moment is what I'd always imagined," her voice is barely a whisper, "you with a man who loves and cherishes you, and you telling me that you're pregnant. The joy that would fill my body finding out I was going to be a grandmother." She wiped a tear. "I love that little girl, Zoe." She added quickly, defensively.

"I know you love Lana, mom?" I was so confused. I didn't understand what was happening.

"You went through all of that alone." She finally said. I inhale, I wished my mother would stop letting the past haunt her so deeply. There was nothing we could do to change it now. "You're entire pregnancy I was just so mad and embarrassed and disgusted that my daughter was going to be a teen mom. I left you alone and then I didn't support your decision to give her up for adoption…every conceivable way I could've stepped up and helped you as a mother, I didn't."

"Mom…"

"I will never forgive myself for what happened to you and all that you have to go through now." She said the words with so much sorrow that I had to look up to prevent my tears from falling. "I'm sorry; this is a happy day and I'm souring it."

"Is it enough to tell you *I* forgive *you*?" I say. I'd never said that to her before, but I did forgive her. I mean, I wish there was a magic wand to wave and make our problems go away, but there wasn't. We were human and we were still working through a lot of our issues. Though I could never see what she saw in Oscar, I know how it feels to crave love, to be blinded by your emotions so thoroughly that it weakens your judgement.

She walked over to me and hugged me again. "Thank you," she cried onto my shoulder. "I love you, baby girl."

"I love you too." I whisper back to her, "…and so does your granddaughter."

She squeezed me tighter and I closed my eyes. There will always be a light …

Chapter Twenty: I do, again…

"You can't tell." My mother lies as she pulls at the waist of my dress.

"It looks like I'm smuggling a cantaloupe." I look in the mirror and all I see is stomach. "I found out I was pregnant so late with Lana because I barely showed the first five months, I look like I'm five months now and I'm three."

"You don't look five months," my mother lied again as she still pulled at my dress, "it's all in your head, you're paranoid."

243

Only six people besides the doctor knew that I was pregnant, me, Aiden, my mother, Lana, Matt and Alicia. I had a feeling seventy plus people were going to find out today.

"Maybe we can run to the mall and get something a little looser… I mean I don't think it's crucial that I wear *white* anyways." I say with a raised eyebrow.

My mother glared at me then rolled her eyes. "*One* we don't have time. We are under the two hour warning. *Two* this dress looks perfect on you and *three* I can't believe my baby girl is getting married." She said with a soft smile, her eyes glistening.

"Mom, we can't get emotional yet, okay?" I say, she nodded with the same heart melting smile on her face. We were still tugging on my dress in front of the mirror when the door opened.

"Hey fatty," I hear Matt say, and barely a second later I hear Alicia punch him. That's why she was my Maid of Honor.

"You just know how to make a girl feel pretty." I say sarcastically not even turning around to see them.

"Oh my goodness!" Alicia gasped as she walked over to me, her eyes watering. "You look like a freaking mermaid, you're beautiful!" She beamed.

"Thank you so much, Alicia." I smile genuinely. "We have a *show no emotions* rule going on," I add as I see her eyes welt more. "We can't freak out before the ceremony." I say calmly.

"It's a stupid rule," I hear my mother say as I catch her wiping a tear away.

It was weird seeing everyone get emotional. Maybe I should cry or act nervous. I was honestly just ready to eat and hang out with the people I cared about. Aiden and I had been married for six months already, nothing about seeing this dress, or putting the makeup on, or seeing the venue got me emotional. I'd already experienced the mecca of joy when I said *I do* over the summer.

"Sorry," Alicia said. "You just look happier than I've ever seen you." She smiled again. I grabbed her hand and squeezed it.

Matt clears his throat, "Okay, okay, as the person walking her down the aisle it is *my* duty to say the sweet words and make her smile and get all emotional and whatever." He grabbed my hand from Alicia's hands and looked at me right in the eyes.

"From the bottom of my heart," he began sincerely, "I just want to say… that I can barely tell you're trying to hide a pregnancy in that dress."

"Damn it, Matt!" I say pulling my hand away and hitting him, the same time Alicia hit him on the other shoulder.

"What? You're camouflaging very well! "

"Matt," my mother said while trying not to laugh. "You have the rings?"

"Yes ma'am." He says with confidence, he pulled them out of his jacket pocket to show her.

"How are your feet?" Alicia asked me. I remember on our real wedding day I'd accused Aiden of having cold feet, his corny response was the first thing to pop into my head.

"Walking on lava," I say with a smile. "I'm more ready than you guys could ever possibly know."

"Baby girl," my mother says as she walks up to me. "I have to go make sure everything at the church is set up properly, if you need *anything* call me. I gave Alicia my cell just in case …"

"Just in case what, mom?"

"I don't know, I just want everything to be perfect okay?"

I laughed and nodded, "We will see you in an hour."

***

My arm was wrapped around Matt's arm as we stood silently behind the closed church doors. He looked at me and then we both burst into laughter.

"Dude," he said.

"I know." I responded.

"I never thought I'd see the day where you would have a dress and makeup on," he shook his head. "You're about to get married... you're going to be Zoe *Jordan* in a few minutes." His voice was full of wonder.

I was silent for a moment and then I thought *why not*...it didn't matter at this point.

"Matt," I whisper, "I have a confession."

He looked down at me with furrowed eyebrows, "What?"

"I'm *already* Zoe Jordan." I say with a smile.

"Wait, huh?"

"Aiden and I are married already."

"What do you mean *married already?*" He asked, I tried so hard not to laugh.

"I mean, last week marked six months."

He just stared at me at first. I looked ahead waiting for the doors to open.

"Then why the hell am I wearing a tuxedo?" He whispered forcefully with surprise and mock anger in his voice. I laughed.

"We just didn't want to wait and my mom wanted to plan this big thing…" I look at him to read his face. "Plus, we *do* want the pictures and stuff to show Lana when she is older and now this little one." I put my hand with the bouquet on my slightly plumped stomach.

"I can't believe you didn't tell me," he said. "I'm hurt." His fake sad face is despicable.

"Well, now you're the only other person that knows aside from Lana." I wink at him. One more person actually knew, but he was irrelevant and I was not going to bring his name up on my wedding day.

"That makes me feel special," he said sarcastically. Before I could respond the music started playing, it was time. The church doors opened slowly.

"You ready?" Matt asked me.

I nodded, "More than I'll ever be."

We slowly began to walk down the aisle, everyone was on their feet. The faces of family members I hadn't seen in years, friends I hadn't seen since high school – I used the term friends loosely. I was absorbing everything about this moment. It was weird having people here to specifically celebrate Aiden and I.

I looked forward and saw my little girl standing there in a white dress, her curly brown hair in a tight bun. She fought my mother tooth and nail trying to get that thing in her hair. I smiled at her and it was almost as if she didn't recognize me. I didn't have too much makeup on, but I did look a far cry from the t-shirts and converses she's used to seeing.

In a trance I look over and see Aiden. I didn't even realize that I hadn't looked at him yet until this very moment when the air was almost knocked out of me. Aiden Jordan was already my husband, we'd already had an intertwined life together, but as I walk towards him I feel an overwhelming sense to run. Not run away from him, but to run towards him.

I see him standing there in his tuxedo and I realize why this wedding was important. It was one thing to devote ourselves to one another six months ago in private, but to declare our love for one another for everyone to see was such a powerful feeling.

Everything was a blur at this point as Aiden and I just stared at each other, the pastor said something, and then my mom said something, and then Matt placed my hand into Aiden's. We still hadn't broken our eye contact. It was amazing how much he and I were able to say without saying anything.

"I love you." I whispered to him as the wedding guests were taking their seats. I said it impulsively, in that moment I wanted him to know how deeply and madly I was in love with him. In Aiden's eyes I saw my future and I saw beamingly bright spots of my past, only the parts he was in. The anxiety and the nervousness that were nowhere to be found moments ago were now invading my body completely.

"I love you more," he said with a smile, his eyes wide and curious like it was the first time he'd ever seen me. "You're beautiful." The words were simple, but the passion behind them made me blush. I was still lost in this moment barely aware of what the pastor was saying or the seventy-six pairs of eyes looking at us. I see Aiden nod, and then reach into his jacket to pull out a piece of paper.

Crap, I need to focus.

Aiden and I decided that we wouldn't write our own vows that we'd keep the traditional ones, but here he was with something prepared.

"Zoe," he said softly, "I know we said we wouldn't write our own vows, but I just wanted to say a few things." He folded the paper and put it back in his pocket, he grabbed my hands as his eyes bore into mine. "Not even an hour into our first date and I knew that I was never going to date another person. We were both young and both stupid, but whatever it was between us was real. It was scary and intimidating and confusing, but I knew I wanted to spend the rest of my life figuring out why. In nearly three years I know that in you I have found a best friend, a safe haven, the love of my life. You, becoming my wife is my greatest accomplishment and the family that we have and will have is what gives me the motivation to keep going every single day."

My hands are trembling and my makeup is already ruined.

"You are the strongest person I have ever met," he continued. "There are people who could not have gone through half of what you've been through and still stand on their own two feet. So today, on our wedding day," he winked, "I'm vowing to always be there, to never disappear, and to be your foundation when things aren't going as planned. I will love you intensely, unapologetically, passionately and unyieldingly for the rest of my days. I will fight for you, I will fight for *us*. I will hold your hand while walking blindly into the unknown. I am yours and you are mine, thank you for being Zoe because without you, I couldn't be Aiden."

His words wrapped around me like a blanket. There are only two people in the room at this moment.

The pastor went onto speak, but I had to say something. I didn't know what I would say, but I needed him to know what I was feeling at this very moment.

"I want to say something," I interrupt the pastor. He nods and tells me to continue.

I take a deep breath, "I've had a lot of darkness in my life." I say, the tears are streaming down my neck, but I don't even try to wipe them, more will just take their place.

"So much darkness that I'd ruled out ever being happy. What makes that sad is that I was okay with it, I talked myself into believing some people just weren't granted that kind of joy in life," I squeeze his hand tightly, "but then you sat down at my table at lunch, you shared your cheeseburger with me, we had all the same afternoon classes, you asked me out on a date… you asked *me* a sarcastic and angry *me*."

I'm smiling through my tears as I speak. "You were like a tsunami, you came in and in one huge wave you washed away all the doubt I'd had. You drew that picture of me, a picture that I still have to this day –you drew that picture and identified a part of me that I was sure I'd been concealing. You shined a light on a part of me that was dormant and it made me fall for you."

Aiden is smiling, his eyes glistening.

"You saved me from myself, you didn't let me push you away, you didn't let me drown myself in my fear and anger –you saved me. You showed me that I was capable of love and of being loved. So, I'm vowing to *you* to continue being your best friend, continue being your safe haven because I am so thankful that you are all of those things to me." I sniffle before I am able to continue.

"You are the love of my life and I could never express in words how thankful I am that you left boring Nebraska to come to boring Ohio." He laughed. "I love you. I love you in a way that makes me want to cry just from saying the words. I'm ready to have that consuming feeling for the rest of my life. Thank you for showing this broken girl that even in the most trying times there will always be life after. There will always be a light. I'm never letting go of your hand."

I can hear the sniffling in the crowd, the crowd that I'd forgotten was there.

I felt so cliché, but I was lost in his eyes. I was lost in the possibilities of our future. I was lost in the *guarantee* of our future. At this moment there was no drama, or court, or arguing. I was standing here with my husband, my little girl behind me, and our unborn child and in this moment I knew that everything was going to be okay. We would face battles, we would have moments where it seemed impossible to move on, but we would come out on the other side. We had each other. We were always going to be okay.

He placed the ring on my finger and I placed the ring on his. Still, the pastor's words were just background noise for me at this point. I was so immersed in this one on one moment with Aiden that everything else around me felt obsolete.

"I do," I hear Aiden say fervently. I smiled, his words snapping me out of my trance.

"And do you take Aiden to be your lawfully wedded husband?" The pastor asked.

"I do."

"With the power vested in me and the state of Ohio, I now pronounce you Mr. and Mrs. Aiden Anthony Jordan. You may now kiss the bride."

His lips touched mine and though we were already married, there was something strengthening and prevailing and magical about this kiss. I hear the clapping and the cheering and I hear the music playing and I am realizing that I am so happy I let my mother talk me into this. I felt euphoric and happier than I'd ever been. I wanted to celebrate this union with every single person I knew.

When he pulled his lips away from mine he wiped my tears as his smile beamed brightly. "Wow," he whispered to me. "This was a good idea." His words confirmed to me that he was feeling what I was feeling, this moment was special and I would cherish it for the rest of my life.

Chapter Twenty One: Ours

I am on our bed flat on my back facing the ceiling. Aiden and Lana would be home any minute. I took a deep breath in, and then placed both of my hands on my stomach. I refused to shed a tear about something I knew was coming.

I just received an email from Mrs. Pierce saying that two weeks from today we had our first court date for custody of Lana. It had been such an abnormally long time waiting for a date that I'd managed to push it to the very back of my mind. It was easier to pretend that she was fully ours and that we didn't have to go to court. Mrs. Pierce was an amazing attorney she'd appealed Oscar's motion for joint and/ or visitation for as long as she possibly could. It was time.

I rubbed my rounded stomach; at least I was able to keep *this* baby safe. I was able to protect this baby from court, and lawyers, and sociopaths like Oscar. I hear the front door open and I inhale. It was going to be so hard telling Aiden this, even though he knew it was coming, I think he was like me he'd pushed it to the back of his mind. Lana was ours we shouldn't have to fight to keep it that way.

"Zoe?" I hear him call out. I hear Lana's little feet running up our small hallway.

"I'm in the bedroom," I call out. Seconds later he was walking in with Lana.

"Hey, I'm sorry were you sleeping?" He sat on the bed and kissed my forehead.

"No," I say softly. He looks at me for a few exaggerated seconds.

"Hey Lana, go in your room and set up the teddy bears, I think they want to have a tea party."

"Okay!" She yells as she runs out of our room to hers.

"What happened?" He asked as soon as she was out of earshot. I couldn't hide anything from my husband even if I tried.

"We got the email," was all I said. I was not going to cry, I would not cry.

Aiden is quiet for a moment. He got up and walked to the other side of the bed lying down on his back next to me, "When?" He asked.

"Two weeks from today."

We both sat there in welcomed silence, and then he grabbed my hand.

"The sooner we get this over with the sooner we can put all of this behind us and just enjoy our family. It's going to be okay."

"I know." I say.

"Aideeeeen!" We hear Lana calling from her bedroom. "It's ready!" she screamed.

I smiled and let go of his hand, he sat up and placed a kiss on my stomach before standing up. "Seriously, she's ours and only ours. Everything is going to be fine."

I smile and nod –very proud of myself for not letting these tears fall. I was almost six months pregnant and my emotions were all over the place. I'd been such a handful for anyone who'd come in a five mile radius of me.

I placed my hands back on my stomach and sighed again "Wait until you meet your big sister and your daddy, they're amazing." I said with a smile. Aiden didn't know that I did this any time I was alone with our baby. I would talk to him or her –we decided not to find out the sex, which I was beginning to think was a horrible idea –I would talk to the baby about everything under the sun. It felt peaceful to have that outlet.

Of course I talked to my husband, but I felt like I was able to bond with this baby. When I was pregnant with Lana, I was alone and angry and terrified and in denial. I didn't rub my stomach, I didn't get excited the first time she kicked, I didn't cry tears of joy when I got my first ultrasound. Everything was shrouded in regret and anger. When I look at Lana now it's hard to even comprehend how disconnected I was with her and myself back then. It feels like another life, like a completely different universe.

I look into her eyes now and I find peace. Sometimes I ask myself how I was doing this. One day would I look at her and only see the horror of the night Oscar raped me? I fear it with every fiber of my being. It would be what Oscar wanted to happen. I wouldn't be surprised if I were called crazy and insane for wanting to be a mother to her, but I couldn't see it that way. I loved her, I loved her so much. She was mine even through the anger and disgust of what happened to me, she was *mine*.

Over three years ago, I gave her away. It seemed like the only way so I hardly questioned myself, but today here I lay almost crippled with the thought of ever having to be without her again.

"Zoweee!" I hear Lana call out for me. I sit up slowly, one of my hands still rubbing my rounded and stretched stomach.

"Yea?" I call out.

"Can you make me food?"

I smiled.

I got up from the bed and walked to her room. Aiden was sitting on the floor in front of her bed while she stood at her pink kitchen that my mother bought for her third birthday. I wished I had my phone on me so I could take a picture. Aiden was a great husband, but he was an amazing father, I felt like he deserved awards for his attentiveness in both areas.

"Hey," I say sitting down on Lana's bed. "I can *tea party* it up, go study until dinner is ready."

He put his arm on my leg. "I think I have another fifteen minutes in me, and besides did you forget? You suck at tea parties," he whispered.

I laughed and nudged his arm off of my leg. "I'm sorry that I'm not as good with the fake accents as you are!"

We both laughed as our eyes stayed locked on Lana. She was walking back and forth placing fake food items on her little table. It was like we both stopped laughing to absorb her energy. Aiden inhaled and rubbed my calf, "she's ours," he said softly.

One tear fell and I wiped it away quickly. "Ours," I repeated softly.

***

My mother took Lana for the day. I didn't want her to be in court for any of this. The judge was rattling off things that I would only understand if I were a lawyer who passed the bar on the first try or something. I just wanted to scream.

I couldn't believe that the justice system had let it come down to this. I hated that my fear and my disgust caused me to make decisions that are now haunting me and my family. I keep rewinding to that night. I should've gotten up and called the police, and then my mother. I should've pressed charges. I shouldn't have sat on all of that for a year before snapping.

I had to take the stand today. I had to prove that I was raped and that my decision to lie about knowing the paternity of Lana was in order to protect myself, my family, and most importantly to protect Lana. I didn't understand why I had to do this, but Mrs. Pierce told me that Oscar's defense would be that it was consensual, that I didn't fear him, and that for my own reasons I gave the baby up for adoption. It all seemed so insane. I wanted Lana now, I needed her. That should be enough.

255

All of this seemed unbelievable and ridiculous. Couldn't they see what he was doing? Couldn't they see the maliciousness and callousness of Oscar, it blared from him even if I didn't know him.

Oscar was trying to stay immersed in my life, he was angry and he wanted revenge, he'd admitted that much to me. How was this not noticeable or plausible to anyone else? I was getting worked up just sitting here thinking about it. I turn to look at Aiden, he was always my compass. He would bring me back.

I turn and the look on Aiden's face is one that I wasn't familiar with and it scared me. He looked so furious and detached. My husband tried so hard to be strong for me that sometimes I forgot that I needed to be strong for him. I mouthed to him *It's all going to be fine* he nodded, but the look on his face did not change. I wish I could sit next to him and not Mrs. Pierce.

"I would like to call Mrs. Zoe Jordan to the stand," Oscar's lawyer says. I take a deep breath in as I stand up and walk towards the bailiff. I swear to tell the whole truth and nothing but the truth.

I sit down and the only person I can see is Aiden –my compass, my foundation, my life jacket. My nerves immediately start to calm down a little bit.

"Mrs. Jordan," his lawyer says, "you just recently got married correct?"

"Yes."

"Congratulations."

"Thank you." I felt like after every word I said I would look at Aiden for confirmation.

"Also, more congratulations are in order, I see you are expecting a child?"

"Objection," Mrs. Pierce says nonchalantly. "Relevance?"

"Your honor," his lawyer says, "I think it is very relevant to know how many siblings or who all is in the household with Lana."

"I'll allow it, but get to your point quickly Mr. Shur." Judge Waldron says. "Answer the question Mrs. Jordan."

I nod, "Yes, in three months."

Mr. Shur walks away and stands next to his table. "This will be your second child, correct?"

"Yes." I was already annoyed because I hated answering obvious questions.

"You did not want your first child?"

"Objection!" Mrs. Pierce yelled angrily.

"Mr. Shur, the wording of your question is speculation. Please rephrase. " Judge Waldron said.

It was like waves of fire shot through my veins.

"I'm sorry your honor," Mr. Shur said. "Mrs. Jordan, your first child you gave up for adoption?"

I nodded, I felt like my jaw was clenching so hard that it could pass for being wired shut.

"I'm sorry you have to verbally answer." He said.

"Yes."

It's quiet in the courtroom for a moment and I look back over at Aiden he looks like he wants to blow this entire building up.

"What were your reasons for opting for adoption?" he asked.

I took a deep breath in as I realized where this line of questioning was going. Oscar sat there staring at me, like he wanted to hear me say what happened, like he wanted to see me cry when saying the words. He was enjoying this. He was basking in the fact I would have to tell a room full of strangers something that I'd tried so hard to conceal before.

"I became pregnant after I was sexually assaulted when I was sixteen." I say the words clearly. I would not let him see me waver. I would not give him that benefit. Though the words burned my tongue, I wouldn't let him see that.

"You were allegedly assaulted by whom?" Mr. Shur asked.

"My mother's husband at the time, Oscar Doyle," Again, the words stung, but I said them.

"When was this?"

"February of 2013." I say.

Mr. Shur nods then walks towards me. "What happened that night exactly?"

There was a war within me, a war with wanting to let the flood of tears pour out of my eyes, but also wanting to be strong. It had been easier to say *Oscar raped me* I was able to say the words over the last couple years without flinching or gagging. There was a time when if the thought even crossed my mind I would get dizzy and sick. But never, not even one time had I ever had to say the details out loud of what happened.

Not even in the police report when I snapped and stabbed him in my mother's kitchen, I never gave details. I felt my calm and collective exterior faltering. I look over at Aiden and my heart drops because for the first time in our entire relationship I don't want him here. I don't want him sitting there as I give details of what happened to me that night. I can feel my hands starting to tremble –the sweat is starting to gloss my forehead.

258

"I..." I say lowly, but I feel like I am choking on my words. I couldn't do this. I felt like I was going to have a full blown panic attack. I was scaring myself because I thought I'd conquered this part of me, the dormant part that I always refer to. I thought I'd finally shined so many lights on it that it didn't exist anymore, but here I was reverting to the old me. The girl who couldn't use her words, the girl who was afraid of what her words would do. I looked at Aiden again and a tear fell from my eye. Damn it!

I just stared at him, wishing and hoping he could see and feel what I was thinking. The feeling was probably one of the worst things to ever experience –wanting Aiden near me but also wanting him out of the room.

"Mrs. Jordan," Mr. Shur said, "please answer the question. What happened on the night of the alleged assault?"

I looked at him then back at Aiden, something in his eyes shifted. His mood and his aura started fading into something else. He nodded then mouthed *It's okay, I love you* at that moment he got up quietly and walked out of the courtroom.

He knew that I didn't want him in here for this, my husband loved me so much that he knew that even after everything we'd been through there were still things in the darkest areas of my being that I didn't want to expose to him, because I knew they would hurt him just as much as they hurt me. It was truer now more than ever that his love for me gave me strength and confidence.

"It happened Feb 9, 2013 around 9:30pm." I say softly, I still have a few escaped tears on my cheeks, but it was okay. Aiden was on the other side of the door and though I couldn't see him, I could feel him. My compass was reeling me back in, my foundation was holding me in place, and my life jacket was keeping me afloat.

I inhale. I would say my truth, "My mom was usually home by 7pm, that's around the time I would get home from my best friend's house every day. The evening of February 8th my mother told me she would be picking up an extra shift the following night and wouldn't be home until around 2am."

As I am saying the words I'm realizing I've immersed myself back into that day and conversation. I can feel the apprehension tightening in my chest. I remember thinking it would be my first time in that house alone with Oscar and it made me feel uncomfortable. I remember wanting to tell my mom that but opting not to because I didn't want her stressing out about it.

"That night I got home at 7pm and Oscar and I got into a disagreement because he thought that I should've been home earlier to cook since my mom wasn't there." I remember that vividly. I remember thinking *who the hell was he?* He and I never got along we would rarely ever spoke and if we did it was a disagreement over something trivial or being fake polite for my mother's sake. "I told him I wasn't cooking and I went upstairs to my room for a while. I took a quick shower and laid down on my bed with my headphones in."

My heart is starting to race because I know I'm going to have to say these words. Words that I never wanted to say, ever. "I had my eyes closed and the music was blasting very loudly." I can feel my voice getting softer, my hands clenching as I sat myself right in that moment. "I felt like someone was standing there and I opened my eyes and he was right there."

"Who was standing there?" Mr. Shur asked.

"Oscar," I say. I'm sitting there quietly though I knew what was asked of me I was hoping I could leave it off there.

"Carry on, Mrs. Jordan?"

I inhale, "I sat up quickly and yanked my headphones out." I swallow and decide that I had to rip the band aid. Telling this courtroom what happened doesn't change the fact that it happened. "I told him to get out of my room and as soon as I said the words he pushed me back down onto the mattress. He told me that I had a big mouth and that I needed to stay in my place."

I bite my lip and blink slowly, "I couldn't believe that he'd pushed me or even touched me at all. I went to get up again but he…" I pause and look directly at him. It enraged me to know that as I sit here telling the world what happened –he knows exactly what happened and yet he thinks *I* did something wrong. "He grabbed me by the throat and slammed me down on the bed."

I remember the shock that traveled through me and even in that moment I *still* didn't realize what was actually about to happen. It all happened so quickly yet somehow still seemed like slow motion. "I couldn't breathe," I continued, "I struggled against his hands trying to scratch them and pry them off of me." I remember the panic I felt gasping for air. His grip was so tight I knew I was going to have bruises, I thought I was going to pass out. I thought he was going to kill me.

I pause. The visuals are flitting across my memory angrily and I am starting to feel depleted, but I knew I had to keep going.

"Then he put his entire body over me, laying most of his weight on me so I couldn't move. I was pinned." I exhale.

Surprisingly, I'm not sad and distraught as I say the words, not like I thought I'd be –I'm furious, I'm full of hate and just pure unmitigated anger. "It clicked, I realized what was happening and I tried to scream, I started kicking and hitting him, but he kissed me roughly trying to muffle my voice, his hand was still gripped around my neck."

I remember what it felt like to try and scream. My own muffled cries for help haunted me for the first few months after. I never felt more voiceless and helpless in my entire life. "I bit his lip and he lifted up and slapped me." I remembered feeling relieved that he hit me because he released my throat and took some of his weight off of me –I could breathe.

261

"I gasped then started screaming again and begging him not to do this. He put his hand over my mouth and told me to shut up. Then he yanked my towel off."

I stop speaking as more moments flashed across my memory. The pain, the loneliness, the confusion, the hate…the drowning…

I clear my throat and exhale a shaky breath before continuing. "I was still begging him, pleading with him not to do this." I wiped a tear. "I was able to get one hand loose from his hold, I tried to jab at his eye and push with all my strength to get him off of me. He yelled something, I can't remember what exactly. Then he yanked off his belt and tied my wrists together before tying them above my head to my bedpost." I swallow. I breathe a hollow, shaky breath and wipe tears from my cheeks with both hands.

"Then he raped me, twice."

My naked body pressed underneath this 275lb man. My mother's husband. I remember feeling like I was in a vortex, it was as if I'd left my body and was watching what was happening to me through tunnel vision in another realm. His hand was still over my mouth as he raped me, as he called me every single explicit name imaginable. My tears were pouring out of my eyes uncontrollably. I wouldn't have had the strength to scream again anyways, what good would it have done?

I was so depleted and sinking beneath the current on a planet I was unfamiliar with. I remember closing my eyes and thinking I wanted to die. I didn't have another thought in my mind except wanting to die. I *needed* to die. What other possibilities did I have?

There wasn't an *after* for me. I was shattered, I was suffocating. I told myself if I just kept my eyes closed it would soon be over. If I just focused on the fact that this moment could not last forever I would survive …but *surviving* felt like the punishment, not the gold at the end of the rainbow.

He moved his hand from my mouth his sweat dripping onto me as he panted in my ear. "I don't hear your smart ass mouth, now?" He breathed angrily before putting his hand back around my throat. "If you bite me again, I'll kill you," his husky voice full of contempt and hate. He crashed his lips onto mine and I did nothing. He forced his tongue into my mouth and I did nothing. I realized the more I fought him the more he hurt me, the longer this would last. So I just laid there, numb, crying, eyes closed, and *drowning*.

I exhaled raggedly when I thought it was over. He crashed himself on top of me breathlessly and just laid there for a moment. My eyes were still closed, but my tears were still managing to boil out. My hands and body were still restrained. He rose up from me slightly and I exhaled again because I was realizing that I'd somehow made it to the *after* –the *after* that seemed so far away minutes ago.

That odd sense of relief was quickly erased when he suddenly flipped me over violently, my wrists bending in an awkward angle from the belt tightening. The leather was pulling painfully at my skin. He pulled my hair roughly and I screamed out, I thought my neck was going to snap. *What if he was really going to kill me?* I remember thinking. I'd talked myself into being okay with it if he did.

I never wanted to have to think about this again and if he killed me I never would.

"Shut the fuck up!" He yelled pulling my hair harder. I sobbed soundlessly –the pain in my neck was excruciating. More tears fell recklessly down my cheeks soaking my face, chest, and my pillow.

I thought that maybe I was wrong; this was never going to end. It would be hours before my mother would be home and my mother worked six days a week. This could happen again? This was going to be my life now? I didn't think it was possible, but I started to cry harder. I was nearly hyperventilating when he began raping me again. "Shut. The. Fuck. Up!" He yelled. He was rougher and angrier than he had been the first time.

The pain was indescribable, but I was almost numb to it now. I felt like a rag doll, I didn't feel like a human being anymore. I was a destroyed outer lining of who I once was.

Just kill me, please kill me I thought, I almost said the words aloud.

He stilled and then yelled out in my ear huskily. He shoved my face forcefully into the pillow, his hot breath on my neck making me squirm. He just laid there on top of me, *inside of me*, for a few more moments before speaking again, "Go clean yourself up before your mother gets home." He says, finally removing himself from me.

He untied the belt from my bedpost and wrists then flipped me back over to my back. He smiled down at me, that evil smile that makes my blood boil to this day and kissed me, his tongue invading my mouth again while his hand gripped my throat and jaw. I was emotionless, staring blankly ahead not able to do anything.

He finally got up, pulled his pants up, and walked out of my room slamming the door behind him. I just laid there naked drenched in my tears, his sweat, and my blood. I didn't move. I couldn't move.

I was frozen in hell.

I laid there on my bed for over two hours, too afraid to leave my room until my mother got home, afraid that he was going to come back for more.

My mother.

I remember an image of her smile flitting across my memory –her smile was always the brightest when she was looking at Oscar. I immediately decided I couldn't tell her, I couldn't destroy her. I couldn't tell anyone. I would take this to my grave. I remember getting angry at the fact that Oscar assumed I wouldn't say anything, I hated that he was right.

For those two hours I didn't move, I didn't speak, I waited. I didn't think about anything else my mind had gone completely blank until I heard the front door open. My mother was home. She was going to walk in and kiss her husband, her husband whose lips had just been all over her daughter two hours ago. She was going to hug him and ask him how his day was and he was going to leave out the part where he violently raped her sixteen year old daughter. She was going to be happy and remain happy because she deserved a happy ending more than I did.

More tears pool out of my eyes, but I am still numb. No expression, no anger, or fear anymore –just empty.

I remember slowly getting up. Every inch of me ached and throbbed. I yanked the stained sheets off of my bed and rolled them into a huge ball. I walked over to my closet and put the sheets in the far back behind all of my clothes. I grabbed an old robe and walked into the bathroom. I turned only the hot water on in the shower, the entire bathroom was gray from steam.

I stepped into the shower and let the scorching hot water burn my skin. I just stood there unmoving for about fifteen minutes before I started scrubbing. I scrubbed until my skin was raw and scratched. Red blotches scattered all over my body, some were bruises.

The soap wasn't strong enough. The water wasn't hot enough. I was disgusting, I was filthy, and damaged, and destroyed. I remember collapsing to the bottom of the tub, pain shooting sporadically through me. I sat in the corner of that tub as the hot water splashed wildly all over me and I sobbed. I cried so hard that I became dizzy. I hated myself. I didn't want to be Zoe anymore. The physical pain was one thing, but the ache that traveled through my psyche was paralyzing.

I needed to scream until I was blue. I needed to scream until I had no voice left to speak. I needed to scream so loudly that every window in my neighborhood shattered. No one had heard me when he was inside of me, no one heard me begging and pleading for him to stop. *No one heard me.*

I wanted to pour gasoline over his sleeping body, light a match, and watch him burn.

I snap out of my memory and absorb my surroundings. That day seemed so far away, so much had changed, so much had happened, but I was still standing. I was stronger, I wasn't voiceless. I didn't hate myself anymore. I was a wife, a mother, a daughter, a student. I was happy and there was nothing Oscar could do to take those things away from me no matter how hard he tried.

Though the tears were falling down my cheeks he hadn't broken me. I did it, I said what happened and I didn't fall apart. I was still here and he was a monster who wanted so badly to relish in my sadness.

Mr. Shur walked back and forth for a few exaggerated seconds before finally speaking.

"Without your mother around, how many *one on one* encounters or conversations did you and Mr. Doyle have before any sexual contact?"

"Ummm," I say shaking my head, "none." My mother was always there. I'd already said that was the first time we'd ever been alone in that house together.

"How many times had you met him before he married your mother?"

"Not too many times, maybe five." I say almost confusingly not seeing why that mattered at this point in the trial.

"In the year leading up to the sexual contact how many conversations had you both had about school? You know, simply *teenager stuff* in general?"

"Objection," Mrs. Pierce said exasperatedly. "What is the relevance?"

"Counsel?" Judge Waldron said.

"I'm trying to see at what point Mrs. Jordan disclosed her age to Mr. Doyle."

I looked at him confusingly and then at my lawyer who was already shouting objection. This was the card that was going to be played. Mrs. Pierce already told me that it wasn't a defense that I didn't have to worry about that catching wind, but here I was moments away from it being a focal point of this trial.

"New line of questioning Mr. Shur," Judge Waldron orders. "Being negligent of the law is not nor will ever be a defense, especially in my courtroom."

Mr. Shur cleared his throat, and then walked directly in front of me.

"The night of the sexual contact, you said you were wearing a towel?" Mr. Shur said.

"Yes."

"Was your door opened or closed?"

"I think it was closed." I say.

"You *think* or you *know*?"

"Objection, badgering." Mrs. Pierce said.

"Sustained,"

"Okay," Mr. Shur said, "you can say that you are not 100% sure if your bedroom door was opened or not?"

"I think it may have been cracked…"

"So, you were lying in only a towel with your door open?"

"Objection, your honor," Mrs. Pierce said again.

"Where are you leading counsel?" Judge Waldron said.

"My client says that the events that took place that night were consensual and that Mrs. Jordan was actually the initiator." Mr. Shur replied. "When he was hesitant she told him she was eighteen and that she wouldn't tell her mother."

I looked at Oscar and he had a glimmer of a smile in his eyes. I was going to throw up. I was going to pass out. Mrs. Pierce tried to prepare me for this, but he had an elaborate story. He'd created a Zoe in this scenario that would never exist in any realm or parallel universe.

"What?" I say exasperatedly and in disbelief. I feel disoriented and confused.

"Your honor," Mrs. Pierce says, "to tell this narrative in the middle of a custody hearing, to accuse someone who was *sixteen* when the assault occurred is barbaric."

"Mr. Shur," Judge Waldron said, "if you are planning on calling Mr. Doyle to the stand you can ask these questions. Our focus *today* will be solely on why Mrs. Jordan felt the need to sign the papers to have Lana Hill put up for adoption without Mr. Doyle's signature and to see who is fit to take custody, reel it in."

"Her reasoning's are the whole basis of my questioning your honor," Mr. Shur rebutted. "I'm trying to show that this was a girl who panicked and lied. She did not put that child up for adoption out of fear or resentment towards my client because it was consensual and had he known the child was his he would've stepped up to take care of her. Mrs. Jordan ripped my client's rights away, robbing him of the opportunity to be a father to Lana Hill."

The room was spinning and the air was not circulating. *I* robbed *him*? I ripped *his* rights away? Being pinned to my bed, my arms restrained over my head, Oscar hovering over me. Those images flood my thoughts again and I feel weak and confused. My breath hitches and the tears are falling one by one.

I had to find my center somehow. I had to grip onto something because reality was slipping from my fingertips.

"New line of questioning," Judge Waldron said and this time he seemed to have frustration in his voice. Mr. Shur sighed, but nodded in agreement.

"So you've had custody of Lana Hill for quite some time now?"

"Yes." My voice cracks. I'm still trying to process everything that was said. I'm still trying to erase the images of Oscar on top of me from my memory.

"It's been quite an adjustment for you and your husband?"

Somehow through the murky haze of this trial just thinking about Lana made a soft, yet timid smile appear on my face, "Yes, it's been an adjustment, but wonderful all the same." I was able to focus my thoughts on my daughter. Her beautiful smile and sweet spirit were able to bring me back. I exhale.

"You're pretty young, especially to raise a child. Let alone two, wouldn't you say?"

Something about Mr. Shur rubbed me the wrong way. Maybe it was the fact he was asking ridiculous and nonsensical questions. Maybe it was the fact he was defending a monster and deep down I knew he knew his client was a guilty snake. I could feel the acid overflowing in my mouth.

"Well it was never my plan to be raped by your client at sixteen and get pregnant. So yea, I'd say that's pretty fucking young." I say angrily.

I spat the words out like they were daggers. For a moment I fell back into the sarcastic snarky teen Zoe who would ward off intrusive questions with dismissive and blunt remarks. I hadn't been *her* in a while. It was weird to be reacquainted with her so suddenly.

269

"Mrs. Jordan," Judge Waldron banged his gavel, "would you like a ten minute recess?"

I took a deep breath in as I looked at my lawyer, I could detect sympathy in her eyes.

"No, I am fine your honor. I apologize for my language," I blink and look back at Mr. Shur. "Yes, I am young, but I am a good mother and Aiden is a good father."

Mr. Shur smiled curtly before continuing, "I'm sure you are." He grabbed a folder off of his table and handed it to me. "Could you open this and explain what this picture is?"

"Objection, your honor I have no clue what this is and it should've been disclosed before the trial." Mrs. Pierce was visibly upset.

Mr. Shur grabbed two more identical folders handing Mrs. Pierce one and Judge Waldron one. She opened hers immediately and the look that shot across her face made me feel nauseas.

Judge Waldron placed the picture back in the folder and nodded, "I'll allow it." I looked at my lawyer and all she did was nod, but her eyes looked like they were a mixture of anger and sadness.

The confusion and nervousness that traveled through my body was almost enough to paralyze me. My hands shakily opened the folder and inside was a photo of Lana, her tear soaked face, her shoulder exposed as a fresh first degree burn rested on her right shoulder. I took in a quick gasp of air and looked directly at my lawyer. I felt disoriented again.

Miss. Ramsey had to take the photo for Lana's file and I was told repeatedly that the accident wouldn't affect this hearing. Rage was boiling inside of me, but fear was the most dominant feeling. I needed Aiden.

"Can you explain what happened here?" Mr. Shur said. His voice was smug and if I wasn't pregnant, if I wouldn't end up in handcuffs, and if it wouldn't affect this hearing, I wanted to reach out and slap him with all of my might.

"She stood on her Barbie stool and pulled a pot of water from the stove." I say angrily.

"Boiling water?"

I inhale, "Yes."

"Where were you? Where was your husband? How was a two year old able to injure herself like this in your temporary custody?"

My hands were trembling and my mouth was dry. "We stepped into the next room, briefly." I say weakly.

"You left a toddler unattended with a pot of boiling water?"

"Objection," Mrs. Pierce said, "she has answered this question already."

"No further questions your honor." Mr. Shur says and walks away to sit down. Oscar's eyes are almost glowing in delight and triumph. I'm still trying to find my placing. This is what was going to happen. A picture of me so unbelievably unfavorable was going to be painted. How was this happening? I didn't seduce Oscar, I didn't lie about my age, and I wasn't a bad mother. I could feel me spiraling scarily close to the edge. My vision was blurry and I wasn't sure if it was from the tears or the anger and hate encompassing me fully.

There was no evidence of what happened, just his words, my words, and Lana existing. I hated that I couldn't change so many things that I should've done. I wanted to go home. I wanted to lay on my bed cuddled next to Aiden and Lana like we did every Saturday morning for the last few months. I wanted to be anywhere but here.

Of course what was being said about me wasn't true, but I was so thankful my mother and Aiden were not here to hear all of this.

"How are you feeling today, Zoe?" Mrs. Pierce said as she stood, pulling me out of my deep thought.

"I feel fine," I say, my voice is shaky and uncontrolled. I wasn't fine, I was far from fine. Mr. Shur's questioning was permanently in court records and permanently etched in my mind. It would stay in both places forever and there was nothing I could do about it.

"When did you find out you were pregnant with Lana?" Her voice was so calm and welcoming. She saw that I was in the middle of losing it. She was trying to pull me back in.

"Towards the end of July 2013," my voice is still shaky and distant.

"So you were what, almost six months pregnant before you found out?"

"Yes."

She walked towards me and nodded. "I could imagine how shocked and scared you were?"

"Objection," Mr. Shur said, "are we getting to a point?"

"Counsel, are you?" Judge Waldron directed towards Mrs. Pierce.

"Absolutely, your honor," she answered swiftly. "We are painting a picture of her thought process leading up to the birth of Lana."

"I'll allow it."

She looked at me and nodded, indicating I could answer the question.

"Yes, I was terrified. I didn't know what to do."

"At the time Mr. Doyle was the only one you'd had sexual contact with?"

Hearing the words were almost worse than saying them. "Yes," I say fighting back the bile.

"You're sixteen and you've just found out you are pregnant by your stepfather. How did you feel?"

I took in a deep breath and closed my eyes before being able to speak. "I wanted to terminate the pregnancy, but decided I would have the baby and give it up for adoption," I sniffle wiping a tear. "I knew I had to tell my mother that I was pregnant, but I couldn't tell her by whom."

"And why was that?"

I bite my lip because now I'm trying to hold in a sob. "I knew how much she loved him. I didn't want to break her heart." My voice cracked over that last sentence.

Mrs. Pierce walks over to me and hands me a tissue. "I'm sorry."

I nod and wipe under my eyes.

She continued, "You decided adoption would be the best option?" She reaffirmed.

"Yes."

"At any point during your pregnancy did you consider keeping the child and parenting her?"

I thought back to a rainy fall day in October, I was eight months pregnant. I remember I was lying on my bed crying. I had just gotten back from a doctor's appointment and they told me how much the baby weighed and that I was barley four weeks away from my due date. I'd had other appointments before, but for some reason on that day this baby finally seemed *real*.

I'd gotten used to pushing the fact that I was pregnant to the back of my mind. I didn't think about the baby I wanted to act as if everything were the same. My mother was the only reason I even went to the doctors. I honestly was so detached that I just wanted to push it out and go back to school. But on that day in October she was kicking so much, more than she ever had in the previous months and I fought the urge to rub my stomach, I refused to acknowledge it was there.

As I laid there on my bed I thought about all the people who told me to keep the baby, who told me they would help raise it. My mother being the biggest advocate, she went from being angry, disgusted, and disappointed in me for getting pregnant to wanting to take the baby and raise it until I was old enough to support us.

I hated that I couldn't tell my mother that the reason I didn't want the baby wasn't because I was young, but it was because it was her husband's baby, that he'd raped me. It was like my mouth was super glued shut, I couldn't even fathom saying those words to her –they weren't an option.

I laid there on that bed and for five minutes I tried to picture keeping that baby, raising it, caring for it, *trying* to love it. Every time I tried to picture holding it I pictured Oscar, it terrified me. I couldn't love something that came from that. I never knew how wrong I could be. Just thinking of my Lana brings a smile to my face. The exact opposite of what I feel when I think of Oscar. He may be part of her DNA, but Aiden was and is her father. That was never going to change.

"Yes, but there was no way looking at the situation that it could've worked or been healthy." I finally answer.

"Healthy? Can you elaborate?"

"I knew I was stuck in that house until college and that there was nothing I could do. I made sure I was never home when my mom wasn't home. I locked my bedroom door every single night. But if I

274

had a child, if I had her in the same house as the monster who raped me…"

"Objection!" Mr. Shur yelled, "Allegedly."

"Continue Mrs. Jordan." The judge said.

I sighed and continued. "I just knew that it would not be good for her to be around him. Had I known I could love her as much as I do I would've done things differently. Had I known I could look at her and not think about that night or see Oscars face I would've rubbed my stomach and spoke to her like I do during this pregnancy. I would've held her when she was born, I would've named her. I would've cried tears of joy instead of sadness… I would've *kept her* if I knew what I know now. I would've reported everything that happened." I pat the tissue under my nose and sniffle. "I would've told my mother so she didn't have to waste another year of her life with him."

Mrs. Pierce nodded with a pitied smile. "You know I'm a mother of two. My boys are adults now."

"Objection," Mr. Shur sounded annoyed, "relevance?"

"Where are you going with this Mrs. Pierce?" Judge Waldron.

"This is just one mother speaking to another mother about experiences, your honor."

"I'll allow it. Get to your point quickly." He ordered.

"Thank you," she said, looking back at me. "When my youngest son was five he was into karate and combat fighting, typical boy stuff." She smiled. "I was so exhausted, I was studying for the bar, and raising two kids trying, to be a good wife, but I just needed a break. I'm sure you can relate?"

I nod. We hadn't discussed this prior to the trial so I had no idea where she was going with this.

"I somehow managed to fall asleep on the couch. It wasn't even two minutes that I closed my eyes. I thought my boys were in their rooms playing and suddenly I hear a loud crashing sound and then a scream. I hopped up and ran faster than I'd ever run before to see my five year old lying at the landing of the steps screaming. His elbow was nearly bent the other way." She walked towards me.

"My little boy tried to jump down fifteen steps and ended up breaking his arm and fracturing his ankle. I panicked and I cried and I just thought I was the worst mother to have ever lived. Had I not dozed off, had I been there to stop this he wouldn't be in pain."

She looks me right in the eyes. "My youngest is now in his second year at Howard University. He doesn't even fully remember that day even though I remember it so vividly. I'm telling you this because *all* parents have regrets, and make mistakes and feel guilty or responsible. Every child will have accidents. *None* of those things make you a bad mother. None of those things is enough to take a child from their mother."

My tears were swimming down my cheeks because I'm realizing Mrs. Pierce did that for my benefit, she didn't have a question she was going to ask. She lied about that so she could tell me this story in front of the judge. She knew that a day hadn't gone by that I didn't feel guilty about that accident. I was so thankful for her and her story.

"No further questions your honor." She says serenely as she walks away.

I close my eyes and exhale slowly.

***

When I walked out of the court room Aiden was standing there waiting for me. We didn't speak, I just ran to him wrapping my arms around him. He held me for a few moments. I've had a lot of hard days in my life, but today was definitely one of the hardest. I felt more exposed than ever. I spent the last few years digging up things that I'd buried deep underground, but today everything came to light. I felt almost as violated and naked as I did the night Oscar raped me.

"I'm sorry," I whisper into Aiden's chest.

"What?" he says, "don't you dare apologize. This isn't about me Zoe."

"I don't want you to think that I can't tell you everything because I can," I was still sobbing into his chest. "It's just with him sitting right there and…"

"Zoe," he said pulling me from him so he could make eye contact with me. "Stop. I don't need an explanation. I'm here to support *you* and whether that means ten feet away from you or in the next room."

I nodded, and then hugged him again. It was quiet for a moment. "How do you think it went?" Aiden asked.

"He's claiming I was the initiator. That I lied about my age." It was hard to say the words. Aiden didn't say anything, but I could feel his body tense up. "They're painting this picture of me and I just have to sit there and listen and it enrages me because he and I both know what happened." I say all of that in one breath. "I can see how much he is enjoying this, he said he would."

"The judge isn't going to believe any of that." Aiden's voice is clipped and angry. I know there was so much he wanted to say, probably things he wanted to do, but he was staying calm.

"They brought a picture of Lana's burn. He basically called me a bad mother. He said I was too young to parent two kids."

"That's bullshit," Aiden said furiously, "you're a great mother, Zoe. You know all this crap they're slinging is not going to change anything. He's not going to get her based off of that."

"He's testifying next," I say softly. "How am I supposed to sit there and watch him lie about me?" I felt so defeated. I felt like instead of Oscar being punished for his actions I was being punished for my inaction. I was being punished for keeping silent for over a year. I was being punished for giving my daughter up for adoption. I was being punished for not wanting to fight for the Hills when Emilia was alive even though I kept vowing that I would.

All my mistakes were being broadcast, all my poor decisions were being thrown in my face left and right all while I had to sit there and watch Oscar smirk at me.

"Do you want me to stay out here or go inside with you?" Aiden says, pulling me out of my thought.

I knew that whatever Oscar had planned to say about me would be graphic, but I also knew it would be false. I wanted Aiden by my side. As hard as it was going to be for me to hear these things, I knew in my heart the truth and I had to hope and pray the truth would prevail.

"If you can handle it, come inside. If not I understand."

He kissed my forehead and grabbed my hand. "I love you, *always*. You do know that at this point?" He said. That was his way of telling me that though there are parts of me that I'm scared for him to know –he will always be there. He will always love me. I felt silly wanting him to leave when I testified. As scared as I was, I never wanted there to be anything Aiden didn't know, even this.

I smiled lightly and wiped yet another tear. We walked into the doors.

Aiden kissed me on the cheek. "*You* know the truth, remember that, okay?" He whispered in my ear. I nodded then he took his seat. I didn't want to let go of his hand. I walked over to Mrs. Pierce and sat down next to her.

"Are you going to be able to handle this?" She leaned over to ask. I inhaled. I'd had an outburst before in court, but I had it under control. I just had to repeat what Aiden said, *I knew the truth*. I wouldn't let Oscar's words hurt me.

"Yes, I'm fine." I say lowly. I hate how small I felt. I felt like a spec on a wall. My emotions and the enormity of this situation were sitting heavily on my shoulders. "Thank you for what you said." I say softly to Mrs. Pierce, she doesn't answer she just gives a subtle nod then looks forward.

"All rise." the bailiff said. Judge Waldron walked in then told us to be seated. Mrs. Pierce stood up and called Oscar to the stand. He limped to the stand with a cane in his hand. If I felt small he was too. My memories of him have always been this shadow of man, huge and scary, but now when I look at him he looks feeble. It made it easier to not be afraid of the lie he was about to tell.

"Mr. Doyle," Mrs. Pierce said, her tone was strong and stern. I hadn't heard this side of her before. "When did you meet Kimberly Oakley?"

"October 2011," He answered. His voice was light, not the angry snarl that plays in my memory when he pops up unwelcomely.

"When did you marry?"

"February 6, 2012."

"Hmm," Mrs. Pierce nodded. "So, almost a year to the date later you raped your wife's teenaged daughter?"

"Objection!" Mr. Shur yells.

"Withdrawn," Mrs. Pierce says quickly. "How many times had you met Mrs. Jordan before you moved into her home with her mother?"

"A hand full of times, I don't know." His tone isn't as light as it was before. Mrs. Pierce had pushed a button. One thing I knew about Oscar was that he couldn't escape his temper.

"How would you describe your relationship with Mrs. Jordan leading up to the night in question?"

"I know it was wrong. Looking back at it now, but we had chemistry in the brief moments we were around each other that neither one of us could deny. Never in a million years did I think she and I would have an intimate relationship."

My heart stopped, then started up again beating quadruple the speed. What did he just say? Is he trying to say we had a relationship? I felt like I was going to throw up. I placed my hands on my swollen stomach and closed my eyes. I had to replay Aiden's words in my head *"You know the truth"*

"Mr. Doyle, what exactly are you implying?" Mrs. Pierce's voice sounded like she wanted to scream.

"I'm not implying anything. She and I had an inappropriate relationship for weeks leading up to the sexual intercourse."

"She was sixteen years old, Mr. Doyle."

"As my lawyer stated I believed she was eighteen."

"Mr. Doyle, you want us to believe that your wife never once mentioned her daughter was sixteen?"

"She did not." He answered matter of fact.

"You're basing your whole defense on her allegedly omitting her age?"

"She didn't omit her age. She verbally *told* me she was eighteen."

I could hear what he was saying, but I had to keep repeating Aiden's words, if I didn't, if I let what he was saying seep into my conscience for just one second I would start screaming, I would lose it, I would be arrested.

"You understand that feigning ignorance is not a defense?" Mrs. Pierce said angrily.

"Objection," Mr. Shur said impatiently.

"Move it along Mrs. Pierce." Judge Waldron ordered.

"When did you find out about her pregnancy?" Mrs. Pierce's voice is clipped.

"In July 2013," he answered, "I remember pulling her to the side and asking if the baby was mine. I knew that she had a few boyfriends here and there. She was definitely not a virgin when we were together. I wanted to take responsibility if it was mine, come clean to Kim and tell her about our relationship, but she got scared and screamed and said I wasn't the father. She decided to end it that day."

You know the truth, you know the truth, you know the truth I kept repeating as tears streamed down my face.

"*Decided to end* what?" Mrs. Pierced asked.

"Our physical relationship," Oscar stated plainly.

"Are you claiming that there was more sexual contact after the night of Feb 9, 2013?"

"Yes," he answered assuredly. It felt like the wind had been knocked out of me. I was grasping onto whatever little air I could get into my lungs.

"We were in an actual physical relationship. Look, I know the age difference was a problem, but the only thing I did wrong was cheat

281

on my wife. I shouldn't have disrespected her or our marriage. Had I known she was sixteen this would have never happened. Zoe and I had a strong connection and it got out of control for a while and I wish there were things I could change, but she lied to me more than once. Lana is my daughter and I deserve to be in her life."

In the split second it took for me to hear the words I was snapped out of my rage when I heard my husband yell from behind me.

"You lying piece of shit!" Aiden shouted, his voice boomed, nearly echoing throughout the courtroom. I turned around immediately as shock swam through me. Aiden was on his feet, his face red with fury, his entire body quaking from anger. "Over my dead body, you sick fuck! You will *never* go anywhere near my wife or my daughter! You will have to kill me, you fucking sociopath!"

I heard Judge Waldron bang his gavel and yell something, but I was too in tuned to my husband. All the commotion going on was nonexistent. I stood up, one hand on my stomach as I walked over to him. He was still yelling, he was completed blinded by hate. I grabbed his trembling hand and placed it on my stomach. I leaned forward and whispered in his ear. "*We* know the truth, okay? It's okay. I'm okay." I say softly, "I'm okay. We're okay." I keep repeating in his ear.

The bailiff and a police officer were already at his sides. His trembling hand was still rested on my stomach as I pulled back from his ear to look at him in the eyes. They were bloodshot red and full of sorrow and anger. I wished I could take these emotions away from him. I wished I could put them in a bottle and throw them in the ocean. I'd never seen him like this.

"I'm sorry," he said lowly. His entire body still quaking, but he was much calmer.

"It's okay, I love you." I said to him.

"Please escort Mr. Jordan out of my courtroom, now." Judge Waldron ordered. Aiden's hand was still on my stomach, I laid both of my hands on top of his and squeezed before he had to pull away. He was out of the doors in seconds.

I inhaled then turned back around only to see that smirk on Oscar's face, that same evil smirk that made my skin crawl, the same evil smirk that was on his face seconds after he raped me. I exhale and sat down.

"I'm sorry about that outburst," Mrs. Pierce said. "I can only imagine how it feels being the husband of a woman who is being continuously lied about and attacked."

"Objection!" Mr. Shur said.

"Withdrawn," Mrs. Pierce said.

"So, you claim you two were in a physical relationship. Then can you explain the night you were stabbed. You are pleading guilty for sexually harassing her. No charges were filed against her because with a witness statement, and my client's age and statement it was deemed self-defense."

Oscars jaw clenched, I could see glimpses of the Oscar I was accustomed to seeing slipping out.

"I was told to plead guilty. I read the signals wrong and I thought she wanted to pick back up where we left off and the next thing I know I was being stabbed in my own home."

"With her mother –*your wife* –and her boyfriend in the very next room, you thought she wanted to pick up where you left off?

"Look," he said angrily, "it was just one of those things okay? I can't explain it, but it was dangerous and a little exciting. She liked playing with fire like that in our relationship and I shouldn't have allowed most of what we did to happen. I think she has problems that are deeper than me because she was all for it and then her boyfriend walked in and all of a sudden I was sexually harassing her. She needed to save face."

283

Aiden was right. He was a sociopath, he was a sick fuck. He needed to be admitted. How was it, that I was the one that spent a month in a mental facility after the incident and not him? He was clearly insane. Hearing these things come out of his mouth was like watching a bad movie. You didn't know where he was going with it but you knew wherever he ended up would be bad and worse than the scene before. Oscar had found a way to twist and blatantly lie about every single aspect of that year.

"Hmm," she nods, "so in this entire scenario, the *only* thing you did wrong was cheat on your wife?"

"Yes."

"You don't see any other faults in any area?"

"Objection, badgering," Mr. Shur said.

"Sustained," Judge Waldron said.

"The only other thing I did wrong was not make her take a DNA test the day Lana was born. I've missed years of my daughter's life because I believed her lies."

I couldn't even look in his direction. The volcano in my chest was erupting. The lava was slowly creeping up and down my limbs and throat.

It wasn't even the lies alone that angered me the most. It was the fact that had I not known the truth –his words seemed believable. I remember trying to figure out how my mother couldn't see the evil that I saw when I looked at him and maybe this is why? He was good, he was manipulative…he was able to come across as the average Joe when truly he was Satan in human form.

"No further questions, your honor." She looked at the judge and raised an eyebrow and sat down. I looked at her like she was insane?

284

That was it? She couldn't be done. He basically got up there and negated every single thing I said in the span of ten minutes and that was all?

She saw me looking at her in disbelief and mouthed, "It's okay, trust me."

"Mr. Doyle how long would you say you and Mrs. Jordan were in a relationship after the sexual intercourse that took place the night Mrs. Jordan alleges an assault happened?"

"Maybe five months,"

"So right up until you found out she was pregnant?"

"Yes," he nods. I'm struggling to keep the bile down again.

"Now, the night in question is the first night you two had sexual intercourse, correct?"

"That is correct."

"Can you please explain what happened that night?"

I closed my eyes and rested my hands on my stomach again. I had to think about Lana and Deuce. I had to think about Aiden and how happy I was that I had this beautiful family. I knew that Oscar was going to continue creating a world that I never and would never step foot in.

"Kim had to work late. Zoe came home and went straight to the kitchen where I was sitting drinking a beer. We already had a lot of sexual tension and a lot of flirting, but I never really thought it would go any further than that. It never crossed my mind because I was happily married."

Breathe in, breathe out.

"We started flirting a little bit and I don't know what it was but I think we both realized it was our only time alone in the house together. She leaned in and kissed me and I know at that point I probably should've pulled away or stopped it, but we just sat there kissing in the kitchen for a good ten minutes."

Breathe in, breathe out.

"She told me she was going to take a shower and she went upstairs. It hit me then that she and I had just made a huge mistake. It may not seem like it, but I loved my wife. I still do. So after what happened in the kitchen I decided to go upstairs and talk to Zoe about it." He paused to take a sip of water. "When I got to the top of the steps her door was open and she was drying her naked body off with a towel right in the doorway, we made eye contact and she invited me in."

I gasped. Loudly, so loudly that Judge Waldron banged his gavel. I was shaking and the tears were blinding me. I had to continue to sit here in total silence while he made me out to look like some horny teenaged whore. Every word out of his mouth was a lie, completely and utterly false with not even a trace of truth. The scream rumbling in my chest was burning a hole through me. I needed to get out of here. I didn't want to hear the rest. I couldn't hear the rest.

"I hesitated and she looked me right in the eyes as she walked towards the door and said '*We're both adults. I'm eighteen. My mother never has to know*' then she dropped her towel. I hate that I was weak and I hate that I didn't try harder to just walk away, but I am flesh and I am man. We ended up having sex in her room that night and many other nights following."

I wondered how close I was to fainting.

"Are you saying that any and all sexual contact with Mrs. Jordan was consensual, as she claimed to be of legal consenting age?"

"Yes sir. Like I said, *ethically* I was wrong and it never should've happened and I regret that things have turned out this way, but I did not rape her. She did not start saying that until her boyfriend came

286

into the picture. I am here because I want rights to my daughter, rights that were taken away from me because she lied to me, the courts, and to the state of Ohio."

He takes another sip of water and looks directly at me. "*My* daughter, Lana deserves to be safe and not have a parent that's in and out of mental institutions, a parent that didn't try to kill a man. She needs to be in an environment that is not hostile with two high tempered people as you've all witnessed. I can provide that for her. I wanted joint custody at first because after the passing of Lana's adoptive mother I gave it a lot of thought and figured it would be in Lana's best interest to have Zoe in her life as a mother figure, but that was before I knew what I know now. I want full custody because I want to keep her safe."

"No further questions, your honor."

I felt Mrs. Pierce grab my wrist, but I couldn't move. I needed to wait for the screaming in my head to subside. I needed to wait until the fire at my feet stopped blazing. I needed to wait until I could move without the chance of collapsing and hurting my unborn baby.

"It's over," Mrs. Pierce said. "You don't have to hear any more of the lies. It's okay Zoe – he dug a bigger hole in his case."

I nodded, but I still had no emotion on my face. It was disorienting trying to navigate through what I was feeling at this very moment. All I could think about was the fact that I was so thankful Aiden wasn't here to hear any of that. I don't know what he would've done. I know this would've destroyed him. It was destroying me. Each second that I sat here one of his lies seared its way into my permanent memory.

"I can leave now?" I ask softly.

"Yes, Zoe …look, I know that was hard, but it's going to be okay."

I nodded again, grabbed my bag, and stood to walk away. I needed Lana and Aiden. I needed them like I needed oxygen.

Chapter Twenty Two: Look Ahead

I tried to roll to my side, but my growing belly wouldn't allow it. I looked over to see Lana asleep completely sprawled out and Aiden sleeping with his body centimeters away from falling right off of the bed.

Aiden and I both had this weekend off and decided that every second would be devoted to family time. Baby number two – *Deuce is what we've been calling him or her* –would be here soon and we wanted to have as much one on one time with Lana as possible before our time and attention was split between the two. I got up as quietly as I could to tip toe into the kitchen. I'd promised Lana I would make chocolate chip pancakes. I'd never made them before. I honestly never made any breakfast foods before. I was a cereal and instant oatmeal kind of girl.

I made it to the kitchen as I studied the box, it seemed easy enough.

"Good morning," I hear Aiden yawn as he came around the corner.

"Ugh," I say, "did I wake you? I wanted you to sleep in for once."

"Lana's feet in my back did the trick," he says as he kisses my neck. "Besides I can't sleep past 6:30 anyways." He said as he went to the fridge. "Why are you up?"

"Pancakes," I say as I continue rereading the back of the box.

"You know, I could run up to Denny's and get her some. She'll never know the difference." He says with one eyebrow raised.

"*I* would know," I say, "and besides I promised her homemade. Gotta keep my word," I shrug.

"Need help?" He offers walking up behind me placing both of his hands on my swollen stomach.

"You don't think I'm capable of making us a homemade breakfast, do you?"

He laughs and spins me around to face him, "We are a cereal and oatmeal family and there's nothing wrong with that."

I'm laughing inside because I'd just thought the exact same thing, but I wouldn't let him know that I saw the humor and truth in what he was saying.

"You think I'm a bad cook?" I accuse.

"To be fair, you haven't cooked enough for me to be a good judge."

I looked at him with my mouth gaping open and he laughed. "I can cook!" I say. "...*certain* things I can cook." I correct after looking at his facial expression, "taco night? Build your own pizza night? Grilled cheese?"

"You make a killer grilled cheese," he amended. We both burst into to laughter.

"I don't see you in here trying to prepare anything?" I laugh.

"Because I know my limits," he kissed my lips then sat at the table. "You're the one who thinks her childhood will be ruined if she doesn't get a home cooked meal *or three* every day."

He was right. Looking at my life I sometimes forget that Aiden and I are still so young. There was a lot of life we hadn't experienced before becoming parents and getting married. I felt like I was playing catch up. It felt like every other parent was playing football, but I was somehow running around in circles with a basketball on a baseball field.

"Can you make the eggs?" I say as I grab a bowl and the chocolate chips out of the cabinet.

"Sure," he says. "But I cannot promise you a shell free product."

I laugh.

I look over to see Lana standing at the door, she looks exhausted.

"Hey, what are you doing up so early?" I walk over to her and rub her –wild from sleep – curls down.

"Can I have milk?" She says as she rubs her eyes. Aiden walks over and picks her up. She lays her head on his shoulder with her eyes closed.

"I'll get you some milk," he said, "if you're still sleepy you can always go back to our room?"

"I want to eat my chocolate," she says, her voice groggy. Aiden and I laugh. She was *definitely* my daughter with that sweet tooth of hers. I was stressing out over these pancakes when obviously all she was going to do was pick the chocolate out of them.

"I have an idea," I say grabbing her from Aiden, "you can help us make the pancakes?"

"Yay!" She popped her head up. Every time she smiled my love for her grew insurmountably. "Are you in, Aiden?" I ask.

"Of course," he smiled.

We spent the entire morning laughing, singing, and making a huge mess in the kitchen. I was at the sink when I turned around to watch Lana and Aiden stir the entire bag of chocolate chips into the large bowl of pancake mix. Lana was giggling from the excitement. I watched Aiden's eyes light up as he watched Lana become so happy. I instinctively placed my hand on my stomach.

It warmed my heart seeing what kind of father Aiden was. We had come such a long way. Our little family was everything I never knew I wanted or could ever want. I was nervous and anxious, but overall I was ready for our new baby to be born. I wanted to see that same light that I see in Aiden's eyes right now when he holds this baby for the first time. I felt privileged to have a piece of our love growing inside of me.

I felt joy knowing that besides our love for one another, this baby would cement us together forever.

At that thought I felt a welt of apprehension overtake my senses. I was cemented to Oscar too. No matter how Judge Waldron ruled, no matter if I never hear or see him again. I was always going to be cemented to him. Lana is my entire heart –she breathes a new life into me that I never knew could exist. I hated that Oscar was in the background lingering trying to sour everything in his path.

"Hey," Aiden said yanking me from my thought. "You okay?"

"Oh, yea," I smile, "just day dreaming. I think you guys put too many chocolate chips in there!" I say walking over to the table.

"*Too* many?!" Aiden said appalled, "Lana, tell Zoe that there is no such thing as too much chocolate!"

"No thing as much chocolate!" She tries to repeat with his same tone, missing a few words in the process, but the infliction is there. I couldn't help but laugh.

I leaned down to kiss her forehead and when I stood back up I felt a strange twinge in my stomach. Off of pure reflex I grabbed my stomach with both hands. Aiden had gotten up and his back was turned to me while he stood at the counter. I breathed out slowly before the feeling passed. I still stood there for a moment, my hands still on my stomach slightly hunched over right when Aiden turned around.

291

"Zoe?" He walked over to me quickly. His hand was immediately rubbing my back in a circular motion. "What's wrong?" I could hear the slight panic in his voice, but he was also trying not to alarm Lana.

"Nothing," I say. I haven't moved, "just a little pressure. Think Deuce is starting to run out of room is all," I say. My voice is a little strained. Not quite sure if I believed my own words. While Aiden was pretending to be calm for Lana's sake, I was pretending to be calm for *his*. I'd read all the books and I'd gone through this three years ago. These weren't contractions because I remember being crippled in pain when I went into labor with Lana. The pain was so excruciating that I thought I was hovering close to death. *This* was not that. Though this feeling was something I hadn't experienced I was sure it was Braxton hicks. I wasn't due for another ten weeks. *There was no need to panic*, I told myself.

"Are you sure?" Aiden says. I can tell he doesn't believe me and that he thinks I'm in more pain than I'm letting on. I was, but I knew I would be fine.

"Yea," I say the words as the same twinge happens again, but this time it intensifies. It wasn't as much of a twinge as it was a tight uncomfortable squeeze that jabbed the core of my stomach. I gasped loudly gripping the table, my eyes closing immediately.

"We're going to the hospital," Aiden says as he walked away to grab Lana's belongings. She is sitting there staring at me and I can see fear and confusion in her eyes. I took a slow and deep breath in.

"Okay," I said softly, I doubted if Aiden heard me, but I wasn't going to put up a fight. I knew that what was happening was not contractions and that I would be sent right back home after discovering I was experiencing Braxton hicks/ false labor. But at this point it would always be safer to go in. "Lana, I'm okay." I add.

Aiden came back into the kitchen with his cell phone in hand, "Okay, can you meet us there in fifteen minutes?" He says on the phone. "Yea, okay. Thank you, Kim."

"Your mom is going to meet us at the hospital to look after Lana," Aiden said as he grabbed Lana's hand to help her off of the chair. "Are you okay to walk?" He asks me.

I nod because the pain that I am now feeling in my back has rendered me speechless. Aiden was at my side again, I hated that Lana was seeing this, but I couldn't walk right now. Not until these cramps stopped. That's what it was starting to feel like. It was starting to feel like really bad cramps.

"Should I call an ambulance?" Aiden's words are a little more panicked.

"No," I breathe out slowly, "this is false labor, I'm fine. Walking will help." I say finally managing to stand upright.

We arrived at the hospital in ten minutes. I was surprised Aiden didn't get pulled over.
We'd been here for a little over forty five minutes. I'd been checked in and tests had been run. Aiden sat in the chair just staring at me. It reminded me of a couple years ago when he would look at me as if I would break if he wasn't there to protect me.

"I'm okay." I say to him with a smile. He nodded and smiled in return.

"They're going to come in here and say –false labor –then they'll send me home on bed rest or something." I add, trying to wipe that scared and concerned look off of his face.

It didn't work. "This is not how we were supposed to spend family day." I say with a smile trying so hard to erase the fear in the room.

He smiled, "Well, we've never been conventional."

"True." I say still staring in his eyes. I loved that when my husband and I spoke to each other it was always like we were having two separate conversations with one another. One conversation was with words the other was behind the lens. He was always telling me he loved me by the way he stared into my being and vice versa. As we sat and had light banter while waiting for the doctor to come back, the sparkle in my eyes were telling him *I don't know what I would do without you* the sparkle in his were saying the same.

"Mrs. Jordan," the doctor came in, with two nurses who immediately started hooking me up to things. "I need to check your cervix." he said. I felt like he and the nurses were in a rush, like we were working against the clock.

"Okay?" I say then I look at Aiden. The nervousness was back in his eyes, the nervousness was resting wildly in the middle of my chest. The doctor did the exam and then immediately looked at the nurses and nodded. One nurse walked over to me and grabbed my arm.

"Mrs. Jordan," she said, "I have to draw your blood." I nodded. I was still trying to figure out why I was being checked again, why wasn't I being sent home?

"So," the doctor said while he walked to my bedside. "We have to move you and admit you to the maternity floor."

I couldn't even ask *why* before he continued, "You are in active labor."

The words sat there in the air before I was able to process them.

"What?" I say. Immediately I begin to cry. Aiden stood up and was next to me holding my hand.

"You are dilated three centimeters," the doctor adds. "The good news is, your water hasn't broken yet, and we do *not* want your water to break. We are going to be giving you something to try and hold off anymore dilation or your water breaking."

I squeezed Aiden's hand as more tears splashed violently out of my eyes.

"And if it breaks?" Aiden asked.

"We don't want to think about that right now," the doctor said. "We are going to do everything in our power to get this baby to stay put. It seems like your bundle of joy is anxious to meet the world."

I just turned seven months pregnant two weeks ago. This baby wasn't ready to see the world. Not even remotely close. I felt panicked and unprepared. My hand was still clutching Aiden's. I felt like I needed him more now than I'd ever needed him before. I wipe my tears as he leans down to whisper in my ear. "It's going to be okay," he kissed my cheek. "Our baby will be fine."

I nodded as a quiet sob escaped my lips.

"Mrs. Jordan," the doctor said, "I know this is scary, but we will do everything we can to get you as close to forty weeks as possible."

I looked at Aiden and his eyes were glossed over. I wish I was strong enough or in the right state of mind to comfort him. I was in my own bubble of sadness and fear. I felt helpless, I felt like there was something I could've done to prevent this. Maybe I should've stopped going on those long walks with Lana —was that too strenuous? Or maybe I should've worked out more and eaten better? Maybe I let the stress of court take too much of my energy? Maybe I shouldn't have picked up extra shifts at work?

There had to have been something I could've done to protect this baby.

The most important thing I was ever going to do in my life would be to protect Lana and Deuce. Between going to court and now this, I felt like I was failing them completely.

"Zoe," Aiden said with pain his voice. "Please, don't cry." He kissed my forehead before one of the nurses asked him to step aside so they could transfer me into my new room.

"Mr. Jordan," one of the nurses said, "we will get her situated and then send someone down to bring you to her room."

He nodded.

I watched his face as they rolled me away and if my heart could break any more than it already was then it would have. "I love you." I mouth. He smiles halfheartedly and says it back. I close my eyes and start to pray, something that I hadn't done in a long time.

***

It had been seventeen hours and thankfully my water hadn't broken, they were able to stop my contractions and I was still three centimeters dilated.

"Go to sleep." I say to Aiden. It's almost two in the morning. I can see how exhausted he is. It's been an excruciatingly long day.

"You first," He says. I sigh because he knows I couldn't fall asleep right now if my life depended on it. Lana was pretty upset that she couldn't stay. She didn't know the extent of what was going on, but she knew that I had to stay here for a few days.

There was a time that I could go days without uttering a single word to my mother. Now, I couldn't imagine my life without her. She was with Lana now at our apartment. She called off from her job for the next three days to help with Lana. I had to make sure she knew how grateful I was for her love and dependability.

"How are you feeling?" Aiden asked.

"Like I'm in prison," I answer deadpanned.

"He's going to be in here to check you again in twenty minutes. Take a cat nap and I promise I'll wake you up."

"No," I say simply and he sighs. We are both quiet for a moment while I rubbed my stomach. I think somewhere in the back of my mind I felt like I could *will* this baby into staying put. That maybe I had some otherworldly bond with him or her and he or she would understand that he or she needed to stay in there for ten more weeks. I knew it sounded crazy, but I was desperate.

"You want something to drink?" Aiden asked as he got up. "I'm going to get some coffee."

"Aiden Anthony Jordan, do *not* drink coffee at two in the morning!" I demanded.

"My mom lives in Nebraska," he raised an eyebrow and smirked. "Ice chips?"

"A steak would be nice," I say sarcastically.

"I'll see what I can scrounge up," he smiled then walked out of the room.

I tried to close my eyes, but every time I did all I could do was picture the worst case scenarios. It sent a chill through me. I was terrified. I didn't know how many other ways to describe it. One of the nurses told me that my pregnancy was currently considered high risk that at any moment I could be doing fine and the next second I may have to deliver.

Though I was thankful for the honest information, a part of me wished I didn't know that. I was paranoid.

I was going to force myself to think positive thoughts. I closed my eyes and pictured Aiden and I sitting in our first home on Christmas morning watching an older Lana pass her sibling a present to open. In this fantasy the baby is a boy who looks just like Aiden. I grab Aiden's hand as we smile looking out at our picture perfect family.

That thought sent a sense of calm through me. I breathed out slowly and tried to turn my body slightly so I could be more comfortable. I immediately felt discomfort so I moved back. That same twinge I felt in my stomach this morning shot through my stomach again and I winced. I was nervous waiting for the next sharp squeeze to happen, but it didn't. My heart was racing as I rubbed my stomach. "It's okay." I said out loud. Aiden walked back into the room at that moment.

"I got you water," he said, walking over to my bedside. "No luck on the steak." He joked, but I couldn't focus on his words as reality smacked me square in the face.

"Go get a nurse," I say as calmly as I could.

"What happened?" His voice was nervous. He grabbed the call button and quickly pressed it twice.

"My water just broke." A tear fell down my cheek. I was too focused on the next step to completely freak out. My only concern at the moment was making sure I did everything in my power to be strong for my baby. What we didn't want to happen had happened. We needed to focus on how to fix it.

"Fuck!" Aiden ran to the door and called out to the nurse's station – too impatient to wait for them to respond to the call button. Two were already on their way.

"Her water broke," I hear my husband say frantically. "She can't have the baby yet she's only seven months?"

His words were circling around in the air, hovering in my energy. I wished I could grab his hand and center him. I didn't know why I was so eerily calm. Yes I was horrified, but it happened, we needed to put our energy into figuring out what to do next. I wiped a tear.

"It's okay," I say to him. The look on his face is one I wished I could never see again "We are going to be okay," I say wiping another tear.

The doctor walked into the room and immediately went to check my cervix. I closed my eyes and tried to envision my happy family on Christmas morning a few years from now. I was snapped out of my fantasy when I heard the doctors alarmed tone.

"We have to do an emergency cesarean. I can feel the baby's foot. Its breech and we don't want to waste any time. Your labor increased drastically in the last two hours. You're eight centimeters dilated."

They were already moving my bed before I could comprehend what was actually being said to me. Just this morning this same doctor said that they would do all that they could do to keep the baby inside of me and now I need surgery. Aiden has my hand and he is walking with me. I didn't respond to the doctor nor did he. We were both quiet and in this moment I realized that we were living out our vows. Aiden told me in his vows that he would *hold my hand while walking blindly into the unknown* I said *I will never let go of your hand...* and that's exactly what we were doing.

We didn't know what the outcome of this would be, we didn't know how it would affect us, and we were both blindsided by life at the same time. All we could do was walk hand in hand silently and pray that this baby was strong enough to fight.

Chapter Twenty Three: Fighting the Wind

At 2:52 am my baby boy was born via C-section. It was a completely different feeling than when I had Lana. I had so much anger and resentment in me during that entire pregnancy and delivery. Her cries made me cry and though I told myself I didn't care –I liked hearing her voice. It was weird hearing something you created speak breath into the world for the first time. As much as I fought it at the time, it was still surreal.

Unlike my delivery with Lana, I didn't get to hear his cries. When he was born there wasn't a sound in the room all I heard was the doctor saying, "It's a boy." I remember all I could do was look at Aiden. His eyes were on our little boy as they took him out of me. I was blocked off from seeing because of the curtain they had separating me from the rest of my body. An odd mixture of astonishment, happiness, and fear lay blatantly on his face.

"Why isn't he crying?" I remember saying through tears, no one answered me. "Aiden?" I said, but now I could see the concern on his face and my heart sank. "Is he okay?" I nearly screamed through tears.

Aiden looked over at me and kneeled beside me. "He's beautiful," he said as tears streamed down his face.

"Why isn't he crying?" I asked again through sobs and hiccups. Before he could answer a nurse walked over.

"Mrs. Jordan he isn't breathing quite well on his own. I know you want to hold your baby, but it's important that we take him to the NICU immediately."

I nodded and more tears swam down my cheeks angrily. "He's going to be okay?" I remember saying. It was almost like I was willing her to answer *"Yes, he will be okay."* even if it wasn't the truth.

"We are working very hard to make sure your baby is healthy." She said serenely.

I nodded again while Aiden kissed my tear soaked cheek and then my forehead. I remember them taking our baby out of the room. I looked through the window and could barely see him in the incubator –he was *so* tiny. I saw his little body with machines hooked up all over him and I let out a shriek. I'd been through this scenario before, seeing them take my child away, a child I hadn't seen, a child I hadn't held, a child who didn't have a name.

There wasn't a feeling in the world that could compare to what it felt like in that very moment. I honestly didn't know if he would be okay. That *thought* alone was debilitating.

I was brought out of the memory of that day –when Aiden walked in, his presence snapping me back into present time.

"Here," he said handing me a cup of coffee. He sat down next to me as we both stared at our little boy. "His color is changing." Aiden said softly before taking a sip of his coffee.

"Yea," I smile, "I think he's getting bigger."

Our baby boy was going on his 4th week in the NICU. He was getting stronger every day. I loved him so wholly it was overwhelming. I wondered how my heart could contain so much love for Aiden, Lana and him at the same time.

"Think of a name yet?" Aiden says as he reaches through the incubator window to rub our sons arm.

"I don't have a clue." I answer honestly. We thought we had two more months to pick a name before I'd give birth. We didn't have it narrowed down to anything. The nurses and his doctor have been calling him *Baby Jordan.* We've continued to call him Deuce. I wanted something that fit him perfectly, something that depicted what he was going through now, something to show how strong he was. I wanted something to show how he was still fighting while the odds were stacked against him.

"Andrew," Aiden said, he was still rubbing our sons arm with his index finger.

"Andrew?" I repeat. I let the name sit in my thoughts for a moment. "After your Grandfather?" I add.

He nods. "It means *strong* and *warrior,*" Aiden smiled. His eyes were beginning to gloss over. "He's our little warrior," he said softly, his smile still intact.

I put my hand on his shoulder and looked directly at him. "I love it," I say softly. We were both on the same page. He was our little warrior, he was strong, and he was going to continue to fight. I stood up and looked at the baby, placing my hand on the glass. "Andrew," I say looking at him and I smile. "Hello Andrew," I beam even harder because the name is perfect and this moment was perfect. Aiden stood up and hugged me.

This was one more *bright spot* to add to the growing list.

Chapter Twenty Four: Final Decision

I didn't want to be here, more than any other time in the last year. I wanted to be at the hospital with my son. I needed to be there so he knew I was by his side every step of the way. I sat in court resenting Oscar more than I ever had before. But, I had to protect my little girl. I insisted that Aiden stay at the hospital with Lana and Andrew. I could fight this last battle alone. I truly wanted to keep these two worlds as separate as possible. This case with Oscar was a different life of mine, a life that seemed so far away. My life with Aiden and my children was my world, I could no longer let it be intermingled with the past me.

Today, I would find out if Oscar got any rights to Lana. His lawyers would flip it back and forth so many times just to rattle things up or make the process more difficult. In a years' time Oscar went from wanting full custody, to visitations, to bi-weekly joint custody, to now and the final request of full custody again.

What he said to me kept playing over and over again in my mind, how he didn't care about Lana one way or the other, but that he was doing all of this because he knew it would make my life more difficult and help make him look innocent because why would the rapist want custody of the child they produced?

He wanted me to know that no matter how much I've tried to move on or how much I try to fight he was always going to be there, he was always going to make my life a living hell. One thing he wanted was for me to see Lana every day and think of him. Little did he know that when I looked at my little girl, all I saw and all I felt was love, pure encompassing love, and that was something he could never destroy.

I sat patiently waiting as Judge Waldron sorted through his papers and his rulings. I was nervous beyond comprehension. I didn't know which way this would go. The last couple years of my life have been the best of my life and I would never take any of that for granted, but my life as a whole hasn't been the luckiest. I'm praying that my bad luck and unfortunate events don't follow me into this ruling. I honestly don't know what I would do if the courts granted him any rights to my daughter.

"Alright, as stated before this case and the information I have gone through is specifically based on the legal rights to Lana Hill, not on any other cases pending. My ruling is based solely on the well-being of the child and only that."

My stomach drops. I hear the emphasis in his words. I felt like Judge Waldron was saying that no matter what I said about how I became pregnant or no matter what charges have been or will be pressed that he had legal rights to Lana. I felt sick.

"With that being said, Mr. Doyle listening to your testimony and to Mrs. Jordan's testimony I feel compelled to give my full *opinion* on the entire situation before divulging my ruling. I can't help but feel like this fight has nothing to do with the well-being of Lana Hill. It's like the story of the two mothers fighting for the baby. One mother would rather walk away from the child in order to protect it from being cut in half and shared equally between the two mothers. *You* Mr. Doyle have been trying to cut Lana in half."

I'm listening to the judge's words and my heart is starting to race, his words are giving me hope.

"I believe you knew there was a chance that Lana was yours from the very beginning and you did nothing and did not step forward when she was given up for adoption. You could have done appeals and contested back then, but you did not. Instead you rip her from the home she'd lived in for over two years. You have changed what type of rights you wanted more times than I would like to count and now this little girl has a home with her birth mother and you want to disrupt that."

Judge Waldron opened up an envelope then continued speaking. "I, as a father of a seventeen year old daughter and a fourteen year old daughter find it extremely hard to sit here in front of you. I have to abide by the law and I will, but Sir, you disgust me."

"Your honor," Mr. Shur said.

"I am speaking, be quiet counsel," He orders. "I believe wholeheartedly that you knew Mrs. Jordan was underage and even if your claims are true you are a forty two year old man who slept with your wife's teen daughter."

"I do believe you raped Mrs. Jordan, I do believe you are vindictive and angry about events that happened as retaliation so now you want to disrupt her life and her daughter's life. People like you deserve to live under the jail and I wish I had the power right now to send you there. If this was a court on morality and gut feelings I would've ruled against you seven months ago, but unfortunately it is not."

I'm staring at the judge dumfounded, I couldn't believe what I was hearing. I looked at my lawyer and she had no expression. My eyes landed on Oscars and he looked like fire was going to spew out of him.

"Now with everything I've just said most of it is hearsay and is not enough to strip you of your rights to your birth daughter." He added.

I almost screamed, I almost leapt out of my chair, everything started crashing around me. My eyes immediately started to water, I needed Aiden. Fuck, how was I going to tell Aiden? I felt my lawyer grab my arm. I was shaking, I couldn't see out of my eyes.

"However, what *is* enough is the fact that thanks to *you* Mr. Doyle there is now DNA evidence to prove that you had sex with a minor that resulted in a child. Charges will be pressed against you immediately following my ruling."

"Your honor," Mr. Shur interjected again, "may I approach the bench…"

"Mr. Shur, do not interrupt me again or you will be escorted out," he barks before continuing. "I will be granting Mrs. Jordan sole custody of Lana Hill and because she is an alleged victim of a crime you allegedly committed, there has been a restraining order filed against you that will be effective starting immediately after this hearing and ongoing through the harassment and assault trial. You are to stay 500 yards away from Mrs. Jordan. As for Lana if you want visitation you will have to meet on middle ground at her social workers office once a month for an hour. If you accept this you will be ordered to pay child support to Mrs. Jordan, and seeing as though you are currently collecting social security as your sole income that won't leave much for your other expenses. Make a decision wisely. Mrs. Jordan, no charges will be filed against you for filing false documents during the adoption process. I believe you were a minor under duress and did what you had to do in order to protect your child." Judge Waldron stood up. "Ruling in favor of Mrs. Jordan, court adjourned." He hit the gavel down and walked away.

I was stunned. I was frozen in place. What had just happened? I felt my lawyer hugging me, I heard Mr. Shur asking to speak with Judge Waldron in his chambers. I'd won? This was over? Aiden and I would never have to step foot in this courtroom again in regards to Lana, it was over? It happened so quickly. All this court, and stress, and tears and… it's just over?

"I won?" I whisper aloud to Mrs. Pierce. "She's mine?"
.

"Yes!" She answered gleefully. I still wasn't able to get out of my seat. "When he testified he said you both hadn't been around each other, but then said you had an inappropriate flirtatious relationship before the encounter. His stories didn't add up and I knew Judge Waldron could see through his lies as well. I petitioned for the restraining order last night. I knew judge Waldron had two teenaged girls, there was no way he was going to torture you like that, no way he would let him be around your daughter without supervision. Mr. Doyle is going to appeal, it'll fall through and he will not accept the visitations, I know how much he makes. You can breathe now, go to the hospital. Go be with your family!"

One tear fell as I listened to her last sentence *go be with your family.* "Thank you," I say. I was finally able to hug her back. I could name on one hand how many moments in my life where I've experienced this level of elation. The first time Aiden said he loved me, seeing Lana walking through those courtroom doors, listening to Aiden's vows at our second wedding, being able to see and touch Andrew for the first time, and now knowing that I was leaving here to see my family.

My family.

"This isn't over," I hear Oscar say loudly. His lawyers start shushing him and standing up as if they could block his words from reaching me. "You're not the victim, you're a whore and you know it!"

This is what it looks like when you have no fight left in you. I almost wanted to laugh, I couldn't and I wouldn't let that bitter man hurt me anymore or ever again. At this very moment in time I found peace within myself. I felt complete, and whole, and happy, and there was nothing Oscar of *all people* could do to change that.

Over the last seven weeks I had nothing to hold onto, but faith. As I sat in that rocking chair across from my two pound baby every day for hours on in the only strength I felt in the situation was prayer. What else could I possibly do? Who knows what's out there, but the comfort I felt in knowing that there could be something bigger than me, bigger than this situation, made me feel like everything would be okay. With that thought I stood up grabbing my purse.

"May God help you and have mercy on your soul, Oscar." I say peacefully as I walked away. It felt empowering to know that I could say those words to him and mean them, after everything. Oscar needed help, there was nothing more that I could do. All I could focus on was going to the hospital and telling my husband everything was over now. I couldn't wait to see the look on his face.

Chapter Twenty Five: A Butterfly's Wings

"The stuff you freak out about is ridiculous," Aiden snaps. He's carrying the last box into the attic of our new home.

"I'm not even freaking out! You're just not listening and I want to punch you and scream and then punch you again!" I snap back following him into the attic.

"He's not even going to remember it, so who cares if it's not a huge party or the exact cake *you* want. He's one. He will eat the damn cake and could care less who was here to watch him do it." Aiden says, sitting the box down in front of the window.

"You would deprive your *only* son of a magical first birthday party?" I accuse, my arms folded across my chest, "Lana got a party?"

"Yea, because she's old enough to actually have friends and can speak in full sentences." He rolls his eyes, walking past me.

Aiden and I had been moving into our new home for the last two weeks or so. Though we are renters, it's so exciting to not be in an apartment anymore *–especially* with two young children. I wanted my babies to have a backyard, a pool in the summer, and a nice neighborhood to walk around. This house wasn't exactly in our budget, but we knew we had to do something to make it more comfortable.

Aiden is saying that two weeks would be too soon and too expensive to have a party for Andrew's first birthday. I don't agree, *obviously*.

"I didn't get to throw Lana's first two birthdays." I state to his back.

Aiden stopped in his tracks, and then turned around to look at me. "Really? You're gonna pull that on me?"

"Pull what on you?" I play innocent. "I am just stating the sad, but true facts."

He paused for a moment while I stood there patiently. "Ugh," he finally says, "*small*."

"Thank you!" I say walking towards him and quickly pecking him on the cheek before walking out of the attic.

"Zoe, seriously like ten people!" He yells. "$150 cap!" He adds, but I don't respond. Andrew's dinosaur replica cake *alone* would cost almost that amount.

The last year has been perfect. I got a fulltime job and have been able to maintain a 3.2 GPA. Aiden got a better paying job and has one more year left before graduating. Lana was the best big sister in the world. She treated Andrew like he was her own. It melted my heart every time she asked to feed him or hold him when he first got home.

Andrew ended up spending nine weeks in the NICU before we were able to bring him home. He was just less than six pounds. He looked so fragile to me. I was always afraid of hurting him. Now at almost one year old he is this healthy Tasmanian angel. He started walking a few days ago and now we can't get him to stay in one room for more than forty five seconds at a time. His name was so fitting he was our little warrior. I loved him and his sister so much that it was scary sometimes.

"Momma!" I hear Lana call out and like every time my heart jumps.

A few weeks after the court ruling, Aiden and I sat down with Lana and told her that she would be staying with us forever. It always baffled me that she didn't have more questions about the Hills. A handful of times she would mention them or something that they did together, but she never directly asked for them and selfishly that made me feel relief. I was fearful that I wouldn't say the right thing.

When I told her she could call me mommy and Aiden daddy only if she wanted to her response was, "I have two mommas and two daddies?"

I told her that she was so special and so loved, that's why she had two families, but from now on she got to stay with our family. It's what made sense to her at the time. I still wasn't ready to tell her about Emilia's death, but I would one day. Aiden and I agreed that we would not try to brush the first two years of her life under a rug. It was very important that she knew and *remembered* she had parents before us.

That night she started calling us momma and daddy.

I know she's going to have more direct questions in the future and I know that I'm going to have to answer them, but I knew that regardless I would be as honest with her as I possible could be. The picture Darren Hill gave me to give to her is taped to her wall in her room. I remember discretely wiping tears from my eyes when I read to her what he'd written on the back of the photo. The smile on her face was radiant as she stared at the picture.

"Yes?" I say as I walk down the stairs to our living room.

"Gamma's here." She said. Standing at the front door was my mother with two large boxes, struggling to open the screen. "I have two more in the trunk." She yells.

"Aiden!" I call out as I walk to open the door. "Mom, Aiden will get the ones from the trunk. What is this?" I grab one of the boxes from her.

She kisses my cheek before answering the question. "Well, I figured since you had more room now you'd want stuff from the house. I tried to pack all of the important things... blah blah blah, where are my grandbabies?!" She walked away from me into the living room where she sat on the floor, only seconds passed before Andrew and Lana tackled her.

"Please don't break Gamma!" I say as I carry the box upstairs. Aiden is walking down.

"You called me?" Aiden asked.

"My mom has a couple boxes in the car, could you grab them?"

"Yea...I have to run to the hardware store that light fixture in the hallway is cracked. I'll be back in twenty. She's staying with the kids?"

"Of course she is," I laugh. My mother was that stereotypical grandmother. She let them stay up later than they're supposed to, she let them eat whatever they wanted, and she always wants to keep them for days at a time which I never allow because I'd miss them too much. They loved her just as much as she loved them.

"Okay," he kissed my lips, and the electricity lingered there for a moment. He put his lips to my ear and whispered. "Maybe Kim can take the kids for a few hours so we can christen this *entire* house tonight?"

I blushed, and then smiled. "Every square foot," I whisper back. He smiled, his eyes smoldering before pecking my lips again and walking away. I loved that after all of this time my chest still got warm and my stomach still fluttered when we kissed.

I took the box to the attic because I figured if I've lived without it for this many years then I didn't have a daily use for it. I sat on the floor of the attic so I could go through the box and see if there was anything worth keeping. There were a bunch of CD's and some books that I'd forgotten I even owned. At the very bottom of the box was a journal. It had butterflies all over it and in that moment I was seventeen all over again.

It was my butterfly diary.

I picked it up and just sat there with it in my hands. I remember doing that same thing every night before I wrote in it. I would count the butterflies over and over until I finally was able to open it. There was something about writing your innermost thoughts down that was horrifying. I remember thinking that it had too much power, it knew a part of me that I never wanted anybody to know.

The words that were in this thing felt so heavy, it felt like I was lifting an anvil when I sat it in my lap. This butterfly diary was my other life. Everything in this diary was some of the darkest days of my life. I knew for a fact the only light in that thing was any mentions of Aiden. I remember when I stopped seeing my first therapist I started writing more truthfully. I never understood in the first place why she had to read my diary at all, why she had to dissect my every word. Didn't that negate the entire point of having one in the first place?

I took a deep breath in and opened to my very first entry I'd written:

February 2014

I'm not really sure how this is supposed to work. Am I really supposed to sit here and pretend all of my problems are going to go away because I wrote them down?

Bullshit.

I mean, I'm not a negative person. But all of this seems like some psychobabble created by therapists to make their jobs easier. Forcing me to write my feelings, only to have you dissect them into something they're not?

Fine, call me a pessimist, but this? This is definitely bullshit.

"Wow," I whispered to myself. It was weird, it seemed so long ago and so distant. I was a completely different person, but I still could remember exactly what I was feeling that day. I remember crying from frustration and throwing my pen across the room. I remember hating my counselor for suggesting I speak to a therapist, hating the therapist for making me write in this thing, hating my mother for agreeing, hating my mother for marrying Oscar, hating that deep down I always expected her to come to me and say she knew the truth. I was so lost and angry. I look at my life now and couldn't imagine ever feeling that way. I never wanted to feel so much hate in my heart ever again.

I still have intrusive thoughts that I have to keep at bay, but I was so much better than I was a year ago, and it was only going to continue to get better.

I sat on that floor reading entry after entry, my words making me cry because I can remember exactly why I wrote them. I pray that my children never feel as secluded and isolated as I felt. I wanted them both to know that until the day I die, I would be there for them.

I finally got to a few entries about Aiden that made me smile. I was so in love with him, before I even truly realized I was. I'd written in this diary everyday about Aiden right on up until the week before I was released from the psych ward. Most of this diary would read like a love story. This diary was a beautiful snapshot of how quickly I fell for Aiden, how quickly I knew he was the one. How quickly I knew I wanted him in my life forever.

This diary almost read as a love letter to my husband.

I smiled.

I wanted to show him this. I wanted him to see the moments from my point of view. The little things like him bringing me Kit Kats or him staying after school so I could catch up on work that I'd missed, him sitting outside with me in thirty degree weather because I just didn't have it in me to sit in that cafeteria. He's seen me on my worst days and is pretty much the reason for all of my best days.

I continued to skim through and found an entry that I didn't remember writing:

June 2014

Aiden is so good, so purely good. I am not. He deserves better. I thought he was my answer to everything, but he is not. I thought he could make everything better, but he cannot. It's not his fault. I was too broken before he found me. I thought I was beginning to swim, but I'm still drowning.

I read this entry six times before I was able to have a clear thought about it. It all came back to me. I'd written this my first night at the psych ward. I remember I was angry and embarrassed that I'd been admitted. Aiden visited me and stayed the entire time before visiting hours were over.

I read the words again absorbing the dark place I must've been in when I wrote them and realized I had it all wrong. This butterfly diary wasn't *just* a love letter to Aiden. It was a love letter to me *too*.

This diary was showing me what rock bottom looked like. It was showing me how far I'd come.

When I started this butterfly diary I was a seventeen year old who was shattered beyond repair. I felt unloved and unwanted. Even though I had people who loved me and cared for me, I was too damaged and too blind to see it or feel it at the time. I didn't think I

313

was worthy of that type of affection. Everyday little pieces of me would break off and drift away and I would let them without a fight.

I was spiraling quickly down the rabbit hole and didn't realize it until I met Aiden. When I met him I was reminded that there was life outside of these obscured and fractured moments. He was a shock to my system. It was like he woke me up from a deep sleep. It was disorienting and confusing, but I was happy that my eyes were finally open.

He loved me, when I wouldn't let him. He loved me, when it was foreign and terrifying. And because of this love, I was able to open my heart more, listen to my gut more. I learned to navigate through my own barriers and road blocks and finally rediscover parts of me that I thought I would never know again. My Aiden didn't come in on a horse wearing shiny armor to save me from myself. He came into my life to show me that I was *already* strong, I was *already* loved, I was *already* a person who could define herself and not be defined by her monsters.

He wasn't the answer to all of my problems. He was my reminder that those problems would not be the end of my story. I had more, I *was* more.

Today, I was more fulfilled. I was at levels I never dreamed of and that was because I stopped shutting myself down. Yes, I snapped and attacked Oscar. I completely lost it, but from that day on a new *me* arose. I no longer put myself second or third, I no longer loathed myself for being afraid, for keeping quiet. I grew new wings, I was finally Zoe.

I confronted Oscar, I confronted my mother, I got my daughter back –I *fought* for her and almost lost Aiden because of it. I sat in that courtroom fighting for not only my family, but fighting for myself. There's a stigma when it comes to putting yourself first, you come across selfish or arrogant, but how I feel now is nothing short of triumphant and strong.

The fragmented pieces of me that I let scatter all over the place, were finally mending back together. I'd grown. I'd blossomed into the person I was *supposed* to be regardless of whether Oscar was able to get into my room that night or not. Somehow my life took the biggest detour and it was painful, and scary, and nauseating at times, but it got me *here.* No matter what I was going to end up where I am now. I was going to find and *be* Zoe one way or the other.

Reading this diary I realized that even in your darkest times, when you feel like you have no choice but to give up, you have to hold on longer. You have to fight for better, you have to stand up for yourself, and have a voice. Almost like a butterfly, you transform into something beautiful and magical, you become all of the things you thought were inconceivable. You look back at when you were a caterpillar, or when you were cocooned and you realize that those moments were there to shape you into who you'd become, no matter how dark and scary those moments were.

I closed the diary and exhaled. I'd cried so many tears that it felt so good to just sit here and smile. I was Zoe Jordan now. I truly didn't need this butterfly diary anymore. I already knew what Zoe Oakley went through. The moments with my husband, I've lived them. They were always with me. I threw the diary back in the *Zoe Oakley* box and closed it.

It wasn't my diary anymore, it was *her* butterfly diary.

Epilogue: Happy Endings and All That Jazz

"Stop fighting!" I shout from the kitchen.

"Drew keeps changing the channel!" Lana screams from the living room. I sigh.

"Television, off!" I shout again and I immediately hear screaming from both of them. "You know the rules. If you can't pick something then neither gets to watch."

I look behind me and smile. "You're my only good child," I whisper before giving Lily a kiss on the forehead. She was sitting in her high chair eating puffs. "Promise me when you start to talk you won't turn into a lunatic like your brother and sister?"

I hear Aiden walk through the front door and instantly he's bombarded, "Daddy can I watch the TV?" Andrew says.

"Sure," he says.

"No, TV!" I yell again.

"Welp, heard your mom," Aiden says and again I hear screaming. "Hey beautiful," he says as he walks into the kitchen kissing my cheek completely unfazed by the hell storm going on in the living room.

"Hey," I say with a smile. "You're home early. Thank God." He laughed as he picked up Lily and sat down at the table.

"They've been like this all afternoon?" He asked while he gave our seven month old a plethora of kisses on her chunky little cheeks.

"Pretty much," I say, "sloppy joes for dinner."

"My favorite," he says to Lily. She was smiling at him trying to grab his lips with her chunky hands.

"Momma?" Lana says as she and her brother solemnly walk into the kitchen.

"Yes?"

"Drew and I decided that we will not fight for three days if we can turn the TV back on." She batted her beautiful brown eyes at me. I

316

was well versed in how manipulative my children were. It was so hard parenting when your kids did and said stuff that made you want to laugh.

"Make it a week." I counter. They look at each other and nod before looking back at me. I was still trying to keep myself from laughing. They would be fighting by time dinner hit the table, but I love the united front they'd started.

"Deal!" Andrew says before they both turn around and run back into the living room.

"Aiden, I love our children. I love them so much, but I am so happy about getting out of the house this weekend!"

"Agreed!" He said with a laugh. "I definitely need time with my wife without a kid hanging off of one of us." He smiled, "Isn't that right Lillian?" He cooed at her and she smiled again, she was such a happy baby.

"Two whole days," I say in wonderment. "Your dad is going to have is hands full. Oh, I packed most of your stuff. You just have to pick up your tux by 4pm Thursday." I add.

"Got it," he got up with Lily in his arms. "Not going to lie, I was beginning to think Matt was never going to propose to Alicia."

"Not everybody is like you Aiden," I laugh. "We were fetuses when we got married."

"True," he shrugged. "But if you know what you want, why wait?" He smiled as he walked over to me kissing my cheek again. "I would've proposed much sooner but I thought you would think I was crazy so I held off as long as I could."

"Whatever." I say.

"No, I'm serious!" he said –Lily was starting to get restless so I handed him a bottle to give to her. "Remember when I took you to meet my mom after you got out of the looney bin?"

I scowled at him, "My *court ordered* stay at a specialized facility." I corrected.

He laughed and continued, "All jokes aside, that last night when we were sitting on the porch, we'd never opened up to each other as much as we did that night. I remember looking at your profile while you were looking up at the sky. You were in deep thought, counting the stars like you always do and you were just so beautiful –you weren't even trying. I remember thinking *I want to marry her, I have to marry her.* At that moment I knew I was going to make you my wife one day, sooner rather than later."

I smiled and again, like every time he told me something from his heart I felt warm all over.

"I honestly felt like I had to bite my tongue in order to keep from asking you right then and there." He continues.

"You didn't think I would've said yes?" I ask, because I definitely would've said yes. "We were together like what? Four months?" I laughed, that sounded like my Aiden contemplating marriage before senior year of high school.

"I think you would've said yes, but there was so much going on that I didn't want that to be something else to stress about or…"

"Aiden, I've told you this before," I interrupted, "marrying you *both times* was the smartest thing I've ever done." I kiss him. "Why is this the first time I'm hearing this though?"

"We have a lifetime together. I can't give you *all* my good stuff at once." He winked and walked out of the kitchen with Lily.

I smiled.

I was excited to journey through this life time with Aiden and our children. I was excited to add more happy words to my life's theoretical diary. At twenty five years old I could say that I was living the life I never in a million years would've dreamt of wanting or having. I was the happiest I'd ever been. I honestly didn't think about the past and if I did occasionally it wasn't to sulk or mull over everything I'd been through. It was to put into perspective how perfect my life was now.

Three years ago I found out that Oscar had a stroke and now needed twenty four hour in-home care. You would think that hearing news like that would've given me some type of joy or solace, but it didn't. I meant it when I told him *may God help you and have mercy on your soul.* There was nothing for me to gain from his pain. Though I didn't get the justice I thought I wanted when I was a teen, I got the only thing I ever really wanted in the end –my daughter.

Oscar ended up serving eighteen months in prison out of a four year sentence after he was found guilty for sexually assaulting me. He was added to the sex offenders list as well, something that Mrs. Pierce was determined to make happen. At the time it was difficult for me to understand exactly how the judicial system worked. I found it hard to understand why just eighteen months would be viewed as *justice* for what he'd done to me, but I could not harp over it. I had to move on with my family. That era of my life was over.

Lana does not know about Oscar and she never will. It's a very difficult decision that I made and I am at peace with it. I just couldn't imagine looking her in the eyes and telling her how dark and sad the very beginning was for us.

Maybe I was making the wrong decision, maybe I was failing her as a mother by keeping this from her, but it's what I had to do. Aiden was her father, she *loved* him –she was a daddy's girl and he loved her and her siblings more than anything in this world. It would have to be enough. It *was* enough.

"Zo," I hear Aiden call out, "your mom just texted and said she and Mike are coming over to visit before they leave for vacation."

"Okay!" I say back. I was happy that my mother was finally able to find love again. I didn't want her to force herself to be alone because she felt guilty for things in the past. Mike was a good guy and I was happy they found each other when they did. On the crappy side, I didn't know what I was going to do without my mother in town for two weeks while she was in Jamaica! These kids liked her more than me, I was sure of it.

"Oh," I hear Aiden say as he's walking toward the kitchen –he put Lily in her swing in the living room. "Almost forgot!" He dug through his work bag and pulled out a Kit Kat bar and handed it to me. I smiled. I sat down at our kitchen table and he sat down across from me.

"Oh, so proper manners would be me sharing this with you since you got it for me?" I say as I'm opening it. He arches one eyebrow and shrugs, looking as if he were waiting expectantly.

"I don't have manners." I say quickly as I stuff an entire piece into my mouth. We both start laughing before I break off a piece to hand to him.

"Thank you," he says as he grabs my hand.

We sat there holding hands and eating a Kit Kat bar in the kitchen while our children sat in the living room. After eight years and three children sitting here with Aiden felt like our first date.

"I love you," he says softly.

"I love you too," I say with a smile. "*Almost* as much as I love this Kit Kat bar."

He laughed and squeezed my hand. "Wow, that's some pretty high praise coming from you. You really *do* love me, don't you?"

I continue to smile, gazing into his eyes. *More than he could ever possibly know*. I thought to myself.

When I was younger I would use *water* as an analogy for my life. I would say I felt like I was drowning, or I was finally at the surface, or I was trying to stay afloat. Looking at where I am now, I realized that I am no longer in the water at all.

I was on the shore. I wasn't in the deep angry water that had been pulling me down for years when I was going through every horrible thing. I was lying back in the warm sand under the beautiful sun, not one dark black storm cloud in sight.

I was watching the tides now. I was no longer lost in them, fighting for survival. I was on solid ground, living in a continuum of *bright spots*. My life was *all* light, there was no more darkness. No more dormant areas, no more skeletons jiggling the doorknob, no more demons waiting for the perfect moment to pull me down with them again. I could see, feel, and breathe, and the air was fresh and sweet.

"Yes," I finally answer him. I interlocked our fingers, pressing our palms together. "I *truly* do."

And now I know that I'd been wrong all of those years ago. Maybe happiness *is* meant for everyone. The scrapes and scratches will heal, the grief and sadness will lessen little by little, and eventually you'll realize that all those *bright spots* that would show up randomly during your bleakest times were actually little lightning bolts of happiness. There to remind you that you are more than your darkest moments, that you are more than your monsters.

That you deserve all the love and happiness the world has to offer and though it may take you a while to get there, you are worthy of it all and you always have been.

The End

74030448R00178

Made in the USA
Columbia, SC
24 July 2017